THE
Two bea

WISHING FOR
A MIRACLE

AND

THE MARRY-ME
WISH

BY
ALISON ROBERTS

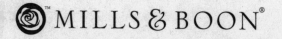

MILLS & BOON

THE BABY GIFT

A gift so special it's priceless

Dear Reader

I'm not lucky enough to have a sister, but I do have an amazing daughter and many truly wonderful friends, so I'm well aware of what an astonishingly powerful thing the bond between women can be.

Friends, mothers and daughters…sisters. I started thinking about the kind of bond that might be created if it encompassed all of these possibilities. Could it be enough to overcome obstacles that seem impossible?

Neither Julia nor Anne Bennett envisages a future that involves children. Their reasons might be different, but the effect their convictions have on their relationships has the potential to be disastrous.

But Jules and Annie are more than simply sisters, and their bond is such that they will go to extraordinary lengths to help each other.

As far, even, as carrying a child for the one who can't.

That kind of bond is amazing all on its own, but I wanted to give these sisters even more. Men who love them for exactly who they are and futures that will allow all their dreams to come true.

Cherish the women in your life. The bond is magic.

With love

Alison

'No.' He spoke softly now. 'Don't you see, Jules?' The words were being forced out. He shouldn't be saying them. But he could no more *not* say them than take in another breath. 'It's not that I *have* to protect you so much. It's that I *want* to. Too much.'

Slowly, her gaze lifted. Caught his and held it.

Mac's hands fisted by his sides as a defence against the urge to reach out and pull her into his arms. He tried to smile but could only manage a brief, one-sided twist of his mouth. 'It's a bit of a problem,' he confessed. 'It has been ever since that…kiss.'

Alison Roberts lives in Christchurch, New Zealand. She began her working career as a primary school teacher, but now juggles available working hours between writing and active duty as an ambulance officer. Throwing in a large dose of parenting, housework, gardening and pet-minding keeps life busy, and teenage daughter Becky is responsible for an increasing number of days spent on equestrian pursuits. Finding time for everything can be a challenge, but the rewards make the effort more than worthwhile.

Recent titles by the same author:

NURSE, NANNY…BRIDE!
HOT-SHOT SURGEON, CINDERELLA BRIDE
THE ITALIAN SURGEON'S CHRISTMAS MIRACLE

CHAPTER ONE

THE train lay like a jagged open wound across the soft, misty Scottish landscape.

One carriage was still on the bridge, anchored by the tangled metal of broken overhead beams. The engine and two more carriages were in the gully, some thirty metres below, partially submerged by the small but fast-moving river. Another hung, suspended somehow by the mess of twisted steel on the bridge, a gigantic pendant that encased goodness knew how much human misery.

'Target sighted.'

The quiet statement from the man staring down from beside the helicopter pilot was superfluous except that the inflection on the second word said it all. This wasn't the usual kind of target they set out to locate. This was, quite probably, a once-in-a-career, major, multi-casualty incident.

This was…huge.

Julia's determined intake of breath was clearly communicated via the equipment built into their helmets.

'How 'bout that, Jules?' The rich, male voice of her partner filled her earphones again. 'Not something you'd see every day back home, is it?'

She wouldn't want to either but it was exactly what she'd come to the other side of the world in search of, wasn't it? In a small country like New Zealand, the chance to be involved with a rescue mission of this size was highly unlikely. Working in the UK was all about getting the experience in case it did happen. Having the opportunities to hone the skills she knew she had.

She hadn't anticipated this sudden rush of adrenaline, however. A sinking, almost sick-making dive occurring in her belly. Julia swallowed hard.

'It's what I signed up for,' she said. 'Bring it on!'

'Hold your horses, lassie.' It had been nearly three months since Julia had joined this new specialist emergency response team and the pilot, Joe, had learned to hide his vague incredulity that such a slender, feminine creature could be so keen to hurl herself into danger but there was still the suggestion in his tone that she had to be at least halfway crazy. 'There's a Medivac chopper taking off. We haven't got clearance to land yet.'

'And then we'll have to check in with Scene Command,' her partner reminded her. 'See where we're needed first.' A hint of tolerance born of understanding crept into his voice. 'Joe's right. Hold those horses.'

The tolerance had been hard won but Alan MacCulloch was used to her enthusiasm by now. Appreciated it, even, now that he knew she wasn't about to rush headlong into a scene and put them both in danger, and this had become a tradition. Julia was the feisty one, ready to leap in and do whatever needed to be done. Mac was the calm one. They both looked but Mac got to give the word before either of them leapt. It was one of the many things they had found that made them able to work so well together. Had forged them into a tight team in a surprisingly short space of time.

The scene commander wasted no time in briefing them. Dealing with the carriages that had crashed to ground level was under control.

'Carriage 3…' The scene commander looked up. 'Still an unknown quantity for victim numbers and status. One bloke got the door open near the top and managed to climb out. He fell.'

Julia exchanged a glance with Mac. They both knew how unlikely it was that someone would have survived such a fall. The dangers inherent in this rescue were becoming very clear.

'Someone else was spotted signalling for help,' the scene commander continued. 'Waving through a broken window at the bottom of the carriage, and cries were heard. More than one voice. We used megaphones from the bridge and the ground to order anyone else in the carriage to stay as still as possible while we tried to stablise things.' He cleared his throat. 'Nothing's been seen or heard since.'

'Needs triaging, then,' Mac said calmly. 'How stable is the bridge?'

'Engineers reckon it's safe at each end, which is where the cables have been anchored. For some reason there was a structural collapse towards the middle, which is what's caused the incident. According to an eye witness who was driving on the road over there, carriage 3 was swinging violently when the first carriages broke free. Presumably it's fairly well caught up to have stayed there but it's anyone's guess how long the connection's going to last.'

'Incident' was such an insignificant title for this disaster. Julia sucked in a breath as she looked up again. The carriage had gone careening off the rails. There must have been one hell of a jolt and then it would have been swinging wildly. Passengers would have been hurled about like puppets and the potential for serious, if not fatal injuries was high.

Her gaze narrowed. The carriage had windows and a door at either end. The door at the top was still open, leaving a black hole that would be an easy entrance. She shifted her gaze back to the men beside her.

'We can winch down from the bridge and have a look.'

There was a heartbeat's silence after Julia had spoken. They all knew it was unlikely they would see as much as they needed to through the windows and impossible to assess the condition let alone treat victims, but if someone climbed inside it would mean disengaging from any safety of a winch line.

This was dangerous. Very dangerous. Weird that Julia's nerves seemed to have vanished.

'I can do that,' she said.

Both men stared at her. Mac opened his mouth to say something but Julia was faster.

'I'm half your weight,' she said. 'We don't know

how much movement those cables are going to cope with and it would be sensible to use whatever advantages we've got. The more gently we can test it, the safer we're all going to be.'

'We've got a crane on the way,' the scene commander added. 'The plan was to lower the carriage to ground level.'

'How long will that take to get here?'

The man responsible for overseeing this enormous scene sighed. 'At least three hours. Maybe longer.'

Too long for anyone struggling to survive in there. Way too long.

Mac's eyes narrowed as he assessed the scene again. Then his gaze was on her and it was just as penetrating. Julia held the touch of those dark eyes with her own and waited. Patiently. She had learned that nothing else she said would make any difference now.

This was Mac's call as the senior officer and she trusted his judgment.

The eye contact went on…and on. Long enough for it to have been unacceptable between people who didn't know each other extremely well indeed. Long enough for it to be intimate but not uncomfortable because they both knew what this was about and it was purely professional.

OK, it was deeply personal as well, of course, because they relied on each other and this was about life-and-death decisions being made—for themselves and others—but they both knew where the boundaries lay and they'd never stepped close enough to even have to define those limits.

Questions were being asked and answered here.

'Are you sure about this?'

'Yes.'

'You don't have to.'

'I know.'

'This will be the toughest yet.'

'I know that too. I can do this, Mac.'

'I know you can.'

And, finally, there it was. Mac's nod.

Slow but resolute. Permission had been granted.

She hadn't expected him to agree so easily.

The flicker of surprise had been there in her eyes. Mac had registered gratitude, too, for the respect his decision encompassed. What he hadn't seen, and which would have been entirely understandable, had been a hint of dismay that he wasn't going to use his authority to stop her tackling this incredibly dangerous mission.

Julia Bennett was one astonishing woman.

Did they breed them all like this in that little country at the bottom of the world? Pint-sized Amazons with rapier-sharp brains and a courage too deep to measure?

No. Mac checked the buckles on Julia's harness and tugged at the carabiner on the front one last time before moving to where he intended to operate the winch. This woman was a one-off. Totally unique. The first female to get through the rigorous selection process to gain access to this elite rescue squad, and he'd been lucky enough to be designated her partner.

Not that he'd felt like that first up, mind you. Neither had any of the guys on the other shifts. Mac had seen the relief in the glances exchanged at that team briefing so many weeks ago now. A foreigner was fine. They had people from all corners of the globe on staff. But a *girl*?

Not that a twenty-eight-year-old could be considered anything less than a woman but her lack of height made her seem much younger. It didn't help that she had such a pretty, fragile kind of prettiness about her either. The spikes of that practical, pixie haircut did nothing to disguise her femininity and if the big, blue eyes that went with those blonde spikes could look like they did with no make-up, it was obvious that Jules could be a knock-out if she chose to be.

Nobody had expected to find that she considered herself 'one of the boys' and was possibly more passionate about this job than they were. She had earned respect remarkably quickly, thanks to an early job that had involved a large portion of the squad when the remains of an old building had collapsed on a demolition crew. Julia had been the only one small enough to squeeze through a gap and she'd hung, upside down, like a determined little bat, for long enough to establish an airway and gain IV access on a man who would certainly have died otherwise.

Respect had become admiration from more than one of the guys but the polite rebuff of any personal overtures had added another dimension to a personality that was intriguing. Any commiseration Mac had received on being partnered with 'the chick' had long since morphed into envy.

Yeah…he was lucky.

But here he was, letting this amazing woman step backwards off a broken bridge, his fingers on the controls that were now lowering her close to the dangling train carriage. If it fell, it would most likely take her with it and there would be nothing he could do but watch. The tension was growing by the second as the small figure in the orange overalls slipped lower.

'Keep going.' Julia's voice sounded clear and calm inside his helmet. 'Seats are clear at the top. I can't see the bottom yet.'

He fed out the steel cable, inch by inch. He felt the jerk as Julia's steel-capped boots touched the side of the carriage and then her gloved hands reached to steady herself and cut the light reflecting on one of the large glass panels.

'Stop!' The command was sharp. 'I can see something.'

CHAPTER TWO

FACES.

Terrified faces. A huddle of humanity in what had been one end of the carriage and was now a narrow base. It was too dark to see clearly. Now mid-afternoon on a typical, drizzly autumn day, natural light was fading fast but the light on Julia's helmet could only go so far through the barrier of glass and deep shadow within. The first two rows of the seats now facing upwards had people on them and were much easier to see. The closest figure was lying slumped.

More people were huddled on the seats on the other side of the aisle.

How many were there?

How badly injured were they?

Julia could see them watching her. A woman on the far side, with a child clutched in her arms, was sobbing but the sound wasn't reaching through the window that was still intact on this side. Or not through the padding inside her helmet and the background noise that included a helicopter hovering directly overhead.

Television crews, probably, capturing the unfolding drama of this rescue. The footage would make international news, that was for sure. Julia spared a fleeting thought for the relatives of everyone involved. Including hers. Thank goodness her sister Anne would be unable to recognise that it was her doing such a dangerous job.

'Can you hear me?' Julia shouted.

'Ouch!' came Mac's voice.

'Sorry.' Julie lifted her microphone, tucking it under the rim of her helmet. She called again and a boy inside, who looked about fourteen, nodded warily.

'How many of you are there?' Julia called.

The boy's eyes slid sideways but he didn't move his head. He looked hunched. Terrified of moving, probably, in case it was enough to send the carriage plummeting to the bottom of the gully. He shrugged helplessly and then winced and Julia could see the way he was cradling one arm with the other. A fracture? Dislocated shoulder?

The woman who had been sobbing in the seat across the aisle tried to get closer, the child still in her arms. She was blocked by the still shape of the slumped man.

'*Help*!' she screamed. 'Please…*help* us!'

Her words were clearly audible. So was the panicked response from others still in there, telling her to stay still, prompted by the sway of the carriage her movement had caused. Julia's hands were still against the window and she simply moved with it, gently swinging out and then back. Not far at all but more than enough for her heart to skip a beat and for a soft curse from Mac to echo in her earphones.

Julia flipped down the small arm of her microphone. 'Pull me up to the door, Mac. I need to get inside.'

'No way!'

'Can't triage from here. I can see at least six people and some look OK to evacuate fast.'

'Get them to climb up and we'll winch from the door.'

Julia frowned. The woman was close to hysterical and wasn't about to let go of the child. The teenage boy had an injured arm or shoulder.

'Not practical,' she informed Mac. 'They need assistance. Anyone else qualified to operate the winch up there?'

'Yes.' The word was reluctant. 'Red Watch is here now as well.'

Another SERT partnership of Angus and Dale. This was good.

'I'll get inside,' Julia suggested. 'You winch down with a nappy harness and I'll bring out as many as I can. Then we'll be able to assess what we've got left.'

Mac must have shifted his microphone but Julia could hear faint voices in animated conversation and knew that her idea was being discussed with others up there on the bridge. A long minute later and Mac was ready to talk to her again.

'On one condition,' he said briskly. 'We're monitoring the cables. We might not get much warning if things aren't going to hold but if I give the word you have to get yourself out of there. Stat. No argument. Got it?'

'Got it.'

Julia did get it and her promise of co-operation was

sincere. She heard the faint wail of distress as she was hoisted away from the faces at the bottom of the carriage despite her hand signals to indicate that things were in hand and rescue was close.

And then there she was. Beside the door. She had to climb inside and unclip the winch line that suddenly felt like an umbilical cord in its ability to sustain life.

Fear kicked in as she did precisely that. Her mouth went dry and her heart pounded so hard it was almost painful. For a horribly long moment, Julia thought she'd gone too far this time. She couldn't do this after all.

'Jules? Talk to me.'

The voice was soft but she could hear a faint reflection of her own fear. Mac was afraid for *her* and it was more than concern for the wellbeing of his colleague. Or was that just wishful thinking on her part?

Stupidly—and so inappropriately it was easy to contain—Julia felt an odd tightness in her throat. A prickle behind her eyes that advertised embryonic tears. She dismissed them with a simple swallow. She didn't need to go there. All she'd needed had been to hear his voice. To remind herself that she wasn't doing this alone. That she had the best possible person in the world watching her back right now.

'I'm…inside,' she relayed. 'Climbing down.' She moved as she spoke. Cautiously. Hanging onto the back of a seat frame as her feet found purchase on the cushioned back of the next seat down the vertical aisle. 'How are those cables looking, mate?'

'Good,' came the terse response. Mac was concentrating as hard as she was.

'These seats make quite a good ladder.' Julia kept talking because she wanted Mac to keep responding. She wanted to hear his voice. Maybe she needed to keep hearing it because it gave her more courage than she could ever otherwise summon.

But when she was halfway down the aisle, the smell hit her. The smell of fear. And she could hear the voices and moans and she knew that within seconds she would be able to speak to and touch these unfortunate people. She could start doing the job she was trained to do and help those who had been plunged into a nightmare they couldn't deal with alone.

Julia felt the power that came with the knowledge that *she* could help and that power gave her complete focus. Knowing that Mac was close gave her strength, yes, but that was simply a platform now. This was it.

Time to go to work.

'Who can hear me?' she called, pausing briefly. 'Keep still but raise your hand if you can.'

She wanted to count. To find out how many were conscious enough to hear her and physically capable of any movement at all.

One hand went up tentatively. And then there was another. And another. Six? No, seven. And dim patches where she could see the shape of people but no hands. The less injured people would have to be evacuated first to allow access to the others.

The woman she'd earlier deemed close to hysteria was still sobbing. 'Please…' she called back. 'Take Carla first. She's only seven… *Please*!'

Julia revised her count to eight. Carla was being clutched too tightly to have raised her hand.

She climbed closer. The teenage boy with the injured arm was silent but she was close enough to see that his eyes were locked on her progress. Searching for her face. Silently pleading with as much passion as Carla's mother.

Julia had to tear her gaze away to try and reassess the number and condition of victims she would be dealing with. To triage the whole scene, but it was difficult. The light had faded even more outside now and it was much darker in here. The light on her helmet could only illuminate a patch at a time and it was like trying to put a mental jigsaw together.

People were jumbled together. Right now it was impossible to see which limbs belonged to which person or even how many people were in the tangle.

'Get me out!' A male voice from behind Carla and her mother was loud. 'I can't feel my legs. I need help.'

Julia saw hands come over the seat back behind the still sobbing woman. Good grief, was the man trying to move himself despite possible spinal or neck injuries? Someone beside him groaned and then someone else screamed as the man's frantic efforts created a shuffle of movement and made the carriage swing alarmingly.

'Stay absolutely *still*, and I mean everybody!' Julia injected every ounce of authority she could into the command. 'Listen to me,' she continued, her tone softening a little. 'I know you're all scared but you've all been incredibly brave for a long time and I need you all to hang onto that courage so you can help me do my job.'

Carla's mother sniffed and fixed wide eyes on Julia. She would do anything, her gaze said. Anything that would, at least, save her child. The man behind her was quiet. Hopefully listening. Even a groan from nearby sounded as if someone was doing their best to stifle the involuntary interruption.

'We're going to get you all out,' Julia said confidently, 'but we have to do this carefully. One at a time. I'm going to help anyone who can move to get to the top of the carriage where someone will be waiting to carry them up to the bridge.'

Would Mac be there yet? Dangling on a winch line with a harness in his hands that he would pass through the door to Julia to buckle onto each survivor?

'I'm here, Jules.' It wasn't the first time that Mac had seemed to be able to read her thoughts. 'Ready when you are.'

'When we've got as many as we can out, we'll be able to take care of all of you that are injured and we'll get you out as well,' Julia told the passengers. 'Do you all understand? Can you help me?'

She heard a whimper of fear and another groan but amongst the sounds of suffering came assent.

'Just get on with it!' the loud man was pleading now. 'Stop talking and *do* something.'

Julia climbed past another seat. She made sure her feet were secure and then anchored herself with one hand. 'Pass Carla to me,' she ordered.

'*No-o-o-o!*' the child shrieked.

'You *have* to, baby.' With tears streaming down her face but her voice remarkably calm, Carla's mother peeled small arms from around her neck and pushed her child towards Julia. 'I'll be there soon, I promise.' Her voice broke on the last word but Julia now had a small girl clinging her like a terrified monkey and she didn't take the time to reassure the mother. She was climbing upwards again and part of her brain was planning ahead. The teenage boy next. She had a triangular bandage in the neat pack belted to her hips. She could secure his injured arm and he should be able to climb with her. Maybe Carla's mother after that, so that her panic wouldn't make it harder for everyone else to wait their turn.

There would be others after that and then the real work could begin. Assessing and stabilising the injured and getting them out of here and on the way to definitive medical care.

By then the weight in the carriage and the potential for unexpected movement would be well down. The cables would have had a reasonably thorough test. Mac or one of the other SERT guys could join her. Someone would have to because there was no way she could carry the injured up herself.

Carrying a slight, seven-year-old girl was proving hard enough. The extra weight made it an effort to balance and then push up to the next padded rung of this odd ladder of seats. Julia's breathing was becoming labored and the muscles in her legs and arms were burning. She had to concentrate more with every step so that fatigue wouldn't cause a slip that might send them both falling down the central aisle.

She couldn't even afford the extra effort of looking

up past her burden to see how close she was to the top or whether Mac was peering down to watch her progress.

'You're almost there. Two more.'

How did he *do* that? Know precisely when she needed encouragement? This time, he could probably see the way she hesitated before each upward push. How each hesitation was becoming a little longer so he wasn't really mind-reading. It just felt like that.

She could do two more. No. Julia could feel the determined line of her lips twist into a kind of smile. She could do *ten* more knowing that Mac was waiting at the top.

'Good job.'

The quiet words were praise enough for her efforts. Julia was too breathless to respond immediately, though. She simply nodded once and then held out her hand for the nappy harness. Then she edged—carefully—into the first space of upturned seats so that she could sit and use both arms and hands for her next task.

'It's OK, sweetheart,' she told the rigid bundle on her lap. 'I'm going to put these special straps around you and then Mac's going to get you out of here and carry you right up to the top.'

'*No-o-o!*' Arms tightened their vice-like grip around Julia's neck.

'I need to go back and look after the other people. Like your mummy. You'll be fine, Carla, I promise.'

But the child was shaking now. Whimpering with fear.

'Mac is a *very* nice man,' Julia told her.

'Cheers, mate,' came with the chuckle in her earphones.

'And he really, really likes children,' Julia added.

'Looking after little girls like you is absolutely his favourite thing to do.'

The earphones stayed silent this time. What was
Mac thinking? Remembering occasions when he'd
poured his heart and soul into trying to save a child?
The heartbreak when he hadn't been successful?

Carla had relaxed fractionally. Enough for Julia to
be able to slip the straps into position and then close and
tighten buckles. She hoped the silence wasn't because
Mac was putting two and two together somehow. That
he had noticed at some point over the last weeks
the way she avoided prolonged contact with paediatric
patients if possible. The way she was so good at dis-
tancing herself by taking on any case that was
preferably complicated *and* adult.

No. She was pretty confident she kept personal
issues well away from her work. Out of her life, in fact,
because she wasn't letting anyone close enough to
discover the truth.

'I'm going to tell Mummy how brave you are,' Julia
told Carla. 'As soon as I get back down to her. Do you
think she'll be proud of you?'

Carla didn't nod but her head moved so that she
could look up at Julia.

'*I'm* proud of you.' Julia smiled. 'Mac will be, too,
you'll see.'

She eased herself to her feet. Carla was still tense and
she cried out in terror when Julia lifted her into Mac's
waiting hands but then she was in his strong, secure
grasp and the child looked up and saw the face of the
man above her.

Mac's smile was as reassuring as a hug.

'Hi, there, peanut,' he said. 'Going to come for a wee ride with me?'

And this time Carla nodded and, as Mac clipped the buckle of her harness to his own and instructed the child to put her arms around his neck and hold on tight, she turned her head and Julia could see that she was—incredibly—smiling herself.

Mac was simply the best when it came to dealing with children. It had made it easier to step back herself and not get people asking awkward questions.

'*Your job,*' she could say to Mac with total sincerity. '*You're the best.*'

He was. He adored kids and she knew him, while he probably wouldn't admit it on station, he was aching for some of his own. And why not? He was in his mid-thirties and by now the absolute obsession with his career had to be ebbing enough for him to realise he might be running out of time to find someone to make a family with. He needed to get on with it.

He'd have gorgeous children and he'd make the best father ever.

And some incredibly lucky woman was going to be his wife and the mother of those children.

Julia turned and began climbing back down as soon as she saw Mac and Carla beginning their upward journey. She had to be just as slow and careful as she had been the first time she had done this despite it seeming easier having done it before. She couldn't afford to fall.

The descent was too slow. It allowed too much

time for errant thoughts and emotions to seep into her mind and body.

Inappropriate things but she was learning to expect the backwash that came from seeing Mac with a child in his arms.

A mix of grief. And jealousy. And…yes…desire.

And, as usual, they had to be stamped out with fierce determination because there was nothing Julia could do to change the way things were now.

Not a single thing.

It took well over an hour for her to help the eight relatively uninjured victims up to the door where they had been winched up to the bridge and into the care of waiting rescuers. Eight heavy people who had required assistance to make the climb. Constant guidance and encouragement, if not actual physical support. Julia had to be exhausted both physically and mentally.

'Angus and Dale could take over the next stage,' Mac suggested.

'No way.' Julia was heading for the base of the carriage again and the crisp words via the communication system put paid to any further suggestions on Mac's part. 'The job's nearly done and there's no way I'm deserting Ken. He knows me, now.'

And she knew. She was deeply involved in this scenario and, knowing Jules, she would be committed to the people and the mission a thousand per cent. If they wanted to get her out of there it would be neither easy nor pleasant. And she was right, the job was nearly done. She had managed to get virtually all the people from the carriage out and Mac knew there was one conscious, injured person, one unconscious and one dead.

So Mac went in to join her because Julia was his partner and everybody knew just how tight a team these two were these days. Inseparable. And darned good at their jobs.

This time when Mac came down on the winch line he brought equipment and the medical supplies they would need.

The bottom two rows of upturned seats had become a kind of triage station.

Julia indicated one of her patients. 'This man has been unconscious since I got my first glance inside.'

The figure was slumped on the seat by the window but Mac could see the end of a plastic OP airway in his mouth. Julia had obviously assessed him and done what she could in the brief window of time that triaging allowed for.

'Head injury,' Julia continued. 'GCS 3. Rapid, weak pulse and query Cheyne-Stokes breathing pattern.'

The man was very seriously injured, then. Unlikely to survive. If they took the time to evacuate him first, others who could survive might die.

'And this is Ken.' Julia was hanging onto the edge of the seat across the aisle now. 'Spinal injury. Paralysis of both legs and paresthesia in both hands.'

A high spinal injury, then. He would need very careful immobilisation before evacuation so they didn't exacerbate the injury.

Julia dropped lower, shining the light of her helmet on the very end of the carriage.

'Status zero here,' she told Mac quietly. 'There were several people on top of him to start with. He's too heavy for me to shift but I've moved enough to be fairly sure there's no one underneath him.'

Mac reached down and caught the arm and shoulder of the heavy body, lifting it further than Julia would have managed. A jumble of luggage, personal possessions like books and drink bottles filled a fair bit of space but there was no sign of movement that might indicate a survivor struggling to get out. He could see shards of broken glass in the debris as well. And so much blood he felt a familiar knot tighten in his gut. He let the man's body fall back gently.

'Let's deal with what we've got first.'

Julia nodded. 'Ken first?'

Mac agreed. The sooner they had his spine immobilised and protected, the better the outcome might be for him.

Julia wriggled into a position where she could support Ken's head while Mac went to get the equipment they would need. A neck collar and survival blankets to start with. Oxygen and IV gear and pain relief. He found her squashed into the tiny gap beside Ken, ready to take the collar and ease it into position, and it wasn't the first time he thought it was a blessing that she was so little and mobile. There was no way he could have managed that feat so competently.

'Do you think I've broken my *neck*?' Ken sounded terrified.

'This is a precaution,' Julia reassured him. 'We don't know what part of your spine has been injured and we need to keep it all in line. It's really important that you don't move even after the collar's secured because the rest of your back isn't protected yet. We'll do everything we can but we need you to help too. Can you do that?'

The huff of sound was still fearful. 'I guess.'

'Just hang in there, mate. You're doing really, really well.'

Mac was busy opening packages but he could hear the smile in Julia's voice as she reassured her patient. He knew exactly how her face would be looking as she spoke even though he couldn't see it. Ken probably couldn't see it either. He might see the way her lips curved back into her cheeks but he wouldn't be able to see the way Julia's eyes always smiled right along with her mouth. The way her whole face—even her whole body sometimes—seemed connected to her emotional state.

Fascinating to watch. Or provoke. Mac wasn't the only one on station who took pleasure in engaging Julia in an animated discussion.

Or delight in making her smile.

'We're going to give you something for that pain very soon.' Julia was swabbing a patch on Ken's forearm. 'Wee scratch coming up. There. All done. Wasn't so bad, was it?'

'Didn't feel a thing. You know what you're doing, don't you, lassie?'

Julia chuckled. 'Sure do. Now, are you allergic to any drugs that you know of?'

Mac flicked the top of an ampoule to move the fluid

inside. Then he snapped it and slid a needle into the narrow neck to draw up the drug.

Ken was right. Julia knew what she was doing. He was right, too. She was involved in this scenario to the extent that it would have been detrimental to try and give her a break. She had established a connection with Ken and he was in exactly the right frame of mind to co-operate with whatever measures needed to be taken to rescue him.

He trusted Julia and Mac knew the trust wasn't misplaced. He had to feel completely dependent on her right now but he knew that she would be treating his vulnerability with the same kind of compassion and skill she brought to the medical practices he had witnessed her administering.

She fitted an oxygen mask onto Ken and hooked it up to the small cylinder from the pack. 'I won't run fluids,' she told Mac. 'BP's down but it's more likely to be neurogenic than hypovolaemic shock.'

'What does that mean?' Ken asked fearfully.

'Any injury to the spine can interfere with nerves,' Julia told him. 'That's why you can't feel your legs at the moment and you're getting pins and needles in your hands. It's not necessarily permanent,' she added firmly, as though she'd given this reassurance more than once. 'We can't know what damage there is but what we can do is take care not to make it any worse.'

A lot of care had to go into the next stage of this rescue. They had to get Ken flat and secured onto a stretcher without twisting or bending his vertebrae. Then they would have to cushion his head and strap him so securely onto a stretcher there would be no danger of movement during the extrication process.

Minutes ticked past swiftly. Mac could feel exhaustion biding its time, waiting for an opportunity to ambush him, and he knew that Julia had to be a long way further down that track. Not that she was slowing down, of course. She never did. Mac was proud of his partner. Not just for her endurance or the way she had crawled into the cramped space by the window to hold Ken's head to support his neck but for the way she effortlessly turned her skills to emotional support for their patient.

'Glasgow's home for you, isn't it, Ken?' she asked.

'Aye. I was just going up to Inverness on business for the day.'

'What do you do?'

'My company makes umbrellas.'

Julia chuckled. 'You must be doing really well. I've never seen so much rain as I have in the three months I've been here.'

'Where are you from?'

'New Zealand.'

'That's a country I've always wanted to visit. Is it as beautiful as they say it is?'

Mac found himself nodding. He felt exactly the same way. He'd love to get down to the bottom of the world for a visit. Always had, but the urge had got a lot stronger in the last few months. Funny, that.

'It is,' Julia was saying. 'Parts of it are very similar to Scotland but I think we get a bit more sunshine.'

'You going back?'

'Yes. I work with an ambulance service that has a

rescue unit back home. I'm here for six months for advanced training.'

'What part of New Zealand do you live in?'

'Christchurch. Middle of the south island. We've got the Alps to the west and the sea to the east. I grew up there.'

'You've got family to go home to, then.' Ken's voice wobbled. He was obviously thinking of his own family and feeling alone right now.

'Only my big sister,' Julia told him.

Mac was busy pulling the extrication device they needed from its case but he was listening carefully. This was personal information. The kind that Jules had kept from her colleagues. He might have been left with questions that would never be answered but Ken wanted distraction from his situation. And Julia was so involved, she probably hadn't registered that others might be able to hear.

'She's like a mum, really,' she told Ken. 'My mother died shortly after I was born. Anne's nearly seven years older than me and she just took over from the various nannies. When Dad died I was only eleven but Anne was old enough to take care of me. She's amazing. Managed to raise me and get through med school at the same time. I love her to bits.'

There was a short silence then. Julia appeared to be checking Ken's pulse. Or was she holding his hand?

'When you get to New Zealand,' she said then, 'make sure you visit Christchurch. It's a very English city but don't hold that against it, will you?'

Something suspiciously like a sniffle could be heard from Ken. 'Nay, lassie,' he said. 'I won't.'

He hadn't missed the conviction in Julia's tone that he would, someday, be well enough to travel to the other side of the world. She had deepened the connection between them by sharing personal information and now her confidence was a boost. She was his anchor right now. Nothing more personal was said because she shifted to professional responsibilities, making sure Ken was fully informed and understood everything going on around him to keep his fear at bay.

'We're getting something called a KED around you now, Ken. You'll feel us tipping you a bit so we can slide it underneath.'

'But I'm not supposed to move!'

'I've got you. Relax. I won't let anything happen to your alignment.'

'What did you say it was?'

'It's like a body splint. It goes right round your chest and waist and up behind your neck and then we do up a whole bunch of straps. Then it'll be safe to get you on the stretcher and out of here.'

'It's dark now, isn't it?'

'Pretty much. Don't worry. We'll have lights all over the place out there now. We can see what we're doing.'

Sure enough, massive lights had been put in place both on the ground and the bridge and, despite drizzle that was determined to become rain, the visibility was excellent. It was still a slow job extricating Ken. He had pain relief on board and was completely immobilised but even the tiniest movement hurt. Angus joined them inside the carriage but it still took an age to inch the stretcher carefully upwards. Julia stayed as close as she could to Ken's head. Talking to him. Reassuring him. Sympathising with the amount of pain he was in. It needed extra help to get the stretcher out of the door and attached to the winch and while that was happening Mac checked the harness he still wore in preparation to accompany the stretcher.

But Julia had other ideas.

'I'll go up with him.'

What he could see of her face looked very pale. Pinched, almost, as though she had been doing more than reassuring Ken and had actually taken some of his pain on board. Mac shook the thought off but whatever the cause she was reaching the limits of her endurance and steadying a stretcher being winched to make sure it didn't catch on obstacles, not to mention helping to lift it over the lip of the destination, was no mean feat.

'I think *I* should,' was all he said.

But then he looked down from Julia's face to where her hand was holding Ken's. To the way Ken was looking up at Julia, his fear only just contained. And, for a weird moment, Mac felt envious. Of that connection. Of that touch.

'OK,' he amended a little hurriedly. 'If you're sure.'

Julia gave a single nod. 'I'm sure.'

There were hand-held television cameras on the bridge now. Journalists eager to interview Julia as Ken was transferred to waiting paramedic crews who had a helicopter ready to evacuate him.

'You're going to the best spinal unit in Glasgow for

assessment,' Julia was able to tell Ken as she said goodbye. 'I'll come and visit you very soon.'

She avoided the media, pushing back to watch anxiously as her SERT colleagues brought out the man with the serious head injury, who was, amazingly, still clinging to life, and were then winched up themselves, one by one. By the time Mac joined her on the bridge, they had been on scene for nearly five hours and their official shift had finished some time ago.

Not that any of them were about to leave just yet. The weather was closing in and the transport that had taken Ken to Glasgow had been the last that would be leaving by air. Joe was grounded so they would have to organise road transport to get back to station and the people who could do that for them were otherwise occupied because the crane had finally arrived and the last stages of this rescue were under way.

Things hadn't quite ended. It made no difference that they had started this shift well over twelve hours ago and that they were both exhausted. This had become 'their' job and they would see it through to the bitter end.

Had she known how bitter that end would be, Julia thought later, she would never have been so willing to accompany Mac back to the carriage for a final check. She would have found some way to ensure that someone other than them were the last people present.

The dead body was sprawled flat on the floor now, debris strewn under, around and over him. Julia edged in beside a seat to give the men in orange overalls room to load the man onto a stretcher and carry him to the temporary morgue set up in one of the huge tents. A space she knew already had fourteen occupants from this disaster.

She watched in silence as the stretcher was eased through the door and outside into the bleak night. Then she turned her head to see Mac also watching. Unguarded for an instant as the beam of her headlamp caught his face, she could see his exhaustion and the kind of defeat that went with every life lost on their watch.

Then he stooped and picked something up from the debris that had been pushed into piles to make way for the stretcher. Julia focused on what he held. It was a soft toy animal of some kind. Probably well loved and shabby to start with but it now had stuffing coming from a ripped-off leg and it was covered with blood-stains.

'Carla's, do you think?'

'Probably. We didn't have any other children in the carriage, thank goodness.'

For a long moment, she held Mac's gaze. Watching the wheels turning in a brain shrugging off how tired it was. For a moment she wondered if he was thinking her statement was another indication of her aversion to working with paediatric cases but then she saw the grim lines in his face deepen and a haunted look appear in the way he frowned. There was another possibility.

They both turned to look back at the space the dead man had filled.

At the door that had been blocked by the body.

It was Mac who moved to open it. He had to put his shoulder against it and push because it was blocked from the inside. And then Julia heard him curse, softly but vehemently, as he dropped instantly to a crouch.

Her view was limited to what she could see over his shoulder because Mac filled the narrow doorway. She could see narrow shoulders and the back of a head covered with long, blonde hair. A woman, then. Had she been thrown to hit her head against the basin during the violent change of direction as the carriage had tipped? Except that there was no obvious injury to be seen from this angle.

Mac had his hand on her neck, searching for a pulse.

'She's too cold.' Mac's voice sounded raw. 'Been dead for a fair while.'

At least there hadn't been a child in here as well. Julia still had to swallow hard as she reached for the portable radio clipped to her belt. 'I'll let the guys know to bring the stretcher back.'

'Wait!' Mac was examining the woman, looking for an indication of what might have killed her. He found nothing.

'Pelvis?' Julia suggested.

Mac put his hands on the woman's hips and pressed. Julia knew it would have been a gentle test but she could see the movement. There were major blood vessels running through that area. If one was cut it was quite possible to bleed to death in a short space of time.

It was also possible they might have been able to save her if they'd got to her first.

Mac was pressing a hand to the woman's abdomen now. It was distended. Even more distended than they might have expected from all the internal bleeding.

'Oh, *God*!' Mac groaned.

Julia didn't ask. She didn't need to. The shape was too regular and obviously too firm to be simply an accumulation of blood. The woman had probably only been in the early stages of her pregnancy but there had been two lives lost here.

Mac straightened. He didn't meet Julia's horrified gaze.

'It's time we went home,' he said heavily. 'There's nothing more we can do here.'

CHAPTER THREE

SOMETHING wasn't right.

They should have been able to debrief and put things into perspective on the long road trip back to headquarters courtesy of a military vehicle. They could have talked through how impossible it would have been to save that young woman. Even if they'd known she was there, they would still have had to evacuate all the mobile people and the time needed to shift the dead man and then extricate her would have put Ken in more trouble. And they couldn't have known. There wasn't even a window that Julia could have looked into from the outside.

These were things that should have been said aloud. Dissected and come to terms with. And maybe then they could have congratulated themselves on a job well done. The fact that ten people had made it out alive when it could have gone in a very different direction and claimed even more victims.

But Mac, for the first time Julia had known him, didn't want to talk and that was confusing. He was the strongest, bravest man she had ever met. Six feet tall in his socks and without an ounce of fat on his body. His strength alone was enough to inspire confidence Julia couldn't hope to impart as soon as he arrived on scene. But there was more to Mac than physical attributes. He was so open and honest and always smiling. Smiling so much that he had deep crinkles around his eyes and grooves on his cheeks. She had seen him tired beyond exhaustion. Frustrated enough to be angry. Sad, even, to the point of his voice sounding thick with tears, but she'd never seen him quite like this.

'I'm stuffed,' he said, when she tried to get him to talk at the start of their road trip home. 'I need sleep. Let's leave the talking till later, OK?'

Which would have been fine, except that Mac didn't sleep. Neither could Julia, Not after she'd noticed the way he was staring through the window on his side. Lost in thoughts he obviously didn't want to share and looking so…bleak.

He closed his eyes, later, but he was feigning sleep. Julia could tell because she could see the way his hands were clenched into fists. So tense.

She wanted—badly—to touch him. To find out what was bothering him and—somehow—make it better.

She cared, dammit. Too much.

And so she said nothing. She kept to her side of the back seat and stared out of *her* window. Her body ached with weariness and more than a few bumps and bruises but her heart ached more.

For Mac.

* * *

Ten years.

It had been a decade ago and Mac hadn't even thought about it for eons.

What was it about that moment that had brought it back so vividly?

The long blonde hair?

The early pregnancy?

Or was it because Julia had been standing so close to him?

It was like pieces of a jigsaw he hadn't intended, or wanted, to solve had come together out of nowhere.

Mac could hear the suck of heavy-duty tyres on water-soaked roadways along with the rumble of the engine and the background buzz of the radio station the driver was listening to. Runnels of water coalesced on the window and then streaked sideways but Mac wasn't really watching. He was seeing an altogether different picture.

No wonder he found Julia Bennett so damned attractive on so many levels. It wasn't just that she was gorgeous and smart and brave. It was that full-on approach to life in combination with an ability to sidestep any hint of a meaningful personal relationship that did it.

Presented the kind of challenge any red-blooded man would find irresistible, it was almost a matter of honour to have a crack at winning such a prize. Or wanting to.

Why hadn't he put two and two together before this?

Because he'd done his damnedest to forget Christine, that was why. To forget the heartache of absolute failure. To move on and make a success of his life.

'You OK, mate?' Julia had asked when they were on the main road and settling in for their journey back to headquarters.

'I'm stuffed,' he'd growled. And he was. Exhausted both physically and emotionally. In pain, actually, because something raw had been unexpectedly exposed deep within. He'd never talked to anyone about it. Ever. And if he did, Julia would be at the bottom of any list of potential listeners. He wasn't about to admit the kind of failure he was on a personal level. Preferably not to anyone but especially not to a woman whom he doubted had ever failed at anything and who would be less than impressed with a man who was nowhere near her equal.

'I need sleep,' he'd added tonelessly, turning away from her. 'Let's leave the talking till later, OK?'

She accepted his withdrawal and why wouldn't she? Today had been tough. This was the best job in the world but it took a day when they succeeded a hundred per cent to reinforce that. A job when no one died or got maimed for life. The way through feeling like that was to talk about it, of course. He knew that. Debriefing was ingrained in anyone who worked in careers that dealt with this kind of trauma and degree of human suffering. It was a part of the job, really, to analyse everything that had happened. To take a quiet pride in things that had been done well and to learn from anything else so they could go out and do an even better job next time.

But he couldn't talk to Julia about this. Not yet. Not when he'd been blindsided by memories and could see danger signs a mile high. Signs that warned him how easy it would be to fall in love with this woman. Hell, he was already quite a way down that track and hadn't even noticed.

He couldn't afford to let her anywhere near him right now, when the scab over that failure had been ripped off and he was feeling raw. Vulnerable, even, and Alan MacCulloch didn't do vulnerable, thanks very much. Imagine if she wasn't unimpressed with his history. If she accepted him, warts and all. He'd fall. Hard. In a way he'd managed to avoid for a whole decade. Nearly a quarter of his life, come to think of it.

She didn't want that.

Neither did he.

Julia was looking at him. He could feel it. He could sense her concern, like a gust of warmth crossing the gap on the back seat in the back of this vehicle. She wanted to offer comfort but Mac didn't want that either. He closed his eyes and pretended to sleep.

Well after midnight, they got back to the outskirts of Glasgow and the station they shared with a road-based ambulance service. They collected their packs from the back of the truck.

'Cheers, mate,' Julia said to the soldier who'd been their chauffeur. 'Hope you get to go back to base and get some shuteye now.'

'Not a chance.' The young soldier grinned. 'I've got to get back to the scene. We'll be there until it's all cleaned up.'

Cleaning up was exactly what he and Julia needed to do. Mac picked up his pack and swung it onto his back. From the corner of his eye he could see Julia struggling to do the same. She was so tired she could barely stay upright, poor thing. The urge to look after her was far too strong to ignore.

'Here,' he said gruffly. 'I'll take them. You go and hit the showers.'

'No, thanks.' The tone was cool. 'I can manage.'

She gave up on lifting the pack to her back and just held it in her arms instead, turning away without a glance in his direction.

It was a slap he deserved so he had no right to feel hurt. Julia had done nothing wrong and hadn't deserved to be treated the way he had treated her. God, how selfish had he been? Maybe she'd been the one who needed the debrief. Praise, if nothing else, for her extraordinary courage and endurance.

He'd made a mistake. A big one. How hard would it have been to talk about the job like they always did? Made a few jokes, even. The kind of black humour that diffused the dark space they were all in danger of slipping into with this kind of job. He could have made her smile and that would have made *him* smile and feel good. She would never have guessed that he'd been thinking of anything other than work.

He'd been stupid as well as selfish. Not only had he created an uncomfortable distance between himself and his partner, it had been the worst defence possible for himself. He'd had nothing to do but think for nearly two hours. Sitting there being so aware of the woman sitting beside him. Wanting her and pushing her away simultaneously.

God, he'd never felt this tired. Exhaustion was becoming confusion. A long, hot shower was what he needed and then he'd head home. Maybe it was better not to say anything more to Jules tonight in an attempt to put things right because, the way he was feeling, he would most likely make things worse. They were due for two days off now. By the time they had to see each other again, she might have forgotten his moodiness or at least forgiven his silence. They could just go back and pick up where they'd left off.

Being colleagues who respected and cared about each other. Julia had called the soldier 'mate' and it was what she often called him as well. That's what they were. Mates. Comrades. Not quite friends because that implied something a lot more personal than they had. Dangerous territory.

The decision to leave things was a relief. The shower and change into warm, dry civvies was a comfort. Mac signed himself out and noted Julia's signature already in the logbook. She'd left before him and that was good.

Or was it?

And why was her car still in the parking lot at the back of the station?

Maybe she'd gone into the messroom to talk to the crew on night shift. Mac battled, briefly, with the desire to retrace his footsteps and find her but solved the problem by turning towards his own vehicle—a hefty, black four-wheel drive that filled his allocated space. Overflowed from it, in fact, despite him nosing it in until the front bumper virtually touched the moss of the old stone wall surrounding this area. There were trees on the other side of the wall. Big, dark shapes that created such intense shadows he didn't see Julia until he was about to pull his driver's door open.

She was sitting on the wall. Wrapped up in a padded anorak and mittens. Waiting for him.

'*What* the—?'

Julia jumped down. Her hood fell away and she wrapped her arms around her body as she took a step forward. And then another. Until she was close enough for him to see that her hair was still damp despite the protection the hood had given her from the drizzle. Close enough for him to smell the shampoo she'd just been using.

'I couldn't go home,' she said quietly. 'Not without knowing what rattled your cage so much tonight.' Her gaze caught his and held it. 'Was it something I did?'

'Good grief, no!' Mac was transfixed. By the smell of…what was it? A mixture of soap and…almonds, that's what it was. Even more by the warmth he could feel radiating off this small, determined woman. Most of all, by the way her eyes seemed to catch the glow from the lights behind him in the parking lot. He knew her eyes were blue but right now they were just huge and dark and full of concern.

'It…it was the job,' he told her. 'It…got to me.'

'Of course it did.' A tiny nod advertised that Julia had already come to that conclusion. 'There'd be something wrong if it didn't.' She frowned now, glancing down and lowering her voice. 'But why couldn't you talk about it? Like we always do?'

Mac opened his mouth to offer the same excuse of exhaustion. Or to say he'd been asleep but it was obvious she knew he would be lying. She was looking up at him again and he could see plainly that she knew he hadn't been asleep. She'd seen through him in the truck and she was seeing through him now. Right into his head. Into his heart. There was no escape and, suddenly, Mac didn't want to find one.

'That woman,' he heard himself saying. 'She...reminded me of someone.'

'Ahh.' The sound was long. It contained complete understanding that there was—or had been—a woman of great importance in his life. Far more important than herself.

Mac could actually see the thought process going on in the way she was standing so still she wasn't even blinking. The almost imperceptible backing away he could sense. The way her lips were parted a fraction as her mind worked.

And that slight parting of her lips was Mac's complete undoing.

She was so wrong to put herself down in any way but that was exactly what she was doing. She was convincing herself that she had been dismissed in favour of the woman he'd been thinking about. That she was somehow less worthy of his attention. So wrong, and there was only one way he could think to prove it as soon as he noticed her lips.

He had to kiss her.

She could have stopped him. Time seemed to slow down to a crawl. He looked at her mouth and then back to her eyes and he could see that she knew he was unable to resist the temptation now that the thought had occurred to him. Slowly and deliberately…so slowly she had any amount of time to duck out of reach, he tilted and lowered his head. He was giving her the chance to move. Part of him was desperately hoping she would.

But she didn't move a single muscle.

Her mouth was there. Waiting for him. Her lips still parted. And even then Mac moved so slowly he could feel the warmth of her breath against his lips before he closed that last, infinitesimal space.

Once his lips touched hers, he couldn't think of anything else at all. Her mouth claimed his. Dragged him in. Drugged him. It was only the need for oxygen that forced him to break the contact but then he heard the sound that Julia made. A soft whimper of desire and he was lost again.

When her mittened hands came up to circle his neck, he surrendered himself without a heartbeat's hesitation. He caught her head in his hands and tilted it. Touched her lips and then her tongue with his own and it felt like the ground had vanished from beneath his feet. He was weightless. Floating. Vaporised in some fashion by the heat being generated.

When he became aware of what he was standing on again, Mac felt reality returning with a jolt. Who had broken that extraordinary kiss? He didn't think he could have if his life had depended on it.

He was breathing hard. So was Julia. She'd stepped back from him. It must have been she who had broken the contact, then, because Mac was sure his feet hadn't moved. What was she thinking? What on earth could he say that might diffuse the intensity of what had just happened? Did he want to?

And then Julia peeped up at him and grinned.

'You have to marry me now, you know,' she said.

Mac's jaw dropped but then it hit him. This was a joke. Maybe Julia's reaction to the kiss had been nothing like his own. Or maybe she was just as astonished as he was and needed enough space to get her head around it. For whatever reason, she was going to make light of it and right now, it seemed the perfect way forward.

'Hey…' He feigned shock. 'It was only a kiss.'

'Only a kiss? Cheers, Mac.' But her lips twitched and there was a glow of merriment in her eyes.

Mac's smile felt rusty but it was still there. And it grew. He could feel it stretching something that had got way too tight inside him. 'It was a pretty good kiss,' he said thoughtfully.

Julia nodded in agreement. 'Exactly.' She sighed. 'So now you have to marry me.'

Mac's smile broadened. 'Is that so?'

Julia nodded again. Firmly. 'Yep. I paid attention at school and Sister Therese *said*…'

The bark of ironic laughter came from nowhere. Oh, God…if only Julia knew that she was making a joke about the very thing that had been haunting Mac so keenly. He could actually hear a faint echo of his own voice from a decade ago.

'I'll marry you, Chris. We can make this work.'

And hers. Scathing.

'You can't be serious! You think I want a kid? Holding me back? Interfering with everything I want to do with my life?'

'It's my baby, too. You can't just—'

'It's my body, Alan. I can do whatever I like and you can't stop me.'

How could he have thought that Julia and Christine were alike? The very idea of marriage had been an insult. A threat, even, to the woman he'd believed himself in love with. Something that could never have been discussed reasonably, let alone joked about.

That Julia *could* make a joke of it was the other end of the spectrum, wasn't it? Maybe he should find that almost as offensive but, somehow, it wasn't.

She didn't know and, at this particular moment in time, it really didn't matter. How could it, in the wake of that astonishing kiss that had taken him somewhere he'd never been before? A place that held release rather than tension. A pleasure so pure it was paradise.

Relief was coursing through him as well. If he wanted to make something out of this new development in their relationship with each other it was going to be up to him. Julia wasn't bothered. She could laugh it off. Even better, any damage done by his behaviour tonight was repaired. They would be able to work together again without a barrier that would have been unbearable.

He could play this game. He could laugh it off too and make it go away.

'Come on, then,' he said, completely deadpan. 'I've

got a full tank in my car and Gretna Green isn't that far away.'

Julia laughed. She turned away, shaking her head. 'Are you kidding? I only listened to Sister Therese's rules, I didn't obey them.' She was walking away now, towards her small car, but her words floated back, still coated with laughter. 'Kisses don't make babies. You're safe, mate.'

Safe?

Safe?

Who was she trying to kid?

Mac wasn't in a remotely safe place right now. What was worse, a part of him didn't think he wanted to be either. The part that wanted to go after Julia right now and grab her and take her in his arms for another kiss.

At least part of his head was still functioning sensibly. He wrenched open the heavy door of his vehicle, eager to shut himself into the temporary sanctuary.

'He *what*?'

'Kissed me. Come on, Annie. This line is so good you might as well be here sitting on the end of my bed. You heard just fine.'

'I'm just…surprised.'

'You and me both.' Julia's laugh was hollow. 'Actually, I have the horrible feeling it might have been me, kissing *him*.'

'Who made the first move?'

'Him. No, me. Oh, God, I don't know. I was worried about him after the job because he'd been so quiet and I kind of ambushed him in the car park. And…and it just kind of happened. The thing is, what am I going to do about it?'

'Why do you have to do anything about it?'

'Because he's my partner. The last three months have been the best I've ever had and I don't want to spoil our working relationship. I might have already!'

'Why? Was it a horrible kiss?'

'No…' Julia's sigh was heartfelt. 'It was even better than I thought it would be.'

'A*ha*!' Her sister pounced. 'I knew you fancied him.'

'Of course I fancy him. Who wouldn't? He's gorgeous.'

'So what's the problem? You're a big girl now, Jules. Go for it. Lord knows, a fling would do you the world of good. How long has it been? Two years?'

'Nearly three.'

'So this is the perfect opportunity.'

'Why?'

'You've only got another three months there. More than long enough to find out if it's a real possibility. An easy way out if it's not. Life shouldn't be all work and no play, you know.'

'That's rich, coming from you.' Julia chuckled. Then she sighed. 'It wouldn't be just playing,' she said then. 'And that's why I can't go there. It's just too scary.'

There was a short silence on the other end of the line. 'You wouldn't say that unless there's something really special about him. You think you're going to fall in love with him and get hurt again, don't you?'

'I'm probably halfway there already,' Julia groaned. 'And if I wasn't before that kiss I certainly am now.'

'All the more reason to try it out.'

'*I can't.*' Julia shook her head even though her sister was half a world away from seeing the decisive action. 'No way. Because he's special. One of us would end up getting hurt. Probably me. Maybe both of us.'

'Not necessarily.'

Julia spoke softly. 'He adores kids, Anne. He's the perfect father-in-waiting.'

'Oh-h-h…'

The sound was so full of understanding and sympathy it brought tears to Julia's eyes.

'You won't believe what I said to him after that kiss.'

'What?'

'I said…' Julia had to catch her breath to swallow a sob that was determined to escape. 'I said that he'd have to marry me now because of what Sister Therese used to say at school. Do you remember? About kissing and babies?'

'Oh, no!' But Anne was laughing. 'Why do you do it to yourself, hon? Every time. Salt in wounds and all that.'

'It's the way I deal with stuff. You know that.'

Her sister's voice was soft. 'I know you're not as tough as you like to make out, Jules. I know how much it can hurt.'

'Better to make jokes than let people feel sorry for me. Or not to tell them and let things go further than is good for anyone involved.'

'Mac's not Peter.'

'No. I doubt there's anyone on earth that quite matches my ex-fiancé in the creep stakes.'

'It's been three years. Maybe it's time to have a look

and see what else is out there. When was the last time you met anyone you were attracted to this much?'

'Three years.' Julia gave an unamused huff. 'Tell you what, if I come across any nice widowers with a few motherless children in tow, I'll pounce, I promise.'

'There are plenty of men who could actually handle adoption. Or surrogacy.'

'Or who would *say* they can. Where have I heard that before?' Julia couldn't help the bitter edge to her voice. 'And then they'll turn up two weeks before the wedding and say, "Oops, sorry, babe. I got someone else pregnant and guess what? It is a major after all."' Neither could she help the spill of words she'd kept bottled up for so long. '"I didn't realise how amazing being a father was going to be and this is the *real* thing. I didn't have to go into some cubicle in a clinic and look at dirty magazines and—"' Julia stopped abruptly, gave a huge sniff and then cleared her throat. 'Sorry,' she added quietly.

'Don't be. You should have said all this a long time ago instead of brushing it off and putting on such a brave front.'

'I guess I've been thinking about it all again, thanks to that kiss. No, actually…' Julia closed her eyes. 'I've been thinking about it since the first day on the job here. Since I saw who I'd be working with. I've thought about it every time I've seen him with kids. The way he is with them.'

She didn't notice the way her tone softened. 'He's a born dad. You should have seen him today. We had this little girl on the train. Carla, her name was. She was only seven and *so* scared and then I handed her up to Mac and he just has to look at her and she's *smiling*. It was—'

'Hey, I think I saw that on the news when I walked past someone's television this morning,' Anne interrupted. 'I haven't had time to check the papers. I knew it was in the UK somewhere but I didn't realise you were involved.'

'Yep. It was up between Edinburgh and Inverness. Bang in our patch.'

'I saw someone dangling off the bridge trying to look in the windows of the carriage. It looked horrific. Was that Mac?'

Julia remembered hearing a helicopter hovering that could well have contained a news crew. 'It was probably me,' she admitted. 'I went down first to assess things.'

'Oh, my God!' Anne groaned. 'Don't tell me it was you who climbed inside the carriage to get people out. Good grief, you must have. You were just telling me about that little girl.'

'Someone had to,' Julia said matter-of-factly. 'And it's what I do, remember?'

'How can I forget?' Julia heard a heavy sigh. 'I want you home safe and sound, Jules. The sooner the better, thanks.'

'Stop worrying so much.'

'It's what *I* do, remember? I'm your big sister. I…miss you, kiddo.'

'I miss you, too.'

Oh, dear. This conversation was supposed to be picking her up after a miserable day of work when she hadn't been able to find anything to take her mind off

Mac. Or that kiss. Or put a stop to the flashes of desire and hope that always spiralled into hopelessness. Now she was going to be feeling homesick on top of heart-sick.

'How are *you*, anyway?' she asked brightly. 'How's work?'

'Flat out,' Anne said co-operatively. 'We had three cases back to back yesterday and they were all compli-cated. The biggest was an ostium primum atrial septal defect that extended through both AV valves into the ventricular septum.'

'Wow! How did that go?'

'Great. Little Down's syndrome girl. Very cute. She was awake when I did my rounds in PICU this morning.'

Julia swallowed. Was the mere mention of a child enough to drag her thoughts back to yesterday? To Mac?

'Any word on that consultancy position?'

'They're going to advertise it soon. Richards thinks I'll be a top contender.'

'You'll get it. Good heavens, you're going to be a consultant paediatric cardiac surgeon by the time you're thirty-five. Go, you!'

'I'm not holding my breath. I've been working towards this for nearly fifteen years. I can wait as long as it takes.'

'Wait until I get home, anyway. I want to help cele-brate.'

'I'll tell them not to advertise for a couple of months, shall I?'

'You do that.' Julia was smiling again but something new was being added to the mix of emotions she'd been grappling with. Three months wasn't very long. She was already halfway through her time here and look how fast it had gone. It would only seem a blink until she was heading home again and then she'd never see Mac again. She'd never know what might have happened if she'd…

'Hey, it's Saturday on your side of the world.' Desperation was providing another distraction. 'You've got a night off for once. You and Dave going out on a hot date?'

'I will if you will.'

Something in her sister's tone made Julia's heart sink. 'Things not going any better, then?'

'Worse if anything,' Anne admitted. 'I get the feeling he wants me to choose between him and my career. He wants a family. How did life get so mixed up?'

'It's crazy, isn't it? You can have kids and don't want any because you've already been a mother to me, and I can't and…' Her voice trailed off. It was the biggest dream of all, wasn't it? A home and family of her own.

It was Anne's turn to try and provide distraction. 'We've got each other,' she said stoutly. 'And we've both got amazing careers. Now, tell me all about this job with the train.'

'It was unreal. It's been all over the Sunday papers here. I'll scan the articles and email them to you.'

'Please. But tell me about it first so I won't have kittens when I see the pictures.'

'OK.' This was good. Anne's career was so much

part of her, it was inseparable from who she was. Julia needed to be more like that. So passionate about her career that anything else got at least a slightly lower priority. Things like relationships. That ordinary kind of family unit she'd never had herself as a child and could never create for any children of her own.

She was a survivor. She'd already survived being orphaned as a young child, hadn't she? And a brush with cancer that had led to a hysterectomy at the age of twenty-two, for heaven's sake. Life couldn't throw anything at her that she couldn't handle.

'We got the call about 2 p.m.,' she told her sister. 'And when we spotted the target, I really couldn't believe what I was seeing…'

CHAPTER FOUR

THANK heaven for uniforms!

If she didn't have a uniform to put on, Julia might have had the entire contents of her admittedly meagre wardrobe strewn over her bed this morning, thanks to a bad dose of what could only be described as 'first date' nerves.

She hadn't seen Mac for two days.

Two days of worrying about how it would be when they saw each other for the first time in the wake of *that* kiss.

Two nights of reliving said kiss and her imagination hadn't held back in exploring what might have happened if they'd been somewhere other than an open car park. Or if she hadn't pulled away and then done her best to dismiss the moment by cracking a stupid joke about it.

The night time was manageable. Private. A guilty but irresistible pleasure.

It was the day time workings of her overactive imagination that was causing the nerves. So many scenarios had presented themselves. The worst was an awkward coolness between herself and Mac that everyone would notice and would make working together a misery instead of a joy.

At the other end of the spectrum, she could imagine an escalation of attraction which drew them together like human magnets. And that would probably have exactly the same effect due to the kind of tension it would create.

The best she could hope for was something in the middle. A return to the status quo but with a connection that had been deepened. A step towards a genuine friendship perhaps.

That was what Julia really wanted.

'Who are you trying to kid?' she muttered at her reflection, pausing in disgust as she realised what she was about to do.

In disgust, she threw the mascara wand back into the drawer. Make-up was an occasional indulgence and only ever used for a night out. Never for work. What *was* she thinking?

As if she didn't know!

'Focus,' she ordered herself, tucking the black T-shirt with the red SERT insignia into her black trousers.

'On your career,' she specified, lacing up her steel-capped black boots. 'Like Anne does. It's all you need to do.'

She tied the knots in the laces tightly. 'You're going to be the best you possibly can be in a job you absolutely love,' she said aloud.

The determined talk to herself was helpful. It worked right through the fifteen-minute drive from the farm cottage she was leasing and got her through parking close to that big, black vehicle and the stone wall that marked the spot where the kiss had happened.

The flashback was so powerful she actually raised her hand to touch her lips, convinced she could feel the pressure of his all over again. Impossible not to push that mental rewind button as she had so many times already. Back to before the kiss had happened. To that delicious *waiting*. Knowing what was about to happen and experiencing a more intense anticipation than she would have believed anything could engender.

Julia tore her gaze away from the wall. She could stop doing this. Stop thinking about it. She couldn't stop that odd kick in her gut, though, or the tingles that shot out from it to spread throughout her entire body but she could—and did—ignore their significance. It was nothing more than a physical thing. She could deal with this.

At least, she could until she walked into the mess-room and saw what it was that she *really* wanted, standing there beside the bench, making coffee.

Mac.

Tall. Solid. Julia eyed his back cautiously, hoping like hell he wouldn't turn around until she got her errant mind—and body—back under control.

He's not even that good looking, she thought somewhat desperately. He's…rugged. His nose and mouth are a bit big and he's got that odd dimple in the middle of his chin. And he looks older than he is. Kind of weathered.

And he's got some other woman he cares about. One with long, blonde hair.

Yes. Maybe this was the track to take. It certainly felt like a splash of cold water. Julia poked her fingers through her own hair, making the spikes more prominent.

A pixie cut, the hairdresser had promised, but it looked more like a hedgehog now that it had grown out a little. Appropriate, really, given her short, little legs.

That blonde woman was probably tall. And beautiful.

And that was fine, because she wasn't interested in Mac as anything other than a colleague.

Oh, Lord. This was going to be every bit as dreadful as she'd feared. That kiss had unleashed something that had to be chained up again. Currently it felt like something far too wild to even begin trying to handle. It was too hard to move her feet and take the first step in any attempt. Her heart was thumping and her stomach was tying itself into a painful knot.

And then Mac turned his head. 'Hey, Jules. Want a coffee?'

It was exactly what he would have said last week. In exactly the same kind of tone. The knot inside began to melt and Julia's heart gave a peculiar kind of wiggle and then settled into a steady rhythm she could ignore. It was going to be OK.

She nodded. 'Yes, please.'

And here it was. The first challenge. Eye contact that would be far too easy to maintain and allow to continue long enough to be significant. To send messages that

Julia had no intention of transmitting. But Mac's glance only brushed hers. Just a whisper of contact. The kind you might make with a complete stranger.

It should have been reassuring.

It certainly shouldn't feel like a physical shove to push her away and even if it did, it shouldn't feel this disappointing.

The Sunday papers were still scattered all over the big table in the kitchen area. Julia made an effort and shifted her focus.

'They took some great pictures, didn't they? I love that one of you and Carla being winched up. You should contact the paper and see if you can get a copy.'

'The TV footage was even better.' Mac came towards her, carrying two steaming mugs. He put one in front of Julia and then sat down. 'They caught you climbing into the carriage. Did you see it?'

'No.' Julia was happy to follow Mac's example and sit down. Maybe she could relax all those tense muscles now because Mac sounded completely normal. As though the kiss had never happened. Her smile was rueful. 'I think my sister did, though. She's planning my obituary in case I don't make it back home.'

Mac smiled. Just one of those crooked, half-smiles he was so good at but Julia was aware of that melting sensation inside again. She reached for her mug and cupped her hands around it as though needing the comfort of its warmth.

'I heard you telling Ken about her. She sounds pretty special.'

Julia risked an upward glance. This was different. A

conversation about something personal? But Mac's expression was simply interested. She couldn't read anything more into this step onto new territory.

She shrugged. 'Yeah…probably not the done thing to share one's life history with a patient but he needed distraction.'

Mac was pulling a section of the newspaper closer, signalling that the personal conversation was over, but then Julia was surprised again.

'Not many people get raised by a sibling,' he said.

'No. She's an amazing person.' Julia was happy to talk about this. This was exactly the kind of conversations that colleagues on the way to being friends could have. 'She was only six and I was a baby when Mum died but Dad always said she grew up overnight and turned into a mother instead of a sister. When she wasn't at school she had to be the one looking after me, and woe betide any nanny who tried to interfere.'

Mac raised an eyebrow. 'Determination is a family trait, then?'

'Yeah…' Was that a compliment of some kind? Way too hard to tell and why on earth was she bothered, anyway? She really, really didn't want this kind of emotional roller-coaster going on in her head.

She could ignore it and it would go away. Julia concentrated on her coffee for the short silence that followed. In the normal run of things, they might have a brief conversation but then they'd probably look at the papers while they finished their drinks. Or discuss what the day might bring. There was no one else on station at the moment, which meant the road crews were busy.

If there were no callouts for the specialist crews they could be used to help cover other work.

Julia was hoping that the silence was only feeling awkward for herself but Mac's abrupt question advertised otherwise.

'She's a doctor? Your sister?'

'A paediatric cardiothoracic surgical registrar, no less.'

'That's extremely impressive.'

'Sure is. I'm very proud of her.'

'But you weren't tempted to go to med school yourself?'

'Tempted, yes. But then I thought about being confined in an ED or a theatre or a general practice and I got cabin fever.'

'You wanted adventure.'

'Yeah.'

'A bit of danger.'

'Too right!'

'No two jobs the same.'

'You got it.' They were both smiling now. Of course Mac got it. They shared a passion for this work and it was a connection far too strong to ignore.

We're talking about *work*, Julia reminded herself. *That's* the connection. We're colleagues.

So why did it feel like something else entirely? That rapid-fire exchange seemed to have derailed them both and led them straight back to where they'd been…the moment before that kiss.

Mac's smile faded and he looked away. 'I'm not surprised she worries about you. She's still being a mother, isn't she?'

'Kind of.' Julia sucked in a breath, pushing this man and her reactions to him out of her head. Trying to concentrate and think about her sister, instead. It was a complicated relationship that had undergone a huge change as she'd left her teens. A rough couple of years, those had been, what with the diagnosis of early endometrial cancer, the surgery and the grief that had accompanied her recuperation with such a huge adjustment needed in what she had envisaged as her future. 'She's like a mother and a sister and a best friend all rolled into one, I guess.'

Mac was silent for a heartbeat. 'You must miss her.'

'I do.'

He cleared his throat. 'Guess you'll be looking forward to getting home, then.'

And there it was. Challenge number two. Had Mac intended any significance behind those words? If she said she couldn't wait to get back to the other side of the world, she could ensure that any thoughts he might have of following up on that kiss would be buried because she would really be saying she wasn't interested in him.

The split second of identifying that significance was enough of a hesitation. Mac stood up and took his mug back to the sink to rinse it. The question morphed into a statement and left the clear impression that the fact she was looking forward to leaving was acceptable.

A relief, even?

He could do this.

That pesky part of Mac's brain that was attached to

something much lower on his body just needed a bit more squashing and it would fit neatly into a box that could be locked and then ignored.

He'd managed well so far today, apart from that tiny prod he hadn't been able to resist this morning, asking if Julia was looking forward to getting home. Alert for a flicker of something other than the impression she was trying very hard to pretend that kiss had never happened. Testing her. Or testing himself?

Whatever. They had both passed.

They'd tidied and restocked the back of the helicopter and then their kits but all they'd discussed had been things like the strength of disinfectant to use or the fact that they were low on IV supplies and morphine. It hadn't helped that the busy start to the day for the road crew had become an unusually quiet day and, once he and Julia had moved inside to do the kits, they were hanging around, keen to hear as much inside detail as they could about the train-crash scene.

'So how did you tackle the fractured femur?'

'Usual protocol,' Julia responded as she pulled pockets of the back packs open and laid out their contents to see what was missing. 'Oxygen, fluids, pain relief and a traction splint. Just the same as you'd be doing.'

'Bit different, hanging in mid-air with a vertical aisle! Must have been hellishly awkward.'

'Jules can work anywhere,' Mac told them. 'She's like a cross between a contortionist and…'

He had to think of something that could describe both her level of endurance and the way she could use her body. Impossible not to let his gaze rest on that body for a moment as he tried to come up with that word. No overalls right now. She was wearing the team T-shirt and it hugged the curves of her upper body. Her arms were bare and he could see the definition of her muscles. She was as fit as he was. If he touched her upper arm, it would be firm. Those curves on the front of her T-shirt wouldn't be firm, though, would they? They'd be… Oh, *God*! Desire seeped out of that mental box, that wasn't secure enough yet, to tackle him like a solid force. He hurriedly shifted his gaze back to that defined biceps.

'A weightlifter,' he supplied.

Nobody had noticed his hesitation. Julia was wrinkling her nose at him.

'Gee, thanks, mate,' she huffed. 'You make me sound like some kind of muscle-bound circus act.'

Mac grinned. And then quirked an eyebrow, keeping his tone very casual. 'I only meant that you're supple. And strong. It was a compliment.'

'Oh-h-h.' The look Julia gave their audience said that this was a one-off, getting a compliment. The look she flashed in Mac's direction said something rather different. There was almost a question there—as though she was puzzled by something.

That kiss was still there. Hanging in the air between them.

'Not that strong,' she said in a tone as offhand as his had been. 'I couldn't have got her onto that stretcher without you, let alone up and out of the carriage.'

Mac leaned past her to drop a new pack of luer plugs

onto one of the piles. 'We make a good team,' he said. 'That's all.'

There. He'd said it aloud and he could feel the way Julia stilled for a moment. As though she was capturing his words and soaking in their significance. The kiss was history. They were colleagues again. Nothing more.

'What about the other guy?' Mac was grateful for the voice of the paramedic. Moving them on and chasing that moment into the past, where it belonged—along with that unfortunate kiss.

'You mean Ken?' Was he imagining any strain in her voice? 'The one with the spinal injury?'

'Yeah.'

'That *was* tricky,' she said. No. She sounded normal. Delighted to be discussing something professional. 'There was a bit more to worry about than there would have been getting him out of, say, a car crash. We knew we had to get him out of the seat and then up the aisle before we could keep him horizontal.'

'Did you use a KED?'

'Absolutely. Couldn't have managed without one.'

'What level was the lesion?'

'Reasonably high. Paresthesia in both hands.'

'Diaphragmatic breathing?'

'No. And he didn't go into a significant level of neurogenic shock, fortunately.'

Mac was only half listening, vaguely irritated by the chatter without knowing why. He kept himself busy sorting an airway roll and putting endotracheal tubes into order by size, finding the guide wires and bite blocks to put back into their correct slots, but he found himself wishing some road-based pagers would sound.

Finally, they did.

'Priority three,' the paramedic said, clearly disappointed. 'Probably a transfer. If you guys get something good happening while we're out, you'll owe us a beer.'

A vaguely tense silence fell once they were alone in the messroom again. Mac fiddled with the kit, making sure everything was perfectly aligned. He was simply too aware of their proximity, that was all. Too aware that the kiss had changed something. It had been a mistake on both sides and they were both doing their best to pretend it hadn't happened, but it had and now it was just…there.

But they couldn't talk about it. If they did, it would be tantamount to admitting attraction and Mac didn't want that conversation. He didn't want to talk about it. He didn't want to *think* about it because if he did, he couldn't control the pull that came in its wake.

A pull towards something he really didn't want. Territory he was more than content to be exiled from. This pull was stronger than anything he'd come across in ten years of voluntary exile. And for the first time it felt like he was in a place he might not want to be in for much longer.

A lonely place.

He didn't like that feeling. It was a relief when Julia broke the silence.

'Mac?'

He looked up. Hell…there was a plea in her eyes. She wanted something from him and if she asked, it might take more strength than he had to refuse.

'Mmm?' It was a noncommittal sound.

'Do you think…if it stays this quiet…?'

She was hesitant. About to ask for something that might not be entirely professional? Mac's mouth went curiously dry.

'I was hoping…' Julia's smile was mischievous '…that we might be able to sneak out and go and visit Ken.'

Mac was quiet again.

He was driving the late-model SUV that was the SERT team's road vehicle, having checked with Control that it was all right for them to head into the city to visit the hospital Ken had been admitted to. If necessary, they could head for the helipad or any other job at a moment's notice.

This car had only the front seats. The back was packed with all the equipment they could need in an emergency but there was no stretcher. It was used as an advance vehicle to get to a major incident first, an area where no ambulance was available or as back-up for a serious case. An ambulance had to be dispatched as well for transporting any patients and sometimes, if the patient required treatment beyond the skill level of an available road crew, they would have to abandon this vehicle to travel to the hospital and then retrieve it later.

Julia was becoming increasingly aware of how quiet Mac was as she listened in on the radio traffic. The blips advertising a new message were coming thick and fast. An ambulance was being dispatched to a three car pile-up. Someone else was reporting an NFA from another scene. No further assistance was required there because it was a DOA rather than the cardiac arrest that had been called in. A crew patched through advance notice of a critically ill stroke patient they were transporting to a receiving emergency department and a vehicle was being sent to a rural area to be on standby while the fire service dealt with a house fire.

Busy but nothing out of the ordinary. Julia had her fingers crossed that a call wouldn't come in the next little while. Long enough for them to visit Ken and see how he was getting on. And long enough to find out why Mac seemed to have withdrawn again.

Not as much as he had the other night, travelling back from the train crash but enough to worry Julia and chip away at this morning's relief when it had seemed like they could get past any awkward aftermath of that kiss. His message had been received loud and clear. They were a good team and that was all, but they'd never had this odd tension between them before. Silences that became loaded so quickly.

And Mac had made a tentative step towards friendship this morning, hadn't he? She could reciprocate and maybe that would be enough to fix things properly.

'So…' Having made the resolution, Julia impulsively reached out to turn down the volume of the radio. 'Fair's fair, Mac.'

He shot her a wary glance.

'I mean, I'm feeling at a disadvantage now. Like I haven't had *my* turn.'

The look was a frown this time. 'I'm not following you. What have I had that you haven't?'

'Information.'

'Such as?'

'Well, you know a lot more about me than I do about you.'

Mac was staring into the side mirror, watching for an opportunity to change lanes. 'Not that much.'

'Enough,' Julia said firmly.She switched off the tiny voice at the back of her mind that was suggesting she might be making a mistake here. 'It's my turn,' she continued. 'I want to know about you.'

Mac was still concentrating on his driving. He changed lanes twice and then indicated an upcoming turn but Julia was watching his face just as carefully and she saw something in the softening of his features that suggested her interest might not be unwelcome. That encouragement was more than enough to switch off that annoying little voice.

'You know heaps,' Mac said. 'How old I am, where I come from, where I did my training. How I like my coffee.' He gave her just the hint of a crooked smile. 'All the important stuff.'

Julia laughed, shaking her head. 'That last one's going to come back and bite you, mate. And I'm not talking about work stuff. I'm talking about the kinds of things friends might talk about. We *are* friends, aren't we?'

Friends. It was such a nice, safe word. She could definitely detect a lessening of any tension in the atmosphere now.

'You want to talk about football? Wrestling, maybe?'

Julia's breath hitched. No, not wrestling. 'That's boy

stuff,' she said dismissively. 'I'm talking family. Like what you know about me. Brothers, sisters, ex-wives…that sort of thing.'

Oh…God! What on earth had made that come out? This wasn't the time to diffuse tension by cracking stupid jokes.

Mac looked as startled as she was herself. 'You want to know about my ex-wife?'

Julia swallowed. 'You *have* one?'

A tiny pause and then a huff of sound that had an unmistakably ironic twinge. 'No.'

She had to laugh again, to hide the flash of…what was it, relief? Elation? Something entirely inappropriate, anyway. This was supposed to be a joke. Something light that would make Mac smile.

'That's two,' she told him sternly. 'Any more and I can't promise you'll survive the retribution.'

Mac chuckled. 'OK, shoot. My past history is an open book.'

Was it? Could she ask about the blonde woman?

No. She didn't want to know. It was none of her business because this was about friendship, not romance.

'Brothers?'

'Nope.'

'Sisters?'

'Nope.'

'You're an only child?'

Mac sighed. 'Did you really get your degree with honours?'

Julia ignored the insult. 'I wouldn't have picked it, that's all.'

'Why? Do I seem spoilt? Self-centred and socially insensitive or something?'

'Not at all.' The idea of applying any of those criticisms to Mac was ludicrous. 'I was kind of an only child myself, you know, what with Anne turning into my mother.'

Mac turned off onto another road and Julia saw the sign indicating the route to the Eastern Infirmary—the hospital they were heading for. This conversation would have to end very soon and she hadn't stepped off first base, really. Mac was going all silent again so it was up to her to say something.

'It's just that you're such a people person,' she said carefully. 'You get on so well with everybody and you love kids. I had this picture in my head of you being the oldest in a big family. The big brother, you know?'

Mac turned into the car park. 'I wish,' he said quietly, choosing an empty slot to swing the vehicle into. 'A big family was something I always dreamed of.' He pulled on the hand brake and cut the engine.

Something inside Julia died right along with the engine.

The tiny hope that this could have been something. That they didn't have to bury that kiss and make it go away.

It was something in Mac's tone. A wistfulness that told her a big family was a dream that mattered a lot. Something he hadn't had as a child but he could—and should—be able to realise it as a father.

The road that led further than that kiss could never go in that direction and she owed it to Mac not to let either of them take it further.

Not that he was showing the slightest sign of wanting to but she could have kept hoping and now she wasn't going to. And that was good. Any potential for an emotional ride that could only end in a painful crash was being removed.

'Come on, then.' Julia reached for the door latch. 'Let's go and find Ken.'

Their spinal injury patient from the train carriage was still in the intensive care unit but he was awake and seemed delighted to see his visitors.

'Hey, Jules! You've come to see me.'

'I said I would.' Julia's smile was lighting up her whole face and it wasn't just Ken who was captured by its warmth. Mac had to make an effort to look away and find something else compelling enough to compete with that smile.

'I probably won't need surgery.' Ken sounded tired but quite happy to discuss his treatment with the person who'd played such a big part in his rescue.

'That's fantastic,' Julia said. 'So the doctors are happy with you?'

'So far. They've warned me it's going to be a long road to any recovery and they said we won't know how bad things will end up being until after the spinal shock wears off, and that can take weeks.'

Julia was nodding, her face sympathetic. Then she glanced up at the wall behind his bed which was plastered with get-well cards.

'So many cards,' she said. 'You're a popular man, Ken. I reckon I'd be lucky to get two if I was lying in that bed.'

'I doubt that.' Ken's tone was admiring. So was the gaze he had fixed on Julia. Mac felt a kind of growl rumbling in his chest. He cleared his throat.

'What was the verdict?' he asked. 'As far as damage?'

'A fracture/dislocation in C6/7 and a fracture in… um…I think it was T8. Does that mean anything?'

Mac smiled. 'Sure does. Any changes in your symptoms in the last couple of days?'

'The pins and needles have gone from my hands. I've got them in my feet instead but they say that's a good thing.'

'It is,' Julia agreed. 'And the earlier you see an improvement, the more likely things are to end up better than you might expect.'

'Pretty much what my doctor said.' Ken had that slightly awed tone back again. 'You really know your stuff, don't you?'

'I'm still learning.' Julia's gaze flicked to Mac and she smiled.

The smile said that she was learning from him and that she was grateful. It made Mac feel important. Necessary. He had things he could give her, like knowledge and new skills.Not that he hadn't already been doing that but it seemed more significant now. The way everything happening between them did.

The pleasurable pride faded abruptly, however, as Mac realised what that significance was. Julia had just reminded him of his position as her mentor. Of her passion for her career and why she was here.

The sound of their pagers curtailed the visit. Julia

promised to visit again on her next day off and Mac was aware of another unpleasant splash of emotion.

Jealousy?

If it was, it was easily dealt with because Mac also realised that Julia had just handed him exactly what he needed.

The key to be able to lock that box.

It wasn't that the reminder of Christine hadn't been enough to warn him off. This was a bonus. Julia wasn't just a woman whose career was the most important thing to her, he was her senior colleague. Her teacher. In a position of authority. To step over professional boundaries into anything more personal simply wasn't acceptable and his reputation and status in his chosen field of work were everything to him.

This was the key.

He would talk to Julia about spinal injuries on their way to this callout. He would quiz her about spinal oedema and paralytic ileus and the scientific evidence that an early infusion of methyl prednisolone could minimise any ongoing damage to the spinal cord.

And when they were at the job they could talk about that patient. Analyse the job on the way home. Anything that would foster professionalism.

Yes. The key was in its slot and Mac was confident that it would turn smoothly.

The danger was over.

CHAPTER FIVE

'Do SEIZURES in the first week after a head injury indicate a risk of future epilepsy?'

'No.'

'Why are they serious, then?'

Julia sat down at the messroom table. 'They can cause hypoxic brain damage.'

'How?'

She opened the paper bag to extract the lunch she had purchased at a nearby noodle house. Hers was a chili chicken mix and Mac had gone for beef and black beans. He was using a fork and she had chopsticks but it wasn't the differences in their meal or implement choices that was bothering her right now. It wasn't even because Joe had taken his lunch out the back somewhere so he could have a chat to his wife on the phone while he ate, thereby depriving Julia of some ordinary, stress-free conversation.

No. What was bothering her was that it had been nearly three days since they'd gone to visit Ken and something had flicked a switch in Mac in the wake of that hospital visit. He'd turned into the mentor from hell. Julia felt like she was either listening to a lecture, taking an exam or demonstrating practical skills to an assessor. He was perfectly friendly and smiling as much as he ever had. He was taking an interest in her training that could only be described as keen and he clearly wanted to help her challenge herself and learn more. He was also very quick to praise anything and everything she did well.

And it was driving her around the bend!

OK, so the kiss had been a mistake. They both knew that. She'd been content that they'd reset the ground rules so that friendship was permissible but somehow, after that visit to Ken, Mac had changed the rules again and she didn't understand why. Julia was becoming increasingly frustrated. No, actually, she was getting seriously annoyed.

He was safe. She wasn't about to ambush him again and jump his bones. No matter how attractive the prospect, she had dismissed any notion of the fling Anne had advocated, never mind anything with more significance.

So why did she feel like the bad guy here? Like that kiss had liquefied and then formed a glass wall that Mac was determined not to crack. Or look through even. By making it so obvious that he was keeping his distance, he was making things worse.

Instead of being able to forget the kiss and move on, this was making her more and more aware of him. He was probably picking up on that and that was making him feel threatened and retreat further.

A vicious circle.

With an inward sigh, Julia tried to distract herself…yet again.

She opened her cardboard box and sniffed appreciatively. 'Mmm. Good choice, going to the noodle house.' Looking up to see if Mac was enjoying his food, she found he had an eyebrow raised expectantly.

'Oh, for heaven's sake,' she muttered under her breath, snapping the disposable chopsticks apart. 'Fine.' She raised her voice and spoke very quickly. 'Brain damage occurs because a seizure involves maximal brain metabolism and increased muscle metabolism. This consumes oxygen and glucose, which leads to hypoxia. Or they may induce airway obstruction and possibly temporary respiratory arrest, which will also cause hypoxia. A brain deprived of oxygen for too long becomes irreversibly damaged. Can I eat my lunch now, please, sir?'

Something that could have been disappointment or even hurt showed in Mac's face but his gaze slid away from hers instantly. The way it always seemed to now.

'Sure,' he said easily. 'Enjoy.'

They ate in silence for a minute or two. Perversely, Julia wanted Mac to ask her something else. She wanted to hear his voice, even if it meant racking her brains to give him the correct answer to a question or an intelligent response to some information.

Or was it because of the feeling she had done something wrong? Upset him in some way? She had a delicious-looking piece of chicken caught between her chopsticks but hesitated with it in mid-air because she couldn't help glancing across the table at Mac as she hit a mental rewind button to see if she had said or done anything unacceptable so far today.

Mac had just put a generous forkful of noodles into his mouth but one hadn't quite made its destination, hanging from one corner. Julia's gaze was captured. And then Mac put out the tip of his tongue to capture the errant noodle and she was aware of a wave of heat that nearly melted her into a puddle on her chair. It felt like a spark had been dropped into a tinder-dry forest somewhere in her abdomen and it caught with a flash like a small explosion. Heat radiated upwards. She could feel it reach her neck and head for her cheeks.

Her hand must have trembled slightly because she lost the grip on that piece of chicken and it fell and bounced down her overalls, leaving a trail of chilli sauce. Julia made a dive for it, snatching it up and putting it in her mouth, hoping she had reacted so quickly her clumsiness might go unnoticed.

She could feel Mac watching her, however. Could feel the tension making the air she was trying to breathe feel like treacle. Oh, *God*! Had he been watching her watching him lick up that noodle? That vicious circle spun faster. Out of control. This awareness was driving her just as crazy as Mac's determination to be Super-Mentor.

Why couldn't it just go away? If Mac trusted her, it would. A flicker of anger at the hidden insult was generated but confrontation was hardly going to help anything, was it?

'Oops, busted!' The old habit of making a joke to defuse emotional overload was too hard to change. She grinned at Mac. 'I'm a piglet!'

But Mac's smile was tight and Julia felt like an idiot.

Repressed anger grew. She was doing her very best to sort this situation out but Mac wasn't co-operating. At this rate, what had been a perfect partnership would be poisoned. They would end up actually disliking each other. Julia was already feeling the stirring of resentment that could very easily express itself as antagonism. She could feel her own smile freezing and her gaze hardening into a glare.

The sound of their pagers going off should have been a blessing but it only added fuel to the unpleasant emotional mix for Julia. Good grief! The enjoyment of her job was going down the drain and now she couldn't even enjoy her food. Scowling, she pushed her chair back and went to the office to get the details of the job they were being dispatched to, ignoring Mac who was following close behind.

Joe was already in the office, looking at a wall map. 'Police callout,' he told them. 'Incident in a known drug house.'

'Great.' SERT training involved the kind of specialist work that could come from this kind of police operation. Dealing with gunshot wounds or scenes where tear gas or pepper spray might be used. They usually involved people who had no respect for authority and for whom violence was merely a form of communication. Way down on Mac's list of preferences any day. Taking Julia into a job like this was even less appealing.

Working with her at all was losing its appeal.

He had been doing so well since that visit to Ken. So confident he could handle this. And then she'd dropped that damned piece of chicken and stained her overalls and that mental key had shot out of its lock. He had lost control big time.

The fabric of those overalls had become invisible and given him such a clear image of what her breast beneath would look like. His body had supplied what it might feel like to touch it. With his fingers…a soft, slow stroke, maybe. Or with his lips…

The effort it had taken to drag his gaze away had been phenomenal and when he had, it had gone in the wrong direction and collided with hers for just long enough to register the way her pupils had dilated. With alarm, no doubt, because his reaction had hardly been subtle. Her skin had been flushed, too, making her look hotter and more enticing that that spicy sauce she had been throwing around.

'I'm a piglet,' she'd said, with that winning grin, and Mac had tried to smile back but he knew he hadn't been forgiven. The look on her face when she'd scraped her chair back. The way she'd ignored him as she'd stomped off to the office. OK, so he'd slipped his control for a heartbeat. It wasn't going to happen again. It was only a matter of weeks until she packed her bags and disappeared from his life. He wasn't going to risk another slip and give Julia another opportunity to dismiss him like that. She could stop worrying. He was going to. He wasn't even going to worry about the potential for this job to be no place for a woman.

'Come on, then,' he growled. 'Let's go and get it over with.'

It was only a short helicopter ride. They landed in an empty car park between railway lines and the back of a rundown housing estate. Moving to a safe point, Mac was all too aware of how deserted it felt. Dark, blank windows towered menacingly overhead. Tattered plastic bags blew around like tumbleweeds and they walked past a burnt-out car chassis and an off-licence with thick iron bars over its door.

Mac did his best to ignore it but every instinct was telling him that Julia shouldn't be here. This was professional, not personal, he decided. For the first time they were in a situation where her size and gender were a liability. He had every reason to order her to stay with the police at ground level until this incident was done and dusted. It was part of being a mentor. It had nothing to do with any desire to drag her away and simply keep her safe because he cared about her in an inappropriate way.

Not that she'd co-operate, of course. Even him thinking about the possibility had given Julia time to march right up to the police van and wait expectantly for their briefing.

'It was a neighbour who made the call,' they were informed. 'Sounds of a fight going on and shots were fired. Then there was a lot of screaming. Still is. As soon as we can be sure it's safe to enter and we've found who's doing the screaming, we'll send you guys in.'

Mac eyed Julia, the words forming that would be an order for her to stay put while he went in alone. Except that he could almost see a balloon over his partner's head right now. One that enclosed the words 'I don't think so, mate!' They would end up having an argument in public and that would hardly be professional. Not only that, she might think he was trying to protect her for personal reasons.

The same kind of personal reasons she had just been disgusted with, having caught him staring at the food stain on her chest. Mac stared back at Julia, aware of how frustrating this was. Couldn't she see that her feistiness only generated problems? If she hadn't been waiting for him in that car park, that kiss would never have happened and he wouldn't be struggling to keep the key in that mental box in his head. Or was it his heart? Wherever. It was huge and heavy and dragging him down. And it was more than frustrating. It was infuriating.

Fine, was the silent message he sent back. *Do what you like. If you won't listen to reason, be it on your own head.*

It took a good thirty minutes for police to gain control of the scene. The occupants of the dwelling, who hadn't been at all eager to allow the police inside, were hauled out in handcuffs. They were cursing and spitting as they were dragged past Mac and Julia and into the back of a secure van. A police officer close to Mac was kicked in the shins and shook his head in disgust.

'There's one more up there,' he told Mac. 'Have fun.'

The man lay on a filthy mattress in the corner of a room strewn with empty bottles, overflowing ashtrays, half-empty cans of food and piles of tattered clothing. His features were sharp, his hair long and scraggly and he clearly hadn't washed or shaved for a considerable period of time.

'Here he is.' A police officer wearing a bulletproof vest stared down at the man, who was groaning loudly. He gave him a nudge with the toe of his boot and the man stopped groaning and began shouting obscenities.

'Oi!' The police officer looked unimpressed. 'Mind your manners or I'll send the medics away and we'll just take you downtown. Do you want to get looked at or not?'

'Not by him.' The man spat in Mac's direction and then bared yellowish teeth. 'I'm no poofter. *She* can look at me.' He leered in Julia's direction.

Julia could see the way Mac's features hardened. He wasn't about to be given orders by someone like this. He was on the point of stepping forward and making this situation worse than it needed to be. She didn't need his protection. She didn't want it.

Those flickers of resentment and anger were easy to tap into. He couldn't make her the bad guy and then step in and get all protective.

Damn the man. She didn't need his attitude or his protection. She could look after herself. It was Julia who took the first forward step.

'What's the story?' she asked the police officer.

'Says he's got a pain in his stomach.'

'I *have*,' the man sneered. 'Don't make it sound like I'm lying. Arghh!' He groaned convincingly and clutched his abdomen. 'I think I'm *dying*. Give me something. Hurry up!'

Julia avoided catching Mac's gaze as she took in their surroundings again. Not that she needed to given the track marks she could see on the man's arms but…yes, there were used syringes amongst the debris. This man was very likely to be a drug addict and this could be simply drug-seeking behavior. Mac would be thinking the same thing. He might disapprove of any intention on her part to take the performance too seriously.

But there had been a fight. Shots had been fired. An intrinsic part of this career she had chosen meant that judgment had to be put aside. Nobody could be left in pain or in danger of a condition being left untreated that could endanger their lives.

'Says he got kicked in the gut,' the police officer added. 'There was a fight going on when we got here.'

Another two police officers were collecting weapons they'd found in the apartment. A sawn-off shotgun, knives, knuckle-dusters and ammunition were already in a pile near the door.

'Have you been shot?' Mac's query was crisp. 'Or stabbed?'

'Get lost,' the man told him. 'I'm only gonna talk to *her*.'

'Come on, Jules.' Mac's tone was icy. 'If he's not going to co-operate, we're out of here. It's obviously not life-threatening.'

'Ahh!' the man screamed. 'Ahhh! *Ahhhh*!'

It was certainly a good impression of someone in agony. Julia shot Mac a warning glance. 'Won't hurt to take a look,' she said.

'I'm dying,' the man howled. 'Give me some-thing…*please*, lady…'

'Let me see.' Julia took another step towards the mattress. 'Pull up your shirt.'

There were no marks visible on an emaciated-looking midriff but it would require palpation to check whether there was any guarding or swelling which could indicate internal damage that might explain the man's apparent agony.

Julia crouched. She hadn't even got down to floor level when a skinny hand shot out and wrapped itself around her wrist, pulling her off balance.

'Stop wasting time.' the man spat. 'Give me some-thing *now*.'

The training given to deal with situations exactly like this meant that her reaction was instinctive. She wrenched her arm down sharply, towards the man's thumb, which had to give way. Then she rolled out of reach, coming to her knees and lifting her head just in time to see her assailant's other hand coming out from beneath a puddle of blanket, a blade glinting in his grasp.

All hell broke loose then. Police officers seemed to come from every corner of the room and within sec-onds the man was disarmed, on his stomach and hand-cuffed.

One of the police officers smiled somewhat ruefully at Julia. 'Sorry to have wasted your time,' he said. 'Looks like we can deal with this ourselves after all.'

Julia nodded. She was on her feet now but the aware-ness of how close that had been was kicking in. Her stomach was a tight knot and she felt absurdly close to tears. Turning, she made an effort to give Mac a smile that would disguise her reaction. Hopefully one that would tell him this hadn't been anything she hadn't been ready to handle. But her smile faded instantly.

Mac looked absolutely furious.

'You just had to do it, didn't you? Jump in without bothering to consult me. Without even *considering* the potential danger.'

'I did consider it.' Julia lifted her chin. She'd had to wait for this but she'd known it was coming.

Mac hadn't said a word as they'd marched along the concrete balcony of that tenement block or down flight after flight of graffiti-decorated stairwell.

'NFA,' he'd snapped at Joe, who'd looked bemused and had then sent Julia a 'what the hell happened in there?' look before scrambling to get them airborne again.

A silent flight. An apparent absorption with a recent emergency medicine journal since they'd been back on station. Until the road crew was dispatched and they were alone in the messroom. Julia had gone to make herself a cup of coffee and had looked at Mac's back where he was sitting at the table and sighed. Her offer to make him a hot drink had finally pulled the stopper from his bottled-up fury.

'I could see he was an addict,' she continued as calmly as she could. 'And the fact that he could be drug seeking was pretty obvious.' She held Mac's gaze. 'So obvious it would have been idiotic to waste time talking about it.'

'No.' Mac's chair scraped on linoleum as he got to his feet. 'I'll tell you what was idiotic, Julia. Getting flattered because he wanted *you* to assess him. Making a unilateral, *idiotic* decision to go along with what *he* wanted.'

Julia? He never called her by her full name. Or spoke to her as if he was disgusted with her performance or—worse—disappointed with her. And he was saying she was an idiot. Her throat tightened painfully.

'Why do you think he was so keen on the idea?' Mac continued relentlessly. 'Because you were young and attractive and he'd do whatever you asked?'

Julia stayed silent. Battling something that felt oddly like grief.

'No.' Mac's breath was expelled in an angry huff. 'It was because you were the weakest link. The person he was most likely to be able to hurt.'

The weakest link? Oh, God! Mac was working up to telling her he didn't want her on the team any more, wasn't he?

He was overreacting. She'd been in a room with a bunch of armed police officers, for heaven's sake.

As he had so often before in their time of working together, Mac seemed to read her mind but it didn't take any of the heat from his anger.

'What if those cops hadn't been there?' he demanded. 'What if it had just been you and me, on a street corner somewhere?'

She wouldn't have gone anywhere near him, of course. Julia opened her mouth to try and defend herself but Mac wasn't going to let her get a word in.

'You would have been stabbed. Or worse. I would have had to protect you and I could have been taken out as well. We're supposed to be a *team*. We look after each other and we communicate. Is that so difficult to remember?'

She was going to cry. It didn't matter that in any other circumstance she could have sucked this up and stayed in control. Or that crying in front of Mac was the absolute last thing she wanted to do.

He didn't want her on his team any more.

He didn't want *her*.

Oh, *hell*!

She was going to cry.

The anger, which had very little to do with Julia's decision-making on the last job and far more to do with the fact that he hadn't protected her—that she had made it clear she didn't *want* his protection—evaporated.

They stood there, facing each other in the kitchen area of the mess, the room dim now because it was getting late in the day and they hadn't turned on any lights yet. How had they got this close to each other? Had he been trying to intimidate her with his size as well as punishing her with his words?

Whatever. He was close enough and there was still enough light to see the glint of too much moisture in her eyes. Horrified, Mac watched as the glint intensified and a single, fat tear escaped to roll down the side of Julia's nose.

Mac could feel that tear. Melting something inside himself, and he knew exactly what that something was.

The lock on that damned box. Things that had been crammed inside started seeping out. Flickers of images like her smile and the way it made him feel. Pride in her courage. The knowledge that he wanted this woman more than he'd ever wanted any woman in his life. He'd give up anything for her. His life, even. And that was extraordinary. Terrifying. Because he'd honestly believed that nobody would ever be able to mess with his head to this degree now he'd finally got over Christine.

'Oh, *God*…' His voice sounded strangled. 'I'm sorry, Jules. I didn't mean—'

'Yes, you did.' Julia sniffed and scrubbed at her face with an impatient gesture. 'And you're right. It was stupid. I let you down and I'm not surprised you don't want to work with me any more.'

'What?' Anger had become dismay. 'When did I say anything of the kind?'

'You didn't have to.' Julia was avoiding his gaze. 'You think me being female is some kind of liability. That you have to protect me or something.' She gulped in a breath that caught somewhere on the way to create a tiny sob.

The sound undid Mac.

'No.' He spoke softly now. 'Don't you see, Jules?' The words were being forced out. He shouldn't be saying them. But he couldn't no more *not* say them than take in another breath. 'It's not that I *have* to protect you so much. It's that I *want* to. Too much.'

Slowly, her gaze lifted. Caught his and held it.

Mac's hands fisted by his sides as a defence against

the urge to reach out and pull her into his arms. He tried to smile but could only manage a brief, one-sided twist of his mouth. 'It's a bit of a problem,' he confessed. 'It has been ever since that…kiss.'

She so hadn't expected this. She had watched and waited for days for some sign of acknowledgement of that kiss that wasn't running in the opposite direction as fast as humanly possible. In the wake of his anger this was such a twist that Julia felt the earth tilt beneath her feet.

Was the anger…the *passion* behind his reaction to that scare today about frustration, not disappointment?

'I thought you wanted to forget about that kiss,' she whispered.

'I did.' This time, both sides of Mac's mouth moved but, endearingly, they seemed to go in opposite directions. 'I tried to. It hasn't worked.'

'No.' Julia's agreement was heartfelt. She knew precisely how hard that kiss had been to try and forget.

For a heartbeat, and then two, they stood there in silence again, watching each other. Julia was soaking in something warm. Joyous, even, because that kiss had had the same effect on him as it had had on herself. Awareness sizzled between them and she finally knew that it wasn't just her feeling it. The acknowledgement that it existed was enough to have unleashed it and it seemed to be getting bigger and stronger with every second that ticked past.

'Bit of a problem,' Mac offered. There was something in his eyes that made Julia want to cry again, but for very different reasons. A vulnerability that tore a piece off her heart. For some reason, that scared him and now it was *she* that felt the need to protect.

'Mmm.' Were they leaning closer to each other or was that wishful thinking on her part? 'Maybe it doesn't have to be,' she heard herself saying.

Mac said nothing but she could sense his stillness. He was listening. Hard. Something Anne had said was trying to filter through this awareness of Mac that was filling her mind. Something about a fling doing her a world of good. That this was a perfect opportunity because it had a clearly defined end point.

Yes. That was the key. Mac was still safe. He didn't need to be afraid. Vulnerable.

'Whatever it is that's going on here,' she told Mac, 'it's got a use-by date. It won't be a problem for very long.'

Yes. She could see the realisation that there was a safety net available dawn on Mac's face. He was being offered a choice here. They both knew the attraction was there. They could live with it for a limited period of time. Or they could give up resisting it. Either way, it would be temporary. And Mac had the choice. She was giving him control. Not that she should be going down that track but if it was what Mac wanted…

'The *problem*,' Mac growled finally, 'is resisting it.'

'Mmm.' Yes. They were definitely closer. Some-how—imperceptibly—they had moved within kissing range. The pull was simply too powerful to resist.

'What…um….' It was hard enough to remember to breathe, let alone form a coherent question. Julia tried again. 'What do you think we should do about that?'

'I can't do a thing,' Mac groaned. 'Unless I don't mind getting fired.'

Julia's eyes widened. She hadn't thought about it from that perspective. Maybe she wasn't giving him a choice after all, just making things worse. 'You mean there's something I didn't see in the contract? About partners being…um…'

'It's unwritten,' Mac admitted. 'But it's also unethical.'

'Why?'

'Because I'm supposed to be mentoring you. Teaching you. Coercing you into any other kind of relationship would be seen as an abuse of power.'

'Oh…' Julia pursed her lips thoughtfully. 'What if the coercion came from the less powerful side of the equation?'

Mac blinked slowly on a sigh. 'It would still be unethical.'

'Because it would interfere with doing our job?'

'In a nutshell. Yes. It's doing that already, isn't it? Look at what happened today. I'm not sure how much longer I can keep up the fight. It's killing me.'

'Maybe you don't have to,' Julia said very softly. Whatever part of her head might have spent a considerable amount of time warning her not to go down this track was curiously silent. Gagged, probably, but it wouldn't have made any difference if it had been audible. She wanted this way too much. More than she'd ever wanted anything. 'What if it didn't interfere with our work? If it was something kept strictly to out-of-work hours that nobody else knew about?'

Mac's eyes were drifting closed again as though his lids had become too heavy. Was he stepping into fantasy or praying for strength? Suddenly, they snapped open.

'It could work.' He spoke as softly as Julia had. 'If we really wanted to make it work. What do you want, Jules?'

'The same as you, I hope.'

Their eye contact had locked. They were breathing exactly the same air. So close now they could feel each other's body warmth.

'Really?' Mac's voice had a seductive edge Julia had never heard before. A low, silky rumble that made her toes curl. 'Do you know what that is?'

Julia could feel a tiny smile playing with her lips but she feigned ignorance because she wanted to hear him say it.

'No. What do you want, Mac?'

His response was a sigh of breath against her lips as he finally closed the last distance between them.

'You. I want *you*.'

CHAPTER SIX

'WHY is it so dark in here?'

Julia peeled away from Mac's kiss before he'd had the chance to do anything more than touch her lips with his own. She dived for the light switch in the kitchen area and filled the room with a neon glare that was almost as much of a wrench as losing that touch had been.

Angus bowled into the kitchen part of the mess. 'Joe's fiddling with that blessed helicopter again. He said he didn't want to come inside because there was something weird going on and here you guys are, standing around in the dark. What gives?'

Mac shrugged, moving back to where he'd left his journal on the table. This was crazy, thinking they could have some kind of affair and keep it secret from their colleagues.

'I was making a coffee,' Julia said in a surprisingly steady voice. 'Want one?'

Angus swung his head from Mac's direction to stare at Julia. 'Something's up. Joe's right. There's a weird vibe. And you look…'

'Like hell, I expect. It's been a long day.' Julia seemed intent on pressing the switch on the electric jug. 'Can't wait to get home. How 'bout you, Mac?'

'Ditto.' Suddenly, Mac was enjoying the undercurrent between them. The totally private innuendo. Maybe this *was* crazy but trying to work with Julia for the next ten weeks or so and not doing anything about the way he was feeling would make *him* crazy.

There was no chance of locking anything away now. The lock was gone. Melted by those tears that had shown Mac a whole new side to this astonishing woman.

An unexpectedly vulnerable side.

Maybe it was just a physical thing for her but she wanted him. Out of all the men on this station who would cheerfully kill to be fancied by Julia Bennett, she was picking *him*.

They were both single, consenting adults so why not?

Mac had forgotten what it was like to feel this level of attraction. What sex could be like when there was more to it than simply slaking lust.

No. He sucked in a breath. He'd never felt like this. He remembered their last kiss only too well and just that tiny brush of contact they'd just had had been even more electric. Sex with Julia would be totally new territory.

Dangerous, exciting, totally irresistible territory.

And maybe they could keep it a secret. Angus knew there was something up but he was frowning. He couldn't make sense of whatever he was picking up.

'The last job wasn't much fun,' Mac told him calmly. 'Some low-life pulled a knife on Jules.'

'Hells bells! Are you OK?'

'I'm fine.' Julia smiled at Angus. 'It was entirely my own fault and Mac told me off. We're sorted. I'll have to let Joe know it's safe to come inside.'

'If you're sure.' Angus seemed to have forgotten Mac. He had stepped closer to Julia and was eyeing her with concern. 'You…um…haven't been crying, have you?'

'As if!' Julia snorted. 'Try and spread that kind of rumour and you're dead meat, Gus.'

Angus grinned and visibly relaxed. 'As long as you're OK. This job throws some curly ones at us sometimes, doesn't it?'

'Mmm.' Julia looked up from spooning coffee to catch Mac's gaze. 'It sure does. Nothing we can't cope with, though, eh, Mac?'

'No.' Mac held her gaze and it felt like a kind of pact. They could make this work.

It would be easy. Fun. More than fun. He was being given an opportunity he would never have again. And if he didn't go along with the affair Julia clearly wanted, he'd be in trouble. He knew only too well how determined she could be to get what she wanted. Look at today's job when she wasn't going to be left behind at a safe point. Working with her would be hell if he tried to back out now so maybe he should just give in gracefully and enjoy the ride.

A half-smile was playing around his lips and he was only half listening to the conversation behind him.

'Dale should be here any minute,' Angus was saying. 'You can get home a bit early if you want. Any plans for tonight?'

'Maybe.' Julia sounded perfectly innocent. 'I'm waiting to see if something comes up.'

Incredulous laughter almost broke from Mac. He managed to strangle it and turn the sound into a cough. Fortunately, Dale arrived on station at precisely the same moment.

They were free to go where they liked and start their time away from work. Mac caught up with Julia as she walked to the car park.

'What comes up?' he muttered. 'You like playing with fire, don't you?'

'I was just testing.' Julia gave him that mischievous grin he was coming to love. 'It worked, didn't it? Angus could tell something was going on and now he just thinks you're mean and I'm a girl.'

She wasn't a girl. She was a woman. The sexiest, most desirable woman in the world. No, there was no going back now. No chance that Mac could turn away from the path he'd stepped onto when he'd confessed his attraction.

'I can be mean,' Mac growled. 'I probably will be, if we don't get the hell out of here to some place we can stop pretending we don't want to rip each other's clothes off.'

He watched the way Julia licked her lips as though they were suddenly dry.

'Your place or mine?'

* * *

Julia's place was the obvious choice.

Private. Discreet.

Mac shared an inner-city apartment with Angus and even though they worked opposing shifts and only saw each other on days off, it felt far too close to work and the possibility of being discovered.

That this was going to be a secret liaison added a dimension to both the connection and the excitement and it seemed more than enough to tip Julia's anticipation into nervousness. Or maybe it was because every time she glanced in her rear-view mirror she could see the big, dark shape of Mac's vehicle shadowing hers.

The intention of this journey resonated in every cell of her body. It became harder to concentrate. Hard to take a deep enough breath. By the time she pulled to a halt beside the overgrown hedge surrounding her rented cottage, Julia had decided she must be crazy.

She had to work with this man. What if this was a disaster? If he found her a disappointment in comparison to that mystery blonde? If someone at work did find out and she was sent home in disgrace? Was the risk really worth it?

Then Mac was beside her and she was fumbling with the key to the cottage and his hand closed over hers and just held it.

Calming her. The way his solid strength always calmed any nerves she might have when facing a job. Julia took the first deep breath she had managed in quite some time. Felt his presence and automatically found courage again. Looked up and saw understanding in Mac's eyes. Heard the same kind of unspoken conversation they had become so adept at.

We don't have to do this.

I know.

We won't, if you don't want to.

I do. I want to. Do you?

You know I do.

Nervousness kicked back into anticipation. Awareness of Mac's presence ignited into a desire so fierce Julia didn't notice that she rose to stand on tiptoe to meet Mac's lips before his head had completed its dip.

A soft kiss.

A promise.

And then Mac took the key from her hand and unlocked the door.

Something changed the moment the front door of the cottage closed behind them.

Whatever it was between them was unleashed and free to roam.

The heat and urgency in Mac's gaze sent a tremor down Julia's spine. The tiny hallway of her house made him seem so much bigger. His hair was dark and tousled and his eyes darker than she'd ever seen them and so intent there was no hint of a smile on his face. It made him look…dangerous.

This was dangerous.

Never mind any complications with work. She could get hurt. Badly. She could find that any chance of the future she hoped for was destroyed because she'd never find anyone who could make her feel like this again. That was terrifying—the thought that she might be sacrificing future happiness for something that could only be temporary. If it was—and she just knew it would be—totally amazing, it was only going to last a matter of weeks. A brief interlude in her life.

But she'd known it would be dangerous and facing danger—embracing it, even—was part of who she was.

She could still say no. For a heartbeat, as they stood there, Julia knew instinctively that this was her last opportunity to back out. That Mac would respect that decision.

But then he reached out and touched her face. A soft brush of fingertips on her forehead that trickled down to end up on her lips, and the touch was so gentle, so *caring*, that Julia knew she was in real trouble here.

Past the point of no return.

Falling in love, with nothing to hang onto to try and break that fall, and even if there had been, she wouldn't be able to summon the willpower to save herself. She felt her eyes drift shut and her head tip back as Mac's lips replaced his fingers, softly kissing her lips and then the corner of her mouth. Her jawbone and then the side of her neck where her pulse throbbed and then skipped.

Yes. It was way too late to save herself.

She looked…perfect.

The last piece of clothing had been peeled away and Julia was small and golden in the soft light of her bedside lamp, the tan of an antipodean summer still glowing over her entire body.

His hands felt like they might be rough against the silk of her skin. For the first time Mac felt big and… clumsy, almost. Yet every touch…every kiss drew a response that made him feel nothing short of amazing.

She seemed to know exactly where to touch *him*. The right words or sounds to make that had him on the brink of losing control utterly, again and again. Dear God—she *wanted* him. As much as he wanted her.

But he had to hang on. To make this as good as it possibly could be. He had to *be* amazing because it was the only thing good enough for this woman. And he could be, because this was time away from reality. The past didn't exist and didn't need to damage what they had. What had Julia said? This had a 'use-by' date. Yes. It was a blink in a lifetime but it had the potential to give them both a memory they could treasure. Something too good to forget.

Ever.

So he took his time. Milking every sense. Revelling in the sounds of her sighs of pleasure or whimpers of desire. The sight of that smooth, golden skin and what he could read in her eyes. The smell of her hair and her skin and her desire. The taste and the astonishing feel of every part of her body. Yes. He took more time than he ever had. He slowed things down until Julia was begging. For *him*.

Even then, he tried to be gentle. To ease himself into her delicious, tight warmth but she cried out his name and Mac was lost.

He buried himself in paradise and knew he was taking her with him with every stroke.

Her cry of ecstasy could have come from his own soul. Nothing had ever been this good.

Nothing else ever could be.

* * *

How amazing—that something so good could get even better.

Mac couldn't get enough of it. Couldn't get enough of Julia Bennett.

With the frustration of trying to fight the attraction gone, life was just about perfect.

He got to spend every minute of every working day with Julia. The way he had ever since she'd arrived. Except that it was nothing like it had been.

Funnily enough, it was easy to keep up the pretence that nothing had changed. When they were on a job and dealing with patients they were both ultimately professional. On station, the banter might have had a new edge and the way they stole glances at each other might be more significant but nobody seemed to notice. Not even Joe, who spent more time with them than anyone else.

Angus didn't guess but why would he? Mac never spent a whole night away from the apartment so his breakfast dishes still littered the bench and the pile of dirty socks grew in the laundry.

But even with all those working hours and those glorious, stolen evenings, it wasn't enough.

'What's wrong with you?' Mac asked himself, more than once. 'You've got the perfect woman with no strings attached. No excuse not to be the happiest man on earth.'

What else did he want?

A clock that wasn't ticking somewhere in the background, maybe, counting down the weeks and days they had left.

A whole night with Julia, perhaps, so he could hold her in his arms while she slept. Fall asleep himself knowing that when he woke, she would still be there beside him.

Strings?

Possibly. That way, he could eliminate the niggle in the back of his head that kept pace with the growth of this relationship. The fear that his bed, his job—his *life*—might feel too empty when she had gone home.

Not that he was going to think about that. Not yet. If it was formed into coherent thought or, worse, words, there would be no escape. It would change things. And something told him that Julia wouldn't like it and, therefore, it carried the risk of finishing this prematurely. Mac didn't want it to finish. Not while it was this good.

He'd known from the point of recognising his attraction that the potential was there to get in too deep and end up being hurt. It was far too late to do anything about it now and he'd been there before. He could take comfort from the knowledge that he could survive. It was simply a bridge he had no intention of crossing before he was obliged to. There was an element of hope encased in denial. If things continued to get better, maybe Julia wouldn't want to let it go either.

It was possible to float through life.

What truly amazed Julia, however, was that it was also possible to have someone else occupying what seemed like every bit of space in your head and heart and soul. Mac was the first thing she thought of when she woke in the mornings and the last thing on her mind before she drifted off to sleep at night and yet she still had room for everything that used to be important as well. She discovered that the presence of someone you were so much in love with could seep into everything else and make it better.

Like work.

Within the first few days of that amazing step into a relationship, Green Watch was dispatched to a hiker who had fallen and broken her leg badly in hilly, difficult terrain. A mountain search and rescue team had located the woman but they had no doctor available and needed assistance.

The flight had taken them over Loch Ness.

'Watch out for the monster,' Joe said with a chuckle. 'She's down there somewhere.'

'I see her.' Julia grinned. 'Look, Mac—three o'clock.'

He looked and laughed. 'That's the concrete version beside the museum.'

'You should take Jules to see it,' Joe suggested. 'On your next day off.'

'I might just do that.' The tone was offhand. The look Julia received was anything but. 'How far are we from target, Joe?'

'Be there in five.'

The searchers had abseiled into the base of a narrow gully but it was too dangerous to winch into from the helicopter because of the trees and overhanging rock ledges. Thanks to the bird's-eye view, they found an area beside a stream less than a kilometre away. Not big enough to land safely but Joe could get close enough to make it possible to throw the gear out and for Mac and Julia to jump and then run, crouched low enough to keep them safe from the still whirling blades of the chopper.

The adrenaline rush of the dangerous manoeuvre was familiar enough. The fact that Mac caught her hand to keep her running in the crouched position was nothing new either.

It just felt new.

Knowing he cared about her safety on a personal as well as a professional level. The way she had wished he did that day when she had been about to disengage from the safety of the winch line and climb inside that dangling train carriage.

A dream come true.

A fairy-tale.

And that was why it was OK not to tell Mac why this could never be more than a temporary fling. Because it *was* a fairy-tale and reality could destroy it. Like the best tales, this had a beginning and it would have an end. That the end wouldn't be that they lived happily ever after was something Julia was quite prepared to ignore because if she didn't, that would spoil the middle.

She was living in the middle. And loving it.

The fractured femur of the middle-aged female patient in the gully was easy enough to deal with. She needed pain relief and a traction splint to pull the bones into alignment and reduce both the pain level and the amount of internal bleeding. She needed oxygen and fluids to replace the blood already lost and she needed urgent evacuation due to hypothermia, having lain outside overnight. The searchers carried the stretcher back to the area by the stream.

Mac was the winch-operating expert so he was the one to climb into the hovering helicopter to set up the operation. Julia had to catch her breath, blown away by the flash of fear for his safety as he ran, crouched, under blades that would end his life in an instant if something went wrong.

The fear should have been crippling and yet Julia could still tend her patient and reassure her. She drew up a second dose of morphine and topped up the pain relief and then she was aware of the wash of relief at hearing Mac's voice in her helmet as the helicopter hovered at a safe height above them.

'Sending the line down, Jules. You OK?'

'All good. Ready when you are, mate.'

If anything, the only difference their new connection made to how they worked together professionally was to improve it. Julia wanted Mac to be proud of her. To not only perform at her best but to improve her skills. He had already seen her intubate critically ill patients and perform chest decompressions to save the life of someone with a tension pneumothorax. On a night shift not long after the mountain rescue, Julia had done her first crico-thyroid puncture to save a man in anaphylactic shock. It had gone perfectly because she'd had Mac there right beside her.

And he *was* proud of her. He'd told her so, in the early hours of the following morning, when they'd stolen some time for themselves in her cottage.

And Julia had never been so proud of herself.

She'd had to tell her sister all about it, later that day.

'It was pretty terrifying. I mean, I could palpate the membrane but it was hard to stabilise the thyroid cartilage at the same time as getting the cannula in at just the right angle and putting traction on the plunger at exactly the same time.'

'It's a good feeling, though, isn't it, when you can aspirate air and know you're in the right place?'

'The best feeling in the world. You know, I can understand the thrill you get out of surgery more now.'

'You sound pretty happy with what you're doing.' Anne sounded almost wistful. 'In fact, I don't think I've ever heard you sound as happy as you have in the last few weeks.'

'I am happy. It's not just work. I'm loving all the sightseeing. Mac took me up to the Loch Ness museum last week. And we've been to look at the Burrell collection and Robbie Burns's wee cottage and heard someone playing the bagpipes on the wall of Edinburgh castle. Mac's determined that I get to see the "real Scotland". He says he'll take me to Oban the next time he goes to visit his mum. Apparently she makes the best oatcakes and shortbread in Scotland. And—'

Anne's laughter interrupted the excited flow of words. 'You're certainly packing in as much as you can. It sounds wonderful.'

'It is.' Unbelievably wonderful. Julia shut her eyes for a moment, remembering one of those outings, when they'd wandered around the Burrell collection, hand in hand, admiring fabulous tapestries and old oak furniture and stained-glass windows. How the beauty had seemed somehow outside the bubble created by that connection between herself and Mac. That the real beauty came from the bright colours and astonishing sensations that only happiness could create.

She sighed. 'I can't believe how fast the time is going, though. It's been six weeks already, Annie. Another few weeks and it'll all be over. I have to make the most of it.'

Anne knew the time frame was all about her relationship with Mac. She couldn't miss the note of sadness in Julia's quiet words either.

'Maybe it doesn't have to be.'

The hope those words generated had to be crushed. 'It has to be, you know that as well as I do. Hey, it was your idea that I get into this, remember? Because it would do me good and it had a time limit.'

'Yes, but I didn't know how happy it was going to make you.' Anne's sigh was audible. 'Do you think Mac feels the same way?'

'He's just as determined to make the most of the time we have. We don't talk about me going home. It's just there…getting closer all the time. Making everything we do together seem, I don't know, more precious, maybe.'

'You'll have to talk about it some time.'

Julia tried to laugh. 'At the airport, probably, when he comes to wave me off. We'll both promise to ring, or email and keep in touch.' Her voice began to trail away. 'But we won't… Don't worry, Annie. I can handle it.'

'I hope so, hon.'

So did Julia but she didn't say so aloud. If she could hide any doubts from her sister, maybe she could also hide them from herself.

CHAPTER SEVEN

'YOU'RE taking Jules *where*?'

'Oban.' Mac did his best to make it sound like it was no big deal. 'To visit my mum.'

Angus exchanged a look with both Dale and Joe, and Mac's heart sank. He hoped Julia wasn't reading more into this invitation than she had let on. Just because he was taking a girl home to meet his family, it didn't have to be an event of major significance. Good grief. His mother had met girls he'd been associated with before, hadn't she? Or maybe she hadn't. Maybe Christine had been the only one he'd taken home. Mac scowled, irritated by the unwanted association.

'He's a good boy,' Joe offered into the silence. 'Visiting his mum.'

Angus raised his eyebrows in Julia's direction. 'You want to meet Mac's mum, then?'

'It's more a case of it being the other way round.' Mac looked up again from the paperwork he was trying to finish. 'Mum's best friend Doreen's son Lachlan emigrated to New Zealand about thirty years ago.

Doreen wants to go and visit her grandchildren and she wants Mum to go with her. I think she'd love it but she's too set in her ways. Meeting Jules might be just the push she needs.'

Julia was smiling. 'Besides, Mac says his mum's house is a slice of "real Scotland" and I can't go home without tasting her oatcakes.'

'Oh…' Angus was distracted now. 'That's right. It's not long to go now, is it?'

'Just under three weeks.' There was an edge to Julia's voice that Mac could feel like a noose tightening around his neck. Time was running out.

At least the others on station weren't reading anything into the revelation they would be spending some time off together. They were all too busy being subdued at the thought of Julia leaving.

Two days later, Mac collected Julia a little after 8 a.m. He drove them north of Glasgow until they reached Crianlarich and then took the road to Oban. Being midweek, the roads were nice and quiet. It was raining but the scenery was beautiful and they knew each other so well now that they could be together in silence and be totally content. On some of the straight stretches, Mac could keep just one hand on the steering-wheel and hold Julia's with the other.

The periods of silence were not uncomfortable but it occurred to Mac that they'd been happening more often lately. As though they each had things on their minds that they didn't want to share. A discomforting thought.

'Won't be too much longer,' he said.

He could swear he felt Julia flinch. As though she'd been miles away and his words had brought her back to reality with a crunch. And then she blinked and nodded, smiling.

'What time is your mum expecting us?'

'Whenever we turn up. She's only expecting me. You're a surprise, but don't worry. She'll be thrilled.'

'She might not be. What if she feels she needs to give us lunch or something? Shall we take some food?'

'We won't stay that long. Mum can talk the hind leg off a donkey. You'll be exhausted by the time we've been there long enough for a cup of tea, and Mum's always got something in the tin for visitors.'

'Is there much to see in Oban?'

Mac smiled. So she didn't want this time together to finish too soon? That was good. Just as well, given the arrangements he'd made a few days ago in the wake of Julia's enthusiasm for the idea.

'We've got somewhere else to go,' he told her. 'Something I want you to see.'

'Oh? What?'

Mac's smile broadened. 'It's a surprise.'

Mac's mother lived in a tiny, terraced brick house in an old cobbled street. She was grey-haired, wiry and stern looking, and right now she was almost flapping her apron in consternation.

'Tch! You know better than this, Alan MacCulloch,' she chided. 'Bringing a visitor without letting me know. I'm all topsy-turvy in here. It's a terrible mess. *I'm* a mess…'

The accent was strong enough to make it difficult for

Julia to catch all the words but the tone was unmistakable and Julia turned, ready to give Mac an 'I told you so' look. But she saw amusement in his face and the kind of tolerance that only came from a mixture of real respect and deep affection. She watched as he caught his mother's hand and stopped her patting the firm-looking waves of her permed hair.

'Your house is never a mess, Mum, and it wouldn't matter if it was. It's you I brought Julia to see, not your house.'

'Och!' Jean MacCulloch shot Julia an oddly shy glance but she was hanging onto her son's hand now and beamed up at him. 'Look at you, lad... Will you ever stop growing?'

'I think you're shrinking.' Mac hugged his mother, lifting her effortlessly off her feet. She emitted a muted shriek.

'Put me down,' she commanded. 'You're not too old for the wooden spoon, you know.'

'That threat stopped being effective when I was about five. You've never used a wooden spoon on me in my life.' Mac laughed but set her down gently. 'Mum, this is my friend Julia.'

Julia met another curious glance from behind wire-rimmed spectacles. 'I'm pleased to meet you, Mrs MacCulloch.'

'Och, call me Jeannie. Everybody does. And where have you come from, Julia?'

'New Zealand.'

Mac's mother blinked, looking flustered. 'That's a very long way away. Good gracious...'

'Julia's working with me for a while, Mum. We've only come from Glasgow today. We're sightseeing.'

'Is that right? New Zealand…Doreen's Lachlan says it's a bonny place. I'm…thinking of making a visit myself one day.'

Mac's lips twitched. 'Are you going to put the kettle on, Mum, or shall we just stand on the doorstep?'

The house was anything but a mess. Mac insisted on busying himself in the kitchen making tea and Jean insisted on giving Julia a tour of her home. It was obvious that everything was dusted and polished to within an inch of its life. Doilies were positioned precisely and most were beneath framed photographs.

'That's my Donald,' Jean told Julia proudly. 'Mac's father.'

The photograph, in pride of place on a bedside table, was of a man who was an older version of Mac. Even more rugged and more serious but Julia could see that his face would crease in exactly the same way if he smiled.

Jean touched the frame in an action that looked so automatic it was unconscious. 'It's been fifteen years,' she said softly, 'but I still miss him.'

Julia's smile went deeper than merely sympathy. Jean would see that image when she woke in the mornings and before she turned her light off at night. Julia knew what it was like to love someone like that. How lucky were Mac's parents to have had so many years together? To have had a family. Jean looked up and caught Julia's gaze and for a moment the two women just stood there, perfectly in tune. Disturbingly so. Julia had the impression that Jean had her son's ability to read her mind occasionally and knew exactly what she was thinking.

'Come and see Alan's room,' the older woman directed gently.

It was an odd mixture of a guest bedroom and a child's room. Rows of toys and books adorned shelves. Boys' adventure stories, Julia noticed. She'd have to tease Mac about that later. There were old, well-loved wooden building blocks, a tiny microscope, cowboy and Indian models and a train set. Nothing had even a speck of dust on it.

'It's not really his room,' Jean confessed. 'I only came here from the farm after I lost my Donald and that was after Alan had gone away to university. I keep it nice for when he comes to stay and…I keep his toys, of course…for the grandchildren.'

She beamed at Julia but it was suddenly very hard to smile back.

Oh…Lord! She had caught the vibe of her thinking about how much she loved Mac and it was patently obvious where her thoughts had moved onto. What would Mac think if he knew what was happening upstairs? She had been so convinced that Angus had been wrong in assuming there was a deeper significance in this visit.

What was the surprise Mac had talked about?

A trickle of apprehension whispered down her spine. Was it possible Mac was planning to ask her to stay longer in Scotland? To propose marriage, even?

She couldn't let that happen. She didn't want to reject him. She didn't want to hurt anybody.

Including his mother.

So she kept up a bright conversation over the late-morning tea. She told Jean how beautiful her country was and how much she loved it. Maybe she was a bit too enthusiastic but there was an element of panic in there somewhere and maybe if she reminded Mac of how much she loved her home, he wouldn't think of asking anything that might interfere with her return.

She praised the oatcakes and shortbread sincerely but Jean just flapped her hand at her guest. 'They're nothing. I'll give you the recipe, pet.'

Finally, they could take their leave and Julia could escape the tentacles trying to wind themselves around her heart. The solid love Mac's parents had had for each other. That row of toys waiting for a new generation to play with them.

'I think you won her over,' Mac said as they climbed back into his car.

'Oh?' Julia hadn't been trying to win anything. She certainly didn't want to have left Jean with expectations that could only be crushed.

'You sold her on New Zealand. Doreen's going to be very happy.'

'Hey, no problem. Happy to help.' Relieved by Mac's cheerful smile, she grinned back at him. 'Do I get to know where we're going now?'

'Nope. Wait and see.'

So she waited, through a delicious lunch of fish and chips near the wharf and then in the car in a queue to get on the ferry to the island of Mull. A short voyage on a calm sea with seagulls circling overhead, their lonely cries a poignant soundtrack.

When they drove off the ferry, Mac took a turn away from the road to the main township of Tobermory.

'Wasn't he a womble?' Julia's spirits were lifting. This was new and beautiful and she was alone with the man she loved. She'd been wrong to read too much into this and she could relax and simply go with the flow and enjoy herself.

Mac smiled but said nothing. He was, in fact, rather worryingly quiet for the whole drive that took them to the very end of the island where they found a narrow stretch of sea and another ferry.

'We have to leave the car here,' he told Julia. 'No vehicles are allowed on Iona.'

It was well into the afternoon now and the sign stated that the next trip would be the last crossing for the day. Julia looked over her shoulder at the car and then raised her eyebrows at Mac. 'How will we get back?' she asked.

'There'll be another ferry in the morning.'

'But…'

'I've booked a room in a guest house. Upstairs overlooking the beach where we'll be able to smell the sea and hear the waves. That's the surprise. A night in a place where magic happens.'

'But I haven't brought anything! Not even pyjamas.'

For a long, long moment Mac looked down at her, his face so serious that Julia's heart stopped for a beat. And then his face softened and he drew her into his arms and bent to place a slow, tender kiss on her lips. 'You won't need them, hinny, trust me.'

* * *

A place where magic happened.

Had it begun even before they'd reached their destination?

Mac hadn't intended anything significant by this surprise he'd planned for Julia. He'd been here once before, as a child, and remembered being overawed by the sense of history, not to mention the sheer number of royal gravesites. The serenity of this isolated little island had stayed with him as well and it was like a cultural jewel. One that he wanted to gift to Julia so she could take it home with her and keep it for ever.

When did that plan start to become something else?

Had it been when he had hugged his mother in farewell and she had whispered in his ear, 'Don't let this one go, Alan. She's special.'

He knew Julia was special. But he also knew that she saw their relationship as simply a bonus extension of her overseas training experience. A secret one.

How could he prevent her from going?

By asking her to marry him?

The very thought was shocking enough to keep him quiet on the rest of their journey. Thinking hard. Confused by the strength of his feelings. Arguing with himself.

She didn't know him well enough. Or, rather, she didn't know all of him. And there were parts of Julia he knew weren't being shared. They hadn't had time. Or maybe they just hadn't wanted to take that final step into the kind of intimacy that could lead to permanence.

She wouldn't want to.

He wouldn't want to.

Or would he? Faced with the alternative of seeing her vanish from his life for ever, it seemed like a lifeline.

Julia didn't know it yet, but this was going to be the first whole night they would spend together. No going home to the apartment to make sure nobody guessed where Mac was spending so much of his time away from work. Would it be enough to chase away that niggle of discontent for Mac? Would it be enough?

Yes. The magic had begun. Things seemed to be falling into place. Or they would, if Mac could stop fighting it. The serenity of Iona was exactly what he needed. The magic.

They explored the abbey and the cemetery, cuddling together to break the bite of a chilly wind from the sea.

They ate wonderful, home-cooked food in the guest house for their dinner and then he opened the window a little in their bedroom so they could hear the rhythm of the sea as they made love.

They knew each other's bodies so well now. It was so easy to kindle passion. To take infinite delight in each touch…each kiss…knowing what depth of fulfilment they were heading inevitably towards.

There was something different about this night, however. Something that touched Mac so deeply it made him want to close his arms around Julia and never let her go. For this one night, he didn't have to.

He couldn't sleep. He listened to the waves and the sound of Julia's soft, even breaths. And he listened, at last, to what his heart was telling him.

His mother was right. He couldn't let her go willingly.

Maybe he didn't have a ring or anything very fancy to say to her but he could tell her that he loved her.

He could ask her to spend the rest of her life with him.

This was a magic place.

Some of that magic might rub off on them and Julia would tell him she felt the same way.

He'd ask her to marry him.

And she'd say *yes*.

Sometimes, in the movies, they slowed down the inevitable crash scene.

Frame by frame, you could see it coming.

That was exactly how Julia was feeling, sitting on a smooth boulder on a tiny beach the next morning.

Ironically, the sun had come out and the day couldn't have been more perfect. The sea was so smooth Mac was skipping stones just beyond the baby waves that rolled gently onto the shingle, and she knew it was coming.

The declaration.

The proposal.

There had been something very different about last night. As if they'd been swept along by the magic of this tiny island and it had taken them to a new level in their relationship. The love-making had been so intense. So heartbreakingly tender.

Julia had woken knowing it would never be like that again.

The crash was coming.

She had seen it, the instant she had opened her eyes

to find Mac looking at her. The way he had been watching her when he'd thought she wouldn't notice, drying herself after her shower and helping herself to the buffet breakfast in the dining room of the guest house. The way he had almost begun to say something, more than once, but had then stopped himself—as though he couldn't find quite the right words or it wasn't quite the right time or place.

Yes. The crash was coming and it would be her heart—and Mac's—that lay in pieces afterwards.

Her body seemed to be almost absorbing the lump of rock she was sitting on. Something heavy and horrible was taking up residence behind her ribs and it got bigger as Mac turned his head, a triumphant grin on his face.

'Did you see that? Seven!'

'Fantastic. You're the best, Mac.'

'I could only ever do three when I was a kid. I thought my dad was the best 'cos he could do six.'

Funny how you could still smile even when you could actually feel a crack appearing in your heart. Julia could see the little boy Mac so clearly. On this beach with his father. Skipping stones on a clear, sunny morning.

She could see him standing here again. With *his* son. Teaching him. A little boy who would think he was the best because he could skip a stone seven times.

The ferry was almost due to take them back to Mull. She could see it over the short stretch of water. A new group of visitors was on board, eager to come and explore this idyllic spot. The pilot had unhooked the rope and he threw it onto the boat and then jumped after it. The small vessel drifted for a few seconds and then she heard the engine catch—the loudest sound they had heard since they had arrived on Iona.

A call to action. She watched in dismay as Mac turned from the sea and walked towards her rock. He looked impossibly gorgeous. Faded denim jeans and his beloved leather jacket over a T-shirt. He hadn't shaved that morning because he hadn't bothered bringing a razor and the shadow on his jaw only made him look a bit more rugged. Absolutely…perfect.

The love she felt for this man squeezed her heart hard enough to be painful. To feel like there was no blood left to keep her alive.

The smile of success was still playing with Mac's face but he had a very intent look in his eyes.

One that looked like…hope?

Oh, God! Julia jumped to her feet, propelled by a stab of panic that she did her best to disguise with a smile.

'Ferry's coming. See?'

The observation was completely redundant but she had to say something. Something mundane. A futile attempt at creating some kind of buffer, perhaps.

This was it.

His last chance before they had to leave the magic of Iona.

Surely he was imagining the impression that Julia was fleeing?

He hadn't imagined her response to him last night. At

the end, when he'd kissed away the tears of an emotion too great to put into words. When he'd simply held her as she'd slid into sleep, saying nothing because he felt the same way and words could only have diminished it.

But now, on a public beach, when words were all he had, she was running away from him.

Well, walking fast anyway, and there was no reason for it. The little beach was right beside the jetty. That was why he'd been skipping stones with his dad all those years ago because they, too, had been waiting for the boat.

Why on earth had he wasted time with that little excursion down memory lane? Looking into the past when it was his future he should have been doing something about?

Why had he held back this morning, when he had watched Julia open her eyes to a new day and he could have made it the first day of the rest of their lives together?

Because he knew that despite the magic of this place, it wasn't right somehow. That trying to keep Julia might be like caging a wild spirit. That even showing her the cage might destroy whatever time they had left and this morning had been too perfect to tarnish.

He hadn't felt this torn since…

No. He wasn't going to do that. He wasn't going to let any memory of Christine intrude. This was about Julia. About now.

Mac caught her hand and held it as they watched the boat come alongside the jetty. Several young children were hanging onto the rail, shrieking with excitement as the boat bumped against a wooden pile.

He smiled. 'Sound like seagulls, don't they?'

'Yeah…'

Something in her tone jarred Mac. Made him pause and wonder what it was. Disapproval? OK, the children were being noisy and it disrupted the serenity of this spot but they were just happy. Excited. Mac watched a little girl bouncing up and down, unable to contain herself, but from the corner of his eye he could see that Julia was looking over her shoulder. Back at the sheep on the rise of a windswept slope.

A last look at Iona?

Or an aversion to the sight of boisterous children?

'The noise doesn't bother you,' he said quietly, 'when they're your own.'

Her gaze flew to meet his and there was no mistaking the way her pupils dilated with what looked absurdly like fear. Horror, even.

'Kids? *Me?*' Her gaze flicked away and she made an odd sound that morphed into a hollow chuckle. 'Not in this lifetime, mate.'

That jarring sensation returned as something rather more solid. He was up against a warning sign, maybe. Or a wall. The kind you might find if you'd taken a wrong turn and discovered a dead end.

He kept his tone light. 'You sound very sure about that.'

'Oh, I am.' Julia wriggled in a kind of theatrical shudder. 'Kids ruin your career and your bank balance and your social life—not to mention your looks—in one fell swoop. Dangerous little critters.'

Her looks? Since when had Julia Bennett been

bothered about her looks? Most women would have had a fit at the thought of being without any make-up or beauty products having being presented with an unexpected overnight stay in the company of a lover. It hadn't even occurred to Julia to worry about anything other than pyjamas.

Something didn't ring true but Mac wasn't about to try and find out what it was. He was too busy coping with something happening in his head that vaguely resembled a train crash.

The echo was uncanny. This could have been Christine talking. No chance of preventing her intrusion now. Her voice was there—loud and clear.

You think I want a kid? Holding me back? Interfering with everything I want to do with my life?

He had taken a wrong turn. Reached a dead end.

Again.

He'd fallen in love with someone who had no desire to follow the same path in life. A path that led to a solid, loving partnership. The kind his parents had had. And, yes, children. To turn that partnership into a family. And not just one child because he knew how lonely that could be.

This shouldn't matter. He'd never intended to get to this point when he'd started this fling with Julia. Thinking about marriage. Imagining children, for heaven's sake. Little girls as feisty as their mother. Small boys he could teach to skip stones.

Not in this lifetime, mate. The words echoed and took on the ring of an inscription carved in stone. So cold and hard it was contagious. Mac could feel it in his heart. Chilling every cell in his body.

At least this time he might be able to escape without making himself look and feel like a complete failure. Before it got spelt out that there were more important things in life than the dreams he treasured. Dreams that made him who he was.

Mac let go of Julia's hand. 'We can get on the boat now,' he said, knowing his tone would be as expressionless as his face. 'Let's go home.'

If he'd been quiet and thoughtful on the drive towards the end of the island of Mull, Mac was very different on the return journey to the big ferry that would take them back to the mainland.

His conversation was as mundane as that observation Julia had made earlier about the approaching boat. Safe things. Buffers. They talked about the scenery and the weather and, brick by brick, Julia could feel a wall being built between them.

The *weather*, for heaven's sake.

Julia responded on autopilot. She knew perfectly well what Mac was doing. That he was upset. And she knew why. It confirmed her suspicion that he'd been intending to propose to her. To offer to share his life with her. She'd also been equally correct in the assumption she'd passed on to her sister all those weeks ago that Mac saw a family as a vital part of that future. Preferably a big family—the kind he'd never had.

She was busy hating herself for what she'd done. Trying to stave off feeling miserable. Bereft, in fact. If she gave it any head room she would have to deal with a grief she'd thought she'd dealt with a long time ago but it was still there. Waiting.

So she talked about the stupid weather and how lovely it had been earlier that morning but how those gathering clouds did indeed make it look like they could be in for a downpour before they made it back to the city.

They were skittering on conversational ice, with occasional silent patches as they desperately sought something safer. Julia thought they'd found it when they began to talk about what would be the start of their working week tomorrow.

'What kinds of things do you think you might have missed out on?' Mac asked as they drove onto the big ferry. 'Anything we can try and fit into the next couple of weeks?'

'I've done everything I hoped for,' Julia told him. 'A lot more, in fact.'

'True.' Mac nodded. 'That train crash was one of a kind, that's for sure.'

Julia simply nodded. The bonus of a major incident like that train crash hadn't been what had leapt to her mind. It had been something much more personal. The unexpected twist that falling in love represented.

'You were amazing that day.' Mac had stopped the car but didn't get out. 'I'll make sure I put it all in that report I've got to write.'

Julia nodded again. 'Thanks. I couldn't have done it without you, though. You've been the best, Mac.' She found she was brave enough to meet his gaze for a moment. A plea for forgiveness, perhaps? 'You've taught me so much.'

Like what being in love could actually be like. How

it could colour every aspect of your life. Make you try harder and achieve more. Be a better person. How had she ever believed she was in love with Peter? Such a pale comparison to what she felt for this man that it would be easy to wipe it from her memory. But she couldn't afford to do that. Especially not now.

'I've already had a look at the logbooks.' Mac's gaze slid away from hers as he led the way up to the passenger lounge and she hadn't seen any response to her unspoken plea. 'I'll pick out the best to put in the report. One thing did strike me, come to think of it.' He held open the door for Julia. 'An area you might be a bit light on.'

'Oh?'

'Paediatrics.'

Julia walked past him and stopped by the rail on the deck. She turned her face away from the brisk breeze and looked back at the island but she wasn't seeing it.

Mac knew that she knew what he'd been thinking of asking. That what she'd said about not wanting children was a deal breaker. But he wasn't going to say anything about it and neither was she. It was for the best if they could shove this back under a mental rug and pretend it had never happened.

They only had a couple of weeks left and then it would all be over. How hard could it be to just let things run their course? Go back to the way things had been only a day or two ago and make the most of what they had?

Very hard, given that Mac wasn't about to forgive what she'd said. She could tell him the truth but what was the point? She knew what Mac wanted. What he needed, and she couldn't give it to him. Maybe it was kinder to allow him to be angry and to shoulder the blame herself. She deserved this pain because she'd known all along that she shouldn't have used Mac like this.

The only problem was that Julia wasn't at all sure she could carry it off for the hour or two it would take them to get back to Glasgow, never mind the week or two until she packed her bags and left the country.

She had no choice. She straightened her back and turned.

'You're right,' she said. 'I'd better do something about that, hadn't I?' Julia even managed a smile as that crack in her heart widened. 'I'd hate to get a black mark on that report.'

CHAPTER EIGHT

THE clouds that had been gathering as they travelled home became a storm that hit the headlines the next day. There were accidents everywhere, with drivers unable to handle dangerous road conditions and the high winds damaging houses and trees, with some unfortunate people getting in the way of the debris. Roads were closed and the emergency services were inundated with calls.

The helicopter was grounded but Julia and Mac had never been so busy. They sped around the city, going from one job to the next with barely enough time to grab something to eat or drink, let alone talk to each other about anything other than the next job. And that suited Mac just fine because he had nothing he wanted to say. Nothing he could say, anyway, until he'd got his head around all this a bit more. The distance created between them yesterday had grown overnight. It had taken a huge leap when Mac had dropped her home and hadn't stayed. He couldn't. He'd needed time to think.

'Angus has been complaining about the state of the laundry,' was all he said. 'It's high time I caught up on some chores.'

There was a lull in the weather, late in the day and Julia and Mac were dispatched to a rural area. A woman was in labour and she was alone in an isolated farmhouse apart from her three other children. It had been the eldest, an eight-year-old girl, who had made the call for help.

'Mummy's bleeding,' she'd sobbed. 'And I don't know where Daddy's gone. I tried to get to the Kendricks next door but the bridge is all covered with water and…I can't swim and…and I don't know what to do…'

Joe had looked dubious. 'We don't know how long this lull is going to last. It's a good thirty-minute flight. No guarantee we'll be able to evacuate her if we do manage to land.'

'She needs help,' Mac said. 'Just how risky is it?'

Joe shrugged. 'We've been out in worse.'

Not much worse that Mac could remember. The flight was rough. Ten minutes into it and he wasn't surprised Julia was looking pale.

'You OK?' He knew his tone was cool but he couldn't help it. The anger that the perfect woman should present herself and then make it clear that she didn't see any kind of future with him was unbearable. She *knew* how he felt about kids. How important a family was to him.

'I'm fine.' She didn't meet his gaze.

She didn't look fine. They hit a particularly vicious air current and the chopper slewed sideways. Joe swore softly but Mac closed his eyes. It had been his call in the end to scramble this mission. What if he'd put them all in danger?

If he'd put Julia in danger?

The thought was unbearable. Never mind that he was so upset. At some level he knew he was being irrational. It wasn't Julia's fault that she didn't have any ambition to be part of a family. It was simply part of who she was. The courageous, clever woman he'd fallen in love with. He'd put his own life on the line, any day, to ensure her safety. Even now with the anger that was a kind of physical pain.

Her frightened gaze met his. He held it for just a heartbeat. He didn't have to smile, thank goodness. He knew the instant the silent message he was trying to send—that they would be all right—had been received. He saw the way she caught her bottom lip between her teeth as she averted her gaze. The movement of her body as she took a deep breath and…he saw just the corner of a determined, albeit grim smile.

And in that moment of courage that he'd contributed to, Mac realised he'd never had this kind of a connection with any other person. That he'd never find someone else that felt so much like a part of himself. It shouldn't matter a bit that Julia didn't share his dream of having kids but it did. It hurt like hell.

'Target sighted,' he said tersely, minutes later. 'Man, that river's high. And look at the trees in it. I'm not surprised the bridge is washed out.'

'Sooner we're down the better,' Joe muttered. 'I don't like the way this wind is picking up.'

The landing was heavy. A jarring thump.

'Sorry 'bout that,' Joe said. 'Everybody all right?'

The wind shook the aircraft and the rotors howled as they slowed.

'What are our chances of being able to take off again, Joe?'

'Soon?' Joe shook his head. 'Nil.'

Mac nodded. 'Right, then. You may as well make yourself useful, Joe, and help us carry some gear into the house.'

A small girl with curly, red hair met them at the door to the farmhouse. She had two smaller boys clinging to her legs.

'Are you Maggie?' Mac asked.

She nodded, her face tear-streaked and terrified.

Mac crouched down. 'You're a very brave girl,' he told her. 'Can you show us where Mum is?'

Maggie nodded again and tried to move but she was impeded by two sets of small arms. One set belonged to a boy of about five who clung to her waist. The youngest boy was about two years old. A toddler who had a firm grip on her leg.

Mac had his backpack on and another bag in his hands which he handed to Julia. He swung the toddler under one arm and held out his other hand to Maggie. She took it without hesitation, her other hand taking her brother's, and Julia had to swallow past a lump in her throat as she followed the chain of small people

attached to Mac. It was so easy for him to win their
trust. So natural.

· No wonder he was so disappointed with her. He
hadn't been able to bring himself to say a single word
to her today that hadn't had something to do with a job.
Except for asking whether she was OK in that turbu-
lence. And even asking that, he had managed to sound
distant. As though it was simply professional concern.
As Joe's had been on landing. He'd known she'd been
scared, too and his expression had told her she had
nothing to worry about, but even then he hadn't been
able to bring himself to smile at her. Her heart heavy,
she trudged in her partner's wake.

They found the children's mother on the kitchen floor
and it was obvious she was in trouble. Gripped by a contraction, she was barely aware of the influx of people.
Mac handed the toddler to Joe and bent towards Maggie.

'We're going to take care of your mum,' he said. 'I
need you to go with Joe and help look after your
brothers. Can you do that?'

Julia was already crouched beside the woman, her
hand on her wrist seeking a pulse. She looked up as
Maggie nodded and turned away.

'What's your mum's name?' she asked.

'Katherine,' Maggie said, her huge, worried eyes
turned towards her mother. 'But Daddy calls her Katie.'

'Katie? Can you hear me?'

The woman's eyes flickered open. She was breathing fast but her respirations were shallow.

'My name's Julia and this is Mac. We're paramedics
with a helicopter crew.'

'Thank God you're here… My poor wee Maggie.'

'She's fine. How long have you been in labour, Katie?'

'What's the time?'

'Nearly 4 p.m.'

'Doug went out after lunch. I guess the pain came on not long after.'

'Suddenly?'

'Yes…well, it got a lot worse. I've had backache for days. And then my waters broke.'

'How many weeks are you?'

'Thirty-eight… No, it must be almost thirty-nine.'

'And were your previous deliveries normal?'

'Yes. Nothing like this…'

Julia gave up trying to get a heart rate. The pulse beneath her fingers was thready and fast. No surprises there. Katie had been in labour for hours. She would have been exhausted even without the fear of being in this situation without medical assistance. And on top of that, she was losing blood. Julia turned to Mac, who was organising their gear. He had an oxygen mask already attached to a cylinder.

'Ten litres per minute,' he told Julia as he bent towards their patient. 'Hi, Katie. I'm Mac. I'm just going to slip this oxygen mask on for you, is that OK?'

He smiled at Katie. The kind of smile Julia had been missing all day. The kind that made a patient, who was exhausted and in pain and probably worried sick about all her children as well as the baby she was about to have, smile back.

'We need an IV and some fluids up.' Julia's voice came out a little more crisply than she had intended.

Mac's smile faded. 'Whatever you need.' His nod was as crisp as her order as he turned back to the pack of supplies.

The message was clear. Julia was in charge of this job if she was confident she could handle it. Or course she was. This was—or hopefully would be very soon—a paediatric case. She needed the experience.

'I'd like the life pack on and a full set of baseline vitals, thanks,' she told Mac. She turned back to Katie. 'I need to check what's going on below. Is that OK?'

Katie nodded. 'Please…do whatever you have to.' Her face crumpled. 'This wasn't supposed to happen. I was going into hospital tomorrow because the doctor said… Ohhh…it's starting again…'

'Hold my hand,' Mac directed. 'Squeeze as hard as you like.'

Julia was cutting away Katie's clothing. She put a towel down to help soak up the liquid on the floor. A mixture of amniotic fluid and blood but she couldn't see any evidence of meconium staining that could indicate that the danger to the baby's welfare might be getting critical. It was hard to estimate how much blood had been lost. Or why it was happening.

'What did the doctor say, Katie?' she asked as soon as she could see the pain of the contraction begin to fade.

'That I had to get to hospital in good time. Something about my placenta being a bit low.'

Julia's gaze flew to Mac's. A placenta that was too low could start to bleed badly as the cervix dilated and ripped blood vessels. How much worse could this blood loss become before the baby arrived?

Her gloved fingers were searching for information. Delivery was well under way but something felt wrong with the baby's head. It was…Julia's heart sank. 'It's breech,' she told Mac.

Katie stifled another sob. 'The doctor said that if she couldn't be turned this week, I might have to have a Caesarean.'

Mac had just slipped an IV cannula into Katie's forearm. He was holding it in place, waiting to secure it and attach the necessary fluids. Waiting to engage in one of those lightning-fast silent conversations.

You want me to take over?

I know what to do. I just haven't done it before.

You'll be fine. I'm here. You can do this.

She could. It was helpful that this wasn't Katie's first baby. An episiotomy was probably not necessary, which was good because it wasn't in Julia's scope of practice.

'Katie? I know you're tired, hon, but could you try and give a good push with the next contraction?'

'I'll…try…'

She did. The baby's buttocks came into view and Julia was able to hold the hips and apply gentle traction until the shoulder blades came into view. She rotated the trunk of the baby until the front shoulder was delivered and then turned it in the opposite direction to deliver the other shoulder.

Thirty seconds, she reminded herself, to let the trunk hang and protect the head of the baby. Longer than you think. Count. Then lift the legs and swing upwards in an arc until you can see the baby's mouth.

Mac was there with the small rubber bulb and nozzle to clear the baby's airway and allow it to start breathing.

Now it was Julia's job to control the delivery of the baby's head to protect it against sudden expansion and expulsion. She slipped her index finger into the tiny mouth and flexed the head.

'*Ohhh…!*' Katie groaned.

Julia could feel the pressure as the contraction built. As gently as she could she eased the baby's head out. And despite Julia's concern for the blood loss, for this moment, there was joy. Amazement.

'It's a wee girl, Katie.' Mac's voice sounded thick. 'She looks a very good weight.'

'Let me see…oh, please… Let me hold her.'

Julia was happy with what she could see. The baby was a good colour and already breathing well. With a nod she allowed Mac's hands to slip between hers and she transferred the precious bundle. He placed the baby on Katie's chest and covered them both with clean, fluffy towels.

Julia clamped and divided the cord and began to massage Katie's abdomen to stimulate another contraction and speed up delivery of the placenta. If that was enough to stop the bleeding, they would be all right until they could transfer their patient to hospital, no matter how long it took.

Darkness fell and the wild weather continued. The bridge was washed away, isolating the farm from any roads. Phone lines were down and the power was off. The SERT helicopter was going nowhere. They were stuck for the night at least and Mac was absolutely loving it.

The old stone farmhouse was solid enough to withstand whatever nature could hurl at it and the tension of any medical crisis was over. Julia had handled everything brilliantly. A difficult birth, the careful monitoring of Katie until the bleeding stopped completely and her blood pressure climbed back to normal limits, and a commendably thorough paediatric assessment of the newborn girl.

'Her name's Fiona, for the birth certificate and paperwork,' Katie told them. 'But we're going to call her Noni.'

'Noni,' the other children chorused from the door, drawn by the sound of a crying baby now the proud recipient of a perfect Apgar score by Julia. 'We want to see Noni.'

'Mummy?' Maggie's face shone. 'You're all better now?'

'I'm fine, darling. Come in, all of you. Come and welcome your new little sister.'

It was Mac's turn to take charge of the scene for a while but he couldn't see any reason to move from the kitchen. It was a vast room, with an Aga, sink and pantry at one end, a well-scrubbed table and half a dozen chairs in the middle and at the other end was an open fireplace, an old, comfortable-looking couch and two armchairs.

With Joe's help, he built up a roaring log fire to warm the whole room. With Maggie's help to locate linen and pillows, they made a bed for Katie on the couch. She directed them to where the bassinette and supplies of baby clothes were upstairs and then to a high shelf in the pantry where they found candles and kerosene lamps.

Mac felt like the hero of the hour when he made use of their sophisticated radio equipment to make contact with the local police, who managed to locate Katie's husband, Doug. He was at a neighbour's property, having been caught on the wrong side of the river when the water level rose. He was safe and so was the farm truck and the four dogs but he had no way of getting home. He had been beside himself with anxiety but, thanks to modern, satellite technology, the parents of the brand-new baby were able to have a brief conversation. Mac had to stay close to make sure Katie had no problems working the radio. Julia was hovering close to Maggie, who sat in an armchair with her baby sister in her arms. There was no way to avoid hearing both sides of the radio conversation.

'Are you all right, love?'

'I'm fine, Doug. I've had the best care you could imagine. Just as good as it could have been in the hospital, honestly.'

Julia looked up and smiled and Mac smiled back. It was true. She had every right to look proud of herself and he was only too happy to share the moment.

'She's here, Doug,' Katie said brokenly. 'Our wee girl is here at last and…and she's gorgeous.'

'Of course she is. Just like her mother.'

'I wish you were here with us…' Tears were streaming down Katie's face now and Mac saw Julia biting her lip in sympathy.

'I am,' came a gruff voice amidst radio crackle. 'I'm there, Katie. I'm with you. In your heart.'

Such an unexpected thing to hear a staunch farmer say. Mac could hear the love. Could see it as he looked around to find the three older children all sitting as still as mice, listening to their father's voice. He could imagine this room in a day or two with no strangers in here. Maybe the dogs were allowed to lie in front of the fire and Doug would be here with his wife and all these beautiful children.

How could Julia not want something like this in her future? He took the radio from Katie and clipped it back to his belt, carefully avoiding a glance in Julia's direction.

'We'll get this all sorted in the morning,' he promised. 'We'll get your whole family back under the same roof, don't you fret.'

And, in the meantime, they had what amounted to a great substitute family right here.

Joe had clearly been adopted as a grandfather by the two small boys, who both wanted to spend as much time as possible on his knee, listening to stories.

Maggie was the responsible eldest child who was determined to nurse her mother and boss the younger children.

Mac stepped into Doug's shoes to cut and haul firewood to ensure the house was warm. He made sure doors and windows were securely latched against the weather and followed Katie's instructions to put a meal on the table and, later, to get the children into their beds.

Julia was a chameleon. A big sister for Maggie, encouraging her and helping only when needed. A medic making sure her patients were comfortable and cared for and that all the necessary paperwork was meticulously filled in. A fun aunty when it came to face washing and teeth cleaning and pyjamas for the little boys. Hearing her laughter mingled with the giggles of small children was like a slap in the face for Mac.

Even harder to see was the way she was another mother for tiny Fiona.

It was Julia who gently washed the baby on a mattress of soft towels in front of the fire and then dressed her in the soft, warm baby clothes available.

'They were mine,' Maggie said proudly. 'When I was a wee baby like Noni.'

Julia sat with Katie as she fed the baby and watched over them both with the same proud smile Mac had shared earlier.

And it was Julia who got up at some ungodly hour from the armchair she was dozing in to pick Fiona up and change her nappy and to sit and cuddle her in the armchair in the hope of giving Katie a little more time to sleep and heal. Joe was asleep on a couch in another room. The children were all tucked up in their own beds upstairs but Mac was in the other armchair close to the fire. He had also woken as the baby had stirred.

'Need a hand?'

'No, we're good. Go back to sleep, Mac.'

It was easy to pretend to be asleep. To tilt his head back so his eyes looked closed in the flickering glow of banked coals in the grate of the fire and the kerosene lamp nearby. It should have been easy to slip back into real sleep given his weariness but Mac soon found what he was watching utterly compelling.

It began with the gentle way Julia was handling the newborn as she changed its nappy and put tiny legs back into the stretchy suit. The soft sound of her voice as she made soothing murmurs. He must be doing a good job of seeming as soundly asleep as Fiona's exhausted mother, Mac decided, because he had the feeling they were both non-existent for Julia right now. Her focus was completely on the baby as she gathered it up in its blanket and sat on the edge of her armchair, rocking the infant in her arms.

The whimpering ceased. The rocking slowed and then Julia simply sat, gazing down at the baby in her arms. Seconds clicked into a minute and then another but Mac was transfixed. Was she waiting to make sure the baby was asleep so that she could put her back in the bassinette?

No.

The light might be soft and Mac could only see her profile but the intensity of the expression on Julia's face made something inside Mac tighten so painfully he couldn't breathe.

He watched her hand move, almost in silhouette against the backdrop of the glowing fire. He could see the way her thumb stroked the top of the baby's head. So slowly it seemed to go on for ever and Mac could feel every millimetre of that touch himself.

He could feel the…*longing*. The word came easily, really, because he could feel it himself. Could imagine Julia sitting just like that. Holding *their* child.

He wanted to close his eyes properly now because he felt like he was seeing something he wasn't meant to see.

Something very private.

The real Julia? A part he'd never been allowed close to?

A woman who wanted a baby—a family of her own—as much as he did?

Why did that impression feel like a knife in his chest? So painful he had to move? To open his eyes and wake himself up enough to shift his thoughts as a means of self-protection.

And Julia looked up.

She knew he had been watching her. That he had seen something she had intended to keep hidden.

She didn't look angry. Or guilty. What Mac could see was a confirmation that he *had* seen what he thought he'd seen. A desperate yearning for a child of her own. He could see sadness as well. An apology?

For what?

The knife in his chest twisted a little. She had lied to him. She had told him she didn't want children. What she'd really been saying was that she didn't want *him*. But that was a lie, too. This relationship might have been intended as temporary and fun but it had never been a game. Nobody could have what they had found together without it being real.

Without love.

Mac didn't understand. One word was echoing in his head.

Why?

He must have spoken it aloud because Julia's eyes widened. Her voice came out softly enough not to disturb the baby in her arms.

'Why what?'

'Why did you tell me you didn't want to have children? It's not true, is it?'

He saw her look down at the baby and could see the ripple in her neck as she swallowed. Hard. Then she lifted her gaze.

'It has to be.'

'Why? Because I'm not the man you want to be the father of your children?'

The way her lips moved in a half-smile that wobbled precariously made Mac sit up and lean forward, ready to launch himself close enough to protect and comfort her, but he didn't move yet. He might miss what she had to say and it was important.

Life and death kind of important.

'No,' Julia whispered. 'Exactly the opposite.'

Mac didn't understand. His brow creased as he stared at Julia.

'If I had to search the world to find the perfect man to be the father of my children, it would be you, Mac. Don't ever think otherwise. But it's not going to happen. Ever.'

As if to punctuate her statement, Julia rose and carried the baby back to her bassinette.

Mac rubbed his forehead with his hand. 'I don't understand,' he said quietly.

Julia straightened, her arms now empty. She wrapped them around her body. Her face looked pale. Distraught, almost.

'Can't we just leave it?' she begged. 'What we've had has been wonderful. *You're* wonderful. We've only got a short amount of time left and I've hated the way we've been today. Please, Mac…' She took the tiniest step towards him. 'Couldn't we turn the clock back a few days and be like that and then I'll go home and we'll have something wonderful to remember for the rest of our lives?'

Mac stood up and moved to close the gap between them but Julia didn't stop talking. If anything, her words became more desperate.

'You'll find someone else. Someone who'll think exactly the same way and she'll have your babies and you'll be the perfect father and—'

'No.'

The word was more than an interruption. It was intended to stop the flow of words he didn't want to hear. Mac drew Julia into his arms and was horrified to find she was trembling.

'W-why not?'

'Because I don't want to find someone else.'

'You have to.'

'Why?'

'Because I can't give you what you need, Mac.'

'I need you.'

'You need a family.'

'We can be a family.'

'No, we can't.' Julia pulled away. Her voice was still low but there was a fierce edge to it that could have been anger. 'This was never meant to get this far. We had a "use-by" date, Mac. I'm not in the market for anything else.'

'But...' Mac still didn't understand. 'You want children. You've all but admitted you feel the same way I do about having a family.'

'I can't have children, Mac.' Julia had turned away from him now. 'I had a hysterectomy when I was twenty-two because of endometrial cancer. There's no way on earth I'm ever going to have a baby of my own.'

Mac couldn't say anything for a moment. He was stunned. Shocked but then...what...relieved? This wasn't about *him*. This was an obstacle that a lot of couples had to deal with. There were ways around it. If this was all that was standing between a future alone or one with Julia, it simply wasn't an issue.

He couldn't help his smile. He opened his mouth to tell her that if she thought it had to be the end of the road she was wrong, but she had turned back. She saw his smile. She probably read what he was thinking in his face.

'Don't say it,' she warned. 'Don't you dare tell me it doesn't matter. That it doesn't make a difference. I've been there and done that and I'm never going to believe anything you think you want to say right now so don't say it.'

'Julia?' A faint voice came from the couch. 'Is everything all right?'

'Everything's fine, Katie.' The tone of Julia's voice changed markedly but the look Mac received was another clear warning. This discussion was over. 'I'm glad you're awake,' she said, moving towards Katie. 'I want to check your blood pressure and things. Noni will probably need a feed, soon, too.'

Mac sat back in his chair. He closed his eyes but he didn't sleep.

OK. This was the wrong place and time but this discussion was a long way from being over. He knew what he was up against now.

He knew he could win.

CHAPTER NINE

S<small>HE</small> couldn't talk about it.

Not yet.

Not when she could still feel that baby in her arms every time she closed her eyes. Could remember the incredible softness of the down on that tiny head, the baby smell, the fierce protectiveness that came with having sole responsibility—albeit briefly—for such a vulnerable little being.

Julia and Mac had been stood down for twenty-four hours after they had finally been able to evacuate Katie and her family the morning after Noni's birth. Mac had wanted to come home with Julia but she found herself brushing him off in precisely the same way he had brushed her off in the wake of what had turned out to be an unfortunate visit to his mother and the island of Iona.

'I need to sleep,' she had said briskly. 'And wash my hair and clean the house and call my sister. I'll see you tomorrow, Mac. At work.'

Hopefully, it would be as busy as it had been during

the storm and preclude any private conversation. She knew they had to talk about it because she owed Mac that much at least.

But not yet.

Not when it hurt this much and when her head and heart were at war with each other. When she was feeling tired and confused and more vulnerable than she'd ever felt in her life before.

There had been some powerful magic going on in that isolated farmhouse last night. A sprinkle of fairy dust that had tipped the balance and turned what could have been a tragedy into a joyous family extension. Some of that dust must have still been in the air when she'd picked up the baby to comfort her in the dead of night.

Magic that had stilled the emotional roller-coaster she'd been on ever since she'd woken that morning on Iona with the premonition of the coming crash. Maybe they'd brought it with them, a coating that was shaking itself free at unexpected moments.

That magic had been well stuck on the beach when they'd been waiting for the ferry. When she'd pushed Mac away as hard as she could to pre-empt the declaration she had known was imminent. Even less in evidence when Mac had chosen to stay away from her that night. Self-loathing had surfaced at that point. Loneliness that she'd brought on herself and deserved. A negative spiral of thoughts that if not wanting children hadn't been such a deal breaker, he would have wanted to talk about it. He would have come and held her in his arms and said the words that had never been spoken.

He would have told her that he loved her.

As a downward swoop of an emotional roller-coaster, the frightening helicopter ride had been a perfect bottom of the dip. She could have died, never having heard those words. Never having told Mac how much *she* loved him.

But then she'd had the challenge of a potentially disastrous medical emergency and the adrenaline rush of success. The joy of hearing a newborn's first cry that had broken a barrier and pulled her into family life. Sharing a meal with young children, supervising bathtime and tucking them into bed.

A roller-coaster. Emotions going from one extreme to another.

And then the moment of utter serenity, holding a sleeping baby. An astonishing stillness that had given her a glimpse into a part of her soul she had been so determined to deny. A part a career—maybe even a marriage—could never hope to fulfil. A part that had the kind of unconditional, absolute love a parent could give a child.

No wonder Mac wanted a family in his future so badly.

Had the yearning been awakened in him long ago as a lonely child himself? Would it get worse for her? Intense enough to take too much joy from life?

It didn't have to. Julia stepped out of the long, hot shower and towelled herself dry. Maybe the real magic had been to realise that she could have taken the newborn Noni home and loved her as her own, no question. Adoption wasn't an issue. She could do that one day. Adopt children as a single mother, if necessary.

'Are you *crazy*?'

The words were muttered aloud as she pulled on a favourite pair of soft leggings and stuffed her feet into fluffy slippers.

Mac had been about to tell her it didn't matter that she couldn't have babies. That they could adopt.

Her heart wanted to rejoice. Her head overruled it.

History repeating itself, it said. History that led to heartbreak. And this time it would be worse because she loved Mac *so* much. In a way she had never loved anyone and knew she never would again. She hadn't told him that and maybe that was just as well because she'd told him the truth about herself too late and now it felt as though everything they had together was built on something too insubstantial to last.

Too flimsy to trust.

It was only early afternoon. The early hours of the morning on the other side of the world but that was probably just as well, too. If she rang and talked to Anne she would probably start crying and her sister didn't need to know how bad she was feeling. Her sister might feel responsible, having suggested that an affair with Mac was a good idea. She was dealing with the disintegration of her own relationship in any case and, when you got right down to it, she couldn't really understand where Julia was coming from.

Anne didn't have any yearning for a child. Why would she when she had mothered Julia from when she was only a child herself? When her career had her working with children and sharing the heartache of parents who had to deal with the dark side of loving their little ones so much? How ironic was it that they were both in relationships where they couldn't give the man they loved what he wanted but for such different reasons?

Things needed to be done and Julia tried hard to distract herself but the housework didn't take much time and the phone calls and email that were waiting for attention were dealt with just as quickly. Sitting around feeling sorry for herself was stupid so Julia pulled on a woolly hat, padded anorak and rubber boots and headed out into the remnants of yesterday's storm, hoping that a blast of damp arctic air might do something to clear her head. She walked for an hour or more, until her fingers and toes and nose were frozen and all she wanted was another hot shower and to tumble into bed and sleep.

Returning to her cottage the back way across farmland, she missed the big black vehicle parked out the front. It was a shock to find Mac standing on her front porch. He looked as exhausted as she felt. Physically and emotionally. His smile was so brief it almost didn't happen. He hadn't shaved. There was a dark shadow on his jaw line and even darker shadows in his eyes. He looked rugged and unhappy and...so heartstoppingly gorgeous Julia couldn't speak. She could hardly draw a breath.

'We need to talk, Jules.'

Julia nodded. Raindrops trapped in her eyelashes were dislodged by the movement and fell onto her cheeks, like tears.

'You'd better come in, then.'

'You're soaked.'

'I'll leave my outside stuff here.' She shrugged off

the anorak and hung it up to drip on the flagged area of the porch.

'Where have you been?'

'I just went for a walk. I needed some fresh air.' Julia was pulling off her boots but she glanced up to catch Mac's wry smile.

'Nothing stops you, does it? I reckon you'd go for a walk in a hurricane if you felt the need for some fresh air.'

Julia's smile felt tight. Unnatural. She unlocked the cottage door and led Mac inside. Her temporary home felt as grey as the weather outside but Julia didn't move to turn on any lights or heating. Neither did Mac.

This felt horribly awkward.

Mac looked as uncomfortable as Julia felt.

'Would you like a coffee or something?' she asked.

'Sure.' Mac followed her to the kitchenette. A tiny space that had always been made ridiculously small when he was sharing it with her. For weeks now, it had been a secret delight, the way she couldn't move in here without bumping into him or brushing past so close he would be obliged to catch her for an extra kiss or a cuddle.

It was the last thing she could cope with now. Why on earth had she offered coffee? She could hardly ask him to go and wait in the chilly sitting room and the only other room in the cottage was the bedroom. Oh…this was awkward.

Mac finally broke the silence.

'I'm sorry,' he said. 'I know you didn't want to see me today and you probably don't want to talk about this but something you said last night has been stuck in my head all day.'

Julia didn't say anything. She just waited, fiddling with the lid of the instant coffee jar, her fingers clumsy because they were only coming back to life slowly, a burning pain in them as the nerves warmed up. It was nothing on the pain lying in wait for her heart, though.

'That you'd been there and done that,' Mac continued. 'That you wouldn't believe anything I had to say. I need to know why.'

'Fair enough.' The jug had boiled but Julia ignored the waiting mugs. She turned to face Mac instead, backing up so she had the bench against her back in a futile bid for a sense of security.

'Three years ago,' she told him, 'I was engaged. To a man called Peter. We were very much in love and he knew my history. He knew I could never have children of my own and he convinced me that it didn't matter. That we could be childless or adopt or use a surrogate…that it wasn't an issue because he loved me and that was all that mattered. We planned our wedding, we dreamed about our future. We even bought a house.'

It was Mac's turn to be silent now. To wait. He stood there as still as a statue. Listening. Only his eyes moved. Scanning her face. Absorbing her words and analysing their significance.

'I believed him,' Julia continued. 'And why wouldn't I? He loved me and I loved him. I chose the wedding dress of my dreams. Everything was organised. All the grief I'd been through when I had to have the hysterectomy and knew I'd never have children was erased. I'd never been so happy.'

A muscle twitched in Mac's jaw as though he was gritting his teeth. 'And then?'

'Two weeks before the wedding date, Peter told me he was very sorry but he'd made a dreadful mistake.'

'What? In wanting to marry you?'

'In telling me that the fact I couldn't have children wasn't an issue. He'd discovered that having a baby with someone was actually quite a big deal. Becoming a father in a normal way. Making a family.'

'And it took until you were practically at the altar for him to come to this conclusion?' Mac sounded incredulous.

Julia looked away. 'I think the timing was more to do with the fact that someone else informed him he was going to *be* a father. A *real* father.'

Mac's snort was derisive. 'The scumbag was sleeping with someone else?'

'Obviously.'

'And he got her pregnant?'

Julia couldn't help smiling. 'And you got your degree with honours?'

Mac shook his head. Either he didn't remember his dig at Julia when she had been asking him about his siblings that day or he simply wasn't amused. 'I'm smarter than you are.'

Julia blinked. She had expected at least some sympathy for having been so badly treated. 'What's that supposed to mean?'

Mac turned away from her as though he had no intention of answering the question but then he swung back to face her. 'You think you got dumped because you can't have children, yes?'

Julia's jaw dropped at the same time as her hackles rose. Surely Mac didn't think this was an appropriate time to come riding in on a white charger and sweep the issue into oblivion? Tell her that Peter was an idiot because it really didn't matter? The arrogance of the man!

'Actually,' she informed him, 'that was precisely why I got "dumped", as you so sensitively put it. Peter spelt it out. With a scarily similar lack of sensitivity.'

Mac shook his head again. 'Sorry, Jules. Seems to me you missed the point entirely.'

Julia's tone was pure ice. 'And the point is?'

'The fact that he was sleeping with someone else in the first place. You don't do that if you love someone enough to want to spend the rest of your life with them.'

You might if you think the person you're going to marry isn't a 'real' woman. One that's capable of having a baby.

Not that Julia was going to say this aloud only to have it dismissed. She'd been nearly destroyed by the pain of what Peter had done. How could Mac belittle what she'd been through? Make her feel like she'd been stupid and had 'missed the point' or overreacted or something?

He didn't understand.

And why was he any different anyway? He'd never said *he* loved her.

He's shown you, her heart whispered. *Every time he's touched you and kissed you and smiled at you in that special way that makes you melt inside.*

That's just what you want to believe, her head countered. '*Just like you wanted to believe everything Peter said.*

Julia was torn. More than anything, she wanted to trust Mac but to do so was terrifying because she would be laying herself open to a pain she couldn't voluntarily submit to.

She couldn't do it.

She couldn't trust Mac. Something too powerful was holding her back.

Maybe she was wrong and she was being stupid and totally missing the point but it came down to the courage needed to trust and if she didn't have it, this was over. That was the crux of everything happening here, wasn't it? If you loved someone enough to overcome obstacles, you trusted them. It was a given.

Mac was staring at her.

Watching the way her head was overruling her heart.

Reading her mind.

'You don't trust me, do you?' He rubbed his forehead as though aware of the furrows of disbelief that had appeared.

'You don't trust me,' he repeated, his tone hollow now.

She didn't trust him.

Man, that was a kicker.

Mac had been prepared to do anything for this woman but he was facing a wall that was so dauntingly solid he had no idea where to start trying to break it down.

He *loved* her, for God's sake. He could no more

think of sleeping with someone else at this point in his life than… Good grief, he couldn't even think of something abhorrent enough to fill the gap.

She didn't trust him because she thought he was the same as the creep she'd been planning to marry. A man who clearly hadn't loved her and had used her inability to have children as an excuse for his disgusting behavior. His betrayal.

She had loved this Peter. She'd said so. She'd trusted him and had been betrayed and had her heart broken.

Fair enough. He got that.

If she loved *him*, she would trust him.

She didn't trust him. He'd made the accusation and she hadn't even tried to deny it.

She'd never said she loved him so why had he assumed she felt the same way he did?

Because he'd trusted her, that's why. He had felt it in every touch and every smile. Every moment of connection and underlying every silent conversation.

They were at an impasse here. Standing in this ridiculously small space with two mugs on the bench that were probably not going to have coffee in them any time soon.

The silence stretched on. When Julia broke it, her voice was tight.

'I'm not the only one who has a problem with trust,' she said.

'What the hell is that supposed to mean?'

'You've got things in your past you haven't trusted me enough to talk about.'

'You've never asked.'

'OK.' He recognised the tilt of Julia's chin. The same kind of determination he'd seen when she was doing something she probably shouldn't be doing. Like volunteering to dangle from a broken bridge or climb into an unstable train carriage. 'I'm asking now. What was it about the woman on that train? Who did she remind you of and why didn't you want to talk about it?'

Mac sucked in a breath. Did he have any hope of breaking through that wall or was this over? Was this the time to try even? But this was about trust and honesty and Julia had told him about the baggage she carried. She deserved the same from him.

'It was ten years ago,' he said slowly, 'and her name was Christine.'

'And she had long blonde hair?'

'Yes.' Mac breathed in. Carefully, as though the very air in this room was a source of pain. 'I thought I was in love with her. We hadn't known each other very long and I wasn't thinking about asking her to marry me but…she got pregnant.'

He'd known it would be rubbing salt into a wound. What he hadn't known was that the flash of pain on Julia's face would feel like he'd given her a physical blow.

'She didn't want the baby,' he continued woodenly. 'She never wanted to have children holding her back, stopping her doing what she wanted to do with her life. She saw it as an obstacle. Unimportant in its own right. And nothing I could do or say would change her mind because I wasn't important enough either. She had the abortion and told me about it in the email that also said she was leaving.'

There. He'd said it. Admitted the failure that had haunted him for all these years. Would it change anything? Make him more trustworthy because he'd been so honest?

'*You* wanted the baby, though, didn't you?' Julia asked softly.

Oh…God. Mac could never forget that moment when he'd been told about the baby. That clutching sensation around his heart. The shock that had become amazement at what had felt like a miracle. *His* baby. He was going to be a father. And hot on the heels of that had come the powerful urge to protect that baby. From anything. For ever.

Julia's gaze was fixed on his face. 'Of course you did,' she whispered. 'So don't try and tell me it doesn't matter, Mac. That we can get past this. We can't because I won't do that to you. End of story.'

This had to be the worst moment of his life. He wanted to tell her she was wrong. That ending this was wrong, but he couldn't find any words. Maybe there weren't any.

Maybe she was right.

That moment was imprinted on his heart for ever. The same kind of longing for his child—his own family—that he'd seen on Julia's face when she'd been holding Noni.

She understood. She didn't want to stand in the way of him finding that moment again.

Could he feel the same way about an adopted child? Or a childless marriage? The honest answer was that he didn't know. That there was an element of doubt. That there was a small but insistent voice suggesting that maybe Julia was right.

She must have seen that doubt in his face.

'Oh, Mac…' With a tiny sob, she held out her arms and offered—or perhaps asked for—a hug.

Wordlessly, Mac gathered her close and held her.

Time stopped as they stood there. Holding each other tightly. Accepting that this was the end of the road.

'It's been good, hasn't it?' Julia asked finally. 'What we had?'

'The best,' Mac agreed. 'You're an amazing woman, Julia Bennett.'

She pulled away but she was smiling. 'Will that be in your report?'

'You can count on it.'

'Is it nearly finished?'

'Pretty close.'

Julia took another step back. 'Do you think you could maybe finish it by tomorrow? Say, drop it into the office at work by lunchtime?'

'Probably.' Mac had the distinct feeling he wasn't going to like where this conversation was leading. 'Why?'

'Because there's a flight leaving from Heathrow tomorrow night. I could get a connection from Glasgow in the afternoon.'

'You've booked tickets? But you're not supposed to be leaving before next week.'

'I just made some enquiries. The tickets are on hold. I've got a few hours until I need to confirm whether I want them but I think I do, Mac. I think it's time to go home.'

She wanted this. She wanted to escape. Maybe it was for the best. How could he work with her now, knowing it was over? That he had no hope of winning the new future he'd begun to dream of? That perhaps she didn't even love him. Not the way he loved her, anyway.

Julia broke their eye contact. Made a movement with her hands that was a kind of plea.

'We knew this had to end, didn't we? If we make a clean cut now, it'll be easier. We'll be able to look back and remember the good bits. The best bits.'

Mac swallowed. He didn't trust himself to speak. He needed to get out of here.

So he gave a single nod and turned for the door. Then he turned back, took two long steps and caught Julia in his arms again. Held her tightly.

'Mac?'

'What?' He didn't want to let her go. Not yet. Not ever.

'Don't come to the airport with me tomorrow. This is goodbye, OK?'

No, it wasn't OK. It would never be OK. Mac tightened his grip but somehow Julia slipped free. What was it he'd said about her that day? That she was a cross between a contortionist and a weightlifter?

She had her back to him now.

'Please go, Mac.' The words were so quiet they were almost a prayer. 'Please go now.'

CHAPTER TEN

IT WAS the longest journey in the world.

Nearly thirty hours from Glasgow, Scotland to Christchurch, New Zealand with only brief interludes of airport time in London and Singapore.

The physical journey was easy enough. All Julia had to do was put herself in the right place at the right time and she was taken to where she needed to go.

The emotional journey was a very different story.

How unfair was it that it didn't seem to help to know that her head had been right in stopping her heart from trusting Mac? It had been a fight to the death in that tiny kitchen between her head and her heart and when she'd heard the desolation in his voice when he'd accused her of not trusting him, it had been all she could do not to fall into his arms and deny it.

To tell him that she loved him. That she would trust him with her life and with her heart. For ever.

Her head had pulled out the big guns then and they had located their target unerringly.

She'd been shocked, hearing him talk about

Christine. Seeing the pain in his face when he'd told her about the baby he'd tried and failed to save. *His* baby. One that he'd wanted so much it had been painful just seeing a pregnant woman who looked a bit like Christine *ten* years later.

If her head had needed any proof that she was courting disaster by allowing herself to take that leap of faith, she'd had it. In spades.

The only way to survive was to run and hide.

Thank goodness she'd made those phone calls to enquire about changing dates on the tickets she already had. Just in case.

And when she'd voiced her intention to leave, she had seen Mac have the kind of heart/mind struggle she was only too familiar with. She saw the moment his head got the strongest position. The moment when doubt had clouded his eyes.

Yes. It had been a fight to the death. The heads had won and the hearts—her heart, anyway—felt like they were dying.

Anne was there to meet her at the airport. She took one look at Julia's face and gathered her sister into her arms.

'Oh, Jules. Poor baby. You're home now, I've got you. It'll be all right, you'll see.'

And it was, kind of. Anne did what she did so well, with unstinting love and support backed up by some stern advice. It helped being half a world away from Mac and back in a familiar place that he'd never entered.

By the time the jet-lag was over and she was back

at work full time, Julia knew that while nothing would ever be the same again, she would survive. Somehow.

Nothing was the same.

Mac had been right on the money with that niggling fear that his work and his bed would feel empty when Julia had gone. His whole life seemed about as colourful as the relentlessly grey Scottish weather they were experiencing day after day.

He would get through it. He'd done it before.

Or had he?

Had he ever really got his head sorted after Christine? He had been so sure he had but now he was beginning to wonder if all he'd succeeded in doing had been to shove the whole emotional mess under a convenient mental rug. If it hadn't still been there, it couldn't have been uncovered so easily by that tragedy of the young woman on the train.

No hope of pushing things under any kind of cover this time. Julia seemed to be everywhere. Waiting to ambush him at every turn—just like she had when she'd waited for him in the car park that night.

When he'd kissed her.

The car park was bad enough with its associated memories. Arriving in the locker room for a night shift on the day she'd flown out was even more poignant. Julia had forgotten her boots and there they were. Half a dozen sizes smaller than any of the men's footwear, they looked childlike and forlorn. Abandoned.

He could hear an echo of Julia's laughter in here as well. Her voice with that determined lilt.

'I might be smaller than you lot but I'm just as tough, you'll see.'

She hadn't looked tough when she'd held her arms out for that farewell hug.

Everybody was missing her.

'I wonder what Jules is doing,' Angus took to musing at irritatingly frequent intervals. 'Has she emailed yet to tell you why she had to go home in such a rush?'

No. She hadn't emailed. Hadn't phoned. Hadn't even sent for her boots.

A week passed. And another. Until Mac couldn't stand the sight of those small boots any longer. He parceled them up and made a call to the administrative offices to get Julia Bennett's home address. He posted them and then wondered if he would get any response to the cryptic note he had scrawled to go in the parcel.

Missing something?

If she'd missed the boots, she would have sent for them. If she missed him, she would have made contact. If Mac was going to get over this any time soon, he would stop thinking about her so often. The hurt at not being loved enough—*trusted* enough—would fade.

He went to visit his mother a week or so later. Jeannie MacCulloch took one look at her son's face and clicked her tongue.

'You let her get away, didn't you, Alan?'

'I couldn't stop her, Mum. She didn't want to stay.'

'Oh?' The look on her face was mischievous enough to remind him of the woman he'd lost. 'New Zealand is a bonny place, I've heard. I'm going there myself, you know. With Doreen.'

* * *

'You need a change,' Anne decreed. 'A fresh start.'

Julia sighed. 'I'm trying.'

'Did you go ahead with applying for that Urban Search and Rescue training?'

'Yes. It doesn't start for a couple of months, though.'

'Anything else interesting in the classifieds in that *Emergency Medicine* journal?'

'There's a road-based position here in Christchurch. A shift supervisor one that comes with a car to back up ambulance crews.'

'You don't sound overly enthusiastic.'

Julia suppressed another sigh. She wasn't. Not because it wouldn't be a great job but because it would be too similar to what she'd been doing with Mac when they hadn't been needed in the air, only she would be doing it by herself and the empty passenger seat in the front would contain his ghost.

'It comes with a ton of administrative responsibilities.' Anne had done more than her share of listening to her heartache and providing support. It really was high time she pulled herself together. 'There's a bit of teaching involved as well. I quite like the idea of that.'

'Sounds good,' her sister agreed. 'Would it mean giving up the helicopter work completely?'

'Yeah.'

Anne was trying not to look relieved. 'You'd miss it, though, wouldn't you? The thrill of dangling on a line that looks like a thread of a spider's web while you save someone's life?'

'You know what? I think the thrill is fading. I'm almost over it.'

It was an ordeal, actually, climbing into a helicopter these days. Just the sound of the rotors was enough to make her look around to catch the echo of the kind of look Mac would have given her if he'd been there.

The kind that said she was safe. That he would look after her. That whatever they were going to face, they would be able to handle it because they were such a good team.

A parcel arrived the following week with Mac's handwriting on it. Her name and address blurred instantly as her eyes filled with tears.

He'd sent her boots back. She hadn't missed them because she had plenty of footwear for work here.

It was Mac she was missing. Every minute of every hour of every day.

There was a letter in the same mail delivery. An invitation to be part of a team that was going to review the training programme for the emergency services. With her recent experience overseas and the glowing report that had come back with her, she would be able to make a valuable contribution. It would take her away from front-line work but the contract would only be for six months to a year.

The boots lay in their shredded brown paper on the table in front of her. The letter was in her hand. Julia had to blink away a fresh burst of moisture making her eyes sting to read it again.

Annie was right. She needed a fresh start and here it was, being handed to her on a plate. A new challenge. A new life, hopefully.

* * *

An advertisement for a locum to cover Julia's position on the specialist emergency response team was put online within days and applications flooded in for the prestigious vacancy. From the wealth of applications, only six were shortlisted but the process would be thorough and each interview was expected to last at least an hour.

The selection committee consisted of the district manager of the ambulance service, a representative from the police and a clinical instructor who was one of the most experienced paramedics in the country. The reputation of the team was important to everyone and it would be better to be down a team member for a while than do damage by employing the wrong person.

At the last minute, Julia was asked to come in on one of her days off to sit in on the interviews.

'But I haven't even seen the C.V.'s,' she protested.

'I'd rather you didn't.' The district manager ushered her into the boardroom. 'I thought it would be valuable to get an unbiased opinion based on what you see and hear here today. This is your job they'll be doing. You're in the best position to assess qualities that may be relevant but don't appear in qualifications or get covered by the interview process even.'

So Julia sat in what had to be an intimidating row of a selection committee, on one side of the huge boardroom table. Applicants came in one by one and sat on the other side of the expanse of polished mahogany.

The first was an Australian. A confident man in his early thirties with great postgraduate qualifications and an impressive history of service in a helicopter squad.

'I've been on the choppers for years,' he told them.

'I'm just looking for a bit more. I compete in target shooting as a hobby and I do combat obstacle courses as exercise training. Working with the cops is an edge that appeals to me.'

'He seems well qualified,' the clinical instructor said to lead the discussion after the interview. 'Young, fit and keen. Ideal.'

'I think he should be looking to join the police force,' the district manager suggested. 'Or the army.'

Two candidates were local. One had excelled in academic achievements and road-based work but would need full helicopter training.

'Too expensive,' the district manager decreed. 'Can't justify it for a locum position.'

One candidate was female. A thirty-four-year-old paramedic from the north island.

'I want to challenge myself,' she admitted frankly during her interview. 'I've just completed my helicopter training and I'm excited by the opportunities this job could provide. I think I'd learn a lot and it would help me gain a permanent position further down the track.'

'She's got no idea how tough it can be,' was Julia's opinion, after asking searching questions during the interview. 'I think she needs more experience in general helicopter work. She's not ready for something like this.'

'We're getting through them,' the district manager reminded them. 'And so far there hasn't been one who's impressed us unanimously. That Aussie seems like the best bet.' He sounded weary. 'Guess we'd better see number five.'

The other members of this committee could empathise with the weary tone. Four hour-long interviews and a discussion after each one with only a short break for lunch. Julia's brain was beginning to feel fuzzy. The room was very warm so maybe she was getting dehydrated. She reached for the water jug to refill her glass, aware that the door was opening to admit the second to last applicant.

The jug was full and quite heavy so she had to watch what she was doing but that didn't prevent the hairs on the back of her neck lifting in an odd prickle of awareness. Maybe it was due to the sudden silence in the room as any shuffling or movement ceased. She had the sensation that everyone on her side of the table was sitting up and taking notice of the newcomer.

Already impressed.

And why wouldn't they be? Looking up as she gingerly set the water jug down, Julia was stunned to see the big, solid shape of Mac directly in front of her.

'Please…sit down,' the district manager invited. 'Alan MacCulloch, isn't it?'

'Mac will do just fine.'

Mac. He was here. Really here. Only a few feet away from her, but Julia couldn't move. These men around her were all well respected, top-of-their-field professionals. Should she step out of this interview, perhaps, because she was unable to be unbiased?

No. No way was she moving any further away from Mac. She was too stunned to make her legs work in any case.

'You have a very impressive C.V.,' the clinical instructor said, his tone slightly awed.

'Thank you.'

'And you've come from Glasgow, Scotland?' The police representative sounded amazed.

'Aye. I have.'

'That's a very long way to come for an interview for a position that's only temporary.'

'It is indeed.'

Julia cleared her throat. It had to be her turn to ask a question.

'Can…can I ask why you have?'

'Of course.' Mac smiled at her and Julia was aware of a melting sensation she'd been sure she would never feel again. It was one of *those* smiles. For her.

'I've been hearing what a bonny place New Zealand is,' Mac said. 'And I've had a yen to come and see for myself.'

Goodness, he was laying it on a bit thick, wasn't he? Even his accent seemed stronger than Julia remembered. It curled around her and seeped into her cells and warmed her whole body. Everybody else on the committee seemed to be lapping it up as well. Everybody had a smile on their face.

'I felt as though I'd reached the full potential my last position could provide,' Mac continued. He glanced at each committee member before making eye contact with Julia again. 'Like it had…gone past its "use-by" date, perhaps. I need something else and I'm ready to meet any new challenge.'

Julia's breath had caught in her throat. Had he known somehow that she was going to be sitting in on these interviews?

Surely not. But he knew where she lived, didn't he? He had posted her boots back.

The district manager's smile had faded. 'I have to say you're almost over-qualified for this position, Mac. We're a small operation compared to what you're used to. The time frame is also somewhat limited.'

'It's more than enough time,' Mac said. 'I'm confident I can find exactly what I need here. I'm confident I can provide exactly what *you* need.'

His words were being heard by the whole selection committee but it was Julia he was looking at. It was Julia he was really talking to.

Her mouth was as dry as the Sahara but there was no way she was about to reach for her water glass because she knew her hand would be visibly shaking.

The implications of this were slowly sinking in.

Mac was here. Because of *her*.

He had left his job.

They'd kept their relationship a secret so that it was no threat to the job he loved with such a passion. But he'd left it. His 'last position', he'd said. Had he resigned from the SERT to come to the opposite end of the earth simply to find her? On the off chance he could carry on with his career?

'I'm sure your skills would be welcome anywhere you chose to take them,' the district manager was saying now. 'You're clearly a valuable asset to any specialist emergency service.'

'Aye.' Mac's smile was modest. 'I've had a few offers. I need some time to choose where I want to be from now on. Where I'm needed the most.'

I need you, Julia wanted to whisper.

He'd said he was confident. He sounded confident. He said he could provide exactly what she needed.

What did he mean? What had changed?

God, it was so good to see him. Unbelievably good. Julia drew in a shaky breath and only then became aware of the silence. Of the fact that everyone seemed to be looking at her.

'So…' The district manager raised an eyebrow. '*Did* you have anything else you'd like to ask Mac, Julia?'

Oh…yes. Absolutely. But not here.

'No,' she said aloud. 'And I have to confess that I know Mac. I can tell you that this man's experience and reputation are unparalleled. If he wants to be here, for whatever reason, we would be privileged to have him.'

There were heartfelt murmurs of agreement from everyone else on the selection committee. It was a done deal but they had to be seen to be going through the process so the final applicant had to be interviewed.

And maybe that interview was the shortest one of the day but it was still far too long as far as Julia was concerned because it was long enough for Mac to have vanished by the time she could escape from the boardroom.

A wave of disappointment strong enough to make her falter and stand absolutely still, feeling utterly lost, fortunately lasted only the time it took to take a deep, steadying breath.

Mac had posted her boots back to her.

He knew where she lived and Julia knew exactly where he would be right now.

Waiting on her porch.

Because they needed to talk.

He had so much he wanted to say to Julia but there wasn't a single, coherent word in Mac's head when he saw her coming up the tidy brick pathway to where he was waiting on her porch.

The need to take her in his arms and hold her close was so powerful it drove any other thoughts into oblivion because she was *running*. Discarding her bag heedlessly at the bottom of the steps. Flying up and into his arms with the force of a small tornado. Mac was actually knocked off balance and laughed aloud with the joy of it as he caught her.

And held her.

Laughter faded then. Julia's head was buried against his chest and he could feel her fierce need in the way her arms were reaching as far as they could around his body. In the tremor that came from muscles held so tightly. The catch in her breath that was a tiny sob.

He tilted his head so that it rested against the top of Julia's. He pressed his lips to her hair.

'It's all right, hinny. I'm here. I'm sorry it took so long.'

'What do you mean?' Julia's voice was muffled. 'What took so long?'

'For me to get here.'

'I wasn't expecting you.' Julia raised her head and Mac could see bewilderment in her face. Tears in her eyes. 'You never called. Never wrote. The only thing I've had was the parcel with my boots in it and I thought...'

'What?' Mac gave her an encouraging squeeze.

'I thought that you were sending the boots back because you didn't want any reminders of me. That you thought my stupid boots were the only thing I could be missing.'

'Weren't they?'

Julia gave his chest a tiny thump. 'You know they weren't.'

Mac let his breath out in a satisfied sigh. 'I didn't know but now I do.' He kissed her forehead gently. 'And I have to admit I'm quite relieved.'

'You are?'

'Of course. Here I am, jobless and homeless and with everything I need for the rest of my life right here. I was a bit worried about what I'd do if you weren't pleased to see me.'

Julia was wriggling in his arms, looking around behind her.

'You've only got a backpack.'

'I travel light.'

'But you said you have everything you need for the rest of your life.'

'I do. I'm looking at it.' He could see the words hadn't connected. Julia was frowning.

'Have you really resigned from your job?'

'Aye.'

'But…you loved that job.'

'I can get a job I love anywhere. I wasn't lying in that interview when I said I had plenty of offers to choose from. What I can't get anywhere…' He turned Julia back to face him properly. To make sure she heard what he was saying. 'Is the woman I love.'

His voice cracked and Mac had to close his eyes for a heartbeat. The porch they were standing on in an ordinary little house in a Christchurch suburb vanished. He was on the beach on Iona now and the magic was strong. He opened his eyes to find Julia's gaze fixed on his face with a look of wonder. She could feel that magic too.

'I've missed you so much, Jules,' he said softly. 'I could have gone looking for someone else, like you suggested. Some woman who could give me ten children, but I would always feel like something was missing.' He had to swallow the lump in his throat and drag in a new breath. 'Part of my heart. My soul. The part I gave to you without understanding what was happening. The part I can only ever have back if you're by my side.' He tried—and failed—to smile. 'I want it back,' he whispered. 'I want *you*. I need you to trust this. To trust *me*.'

Her heart was filling to bursting point with something that felt like music.

All the time Mac had been holding her and telling her how much he loved her, Julia had been searching his face. Sinking into the depths of his eyes and trying to locate even the smallest hint of the doubt she'd seen there the day they'd said goodbye.

It wasn't there. Her head had to surrender to her heart this time. There was no reason not to trust this.

'I *do* trust you, Mac,' she whispered back. 'And I love you. I've missed you *so* much but…I don't understand…'

Mac's hold on her was gentle now. He raised a hand

and brushed tears from her cheeks but didn't say anything.

'I know how much you wanted that baby,' Julia said bravely. 'Even after so many years I could see how much you wanted it and how important it had been.'

'Aye…'

A shiver ran down Julia's spine at the quiet confirmation. Mac must have felt that shiver because he pulled her closer.

'I didn't understand either,' he told her. 'I hadn't thought about Christine or the baby for years. Not until I saw that woman on the train. Until you made me talk about her. I did a lot of thinking after you left, Jules, and the pieces finally came together. The whole picture.'

'What did you see?' The porch was an odd place to be opening their hearts like this but it didn't occur to Julia to invite Mac inside her home just yet. There was magic happening here and it wasn't about to be broken.

'I thought I loved Christine,' Mac said, 'but what I actually fell in love with was that baby. The feeling like something had already been born that I could protect from anything and love for the rest of my life. It was…the feeling of family, I guess. Or something more important than myself. Something huge and warm and…more important than anything else could ever be.'

Julia could feel her whole body tensing. She'd been right. A baby…*his* baby…was that important. Something that had been ripped away from him and something she could never give him. So why was he here, holding her like this? How could she ever persuade him that he would regret giving up the chance to have that family?

'I was missing you so much I couldn't breathe without it hurting,' Mac said then. 'And, finally, I understood.'

'Understood what?' Julia's words were a whisper of hope.

'That I don't need a baby. That I already had that feeling when I was with you. That urge to protect you from anything. So much love I know it will last for ever. I love you…' he smiled '…and that's all that matters.'

'But…'

Mac gave his head a tiny shake. 'We could have children,' he said. 'Our own with a surrogate or adopted. We could foster some or just borrow some from a friend for a weekend but it would be a bonus. We could have a puppy or a tank of goldfish or an elephant in the back yard if we wanted but we don't need any of that to be a family. We're the lucky ones.'

'We are?' She certainly felt lucky. Blessed beyond measure, but hearing Mac say these things was unbelievably wonderful. Maybe she'd heard them before but only with her ears. This time she could hear them with her heart and soul and she couldn't doubt a single syllable of them.

'Some people have to have children to make a family and then the kids grow up and leave home and they haven't got it any more. We've got it now. We'll still have it when we're old and grey.' His brow furrowed. 'If that's what you want, too?'

'Of course it is. I want to be with you, Mac. I want

you by my side just as much as you want me by yours. And you're right.'

'About?'

'I hadn't thought it through, really. I thought about adopting children and that I could do it by myself if I had to and I would be able to love those kids as if I'd given birth to them myself. I could have made a family but it would never have stopped me missing you. I love you, Mac.'

'Will you marry me?'

'Yes.' Julia's joy bubbled out in laughter. 'Absolutely, yes.'

Mac's lips touched hers almost reverently and those dark eyes Julia loved so much were suspiciously bright.

With love. For her.

'Thank you,' Julia breathed.

'What for?'

'For making a dream I didn't dare have any more come true.'

'We can make all our dreams come true if we do it together.'

Julia's smile wobbled. 'You know what?'

'What?'

'I actually believe that.'

Mac's brow creased thoughtfully. '*You* know what?'

'What?'

'Bed's a very good place for dreaming.'

Julia's laughter sounded like a joyous peal of bells. 'You'd better come inside then.'

EPILOGUE

'I'LL give you a moment to yourselves,' the doctor said. 'To let you make a final decision.'

He shut the door behind them and they were alone in this treatment room of the specialist private fertility clinic.

Julia's hand was being held tightly by that of her husband.

Her other hand was being held almost as tightly by her sister.

Anne lay on the bed, wearing a hospital gown, a sheet covering her bare legs.

Mac was eyeing the stirrups attached to the end of the bed. Julia followed his gaze and then looked back at her sister.

'Are you sure about this, Annie? It's not too late to change your mind.'

'I'm hardly about to take back my wedding gift to you guys,' Anne said calmly. 'Not when it's taken this long to get you to accept it.'

It had taken a while but there had been good reasons for that.

The first month after Mac had arrived in New

Zealand had passed in a blur of happiness and making plans. At the end of that month, they had been married in a simple ceremony on a beach.

Anne had been there, of course. She had loved Mac from their first meeting but the short engagement and low-key celebration of their commitment to each other had concerned her a little. When Julia had chosen a pretty sundress for the occasion, Anne had shaken her head.

'Are you sure this is all you want? I mean, you wanted to do the whole meringue thing last time.'

Julia had grinned. 'The dream wedding dress. Yeah…but this time I've got the dream man, Annie. I don't need anything else.'

'This is all happening so fast. I haven't even thought of what to get you for a wedding gift.'

'We don't need one. We love each other. We've got a week on a desert island for a honeymoon. We couldn't be happier, honestly.'

But she'd been wrong.

When they came back from their honeymoon, Anne had a gift waiting for them. A promise.

'I want to be a surrogate mother for you,' she said.

Julia's hand had found Mac's and they'd sat there, stunned by the incredible offer they were hearing.

'You'd be doing me a favour, really,' Anne said in the end. 'I don't want motherhood but if I missed the experience of childbirth I might regret it one day. And, hey, this way I'll be getting nieces and nephews and I can guarantee I'll always get an invitation to a family Christmas dinner.'

At first, both Julia and Mac had been too blown away to really consider the offer seriously.

And they were busy. Julia had loved her think-tank contract so much she'd accepted another one to set up a training programme in dealing with multi-casualty incidents.

Mac had been persuaded to accept a permanent position on the local specialist emergency response team with invitations to travel and train teams in other centres if he had the time and inclination.

They bought a house together, on a bush-clad hill overlooking a tiny private beach in a secluded harbour bay. They called the property Iona.

Jeannie MacCulloch came to visit them as she toured the country with her friend Doreen.

'You're a clever lad,' she told her son. 'I knew you'd see sense. But will you *ever* stop growing?'

Anne reminded them periodically that she wasn't getting any younger. 'I've got a sabbatical due half way through next year, so if you're ever going to accept this gift, this is the best possible time.' She had given them a knowing smile. 'There's some fine print you might have missed concerning a "use-by" date.'

They'd talked and talked about it.

Walking on what rapidly came to feel like their own little beach.

Holding each other at night after making love.

During telephone calls when one of them was out of town for a day or two. Separation that was only made tolerable by long, long conversations last thing in the day.

And, finally, they realised they were being offered a gift that was beyond price.

A bonus to their lives that they might not need but which would add to their happiness immeasurably.

Julia underwent treatment to stimulate her ovaries and then Mac held her hand while the egg collection procedure happened.

Mac did his part without a murmur of complaint at any indignities involved.

And here they were, nearly a year after their wedding, and a decision had to be made about how many embryos to implant in Anne's womb.

'Two's good,' the specialist had advised. 'If it's successful, twins are manageable and don't present too much of a risk of complications to the mother, and if one embryo fails to take, you've got back-up. Three is acceptable and gives you more chances for implantation but a riskier pregnancy if they all take.'

They agreed on two.

Mac went to call the doctor back to the room but paused at the door and turned. 'I can stay in the waiting room for the next bit if you prefer,' he told Anne.

Anne snorted. 'You're the father of these babies, Mac. You won't be in the waiting room for their birth so you may as well be here for the opening act.'

Mac grinned, clearly delighted. He came back a minute later with the doctor and the lab technician who carried a petri dish. A nurse also came in to uncover the trolley that had the sterile cannula and other equipment needed for this brief procedure.

Julia still held her sister's hand.

Mac stood just behind her, his hands resting lightly on her hips, holding her so that she was touching his whole body.

'Here we go then,' the doctor said cheerfully.

Anne Bennett thought about closing her eyes for this but looked up instead.

Julia was still holding her hand but she had tipped her head back to look up at Mac and he was looking down at her.

She saw the hopes and dreams of a young couple who were born to be parents in that glance.

She saw a love so solid and huge it brought tears to her eyes.

So she did close them.

And she made a silent plea that this part of their story would have a very happy ending.

THE MARRY-ME
WISH

BY
ALISON ROBERTS

MILLS & BOON

All the characters in this book have no existence outside the imagination
of the author, and have no relation whatsoever to anyone bearing the
same name or names. They are not even distantly inspired by any
individual known or unknown to the author, and all the incidents are
pure invention.

First published in Great Britain 2010
Harlequin Mills & Boon Limited,
Eton House, 18-24 Paradise Road, Richmond, Surrey TW9 1SR

© Alison Roberts 2010

ISBN: 978 0 263 87908 7

Harlequin Mills & Boon policy is to use papers that are natural,
renewable and recyclable products and made from wood grown in
sustainable forests. The logging and manufacturing process conform
to the legal environmental regulations of the country of origin.

Printed and bound in Spain
by Litografia Rosés, S.A., Barcelona

'You're *selling*?' The word was a gasp. 'But…you love this place. It's—' She was going to say *it's your home* but the words caught. It wasn't any more, was it?

David still wasn't looking at her. 'You can't always keep the things you love, Annie.'

The edges of his words were rough enough to negate the fact that he'd softened her name. They grated, like the way David's chair did as he pushed it roughly back to stand up. 'Sometimes you have to let them go in order to move on. That's life.'

He walked to the fridge and opened the door. Anne found herself staring at his back.

Fighting tears. He hadn't been talking about the house, had he?

Praise for
Alison Roberts:

'Written with plenty of warmth and heart,
TWINS FOR CHRISTMAS is bound to touch the heart
of every single reader!'

—*cataromance.com*

CHAPTER ONE

'WE NEED you, Anne. I wouldn't ask but this is a real emergency.'

'What's up, Jeff? I thought you were in Theatre with a complicated valve replacement case.'

'I am. Got to scrub back in in a sec. We've got a theatre free up here but no surgeon. Six-year-old kid coming up from Emergency that I don't want to give to a registrar.'

'Trauma?'

'Hit by a car. Chest injuries, possible tamponade. There's an ED team coming up with him.'

'I'm onto it. Which theatre?'

'Three. They're setting up now. Are you sure, Annie? Your back all right?'

'I'll cope.'

A wry chuckle came down the phone line. 'As long as you can still reach the table. I'll come in to assist as soon as I can leave my reg to close up.'

'I'll be fine, Jeff.'

Anne hit the 'save' button for the paper she'd been

working on and pushed her chair back. It hadn't been so long since she would have leapt to her feet to respond to a call like this. Her brain was still fast enough but her body had somewhat different ideas.

Almost eight months pregnant. With twins, and her bump was impressive by anyone's standards. Her feet were swollen as well and she had permanent backache these days. Due to start a sabbatical break in just a week, Anne was using these last days to catch up on things there was never enough time for. Like journal reading to keep up with new developments in her field and departmental administration tasks, and her favourite—writing up papers to submit to specialist paediatric cardiovascular surgical journals. Already, her list of peer-reviewed papers was something to be proud of and the main goal of the upcoming break in her full on career was to recapture the joy of producing something to interest, if not challenge, like minds.

She couldn't turn away from this call, however. Not when the life of a six-year-old child was at stake.

The route from her office to the theatre suite only involved one flight of stairs so there was no point waiting for the elevator. Annoying to be so out of breath by the time she pushed open the fire-stop door in the stairwell but at least she was here before her patient.

A 'ping' announcing the arrival of an elevator sounded as Anne stepped through the swing door of the stairwell. The metal doors of the lift slid open by the time she was directly in front of them and there could be no doubt that this was the emergency she had been called upstairs for. The small space behind those doors was crowded.

A bed with a small person on it. A nurse holding bags of fluid steady on an IV pole. A doctor at the head of the bed holding an ambu-bag to assist breathing if necessary. A frame over the bed supported a defibrillator and other monitoring equipment. Another nurse was wedged in, carrying an oxygen cylinder, and leading the team was a consultant from the emergency department.

That consultant was someone Anne knew very well indeed but had never expected to see again. For just a heartbeat, she totally forgot what she was here for.

David?

He'd left St Patrick's hospital almost a year ago. He'd made no bones about being prepared to give up his senior position in the emergency department because it was the easiest way to end their relationship. Probably the only way they could finally tear apart a connection that was strong enough to be irresistible, but they had both known it was going nowhere.

How ironic that they should meet again like this.

For David to see her pregnant.

And in that same heartbeat, as his gaze lifted to meet hers, Anne tried desperately to signal a message.

It's not what you think.

Oh, my God!

The shock was a physical thing. A kind of detonation somewhere behind his ribs that sent shockwaves rippling through his body. Unpleasant, electrical sort of jolts.

Anne was pregnant.

Enormously pregnant.

Glowing with it. Looking more beautiful than he ever remembered, with her rich, dark hair flowing over her shoulders and a loose, soft cotton top that caressed the huge bump of her stomach.

So it hadn't been that she hadn't ever wanted a family.

She just hadn't wanted one with *him*.

David didn't need to catch the flash of guilt in her eyes to confirm what was so blindingly obvious. Shock morphed instantly into a pain that he knew would become anger.

But not now.

'Keiran Burroughs, aged six,' he snapped. 'Hit by a car going approximately forty-five kilometres an hour. Flail chest, tension pneumothorax. Three-fifty mils drained so far. Cardiac arrhythmia—runs of VPBs. Arrested in ED prior to chest drain insertion and pericardiocentesis.'

The bed was moving forward as he spoke, underlying the urgency of getting this child into Theatre. Anne was assessing the boy visually, noting his lack of consciousness and pallor. She was also trying to read the figures on the monitor screens.

'X-rays?'

'I'll put them up while you get scrubbed.' He could see the anaesthetist waiting at the entrance to the theatre anteroom. As the bed was manoeuvred through the doorway, an alarm sounded from the life pack monitoring the heart rhythm. He was turning away from the surgeon as he spoke again.

'My shift has finished,' he said. 'I'd like to stay in Theatre if that's okay with you.'

Anne was also turning away, heading at speed towards the locker room.

'Of course,' was all she said. 'Fine by me.'

The bristles of the small, soap-impregnated brush were tough enough to make her skin sting. Or perhaps that was because she was scrubbing so hard and fast. Under her nails. Over and between her fingers. All the way up to her elbows.

Thank goodness she had something so automatic to do and something to think about that was so urgent it could override her reactions to seeing David again and knowing that he would be somewhere amongst the gowned and masked figures in Theatre with her.

Anne began rinsing her hands, angling them so that the water went from fingertip to elbow. Okay, maybe she wasn't being quite as successful as she thought. Had it only been this morning when she'd had coffee with her sister, Julia, and they'd been laughing? Excited about the imminent birth of these babies. Discussing names. Planning and dreaming for what lay ahead as they came so close to the culmination of a long-awaited dream.

Life could turn on a sixpence, couldn't it?

Happiness could be twisted and become unrecognisable. Get replaced with sadness and guilt and a tension she couldn't begin to analyse because there was someone far more important that David or herself or even her babies to consider right now. A small boy and his family whose lives had been derailed far more dangerously than her own.

This time, her success was complete. As a nurse tied the strings of her gown—not without difficulty given her new size—Anne Bennett had nothing on her mind other than the task that lay immediately ahead of her.

Saving the life of little Keiran.

It was unusual enough to have a woman who was only in her mid-thirties holding a senior position in a specialty as tough as this one. Even more unusual to see one working around the challenges presented by advanced pregnancy.

So advanced, it looked as if Anne might need to put her scalpel down and give birth at any moment.

David had only been gone for a year. Not quite a year, in fact, which meant that she must have become pregnant within weeks of him leaving the country.

Oh, anger was there all right. When he thought back to the sheer torment of uprooting himself. Trying to settle in a new place and a new job with the background misery of mourning a relationship that had died. Wishing it could have been different. Feeling displaced and…downright lonely.

And what had Anne been doing? Starting again. Sleeping with some other guy. Planning a family and a future. Disgust mixed with anger and hardened the stare David had fixed on the surgeon. Not that Anne was remotely aware of it, of course, and something else got mixed into that nasty emotional brew.

Jealousy. Not just for the fact that she'd been enjoying life while he'd been suffering. Or for the man she had chosen to be the father of her child. Right now, it was for her focus. Her career. The way she could be so totally absorbed in what she was doing that anything personal ceased to exist. Anne was completely free of the turbulent, painful thoughts David couldn't quite distract himself from. But it had always been like that, hadn't it? That focus. The passion that was more important than anything else in life.

If he was scrubbed in and right alongside the table he could have emptied his head and heart of anything other than this case. Even where he was, close to the anaesthetist at the head of the table where he was getting the best view without being in anyone's way, he could lose himself often enough to keep him from walking out of the operating theatre.

The tension was contagious. The difficulty in controlling the bleeding enough to see what damage lay inside that small chest. The time-critical period of starting cardiac bypass to allow repairs to the heart itself. David had to wait long enough to see what he'd been trying to deal with in the emergency department. The damage that the sharp ends of fractured ribs had caused to the vital organs they were supposed to protect. And then he had to see it though.

He was here because he had worked so hard already to stabilise this child and get him to Theatre. His determination to save the boy was still there and however irrelevant it now was, it was compelling to still be part of this equation. As though he could still make a contribution to the outcome. Staying long enough to know what that outcome was going to be was important. David had to wait and see if the heart could be restarted and whether the patchwork of repairs would be up to the job of supplying blood and oxygen under sufficient pressure to sustain life.

In between the dramatic start and finding out how this story would end was a lull as far as David was concerned, however. It was too hard to see into the chest cavity clearly enough to admire the tiny, neat sutures the surgeon was making. He could watch the monitors and follow any deterioration or improvement in the little boy's condition and he could listen to the verbal exchanges between the surgical team members and watch the instruments and equipment being used, but too much of his own head was free to wander. To stand back, like the observer he was physically. And how could he stay completely focused when he could hear Anne's voice giving quiet but clear instructions to her scrub nurse or registrar or asking for information on what the monitors were recording?

When he could see the shape of her body every time he looked up from the open square in the sterile, green drapes.

This was just so…wrong!

It had been *him* who'd wanted a family so much it had begun to poison what had been the love affair of his life.

Anne had been so adamant she couldn't give him what he wanted.

She'd been there and done that. Effectively been a mother from when she was still a child herself to her younger sister, Julia, when their mother had died shortly after Julia's birth.

They'd lived with a series of nannies in the household and she'd said she'd never wish that on a child of her own.

She'd fought hard to win the career of her dreams and no matter how much she loved David she couldn't give that up because she would be giving up too much of who she was.

But here she was. About to have a baby and, if she intended to keep her career, that child would be raised, to quite a large extent, by nannies. Or had she found a lover whose ambition was to be a house-husband?

Surely not. With a mind as sharp as Anne's, she needed someone she could talk to. Discuss her career with and medicine in general. The fascination she had with research and the ethical issues involved. The kind of animated, satisfying conversations she had always had with him.

When they hadn't been in each others arms, that was, indulging in a physical passion so powerful they had both known that being with anyone else could only be a compromise.

A compromise Anne had only too clearly been willing to make.

For someone else. Perhaps she'd planned it even before he'd made that final, excruciatingly painful decision to leave? Had the father of that baby already been waiting in the wings?

'Looking good,' he heard Anne say. 'I think we've done all we can. Let's start getting this lad off bypass.'

She sounded confident.She'd done all she could and, knowing Anne, it was probably enough.

David had done all he could as well, and not just for this little boy when he'd been under his care in the emergency department.

He'd done all he could to make their relationship work, hadn't he? And it hadn't been enough.

Suddenly sickened, David had to turn away. He didn't want to be here any longer. If he met Keiran's parents on the way out he would be able to tell them honestly that everything was going as well as they could hope for and that their son was in the best possible hands. He could go into Recovery in a little while and catch up with what was happening to this small patient.

And, in the meantime, he could spare himself the agony of seeing what had been going on in the life of the woman he loved since he'd removed himself from it. Spare himself the pain of hearing her voice.

Why on earth had he come back? Had he really thought that a three-month locum position here until he started a new posting overseas would be a good idea? It had seemed like a sensible punctuation mark in his life. He had loose ends to tie up that had been left. Just in case. Part of him hadn't been able to give up hoping that the separation might be all that had been needed to change Anne's mind.

If it hadn't, he'd be able to tick the box that said he'd done the right thing in leaving in the first place. That the misery of the last year had been worthwhile. He had achieved knowing he'd been right to leave in one fell swoop by simply catching sight of Anne. Killed that 'just in case' scenario stone dead. Now the problem was that he'd been through hell for no good reason whatsoever.

He'd given his heart to a woman who hadn't been honest with him. Hadn't actually been the woman he'd fallen in love with at all.

He could hate her for that. Hopefully.

'Sinus rhythm.' He could hear the triumph in Anne's voice behind him as she noted the normal activity in the small heart they'd just restarted.

He couldn't share the triumph. Utter defeat was dragging at his spirits. So much so that David left that operating theatre wishing fervently that he would never have to hear Anne Bennett's voice again.

CHAPTER TWO

'DON'T cry, Annie. Please don't cry. You *never* cry.'

'It's hormones.' Anne gave a huge, gulping sniff and pulled back from her sister's fierce hug. 'It was just…he looked like he *hated* me, Jules.'

'He doesn't hate you. He just doesn't understand what's going on.'

'I should have told him.'

A tiny silence. Long enough to let Anne know that Julia agreed. But how could she have told David? His emails had been infrequent and, oh, so polite. The 'I hope everything's going as well for you as it is for me' kind of communication. He had been getting settled into a new job and a new country. Getting over her. There just hadn't been a good moment to drop in the 'I decided to be a surrogate mother for my sister and I'm pregnant with twins' kind of message.

'Here, come inside.' Julia was tugging Anne into the little house she shared with Mac on a bush-covered hillside overlooking the harbour. Into the kitchen with its old wooden cupboards and enamel sink and a wide window with a view to die for with one of the larger harbour islands centre stage. 'Sit down. I'm going to make us a cup of tea. Unless you'd like something stronger?'

Anne shook her head, grabbing a handful of tissues as she passed the box on the end of the bench. She'd been alcohol free for nine months now. They all had, in a kind of supportive pact, and this was no reason to break that pact. No reason to feel like the world had ended.

This time Anne blew her nose far more effectively. She wiped her eyes with more tissues and took a deep, steadying breath. Then she sat down, buried her face in her hands and groaned.

'It couldn't have been worse, you know? There we were with a critically ill child between us and he was looking at my bump and then he looked up and... Oh, *God*...it was like I'd slapped his face in public or something.'

'You just need to talk to him. You can tell him it was at least partly *his* idea all along.'

'What?' Startled, Anne raised her head to watch Julia as she busied herself at the bench, making the tea.

'Remember back when we were first talking about this whole surrogacy thing?' Julia poured boiling water into the teapot and put the lid on it. 'When you were trying to persuade me and Mac to accept your incredible wedding gift?'

'Yeah...I guess. Seems a long time ago.'

Julia brought the teapot and mugs to the table. 'You said that Dave had told you over and over again that you could be missing the most amazing experience of your life by not wanting to be a mother. That you would regret it one day.'

Anne sighed as she nodded slowly. 'And I told you that part of all that angst had taken root and while it hadn't changed my mind about trying to juggle a career with being a parent, he could be right about the experience of being pregnant and giving birth.'

'So there you go.' Julia's smile was encouraging, albeit still worried. 'You said you'd found the perfect compromise. You get the whole experience and get to watch babies growing up but you can be an aunty and not a mum.' She bit her lip. 'Do you still feel like that?'

'Of course I do. Why wouldn't I?'

'Because you've seen David again and you're so upset. You still love him, don't you?'

'Of course I do,' Anne repeated, her tone hollow. 'I'll always love him but it would never have worked. He's desperate for a family and I can't give him that. We both knew it wouldn't be enough, not having one. He would have ended up resenting me.'

'I thought that about Mac and look what happened.'

'Mac adores you.'

'Maybe David feels the same way about you.'

'I don't think so.' Anne could feel her face settle into grim lines as she picked up the mug of tea Julia had poured. 'If he did, he wouldn't have agreed it was time to pull the plug. He wouldn't have gone off to start a new life on the other side of the globe. He wouldn't have sent horrible, polite emails that sounded like they were coming from a stranger. And he certainly wouldn't have been looking at me today as if I'd just stuck a knife in his heart.'

'Oh, Annie…'Julia leaned over the corner of the table to give her sister another hug and, as she did so, a door banged from outside the kitchen.

'Is that Annie's car out there?' The delight in the male voice changed to concern as Mac entered the kitchen. 'Oh, no…what's happened? Are you all right, Annie?'

'Yes, I'm fine,' Anne said, and burst into tears again.

Mac was by her side in an instant, his face stricken. She could feel his concern wrap around her like a blanket. It was partly the close bond they'd made in the last year but she could feel another part. Professional concern. As a paramedic, like Julia, he was assessing her physical condition. Looking for reasons for this highly unusual breakdown.

'It's hormones, that's all,' she sobbed. 'Take no notice of me.'

The box of tissues materialised beside her on the table and, as she reached for a fresh handful, Anne could see Mac looking at his wife with a question in his eyes.

'David turned up at the hospital today,' Julia told him. 'He saw Anne but she didn't get a chance to tell him why she's pregnant.'

'Ohhh…' Mac dragged out another chair and sat down right beside Anne. He squeezed her arm. 'And you think he thinks you've gone from breaking up with him to start a family with some other bloke.'

If Mac could see it so clearly it was a no-brainer, wasn't it? She *should* have told him. Why had she been so stupid? Because she'd been stamping so hard on any of those fantasies where he turned up in her life again and said he couldn't live without her? She had been trying to be realistic. Trying not to expect to ever see him again. Getting on with her life. Giving the only other people in the world she loved this much of a gift.

'Well, that's easily fixed.' Mac sounded satisfied. 'You just need to talk to him. And if that's too hard, I could talk to him. Bloke to bloke, you know.'

Anne shook her head. 'It won't help. He'll think if I could get pregnant for you guys I should have done it for him. That's why I never told him in the first place. He wasn't meant to know anything about this.'

A silence fell over the small group.

'You know…' Julia sounded tentative. 'There could be another way around this.' She had been staring into the depths of her mug but now she looked up at Anne. 'I could give you what you've given me and Mac. A…chance at a family.'

Both Mac and Anne were staring at her. Anne felt a fond smile tug at her lips. They were so different. She was tall and dark and Julia was like a little imp with spiky blonde hair. And thanks to the unusual circumstances of their childhoods, not to mention the trauma of going through the hysterectomy Julia had had to have when she had only been in her early twenties, they were far closer than most sisters ever got to be. She loved Julia with all her heart but that familiar, determined light glowing in her eyes right now would have to be dampened.

'I don't think so, hon,' she said gently.

'I'm going to be at home with the twins.' Julia was undeterred by the soft warning in Anne's tone. 'I'm happy to be giving up work to be a full-time mum. Couldn't be happier. I'll be at home for years and years and what could be better than having cousins around for our two?'

'A kind of blended family…' Mac was absorbing her idea. 'You know, it might work. Jules is an aunty so it wouldn't be like having nannies that didn't love your kids as much as you do. She's going to be the best mum in the world, I can guarantee that.'

Mac was smiling. Anne could see the way his gaze was drawn irresistibly to Julia's. The way it held.

She knew that look. That kind of bond you could only get with the love of your life.

The kind of bond she and David had had. Way back. Before there had been any question of just how disparate they saw their future paths in life.

She missed that bond.

Here she was, sitting with the people she loved most in the world. About to have an experience they'd all been dreaming about for so long, and she'd never felt so utterly miserable.

So lonely.

It was too much. Something deep inside her snapped.

She pushed her barely touched mug of tea away so sharply it slopped onto the table. Her voice came out high and tight.

'I don't *believe* this,' she said. 'You're both starting to sound exactly like David used to. Pressuring me into doing something I don't want to do by finding ways around it.'

She pushed herself to her feet, shaking her head with an angry gesture. 'This is it. A one-off! Why won't anyone understand that?'

'We do understand,' Julia said urgently. 'I'm sorry, Annie. It was just—'

Anne cut her off. The anger and misery were coalescing now. A volcano that had to erupt.

'You don't understand anything,' she said bitterly. 'How could you? You have *no* idea how hard it's been to do my job ever since I got pregnant. Feeling rotten with morning sickness…being tired all the time. Having backache that's been killing me every time I've been in Theatre for months and months.'

Julia's face had gone pale. Mac was standing up, looking unsure of whose side he should go to. His wife or the angry pregnant woman who was shouting at them both?

Anne spared him having to make the decision. 'I'm leaving,' she announced. 'And I don't want to talk to either of you right now so don't try and stop me.' She got to the door but had to turn back for a parting shot. 'You might be happy to give up your job to be a mother,' she told her sister. 'That's great. Absolutely peachy. But that's *you*, not me. I'm *not* happy to give up mine. I thought I'd manage a lot better than this but, if I'm being honest, it's been extremely hard and I'm not doing it again. For you *or* David.'

Julia's face had crumpled now, on the verge of tears. Could this day get any worse? Anne closed her eyes.

'Look…I'm sorry.' She opened her eyes again and took a deep breath. 'Blame it on the hormones. I chose to do this for you and I'm happy about it, honestly. Presenting David with a baby isn't going to fix what went wrong. It's…like you guys. A family has to be a bonus, not something to patch up a relationship that's come apart.'

Somehow they were all within hugging range again now. There were tears but the knowledge that they would all get through this and come out stronger on the other side.

It was Anne who pulled away. 'I really do need to go,' she told them. 'I've got a ton of stuff I have to get done. Nesting urge or something probably but I really do need to get to the supermarket and buy enough toilet paper to last the next six months.'

Shaky laughter was following her as she headed for the door.

'It's bad luck that David's happened to come back at this particular point,' she added by way of farewell, 'but I can deal with it.' She smiled to prove it. 'You're both right. I just need to talk to him.'

Weird that having an emergency department crowded with sick and injured people and a team of medical staff depending on his skills to make sure it was running smoothly enough that no one fell through any cracks had often seemed too stressful to be enjoyable.

But this was great! Perfect.

'Get Security to cubicle three,' he instructed the receptionist.

'Set up the trauma room for incoming patients from that MVA,' he told a hovering nurse. 'And Resus 1.

Page the team. We're expecting three status 1 and 2 patients.'

David took just a moment to survey the spaces on the whiteboard beside the main triage area. 'We need to juggle beds,' he said to the registrar by his side. 'I want Resus 2 clear if possible. Has Cardiology assessed that patient yet?'

'No.'

'Chase them up. What about Orthopaedics for that neck of femur?'

'She's gone to X-Ray.'

'Head injury in cubicle seven?'

'Gone for a scan.'

More staff were already streaming into the department in response to their pagers.

'Incoming trauma?' a young anaesthetist queried.

David gestured towards the doors where ambulances could be seen, red and blue lights still flashing, turning to back up to the loading bay. With a nod to another knot of ED staff, already gowned and gloved, he moved to help intercept the incoming stretchers.

For the next hour they were all too pushed to do any more than manage the most critical cases under their care. Troubleshooting bleeding that couldn't be controlled. Fluid resuscitation. Airway management. Chest drains and fracture management. A fragile cardiac case that came hot on the heels of the road-accident victims. A baby with febrile seizures and a hysterical young mother whose sobbing could be heard from the other side of the department.

Chaos. Controlled but exhausting.

Yes. This was great.

David was every bit as focused as Anne had been in Theatre yesterday. Totally committed to doing his job to the best of his ability. No worries about getting distracted, although somewhere in the back of his mind he knew an account was being registered and that there would be a price to pay for this escape.

Another virtually sleepless night, probably, with the kind of emotional turmoil that was just as draining as running a large emergency department at full tilt, but he was quite prepared to pay that price.

And, with a bit of luck, by the time this shift ended, he'd be too whacked to even care.

Making another visit to the paediatric intensive care unit when his working day *was* finally over was pushing things a bit too far, really, but David could already feel that odd kind of calm that came when all reserves of adrenaline were depleted.

The worst that could happen would be that he could find Anne in the unit, which would be unwelcome but quite manageable. Thanks to the windows in the doors and the fact that little Keiran's space was almost opposite those doors, he would be able to see her before she could see him. He could simply turn around in that case and come back another time. It would be slightly more awkward if she arrived while he was there but, hey, it was a crowded area. As long as he avoided any direct eye contact, he would be fine.

After all, what could she possibly do or say that would be any worse than yesterday?

'You've just missed Dr Bennett,' a nurse told him

helpfully as he neared the desk. 'She can't be far away and she'd be able to update you better than me. Would you like me to page her?'

'Good heavens, no.' David gave the pretty, young nurse his most charming smile. 'I'm sure she's even keener than I am to get home and put her feet up.'

'Mmm.' The nurse's cheeks had gone very pink. 'It must be hard being at work when you get to that stage of pregnancy.'

David's smile felt as though it had been flicked off with a switch. 'I'll read the notes, if that's okay. He's looking good from here.'

The nurse nodded. 'Dr Bennett seemed very happy and she spent a bit of time reassuring his mother. Poor woman… She's a single mother and he's her only child and I don't think she's even closed her eyes since Keiran arrived in here.'

David followed her line of vision to the woman who sat beside the small boy attached to the bank of monitoring equipment. Lines of anguish were ingrained on her face and her eyes were deeply shadowed. She looked up, as though sensing the attention she was under, and David smiled at her. A very different kind of smile this time. Sympathetic. Encouraging. One that put him in her corner.

'I'll have a chat to her when I've caught up on the notes,' he told the nurse.

'See if you can persuade her to go to the cafeteria or something and get a meal. She needs a break.'

David was happy to take on the mission. Having read all the documentation and reassured that Keiran was doing extremely well, he was able to add to his mother's reassurance.

'Looks like he might even come off the ventilator tomorrow and then they'll be able to lighten the sedation and let him wake up. He'll need you even more then, so it's important that you look after yourself. Rest. Eat.' David softened the commands with another smile. 'Doctor's orders.'

Keiran's mother nodded but she sounded vague. 'I'll go to the cafeteria,' she promised. 'I think I know where it is.'

'Why don't you come with me now? I'll be walking right past it to go home and if you go now you won't miss out on their macaroni cheese. It's legendary.'

'Is it?' For the first time, David saw a hint of a smile. 'That's our favourite, me and Kerry.'

'You'll be able to tell him how good it is, then. Something for him to look forward to once he's up on the ward. Come on.'

'He won't wake up, will he?' Her frown deepened as she reached out to touch her son. 'While I'm gone?'

'No chance. He's being kept asleep until he can breathe properly for himself. And he has his nurse right here. She'll be with him the whole time.'

'I will,' the nurse assured her. 'And I know where you'll be. I can send for you if anything changes.'

'Okay, then.' This time David received a real smile. One that said he was trusted. 'Let's go now, before I change my mind.'

The busy part of the day was well over now and the lighting in the corridors was dim. Visitors would start arriving for the evening hours soon but this was a hiatus where routine activity had ceased and, apart from emergencies, the hospital would rest until tomorrow. All was calm, including David. His critical patient from yesterday was doing well, he had avoided any unpleasant confrontation with the woman he didn't want to see and any moment now he would be leaving the hospital grounds and heading for the safety of his own home.

The turn-off to the cafeteria was not far from a back entrance to the emergency department, which suited David very well. He needed to collect his jacket and briefcase and indulge a long-ingrained habit of walking through the department after his shift finished to make sure that it was still running smoothly. That he hadn't left anything undone that could have repercussions later on.

The couple standing against the wall opposite the door that led through the orthopaedic department and into Emergency didn't notice David going past because they were too wrapped up in each other.

But David noticed them.

The man was tall, dark and good looking and he wore the overalls that advertised he was part of an elite helicopter rescue team. The kind of paramedic that David had enormous respect for as an emergency consultant. Taller than the woman beside him, he was looking down at her. Or maybe he was looking at his hand which was resting on the bulge of her pregnant stomach. His fingers were splayed and his expression suggested that he was very comfortable doing this. That he was experiencing the kind of delight and wonder at what he was feeling beneath his hand that…a father would experience connecting with his unborn child.

Anne was watching this stranger and she had a dreamy half-smile playing on her lips. They were both standing very still and all that mattered to either of them was the baby inside her.

He only saw the tableau for a heartbeat. Or maybe it was two before he could wrench his gaze away, but there was no way of erasing it from his brain as David shoved the fire stop doors open and walked towards his office as though the hounds of hell were nipping at his heels.

Jealousy gripped him, hot and bitter. They had looked so content. So *happy*.

So much for all those impassioned conversations with Anne where she'd pleaded the importance of her career. The importance of a mother being more than part time. The fact that she worked with children and gave so much of herself to her patients that she would not have enough left for any of her own.

Lies, all of it. But he'd believed her. *Trusted* her.

At least the way forward was crystal clear now.

He would put his house on the market. He had a couple of late shifts to get through but then he had the two days off and could start tidying up the property. Uninhabited for some time since his tenants had broken their lease and left, the garden was seriously overgrown and there were numerous maintenance jobs that needed doing urgently. He could organise a team of workmen and get everything sorted and then get it sold. He would give notice that he couldn't complete this locum for personal reasons. He'd tie up every damned loose end he could think of and then he'd be out of here.

And this time there would be no coming back.

Oh…Lord! Had that been *David*?

She only saw his back as the man pushed through the doors but, yes, Anne was sure it had been.

He'd seen her, standing here with Mac. A chance meeting after Mac had delivered a patient to Emergency and was heading for a vending machine for a snack and Anne had been coming back from delivering an urgent test to Pathology. The babies must have sensed it was time for her to be heading home because while they were normally quite quiet while she was busy working, they had chosen that moment to have a wrestling match or something in her womb.

Both Julia and Mac loved to feel their babies moving. It was a treat. A gift that Anne had been delighted to share. It was usually something kept very private but tonight the opportunity had presented itself like an apology for her outburst yesterday. Any resentment of the discomforts of this pregnancy had been transitory and Anne had been feeling terrible at leaving Mac and Julia worried.

And, yes, in the back of her mind had been the thought she might duck into the emergency department and try talking to David so the chance to stand here for a few minutes and gather courage had been welcome.

Maybe it wasn't too late.

'I need to go,' she told Mac. 'There's something I want to do before I head home.'

'Sure thing.' Mac took his hand off her stomach. 'Thanks for that. I'll be able to tell Jules we've got a couple of little rugby players in there. She'll be sorry she missed it.'

'I'll see her tomorrow. We're going shopping.' Anne threw a smile over her shoulder as she moved towards the doors. 'Have you any idea of how much your wife is spending at the baby shops?'

Mac grinned. 'Tell her to go for gold. Nothing but the best will do.'

Anne's smile vanished as the doors closed behind her. She went directly for the office area the consultants shared before she could lose the small amount of courage she had.

But David was nowhere to be seen.

She went into the department, trying to keep the urgency out of both the way she moved and spoke.

'Is Dr Earnshaw around, by any chance?' she asked the triage nurse.

'He just left. Did you need him for something in particular?'

'No… Um…' Anne tried to stop herself looking towards the exit in case she saw him. If she was honest with herself, there was an element of relief in finding she had missed him. It would have been bad enough anyway but in the wake of him seeing her in what could only have appeared a compromising position with Mac it would have been much worse. 'I was just going to update him on the little boy he treated yesterday. The one hit by the car.'

'Oh…Keiran. How's he doing?'

'Really well. Could you pass that on, maybe, when Dr Earnshaw's in tomorrow? Or…tell him to page me.'

The nurse was nodding but clearly hadn't noticed the way Anne clenched her fists at her final words and she couldn't know how her heart was hammering at the thought of hearing David's voice on the phone. She was distracted, in any case, by the arrival of a stretcher. Someone with a neck collar and padding in place that suggested a spinal injury.

Anne left the department. It should feel like a reprieve but, instead, she could feel a new tension in the wake of realising how fast David must have left the building.

Was he avoiding her?

Quite probably, she decided the next day when several pager messages went unanswered.

He was nowhere to be seen when she found an excuse to go into the emergency department on her way home the day after that either but Anne hesitated before making a query about when he was next rostered on.

If she started asking questions, where would she stop?

Would someone know why he was here at all? Or how long for? Where he was living?

He'd leased out his house long term when he'd left so he couldn't have gone back to the fabulous property he'd inherited from his mother. That huge old house in the exclusive, leafy suburb that Anne was as familiar with as she was with her own home.

How weird would that feel, to come back to the city you'd lived in virtually your whole life but not be able to go home?

It probably paled into insignificance compared to seeing the woman you'd loved, who'd sworn she never wanted children, looking ready to give birth at any moment.

She was getting used to the startled looks people gave her belly—as though it was a miracle she could still function with such a massive bump. Anne's smile was wry. Just as well they hadn't decided to implant all the embryos and she wasn't pregnant with triplets.

It was becoming seriously difficult to fit behind the steering-wheel of her car now. Maybe she shouldn't be driving any more? Imagine what could happen in even a minor collision? Fortunately it was only a short drive to her inner-city cottage and when she arrived safely she threw her car keys into a drawer and shut it firmly. From now on she was going to walk or take a taxi.

She'd cut her hours at the hospital for the next few days too and then she was going to turn into the world's biggest couch potato.

And maybe…hopefully…she would be able to get her head around David's reappearance in her life and decide what to do about it.

She was overdoing things. No wonder she felt too emotionally fragile to cope with talking to him.

And no wonder her back was aching so much.

Six hours later, just after midnight, her backache still hadn't eased and that was when Anne felt the first contraction.

She rang Julia and Mac immediately.

'I just had a contraction,' she said tersely. 'Damn it! It's way too early.'

'You're a little bit over thirty-six weeks,' Julia said, clearly struggling to sound calm. 'That's not early for twins. You'll be fine, Annie. Mac's on a night shift. I'll ring him and then I'm on my way. It'll take me a good thirty minutes to get into town, though, so if the contractions speed up, you should get yourself to hospital. Don't drive. Call a taxi.'

'Ah…' Anne could feel the grip of a new contraction starting already. She could also feel an ominous trickle of fluid down her legs.

'Annie?' Julia's voice lost any pretence of calm. 'Are you all right?'

'I think…my waters just broke.'

'Forget the taxi.' She could hear Julia's sharp intake of breath. Could almost hear her sister's mind click into professional mode, so she wasn't surprised at the authority in her voice when she spoke again. Crisply this time.

'I'm going to call an ambulance for you. Hang in there, Annie. Help's on its way.'

CHAPTER THREE

THIS was a first.

In all his years as an emergency physician, David had faced just about everything. He had dealt with terrible trauma and heart-breaking tragedy. He had seen mistakes happen or grappled with the futility of attempting the impossible. He had even managed violent situations when his own life might have been at stake.

But he couldn't face this!

This pregnant woman on the stretcher with the extra paramedic in the crew. One that was holding her hand to advertise their connection as she was wheeled through the doors of the emergency department. David bent his head over the notes he'd been reading, pretending to concentrate but aware of little more than the way his heart rate had accelerated.

'This is Anne Bennett,' he heard the crew leader tell the triage nurse. 'Thirty-six-year-old primigravida. She's thirty-six weeks pregnant with twins. Waters broke approximately fifteen minutes ago and contractions are now three to four minutes apart.'

Twins?

Good grief. An instant family. David couldn't help looking up. The head of the triage nurse was turning now. Looking for him. David found his own head turning. Looking for someone else. Anyone else would do.

Staff numbers were at a minimum, of course. After midnight on a weeknight, things didn't generally get that busy. Three consultants were more than enough, with their registrars and the nursing staff. But one team was on a meal break and the other consultant was in the trauma room, dealing with a lacerated artery on a young man who'd put his fist through a window.

Which left him. Or a registrar.

'Any problems with the pregnancy so far?' the nurse was asking.

'No.' It was the man who answered the question. 'Everything's been perfect.'

David almost snorted. Perfect? Was that what Anne had told him? Perfect relationship. Perfect pregnancy. About to produce a perfect little family.

Yes. A junior doctor could handle this. All that was needed was a quick check on the stage of labour, filling in all the admission paperwork and a transfer to the maternity department.

Where *was* his registrar?

'Dr Earnshaw?'

David turned back, still trying to think of some way to escape this situation. He had to. He was too involved. It would be unethical to examine this woman and…and he didn't want to. He didn't want to have to touch her. Or see parts of her body that had haunted his life for what seemed like for ever.

But he had to turn back. He had to look at Anne and then he had to take a step closer because he'd never seen her look quite like this.

Pale. Frightened.

She tried to smile at him in a show of bravado but her knuckles were white where she held her companion's hand and her eyes were huge. Fastened on his, and there was a plea there.

She needed help.

She was asking for *his* help.

'Resus 1,' he ordered, his voice firm enough to disguise an inward groan. 'And page Obstetrics. Get them to bring an incubator down here as well, just in case. Actually, make that two.'

Thirty-six weeks wasn't that much of a worry in terms of prematurity for a single baby but these were twins who were likely to have lower birth weights anyway. Plus, he knew nothing about this pregnancy. He hadn't even known it existed, dammit. Was it unreasonable to feel so hurt by that? He'd been starting over, for God's sake. Struggling to let go of the past and start a new life. Surely it would have been courteous at the very least to inform him of something that might have allowed him to move forward with a semblance of enthusiasm?

The flurry of activity that followed his instructions gave David a minute or two to collect himself. Anne was taken into the well-equipped resuscitation area and transferred onto the bed. Nurses helped peel off extra clothing and blankets. A blood-pressure cuff was wrapped around her arm. Someone was sent to find an Entonox cylinder.

David donned a gown and gloves. Professional accessories that somehow helped him switch off the personal issues he had with this case. He could do this. He had to, because no matter how hurt and angry he was at the way he'd been treated, he cared about Anne. He would never forgive himself if he didn't make sure she received the best assessment and treatment he was capable of providing. An IV line was a priority. So was some form of foetal monitoring. Checking the position of the babies and how far along her cervix was in dilatation.

'Ohhhh!' Anne's groan cut through the air, ripping into David and threatening to undermine his resolve. 'Oh, God…*Mac*…'

'It's okay, love.' The big man with the tousled dark hair had his arm around her shoulders as Anne leaned forward in her sitting position, drawing her legs up so that she could hang onto her knees. 'You're doing great.'

'Where's the Entonox?' David picked up the blue plastic kidney dish that contained everything he needed to start an IV line, doing his best to stamp on the flash of resentment he was feeling towards this Mac. The way he was holding Anne. The kind of anxiety on his face that every man would have if the woman he loved was in such pain.

'Here.' A nurse held the tubing attached to a large cylinder that had just been wheeled through the curtains. 'I was on the phone to Obstetrics. The registrar is tied up with a forceps delivery. They've paged a consultant but it'll be twenty minutes before they can get here.'

It was looking more and more likely that Anne was going to have her babies here. Especially given the way she kept shifting position, looking restless and irritable, which could well indicate an advance into the second stage of labour. She pushed away a hand that was offering her the mouthpiece to the inhaled pain relief.

'It's nitrous oxide,' David reminded her. 'A fifty-fifty mix of—'

'I know what Entonox is,' Anne snapped. She dragged in a breath as her contraction eased.

'I'm going to have a feel of your tummy while you're between contractions,' David warned her.

'Fine.' Anne closed her eyes.

The nurse pulled up the nightshirt Anne was wearing. An oversized T-shirt that he didn't recognise, but when had she ever worn clothing to bed when he'd been around?

The feel of her skin was all too familiar but at least her abdomen had never felt remotely like this. Hard and firm and stretched to what seemed like breaking point. Full of lumpy shapes. An elbow there. A foot here. David remembered seeing Mac with his hands exactly where his own were now. Entranced by feeling all those tiny limbs moving. He wasn't feeling any movement at the moment.

'Have we got a Doppler here?' he asked his registrar.

'I think so.'

'Maybe you could find it, then,' David heard himself snapping.

He looked up to catch the way his junior colleague's eyebrows rose. And no wonder. A flash of temper was disturbingly unlike the way he treated the people he worked with. David offered a quick smile. 'I'd like to check on the foetal heart rates after contractions.'

'Is something wrong?' Anne had picked up on the exchange.

'Not that I can pick up,' David reassured her. 'Have you had a scan recently?'

'I've been getting them weekly. To check on the growth rate. It's been within normal range and they're pretty even in size.'

'Do you know the presentation?'

'Cephalic-cephalic.'

'Good.' The babies were both presenting head first. 'As normal as it gets, then.'

Anne groaned again. 'Mac, where's Jules? She's supposed to *be* here.'

Yes. Definitely irritable. The sooner he could check on her dilatation the better. David moved towards the end of the bed.

'She's on her way,' Mac told Anne.

'Oh...*God*...' Anne flopped back onto her pillows. 'I don't believe this. I must have been mad to offer to have these babies for you. This *hurts*.'

David stiffened at her words. She had 'offered' to have babies for this man? She made it sound as if she hadn't actually wanted to. Ha! No surprises there.

'Try the Entonox.' His tone was cool. 'The pain relief can be very effective. I need to check your cervix, if that's all right.'

Anne gave an incredulous huff. She didn't want it to be him doing this any more than he did. 'Just get on with it, David. I'd rather get this over with as soon as possible. If that's *all right*.'

It was fine by him. Even making allowances for how women could lash out at people they cared most about during labour, her sarcasm had hit home. This was intolerable. And about to get worse. As David lifted the sheet, Anne muttered something that made him pause.

'Sorry?'

'I said, Jules was right. This is just as much your fault as Mac's.'

'Oh?' The distraction was all he needed to be able to continue this examination. His hands did what they needed to do while his brain focused on his patient's extraordinary statement.

'You said I'd be missing one of life's great experiences by never giving birth,' Anne said. 'So here I am. And…and right now I wish I wasn't.'

That made two of them. 'You're fully dilated,' he informed Anne. 'You can start pushing any time you feel the urge.'

David straightened to find he was being stared at by the man still holding Anne's hand.

'You're David?' He looked both startled and sympathetic. As though he knew a little too much about how Anne's ex might be feeling in this situation. What had Anne told him? That she'd had to end their relationship because she had no desire to have a family with him? But that she was prepared to go through it for *him*?

David glared at him. 'And you are?'

'Mac.' A fleeting grin. 'Annie's brother-in-law.'

David's jaw dropped. So did those of the nursing

staff. Before anyone could say anything, however, the curtains parted and a small figure dashed into the resus area.

'*Annie!*'

'Jules. About time, kid. You nearly missed the action. Ohhh…' Anne extended her hand. 'I'll try some of that Entonox now, thanks.'

Now Anne had a figure on both sides of her bed. Her sister and her brother-in-law. David was missing something here. Something big.

'I rang Emily,' Julia was telling Mac. 'She'll be here any minute.'

'Who the hell is Emily?' It was about to get absurdly crowded in here, given that a new arrival was pushing a large incubator into the space. David had the feeling he was losing his grip on reality. Assumptions were being splintered but he didn't know how to put the pieces into a picture that would be comprehensible.

'She's Annie's O and G consultant,' Julia told him. 'Assisted fertility specialist and a friend. She's been managing this pregnancy all along and she wants to be present for the birth. Oh, my God!' Anne's sister's eyes widened. 'David—it's *you*!'

'I want to push,' Anne announced. '*Ohhh!*'

However complicated this situation was, the birth itself was apparently going to be straightforward. Within minutes, David found himself controlling the descent of a tiny head covered with crinkly, dark hair, keeping it flexed until crowning to protect Anne from tearing.

Waiting for the next contraction, David was aware

of yet another arrival at this bedside. A female voice overrode the reassurance and encouragement Anne was receiving from both Mac and Julia.

'I'm Emily Scott,' the woman said. 'O and G. Need a hand?'

'We're good for now.' David could see the first shoulder appearing. This wasn't the moment to hand over management, even to a specialist already familiar with the patient.

'Fabulous.' The voice was being directed at someone behind him now. 'Can we get another bed in here, please? I'd like the mother to be able to get some skin contact with these infants.'

David's breath caught somewhere in his chest. His brain registered the odd statement from the most recent arrival but he couldn't process it because he was stunned by the fact he was now holding Anne's newborn baby.

'It's…' His voice sounded raw. He had to blink and then look up from the baby who was drawing its first breath to catch Anne's gaze. To make contact. 'It's a boy.'

He began to lift the baby to put it onto her chest but Anne was shaking her head. With tears streaming down her face, she still produced a wobbly smile.

'Give him to his mother,' she said.

Julia was crying as well. She held out her arms and a nurse draped a clean towel across them. David placed a wriggling and healthily pink baby carefully onto the towel and Julia gathered him into her arms, lifting him to nestle against the only available skin she had, where the top of her shirt was unbuttoned.

'We need another bed,' Emily ordered. 'Let's make some room, people. Any unnecessary staff can leave.' With gloves on, she was moving to check Anne's belly and she had a Doppler to assess the remaining baby's condition.

It was probably just as well she was taking over the management of this birth because David was staring at Julia, the pieces of this puzzle finally falling into place.

This was a surrogate pregnancy.

Anne hadn't replaced him with someone she wanted to have a family with. Fragments of distant conversations were appearing in his memory. Julia had been diagnosed with endometrial cancer in her early twenties. Early stage, thank goodness, but it had meant having a hysterectomy, and dealing with the certainty of never being able to have children had been difficult to work through. There had been a disastrous relationship as well, years ago, when he had first dated Anne and he'd been envious of the close bond between the sisters. And a little put out by having to wait his turn for her time and attention.

Anne was doing something for her sister she'd never wanted to do for herself. Extraordinary. Impressive even, but David wasn't going to try and analyse the turmoil of his own reaction right now. Not when the Doppler was relaying the rapid 'clop clop clop' of an unborn baby's heartbeat and advertising that there were far more important things he should be thinking about.

'Do you want an oxytocin infusion set up?' he asked the obstetrician.

'Set it up, but we won't use it immediately. Let's wait

and see if we get a spontaneous onset of some more contractions. Baby sounds like she's coping. How are you doing, Anne?'

'Um…I'm good…I think.' Anne was watching her sister holding the baby. Mac had moved to that side of the bed and he was holding Julia as she held the infant. Everybody seemed to be crying and David could feel an ominous prickle behind his own eyes. He cleared his throat and reached for some clamps.

'Would the father like to cut the cord?'

'Sure.' Mac was grinning. And sniffing. David caught his glance and read a trace of something that could have been embarrassment there. Because he was being so emotional in public or was it because he was the father here and not David? Whatever it was—joy or sympathy—he could feel a connection to this stranger who was realising his dream of having a family against what had probably seemed impossible odds. Besides, he was obviously a nice guy. Impossible not to like him instinctively.

'Scissors are on the trolley, mate. Cut here, just between these clamps.'

Somehow, another bed was being slotted into this small area. Julia climbed onto it and unselfconsciously bared her chest to hold her tiny son.

'Perfect Apgar,' Emily announced a minute later. She swivelled back to the other bed. 'Now, Anne. Let's have another look at you and see how things are shaping up for number two.'

He could have escaped before the arrival of the second baby. If a serious case had come into the department, he would certainly have made the effort to squeeze past the extra bed and all these people and leave them to it.

Part of him wished a nurse would put her head around the edge of the curtain and summon him to somewhere he was actually needed but he couldn't just leave. Not while Anne was still in labour and the potential for something to go wrong still existed.

He was also held here by the obscure notion that the emotional punishment this represented was deserved because he'd thought so badly of Anne. He'd thought she could have fallen into the arms of another man within weeks of his departure. Even—in the wakeful hours of a particularly dark night—that the whole disintegration of their relationship had been engineered as a way of escape because there had already been someone else in the wings.

He'd almost convinced himself that Anne had arranged to have all those dates or times together interrupted by urgent calls so that he'd never seemed to be a priority in her life. That she'd discovered what he wanted most in life—a future with her that included a family—and had simply taken half of that equation away from him.

No negotiation but compromise wasn't in Anne Bennett's vocabulary, was it? He stood there now, as Emily waited to catch the second twin, and saw the lines of effort and pain contort Anne's face as she pushed.

What an extraordinary thing to be doing for someone else. Months of discomfort and change. Physical risk. Pain.

It was typical of the woman he knew, though, wasn't it? She was such a black-and-white person. All or nothing. If she had decided to help her sister because she couldn't have her own baby, then she would have gone all the way.

Anne was gasping now, between contractions, clearly very tired. Mac had his hands on her shoulders, trying to encourage her to slow her breathing.

'In, one…two…three… Out, one…two…three…'

Julia was still holding the baby boy, now wrapped in a warm cover but her gaze was fixed on her sister.

'You're doing great, Annie. I love you…'

'Another push should do it,' Emily said. 'Wait for the next contraction and give it all you've got, Anne.'

David found himself holding his breath, as caught up in this as everybody present was. Along with some excited staff on the other side of the curtain, eager for news. Successful birth stories were actually quite unusual in an emergency department and this was no ordinary story. It had captured imaginations.

Anne would be considered a heroine doing this for her sister.

His thoughts circled back to what he knew of her personality. So black and white. She wanted her career and was, therefore, not going to have children of her own. She had wanted the experience of childbirth but not to be a parent.

Heroic? Or…selfish?

Lord, where had that come from? Some pocket of envy because Anne was prepared to do this for someone other than himself? He knew it was unfair. He knew that what he was seeing here was total commitment. The positive side of being black and white.

He'd experienced that commitment himself. Maybe that was why the thought of Anne being with anyone else had been such a shock. She didn't do half-measures. She did total commitment and he'd had it in their relationship. He'd known that every time he'd touched her. When she allowed herself to succumb to passion she had given everything she had to give.

Demanded all from him.

An explosive mix that had always left them completely satisfied. Drained so that the cares of the world trickled away. Content to the point of utter bliss.

Nobody else had ever given him that. Or demanded it from him. Not that he'd want to give that much of himself to anyone else. He couldn't. He'd already given it away.

To Anne.

The second baby was emerging now. A girl who looked to be pretty much the same size as her brother. Small but not enough to need special care. She was crying already, sounding healthy.

The beds were manoeuvred so that this baby could lie on Julia's stomach cradled by one of each of her parents' hands as they waited for the cord to stop pulsing before it was cut. For a minute, they were all joined. The babies, their biological parents and their birth mother.

An incredible family unit. No wonder there were smiles and tears amongst the soft words being spoken as the babies were introduced to each other and the world. Angus was going to be the boy's name. The girl was Amy.

* * *

When Mac cut the cord of the second baby, Anne could have sworn she felt it herself.

It had been weird lying here, still connected to the tiny girl who was lying on Julia's stomach. She could see the miracle of this gift in her sister's face. The wonder and the joy of it. And she could see—and feel—overwhelming love. Between Julia and Mac and between these new parents and their babies. A solid force that she was part of but separate from.

And then the cord was cut and she felt the separation increase.

Almost desperately, she scanned what she could see of the twins. Imprinting the memory of their bare skin and crinkled little faces. All those fingers and toes that Mac and Julia were touching in reverence. She wanted to touch them herself.

To count them, as all new parents did.

She wanted to hold them and have those serious dark eyes calmly watching *her* the way these babies, now quiet, were watching Julia. Imprinting their mother's face on their brains the way she was with them.

Her breasts ached. Anne was barely aware of what Emily was doing at the end of the bed. The calm voice telling her that the placentas seemed fine and that she hadn't torn at all and wasn't it great that she wouldn't need a single stitch? She was too distracted by pulling advice from her head. The words of the counsellor that had seemed so sensible to all involved at the time.

Don't breastfeed, even once, no matter how strong the urge might be. It's a mistake physically because it will stimulate milk supply and make the drying-up process a lot harder. It will also create an emotional connection that could have repercussions none of you will want.

They had all been so clear about what they wanted. Anne would love and cherish these babies, of course, but she wasn't their mother. Julia was. She'd been a human incubator but she was only their aunt. A very special aunt, certainly, but she had to be one step removed. She had to allow Julia and Mac to parent these children without interference or pressure of any kind. For the next few weeks, in fact, she was going to have nothing more than minimal contact while the new family bonded.

She needed time to recover from the ordeal her body had been through. So many changes with the grand finale of birth. The power of those changes had been a revelation to Anne and it was helpful to remember that. This desperate urge to hold the babies and feed them was probably nothing more than a fresh burst of hormonal activity.

Astonishingly powerful, these hormones. It was incredibly hard not to reach out her hand. Almost impossible to drag her gaze away from the infants. And when she did, she found David watching her with an oddly intense expression.

Or maybe it wasn't so odd. It hadn't been that long ago that they'd been deeply in love and so in tune with each other they could pick up on thoughts and emotions in a kind of telepathy. Was he picking up what she was thinking now? Would he interpret her desire to hold these babies as an admission that she'd been wrong all along? That she just hadn't known how much she did want children of her own?

She *didn't*. She hadn't been wrong. Oh, no. She had to escape David's gaze. It was making her feel confused. Maybe she *had* been wrong.

Anne closed her eyes, which made it much easier to think straight. No. It was still there. The conviction that she wasn't wrong. She'd given up too much of what she wanted in life already. Her childhood, to become a mother to the baby sister she'd adored. Her social life as a teenager and medical student. Sports and hobbies and anything else that took up too much time or money. Things had always been put on hold. She had always promised herself that she could have her life on her own terms once Julia didn't need her any more.

That time was now.

Julia had Mac. They had their babies. This moment was more than the birth of a family. It was the birth of her own future as well. Life without sacrifice for someone else. Was that selfish?

Maybe, but she deserved it, didn't she? After everything she'd given up? Everything she'd been through for the person she loved the most?

But she had loved David too. Still did, even though she didn't dare admit how much.

This was so hard. So confusing. Anne opened her eyes to find that David was now looking at the bed beside her. Somehow, Mac had made room to get onto the bed and cradle Julia in his arms and her arms were full of babies. Two dark little heads, one in the crook of each elbow. They seemed to be asleep now. Mac's head was tilted and Julia's forehead rested against his cheek. They were both looking down at the babies and someone, bless them, had produced a camera and was taking the first family photos.

David didn't seem to be as entranced by the photo shoot as everyone else. When her own gaze shifted she found him looking at her again. No worries about telepathy now. He looked distant. Cold, even.

As though it was sinking in that she'd given her sister something she was never willing to give him.

How could she be like this?

To give birth and not want to hold the babies? Fair enough that she didn't want to breastfeed but to not even touch them?

Cutting that second umbilical cord had seemed to sever Anne's involvement. Her sister and her brother-in-law and the babies were a unit. On a separate bed. Might as well have been on a separate planet.

How ironic that he should have been present to witness Anne deliver babies that she had no desire to parent in any way. Fate was handing him a graphic illustration of everything that had gone wrong with their relationship, really. There wasn't any point in him being in here any longer. Emily was in charge.

'We'll get you up to Maternity,' she was telling Julia. 'I think we'll keep you all in overnight. The babies are a reasonable weight but I want a full paediatric check on them both and we want to make sure they're feeding well.'

The consultant turned back to Anne then. Oddly, David got the impression that there was sympathy in her smile and gentle tone. 'I'd like to keep you in overnight, too, Anne. In another ward, maybe?'

David sucked in a breath. Had they already discussed these arrangements? Emily seemed aware that Anne wanted as little contact with the babies as possible. She was shaking her head.

'I don't want to stay.'

'Do you have anyone at home?'

'No.'

The thought of her going home alone after an experience like this was too sad for words but David strangled the desire to offer comfort or support. She'd chosen this path. She didn't have to be alone. She wanted to be.

'It was a normal delivery,' Anne said wearily. 'And I feel fine. What's the minimum time you keep women in these days?'

'We let mothers go home after six hours if they choose but…they're not usually by themselves.'

'I've got a phone. I'll call for help if I need it.'

'I could come home with you, Annie,' Mac offered.

David could feel a muscle in his jaw begin to ache from tension but again Anne shook her head.

'You stay with Jules. With your family. They need you.'

Julia was chewing her bottom lip. 'This is wrong,' she said with a wobble in her voice. 'We need *you*, too, Annie. We want to look after you.'

David could see the shine of tears in Anne's eyes. So she wasn't being as hard hearted as he thought. Again, he had to fight an urge to step closer.

'I know, hon,' she said to Julia. 'But I'll be fine, honestly. We made a plan, remember?'

Julia nodded, dislodging unshed tears. 'But…'

'I'll visit tomorrow.'

They were getting ready to start moving the bed. Mac climbed off. Julia turned her head so that she could still see Anne. 'Call me?'

'I will. First thing in the morning when I'm home.'

David found Emily by his side. 'Perhaps Anne could stay down here for observation?'

'Sure.' He would be going home soon enough. As Anne had said herself, the delivery had been uncomplicated. Any registrar could monitor her condition until she was discharged in a few hours. He didn't have to go anywhere near her.

Except he couldn't stay away.

An hour later her found Anne asleep in the side room but with a second check in another hour or so, he found her awake.

'How are you feeling?'

'Kind of like I've been run over by a bus.'

'I'm not surprised.' David stood at the end of her bed. The silence grew and became awkward. There was so much he could have said. Wanted to say. Impossible to know how to start. He needed to apologise but there was a barrier there created by hurt. He wanted to ask why but was so sure he wouldn't like the answer that even that tiny word stuck in his throat.

Finally, he picked up the observation chart. 'Your blood pressure's fine,' he told her. 'Everything's looking good.'

'I could go home then.' Her voice was flat.

'Soon. I…guess you'll be taking some time off?'

Anne gave a small huff of sound. 'Three months. I was due a sabbatical but the first few weeks were supposed to be resting in late pregnancy.'

'You'll still need to rest and recuperate.'

'That was the plan for the second month. Then I'm negotiating to spend a month in an overseas unit that specialises in paediatric chest trauma.'

'Oh…' David had a three-month locum. By the time Anne returned for work, he'd be gone.

It should be a relief.

'Maybe I can bring it forward,' Anne said.

Which would take her out of the country. He wouldn't see her again. Possibly ever.

'Maybe we could…meet up before you go,' he heard himself saying aloud. 'We haven't had much of a chance to…talk or anything.'

'No.' Another tiny huff at the understatement. Anne closed her eyes again but not before he'd seen a flash of agreement. Even…what, *hope*?

'I'm really tired right now,' she said.

'I'll leave you to rest, then.' He couldn't push her, however much he'd like to find out what she'd been thinking before she'd closed her eyes. She had to be totally exhausted, both physically and emotionally. He understood that. He knew this wasn't the time to talk but David still hesitated. Opened his mouth to say something else.

As though sensing his intention, Anne turned her head to face away from him. There was nothing for it but to respect the dismissal and leave.

* * *

Anne kept her eyes tightly closed.

She wanted to talk to David. Of course she did. He deserved an explanation. An apology even, but she couldn't find the words right now. Not while she was feeling like this. As though she had lost something infinitely precious.

Something she would never be able to find again.

It didn't seem to matter how tightly she kept her eyes squeezed shut.

Her tears still managed to escape.

CHAPTER FOUR

SHE couldn't stop thinking about him.

The way he'd looked, standing at the end of her bed the other night. The light may have been subdued but there had been no mistaking the look of pain on his features.

She'd seen that look before. More than once in those difficult, final weeks of their relationship, when the distance between them had become an unbridgeable gulf. The unspoken messages were so eloquent.

I don't want this.

It's unbearable.

Why has it come to this?

How did it all go so terribly wrong?

Can we fix it?

No...

The lines etched on David's face may have been personal but his body language and actions had been nothing but professional. The way he'd stood with the length of the bed between them. The way he'd reached to pick up her chart instead of touching *her*.

'Everything's looking good,' he'd said.

Couldn't he see that she was desperately unhappy? That it was beginning to seem like a huge mistake, being a human incubator for someone else? It had become such a huge part of her life, being so intimately connected to the two tiny beings growing inside her.

She would never forget feeling those first movements. So subtle they had felt like nothing more than a stream of tiny bubbles. Being so aware of the strength increasing as the weeks went on. Strong movements then, that had often startled her. An uncomfortable prod from an elbow or a kick that could make the skin on her stomach bulge and make her laugh in a mixture of amazement and amusement.

And the hiccups that had felt like a clock ticking inside her. The soft flutters that could only be felt from deep within and she would imagine her babies sleeping. A leg brushing against another limb perhaps or a reach to hold hands as she'd seen ultrasound pictures of twins doing in the womb.

Whoa! *Her* babies?

Anne sighed deeply and dragged herself up from the armchair she'd been sitting in for hours now. A still unopened medical journal slid from her lap to the floor.

That was the problem in a nutshell, wasn't it? They had never been *her* babies. Julia's eggs. Mac's sperm. Yes, she'd had custody of the precious little lives for eight months but they'd never been *hers*. She'd known that all along. She'd thought she was more than prepared for how it would feel to hand them over. She'd never for a moment expected it to feel as though something was being ripped away from her soul.

For it to have been *so* hard.

Tears were slipping down her face and she scrubbed at them angrily. What had Jules said that day? That she never cried. Well, she'd made up for it in the last few days, that's for sure, and today was the worst yet. She was like a tap in dire need of a plumber's attention today.

So many sad thoughts that she couldn't shake off. Of babies she ached to hold. Of David's face as he'd stood there at the end of her bed. Of how much she'd missed him over the last year and of how unbridgeable that gap between them was. Especially now.

How ironic that he should have been there when the babies were born.

How unfair!

Intending to go into the kitchen to make a cup of tea, Anne had to pause before she got more than a step or two. She had to reach out and grasp the back of the armchair as a wave of dizziness threatened to make her knees buckle.

Oh…*God!*

Blindly, thanks to a fresh spurt of tears, she felt her way back to a sitting position and then buried her face in her hands with a groan of despair.

What was wrong with her? She was a doctor, for heaven's sake. She should be able to figure out what was happening here and then do something about it.

What was the main problem?

Her breasts hurt. They were as hard as rocks and

aching so much she couldn't bear to wear a bra despite knowing that the support might help. She had taken some anti-inflammatories and had tried an ice-pack earlier today but neither remedy had helped much. Maybe she should try that old wives' treatment of cabbage leaves or something. Another dose of drugs, anyway.

What else? She felt hot, which could be because her armchair was in front of a window in direct sunlight she hadn't been aware of. She also felt faintly nauseated but when had she last had something to eat? It was probably lunchtime by now. A glance at her watch startled her. It was well into the afternoon. Where had all those hours gone? Hard to feel hungry when her belly hurt as though she was in the middle of a particularly heavy period. This amount of discomfort had also been unexpected but her postnatal bleeding hadn't been heavy enough to be a concern.

The main problem was something that was simply making everything else seem worse. The fact that she was alone. That it was day three after giving birth and, while she might have been prepared for the so called 'baby blues', she hadn't realised how hard it would be to deal with them alone.

She could ring Julia but she'd probably burst into tears on the phone and that would worry her sister. What if she heard the babies crying in the background and was unable to get any words out at all? Julia would dispatch Mac to find out what was wrong and he would probably insist on staying or taking her home with him so that she could have company and be looked after.

And that wasn't part of the plan they had stuck to so well so far.

She had gone to visit after her discharge from the emergency department. She had been able to admire the sleeping infants and be as delighted as Julia and Mac that the feeding was going well and they would all be able to go home later that day. She hadn't touched the babies because she needed to create some distance. Not for ever. Just for as long as it took for her hormones to settle down a bit.

And that was all this was all about. Baby blues. Hormones. It was a form of depression and the best treatment was distraction. Physical exercise.

Pleased with her clinical assessment, Anne tried to stand up again. This time her head felt fine. She'd just been sitting still for too long. She hadn't been eating enough. What she needed to do was get a grip and ride this out and in a day or two she would be feeling much better. What on earth had she been thinking, letting herself just sit around latching onto sad things to dwell on?

She had so much to look forward to, didn't she? Being an aunt to the two most beautiful babies in the universe. Time away from work to do something that she would love—like spending time in a clinical facility that was achieving results she admired tremendously. And right now she could go out and enjoy this gorgeous day. It wasn't too late to feel the warmth of sun on her skin. To get a bit of fresh air and escape four walls that were closing both her body and mind into an unfamiliar, and very unwelcome, prison.

Good call, she congratulated herself a short time later. She felt better already, even if the bright light was hurting eyes that had been bathed in far too much salty fluid today.

Planning a route for this gentle walk was too hard. Her brain was crying out for a rest. An escape from sad thoughts and decision-making. With a sigh of relief, Anne surrendered to just following her feet, content to enjoy the warmth and the colours in the pockets of the inner-city gardens she passed. For the first time in her life, she actually had the chance to stop and smell the roses.

That had to be another good thing, surely?

He couldn't stop thinking about her.

The way she'd been lying, alone on that hospital bed, radiating unhappiness.

He'd been contributing to that misery, hadn't he? The feeling of distance between them was all too familiar. He'd pushed and pushed to try and get what he'd wanted in the past and all he'd achieved had been to push her so far away he'd lost her.

With an outward breath verging on a sigh, David tapped a finger on the X-ray image on the screen.

'Right there, see? Probably a stress fracture. Not major but it'll be causing the pain. She needs to go to the bone shop and get a cast on.'

'She won't be happy. She's training for a triathalon.'

David grimaced, unconsciously rolling his head to try and ease the ache between his shoulder blades. 'Try telling her that exercise is overrated.'

His junior colleague grinned. 'You still suffering, then?'

'I think it's getting worse. I'm seizing up.'

'Keep moving, then,' the registrar advised cheekily, trying to stifle his amusement. 'It's the best cure for soft-tissue injuries.'

'No. The best cure is prevention.' David straightened his back with a groan. 'Which is why I'm going to find a landscaping firm to come and tame that jungle that used to be my garden. Know anyone with a bulldozer?'

'Talk to Di on the front desk. I think her son is some kind of gardener.'

'I'll do that. Thanks. Was there anything else you needed to talk to me about?'

'No. Sorry to hold you up. It's past home time for you, isn't it?'

'Sure is.' David took a final glance around the department. He eyed a telephone on the triage desk and once again the thought of Anne crossed his mind.

It wouldn't hurt to call, would it? Just to see how she was doing?

No. He turned towards the reception area instead, intent on tracking down the woman who might have an expert gardener for a son. Anne wouldn't want to talk to him. Not yet, anyway. In a week or two, maybe, when she had recovered a bit more from the birth.

The desire to talk to her was getting stronger every day, along with a faint hope that they could possibly salvage some kind of friendship from the ruins of the relationship they'd had. One that would give him a new base from which to move forward. One that wasn't built on anger and hurt and loss.

He could afford to wait. His two days off had made him realise what an enormous job it was going to be trying to get his property in shape to do well on the market. The garden was impenetrable in places and while he'd actually enjoyed wielding a pickaxe and clippers, despite the after-effects on his body, he hadn't made much progress.

And the garden was only part of what needed to be done. Trying to distract himself from thinking about Anne when he wasn't sweating outside had led him to wandering around the big house, cataloging tasks that needed attention inside. Plumbing needed work. There was dry rot in some of the windowsills. The paint and wallpaper were tired to the point of being shabby but if they were improved the carpets and curtains would look infinitely worse. He needed a team of interior decorators as well as some landscaping experts.

Maybe Di would have some more useful contacts.

Twenty minutes later, David emerged into the late afternoon sunshine, armed with a host of suggestions and phone numbers gleaned from the *Yellow Pages* and Di's advice. Feeling far more positive, he decided to leave his car in the parking building and walk home. That registrar was quite right. Keeping his sore muscles moving was the best thing he could do for them.

It was a pleasant walk. The small river that wound through the central city had wide grassed banks and huge, ancient chestnut trees dotted at regular intervals. Park benches had been sited beneath many of the trees and there were a lot of people out enjoying the late afternoon warmth. A man reading a newspaper. A couple with young children who were feeding stale crusts to an expanding group of enthusiastic ducks. A woman, sitting alone with her head drooping, as though she was being lulled to sleep by the peaceful surroundings.

Something made David take another look at the lone woman as he came closer. And his heart missed a beat.

'*Anne.*'

She looked dreadful. As white as a sheet, and she seemed to be shivering despite the warmth of the day. She also seemed to be having trouble focusing on his face. Or maybe she didn't want to look at him. She was looking down again now, her eyes drifting shut. He couldn't walk away, however. No way.

'What are you doing here?'

'I…I came out for a walk.' Good grief, were her words a little slurred? 'Such a nice day…'

'But you're a long way from home. You're almost at the hospital.'

'Am I?' She looked up and blinked in bewilderment. 'I hadn't noticed.'

'Anne…' David crouched in front of her and touched her knee. 'Are you all right?'

She was looking at him now, her eyes wide. Startled, almost.

'No,' she whispered. 'I don't think I am.'

David swallowed. Hard. 'What's happening?'

Anne drew in a long, shaky breath. 'Things hurt,' she admitted.

'What things?'

'Um…my tummy.' The huff of laughter was pure embarrassment. 'My…ah…boobs.'

David couldn't help the quirk of his lips but it was a poignant twist. If he'd needed any indication that Anne was not herself right now, this total lack of medical terminology did the trick.

'Anything else?'

Anne nodded but said nothing. David waited, holding the eye contact. Encouraging her to tell him what was going on. She didn't look away. She was hanging onto his gaze as though it was a lifeline, in fact.

'What else, Annie?' he prompted gently.

'I…I've *missed* you,' Anne said. And burst into tears.

Oh…Lord! What could he do but ease himself onto the bench beside her and take her into his arms? Hold her until the sobs—that were as uncharacteristic as her layman's anatomy—finally dwindled into a kind of ripple he could feel but no longer hear. And he had to try very hard not to put any undue significance on the words she had just uttered. She had *missed* him? As much as he'd missed her? Enough to make compromise an acceptable alternative?

'Sorry,' Anne muttered. 'Oh, I'm sorry, David.'

'It's okay. It's fine.' He didn't want her to be sorry because it might mean she wanted to take back what she'd said.

'No. No, it's not. I'm…' Anne was pushing at him. He had to fight the urge to tighten his hold. He had to let her go.

'I'm *so* sorry.' She was scrubbing at her face. 'I don't know what's wrong with me.'

'You've got a lot going on. Mentally and physically.'

She wasn't herself. He had to remember that. She'd said she'd missed him like she'd meant it but she wasn't herself so it didn't mean anything. 'You're not…well.'

'I'm not sick.' Anne gave her head a shake. 'Child-birth is a natural process, not some kind of disease.' She gave her face a final wipe, pushing her hair back and then holding it in a ponytail with one hand behind her neck. It made her look much more in control.

'I'm fine, really,' she said as she stood up.

David watched her. He could almost see the way the strength it had taken to stand up ebbed from her body. The way her eyes, made so much darker by her pale face, seemed to glaze over. He was on his feet by the time she began to sway. He had scooped her into his arms by the time she lost consciousness.

Ignoring the horrified stares of people on the river-bank, he strode back towards the emergency depart-ment of the hospital. He was barely aware of the weight in his arms and it certainly didn't slow his pace.

She was waking up from the deepest sleep.

Or maybe she was still dreaming. She could feel the strength of a man's arms around her and feel the warmth of his skin close to her face. Anne's eyes flick-ered open. It was his neck. Her head was cradled on his shoulder and he had one arm around her back and the other under her knees.

Her bones had melted away. She had never been this relaxed. So secure she didn't want to move in case she broke the spell. The ground was moving fast beneath them and it made her feel sick so she closed her eyes again, rolling her head a little so that her mouth and nose were even closer to that skin.

She could even imagine she recognised the smell of this man. That the arms around her were David's. That he was carrying her somewhere safe where nothing could hurt any more and she would never feel lonely ever again.

The rocking continued. Even more comforting was the murmur of his voice, telling her she was going to be fine. That she would be looked after. That *he* would look after her because he cared. He'd missed her *so* much. The words weren't all that clear, maybe, but she could understand them perfectly.

But the movement changed and became jerky. The words became clearer.

'Complained of abdominal pain...'

'Gave birth three days ago. Twins.'

A new voice then. 'She's lost a fair amount of blood.'

The security of those arms was loosening. Anne felt herself being tipped. Put down on something firm and cool. Felt the softness of a pillow next to her face. The loss of those arms was enough to make her groan in distress.

'You're all right, Anne. You're in the emergency department now.'

'W-what?' She forced her eyes open and blinked, trying to focus on the face close to hers. 'What happened?'

'You've had a bit of a postnatal bleed. You fainted, down by the river. You don't remember?'

'I...' How much had been reality and how much a dream? Had David really been telling her how much he'd missed her? How much he still cared? It would be safer to assume that those impressions had been the workings of an unconscious mind. 'No,' she said softly. 'I don't remember much of anything.'

Surely that wasn't disappointment she could see in his eyes? She tried to hang onto the contact so she could interpret the fleeting expression properly but David was standing up now. And the sharp pain in her arm was distracting.

'Ouch!'

'Try and keep still.' David had a hand on her arm. 'We're just getting IV access. Your blood pressure's well down and you need some fluids. Possibly a transfusion.'

She heard orders being given. For blood tests that needed to be done. For an urgent call for an ultrasound technician. The blood-pressure cuff she hadn't been aware of tightened on her other arm. Someone was hanging a bag of saline overhead. An oxygen mask was being slipped onto her face and someone was peeling away her clothing.

Anne shut her eyes. This no longer bore any resemblance to a dream. It was far more like a nightmare.

Except that David was still here. Looking after her. He didn't have to be because Anne had heard someone sounding very surprised that he was here at all because his shift had finished ages ago.

'I'm staying,' he told whoever it was. 'Anne and I go back a long way. We're…friends.'

Friends?

Were they?

It didn't feel true but it would be nice if it was. Friends

cared about each other and made life less lonely. Anne didn't have many close friends. She had her work and colleagues and she had her family and…not much else.

Fighting a strong need to sleep, Anne pushed her eyelids open, hoping to find David amongst the people crowding around her bed. A technician was squeezing gel onto her stomach.

'Sorry, this is a bit cold.'

Anne ignored the apology, looking from one person to the next. If David was there, she could smile at him, maybe, to let him know that she liked what he'd said. That she wanted the statement about being friends to be the truth.

But she couldn't see him anywhere.

He could have been home again by now.

Why on earth had he said he'd stay? That he and Anne were friends. An unfortunate distortion of the truth…or wishful thinking?

David was pacing back and forth in his office. He'd said he would stay but that didn't mean he had to be in the room with her the whole time, did it? She was safe. The doctors on duty were taking good care of her and treatment was under way. He could go and check up on how she was doing and then go home.

He wanted to leave.

He wanted to stay.

No. What he really wanted was to be in that room with Anne. Beside the bed. Holding her hand.

How stupid would it be to get sucked even further into what was going on in her life?

It wasn't going to happen.

So what if the attraction was still there? That it had hit him like a brick that moment he'd first seen her again, looking so rounded and luscious and glowing with her pregnancy. There had been nothing sexual about the way he'd held her as she'd cried today but it had revealed something a lot deeper. That he still cared. A lot. Too much. Carrying her towards medical help like that, not knowing what was wrong or how serious it might be, had smashed through more than one of those defensive barriers he'd carefully constructed. Or maybe that first wall had fallen when she'd said she had missed him.

With a sound rather like a growl of frustration, David circled his office again, ramming his fingers through his hair as he tried to think through the turbulent mix of emotions tearing him apart.

There was absolutely no point in this agonising and he'd done far too much of it already. He knew the way forward, he just had to pull himself together. He could deal with this. The whole purpose of coming back here had been to tie up loose ends. The end of his relationship might have seemed like a tight knot but it had completely unravelled in the last week. There were loose ends all over the place, snapping at him like tiny emotional whips.

David left the office only a minute or so later. Much calmer.

In control.

He would check up on Anne's condition—as any friend would. He would offer support if she needed it because there was very little danger of her accepting, and then he could escape. Never mind that daylight was fading fast. He would go home, ignore his aching muscles, and find something that needed doing with a pickaxe in his garden.

The feeling of safety that being carried here in David's arms had engendered was long gone.

Anne was in a side room now, with the kind of privacy a consultant automatically received if it was available. A privileged space that should have been a peaceful refuge from the bustle of the emergency department.

But there were two tiny babies cocooned in their car seats on the floor beside Anne's bed and they were both whimpering. Their mother wasn't any happier.

'I still can't believe you didn't call when you were feeling so lousy. My God, Annie…'

'Don't fuss, Jules. I'm all right.'

'You might not have been. We should never have let you go home by yourself. The plan was stupid.'

'No.' Anne shook her head wearily. The whimpering of the babies was increasing in strength and the sound felt like a chainsaw inside her head. 'I was doing fine.'

'Are you kidding? Mac's at your house right now, collecting the stuff you'll need. You left the stove on, Annie. *And* the tap.'

Anne winced. Again. 'I know. I'd been planning to make some lunch before I went for a walk. I…must have got distracted, that's all, and forgot I'd turned anything on.'

'You're lucky the house just flooded and didn't burn

to the ground with you lying unconscious on the floor.'
Julia was shaking her head in consternation but then her
chin jerked up. 'David!'

'Is that true?' came the familiar voice from the
doorway. 'Anne flooded her house?'

'Tried to burn it down as well. It's my fault. I should
never have agreed to let her go home by herself.'

David was staring down at the babies. 'Are they
hungry?'

'I'll feed them in a minute. I had to come and see
Anne first. We just threw everything and everyone in
the car when they rang to say Anne was in here.
Someone found her down by the river, would you
believe? Carried her here, unconscious.'

'Mmm.' David's glance towards Anne held a
sparkle of amusement. 'I would believe it. It was me
that carried her.'

'Oh...' Julia's jaw dropped and she dragged her gaze
from David back to Anne. 'You didn't tell me that.'

'You haven't given me a chance to say much at all.'

Julia ignored the implied reprimand. 'Mac's gone to
collect Annie's stuff,' she informed David. 'We'll be
taking her home with us.'

'No.' Anne managed to find the strength to sound
decisive. 'I'm not going home with you, Jules.'

'But you *have* to.'

'No, I don't.' The babies were howling now. Anne
closed her eyes in a desperate attempt to shut out her
surroundings, but not before she caught sight of a nurse
entering the room, closely followed by Mac who was
carrying a suitcase.

'Dr Bennett really needs some peace and quiet to rest,' the nurse told Julia.

Mac looked at David and then at Anne. He put the suitcase down and picked up a handle of a car seat in each hand. 'Come on,' he ordered his wife. 'Let's go and deal with these two. We can come back when they're quiet enough not to be upsetting anybody.'

The nurse nodded her approval. 'I'll take you to the relatives' room.' She closed the door behind the noisy procession.

Anne cautiously opened her eyes. David was still here.

'How are you doing?' he asked.

She gave a tiny huff of sound. 'Better now, thanks.'

David glanced at the door as though still seeing the babies being taken away. His face was expressionless as he turned back.

'I hear the final verdict was a patch of retained placenta.'

Anne nodded. 'Probably a succinturiate lobe that didn't get missed at the time, being an extra bit. Hardly surprising when they had two to check in somewhat unusual circumstances.'

David ignored the reference to her surrogacy. 'But you're not up for a D&C?'

'No.' Anne's sigh of relief was heartfelt. 'Not that they'd do one immediately anyway, with the uterus being so friable, but Emily thinks that bleed I had when I fainted must have cleared the last of it. Going by the ultrasound, it's all good.'

'Infection? You looked a bit feverish.'

'Yeah, I've been cooking a few bugs. Nothing that the antibiotics I'm on now won't fix.'

'And your haemoglobin?'

'Down a bit but not enough to warrant a transfusion, thank heavens. I'll be a bit wobbly for a day or two, that's all.'

'So you'll go and stay with your sister?'

Anne shook her head slowly. 'I'd prefer not to.'

'Why?' The word was crisp. Cool, even. 'Because you'd rather not see the babies?'

Anne bit her lip to stop the prickle of tears. She couldn't expect him to understand, so why did it hurt so much? She might have won the battle with the tears but she couldn't help the tremor in her voice.

'It's more that I want to see them *too* much.'

David's face went very still. It was impossible not to let her gaze rest on him. Tracing lines she knew so well while she tried to gauge whether he was prepared to try and understand. Those tiny crinkles at the corners of his eyes. The deep furrows that joined his nose to the corners of his mouth that would deepen when he smiled. Not that he was smiling right now. He seemed to be returning her gaze with equal intensity.

'They're not my babies,' she explained softly. 'Not even part of them. Jules had her eggs collected and Mac's sperm fertilised them. I had the embryos implanted. My head knows perfectly well that they're not *my* babies but…but my body's not quite singing from the same hymn book yet.' Her smile was even more precarious than her voice. 'I'm a bit of a mess emotionally, to tell you the truth.'

An eyebrow quirked on David's forehead. 'Really? Can't say I noticed.'

His smile was as gentle as his humour. It was the kind of smile that Anne hadn't seen since way back… way before things had begun to fall apart. It touched something deep inside her. Something that brought tears to her eyes that were even harder to control this time.

She blinked. Hard. 'I'll be fine,' she said with a good attempt at bravado. 'In fact, I think the worst is over now. I probably didn't realise how much it was all due to this complication. Being sick on top of everything else. I'll bounce back in no time now.'

'But you can't go home by yourself.'

'No. She can't.' Mac, with a sleeping infant in his arms, had come quietly into the room.

David saw something like fear flare in Anne's eyes. Did she think that Mac might have overheard what she'd been saying? It was obvious she didn't want her sister or Mac to know how difficult she was finding this situation. She was still protecting her baby sister, wasn't she? Prepared to go through hell herself. By herself.

He almost groaned aloud as he felt himself getting entangled a little further in that complicated web of emotion, past and present. There was respect. And caring. And…a moral duty, perhaps.

'I could stay here overnight, I suppose,' Anne said. 'If things don't get too busy. I'll have to go home in the morning anyway and sort out what needs to be done to sort out the mess.'

'I'll take care of that,' Mac said. 'I'll get hold of your insurance company. They can send their assessors and they'll know what needs to be done to dry things out and what will have to be replaced.'

Anne looked like she was trying hard not to cry. Seeing the damage to her home and belongings was the last thing she needed when she was, by her own admission, an emotional basket case.

Julia had come into the room again now and she was holding a baby in her arms that was as quiet as the one Mac was holding. She stood beside her husband. Had the babies been fed and changed already or had they only needed a cuddle from their parents to settle? Not that it mattered. They were content and their parents stood close enough for their bodies to touch. They were the picture of the perfect family and suddenly David could see that picture through Anne's eyes. Could see the babies she had given birth to but had to distance herself from.

How much harder would it be to have to stay in the same house?

'I have an idea,' he heard himself saying aloud. His words held the confidence of a brainwave and it was no surprise to find three sets of adult eyes focusing on him. He couldn't not say it now.

'Anne could come home with me.'

CHAPTER FIVE

GOOD grief!

Had David really said that?

Anne stared at him, her lips parted but there were no words available to emerge. Her brain felt fuzzy. Short-circuited in some way by that simple statement.

Come home with me

Could it be that simple? Did he want her back? Enough to compromise the dreams he'd had for the future? How good would that be, to have David in her life again? And her career uninterrupted. And a little nephew and niece to include in their world. It was going to be enough for her to have that extended family. Maybe it could be enough for David, too?

No. Of course it couldn't. The stupid, romantic fantasy was just an indication of what a basket case she was at the moment.

'No,' she said aloud into the stunned silence.

Julia was biting her lip. She looked up at Mac.

'It's a big house,' David added. 'And I'm working pretty long hours. I'd be around but she probably wouldn't even see that much of me.'

'She' ? They were talking about her as if she wasn't there. Mac was actually nodding at what David had said. 'Be more peaceful than our place,' he said. 'And it *would* only be for a few days.'

Anne tried very hard to keep any tremor out of her voice. 'So I'd be by myself in a big house. And that would be better for me how? I could go to a hotel. I'd have plenty of peace and quiet that way. Room service as well.'

'You wouldn't be alone at my place,' David said.

He said it so calmly. As though she shouldn't be surprised. But she was. More than surprised. She was shocked. David was sharing his house with someone. Another woman? Entirely plausible. It had been more than a year after all. How many men went that long without finding a companion? Especially when they were pushing forty and they'd made no secret about their need to find a life partner that shared their dreams.

David was still talking. With an effort, Anne tuned back in.

'…coming and going all day. The guest suite is private enough but there would certainly be company, or assistance, if it was required.'

Anne tried to fish missing clues from her head. Words that had floated past without being listened to while she dealt with that shock. He'd mentioned builders. Decorators. Gardeners perhaps?

Yes. He was talking about a restoration job on his property. Contractors. Julia didn't seem to be listening any more than Anne had been. She was looking at her sister and as Anne met her gaze, she was drawn into the close connection they had always had. The ability to communicate without words so easily. And this was such a familiar pattern of reassurance. Julia was worried. More than that. In that glance, Anne realised she hadn't been hiding her confusion about the babies as well as she'd thought. There was an awful lot riding on how she handled this.

I understand, she signalled silently with a tiny smile. *But everything's going to work out just fine, you'll see.*

'What do you think, Annie?' Mac was looking just as anxious as Julia.

'No,' she said again. The word lacked the conviction of her earlier refusal, however. She was trying to think of an alternative.

David was looking uncomfortable. Maybe he was regretting his offer? 'Do you have any other friends you could land on at short notice?' he asked.

'No.' A quiet word this time. Was David implying that he could be a friend? A *friend*? How could it sound like such a small, insignificant thing when only an hour or two ago she'd been trying to catch his gaze? To smile at him and let him know that she approved of him describing her as nothing more than that.

This was really rock bottom, wasn't it? Here she was, virtually incapacitated and faced with two choices that were equally undesirable for very different reasons. Both of them were emotional minefields.

Another glance at Julia finally made the decision simple. Neither choice would be great for herself but one would definitely be much better for her baby sister. She couldn't stay here using up a bed in a busy emergency department when she didn't need to. Nobody in this room was going to allow her an independent choice like a hotel and she was too tired to fight. It would only be for a day or two after all. A mere blink in a lifetime.

'David's house is a lot closer to mine,' she said. 'It would certainly make it easier to supervise getting my place sorted.'

'And you'd be doing me a favour,' David nodded. 'For the same reason. I've only got a limited time frame to get the work done on my house. Having someone they think might be looking over their shoulders occasionally would keep the workmen on track.'

There. It was settled. Anne managed to smile. Now that the decision was made she had a goal. All she had to do was focus and get her home and then her life back in order. Knowledge was power. Strength. She could do this.

'I'd like a quick cuddle with those babies, please,' she said calmly. 'And then you'd better get them home.'

'Before they start howling again, you mean?' Mac's tone was gentle as he stepped forward to place one of the neatly wrapped bundles in Anne's arms.

'Exactly. One of the many benefits in being an aunty.'

The guest suite was next to the garage complex but the bedroom had a pretty bay window that would have a lovely outlook into the garden in the daylight. It also had a small sitting room with a desk and couch and, thankfully, it had its own bathroom. No need to risk running into David elsewhere in the house.

'No shower, sorry, but you're welcome to go upstairs and use the main bathroom when you feel up to it.'

'This is fine,' she assured him. 'What a fabulous old bath.'

'The feet look a bit rusty.' David poked one of the cast iron claws with his foot, sending flakes of rust onto cracked linoleum. He turned a big, brass tap on and a stream of rusty water came out. Something clanged ominously within the walls.

'Maybe this isn't such a good idea,' he muttered.

'No…' The prospect of David changing his mind was disturbing. Now that Anne had made the difficult decision she wanted to be here. Kind of. 'Look…the water's coming clear now. It just hasn't been used for a while.'

'There's a plumber due tomorrow to have a look at things. There's someone coming from an electrical firm as well. I used the time you were in ED to make a few calls and found a representative from an interior design company who's keen to come and do a quote. She says they've won all sorts of awards for their restoration work. They all know I've left a key for them outside but I hope they won't disturb you too much.'

'No problem.' Anne moved back to her bedroom. The suitcase David had carried in was on the floor beside the old brass bed. 'Do I need some linen?'

'I'll take care of that.'

The thought of David tucking in sheets and putting fresh cases on the pillows for her was embarrassing. Too personal. The tension in the room suddenly escalated.

'You need to rest,' he reminded her. 'Hauling things around or lifting heavy stuff is not on the agenda.'

Anne couldn't help smiling.

'Hey! I'm not joking here.'

'I know. Thank you for your concern.'

His eyes were still narrowed suspiciously. 'So why were you smiling?'

'You sounded as stern as Mac and Julia did back when I first got pregnant. It always amused me because I felt like I'd spent my whole life worrying about Jules. It was a bit of a U-turn to have her fussing over me.'

Special, though, to have someone so concerned about her physical well-being. To feel so cared for.

'I'm not fussing,' David assured her. 'Just being sensible. I don't want to be scooping you up and carting you back to the emergency department again.'

'Perish the thought.' One that was even more embarrassing than having household chores like changing bed linen being done on her behalf.

Was David also embarrassed by the reminder of being forced to hold her in his arms for so long? The silence certainly felt horribly awkward.

'I haven't even thanked you for rescuing me.'

David shrugged. 'Just in the right place at the right time, I guess. Now, why don't you find the kitchen and make sure you'll be able to find everything you need in the morning? It'll only take me a minute to sort this lot out.'

Obediently, Anne made a slow circuit of the ground floor. Things were just as she remembered them in the big, farmhouse-style kitchen. A glance into the refrigerator was a surprise. So was the pantry.

'You look like you've prepared for a siege,' she said when she returned to her room to find David stuffing the last pillow into a fresh white case. 'So much food!'

'Mmm.' David put the pillow down and gave it a prod. 'I've discovered the convenience of online shopping. Guess I went a bit overboard.'

No surprises there for a man who loved to plan things in meticulous detail. He was like that in his work, too. Nothing got missed. He'd wanted to plan his future like that, too, hadn't he? To make sure he didn't miss out on anything. Like a family.

Again, the silence was awkward. So full of shards of the past that had to be avoided to risk injury.

David cleared his throat. 'It's getting late. I'll leave you to settle in. I put towels in the bathroom.'

'Thanks.' Exhaustion was setting in. The aftermath of the physical and mental roller-coaster she'd been on for days now. Anne eyed the high bed and soft looking pillows. 'Sleep is looking like a very good idea.'

David turned back again as he was going through the doorway. He wasn't smiling but there was a softening to his face that deepened the lines around his eyes and made his lips look fuller. Softer. A kind of precursor to a smile. Or a kiss...

'I'm only upstairs,' he said. 'If you need any help in the night.'

Anne opened her eyes to bright sunlight coming in through windows she had neglected to pull curtains on. The moment of wondering where the hell she was turned into astonishment that she must have fallen into a deep and dreamless sleep the instant her head had touched those wonderful feather pillows.

She felt rested. So much better, in fact, it was a shock

to find her head reeling when she tried to stand up. It took a good minute for the dizziness to recede but making it to the bathroom and finding that her bleeding had virtually ceased made up for feeling as weak as a kitten. The pain had gone from her belly as well. Even her breasts felt much less tender.

Not that she had time for more than a quick physical self-assessment. A glance at her watch made her jaw drop. She had slept for nearly twelve hours and it was 9:30 a.m. She would be lucky to have time to make herself look respectable and find time for a coffee before the first of the contractors arrived.

There was an eerie silence to the house when she made her way to the kitchen. David would be long gone. Had he felt her presence in the house this morning, the way she was aware of his absence?

Maybe. There was a note held onto the fridge door with a smiley magnet button.

Checked on you before I left, it said. *Didn't want to wake you. Be home around 7 p.m. Call or text if you need to.*

He'd checked on her? Been in her bedroom and watched her sleeping? For how long? The thought of him standing in the same room while she had been in bed created a warmth that moved from her belly right up into her cheeks. It wasn't embarrassment this time. It was…

Not something she was going to analyse. She read the note again instead. It finished with his mobile phone number but she had no intention of interrupting his working day if she could help it.

She almost changed her mind less than an hour later.

'What sort of fittings are going in?' The plumber had come looking for her.

'What do you mean?'

'Well, you can go reproduction. Some of it's lovely stuff, like copper cisterns and slippers baths and the like. But if you're looking to modernise, it will affect the pipes. You can conceal cisterns in the wall, for instance. And have a hanging loo that leaves a gap underneath. Easier for cleaning around, you know? Any idea which way you might be heading?'

Anne had to shake her head. 'Sorry but it's not up to me. I can make a note and get the owner to call you.'

'Oh…' the plumber looked disconcerted. 'I thought you were the missus.'

Whatever could have given him that idea?

Had it been because she'd complied with his request on arrival to show him where the main bathroom was? Had something shown in her body language? It had been impossible not to have those flashbacks to the first time David had ever led her up that magnificent sweep of ornate wooden staircase. Holding her hand. Stopping, too many times to count, to kiss her senseless on their way to his bedroom.

'No,' she told him. 'I'm just a friend.'

It was surprisingly easy to say. After a good night's sleep, the implications of that word had changed again. Become something if not desirable then acceptable.

Better than nothing, anyway.

Anne found a pad of paper and a pen and noted all the plumber's immediate queries. He went off to measure the pipes and a couple from an interior design firm

arrived. They sailed around the house, becoming pro-
gressively more enthusiastic and bouncing ideas off
each other after the initial, somewhat awed inspection.

They ended up in the main living room. A wonderful, warm room with a fireplace big enough to roast the
proverbial ox, ancient but supremely comfortable
leather couches and armchairs and French doors that
opened to a terrace and the garden beyond.

It was a room Anne had always loved so it was too
hard not to stop and eavesdrop as she went past on her
way back to her room.

'It's divine,' the slightly effeminate voice of the male
decreed. 'The feature ceiling. That fireplace!'

'The stained glass is fabulous,' the woman added.
'But it's all so dark. Positively medieval.'

'It's the wood. And those dark drapes. Ugh!'

'We could paint the window frames. And the fireplace. Cover the floor.'

'Get rid of all this antique furniture. It's so mascu-
line it's virtually *phallic*.'

'White on white,' the woman said dreamily.

'Oh….oh, yes, darling. I'm loving it.'

'The fireplace would be the feature.'

'Yes. *Yes*. I'm seeing it full of… Ooh, silver spheres.'

Anne had to walk away. She definitely needed to lie
down for a while. What on earth was David thinking?

Part of that first afternoon was taken up talking to the
insurance assessor. The carpets in her cottage would be
lifted tomorrow but he couldn't be sure what was happening underneath. Some of the boards felt suspi-

ciously spongy. Tiles in the kitchen were lifting as well. They would have to be taken up.

'It might take a few days to get things dry enough to do anything,' he warned.

The prognosis sounded bleak enough to make being able to escape into the glorious tangle of David's garden, and not think about any of it for a while, a blessing. There was almost an acre of lawns and trees that had one of the city's small rivers as a boundary. Paths through herbaceous borders led to secret corners and there were any number of lovely nooks to sit in. Or there had been. Some of them were so overgrown only a patch of a stone or wooden bench or a sliver of a pathway flagstone could be seen.

Meeting the landscape architect David had employed negated the pleasure the lengthy ramble had provided. The young man was busy sketching on a large sheet of paper and Anne smiled at his enthusiasm.

'Gorgeous spot, isn't it? This should be an exciting challenge for you.'

'You bet it is. I've never had the chance to work with a house that's crying out for the kind of dramatic foil this one could have.'

'Oh?' All it really needed was to have its original bones uncovered, surely?

'A sweep of lawn, I think, all the way down to the river. Buxus hedging and some gorgeous standards. Bay trees, maybe.'

'Spheres?' Anne suggested drily.

'Exactly. And a water feature. Piped music. Dramatic lighting when we've cleared enough of that jungle from under the trees. That gazebo will have to go, of course. Or get moved. It's completely obstructing the vista from the main entertainment area.'

'The main entertainment area? What's that?'

'I presume he meant the big living room and the terrace.'

'And the vista?' David was popping the tab on a can of chilled lager, having found Anne at the kitchen table with a cup of tea and a notepad full of scribbles.

Her tea was cold now because she'd been sitting in here for an hour, trying not to think about how things might be when David got home. What on earth they could find to talk about that would be safe? The kind of thing that friends might talk about.

She needn't have worried. Reporting back on the visitors to the property was quite enough of a topic.

'The straight line from the terrace to the river,' she explained to David. 'At least, it'll be a straight line once the gazebo gets shifted. Or bulldozed along with the outdated herbaceous borders.'

David put his can down on the old kauri table. He loosened his tie and undid the top button of his shirt. Anne averted her gaze hurriedly but couldn't help the way it was drawn back. Just in time to see him pushing his fingers through his hair. She recognised both the action and the gesture. David was feeling trapped. Unsure. It reminded her of a lion pacing a cage but how much of that tension was to do with what she was telling him? Maybe it was due to her presence. The fact that they were together in a confined space.

'My parents must be rolling over in their graves. The years my mother spent on making that into a prize-winning garden.' He sat down and sighed. 'What did the decorators have to say?'

Anne didn't need to consult her notes. What she'd overheard had been echoing in her head all afternoon. By the time she finished telling David, he was staring at her in utter bemusement.

'Balls?' he finally muttered. 'They want to fill the fireplace with silver *balls*?'

'Spheres,' Anne corrected. A corner of her mouth twitched.

David held her gaze. 'Balls,' he said again.

Anne couldn't help her unladylike snort of mirth. David held out for a moment longer but then tipped his head back and laughed.

A sound Anne hadn't heard in *so* long.

It opened doors she had avoided, assuming they were locked. Avenues to happy times together. The kind of silliness that could only be engaged in when you were so closely connected to another person that it didn't matter. When you loved them so much that trust was a given.

And then David's head straightened and his gaze brushed hers and then held it. Just for an instant. Long enough to know that he felt that old connection as well. For a heartbeat, they stared at each other. And then they both looked away.

'I'm not having any balls,' David said. 'Inside or out. I'll be telling these people exactly what they can do with their quotes.'

'The plumber wasn't so bad. At least he suggested fittings that would fit the era of the house and restore a bit of its former glory.'

David was silent while he took a long mouthful of his drink.

'That's what I had in mind, I guess. I know this place looks tired and the garden's a mess but I don't want to *change* it. I certainly don't want it to end up looking like some professional template of what's trendy in landscaping or interior design.' His tone softened and became almost wistful. 'I wanted it to look like a home again. Like someone loves it.'

Anne's heart skipped a beat. This mattered. But why? Was David thinking of living here again? And why should that cause a frisson of excitement? She kept her nod neutral, hoping it was one of sympathy. An encouragement to keep talking, perhaps, but David wasn't looking at her. He was staring at his can of beer and shaking his head.

'There's no point going any further if it's going to be like this. I might as well just put the place on the market as is and let someone else do the restoration.'

'You're *selling*?' The word was a gasp. 'But…you love this place. It's—' She had been going to say 'it's your home' but the words had caught. It wasn't any more, was it?

David still wasn't looking at her. 'You can't always keep the things you love, Annie.' The edges of his words were rough enough to negate the fact that he'd softened her name. They grated, like the way David's chair did as he pushed it roughly back to stand up.

'Sometimes you have to let them go in order to move on. That's life.'

He walked to the fridge and opened the door. Anne found herself staring at his back.

Fighting tears. He hadn't been talking about the house, had he? But it hadn't been an angry statement. Sadness was swirling in her head like a mist his words had created.

And the subject was apparently closed. 'You hungry?'

The query was polite. Friendly, even. 'Not very.'

David looked over his shoulder. 'You need to eat. So do I. How 'bout a steak? And…um…' he peered back into the fridge '…eggs.'

'You don't need to cook for me.'

'I'm cooking for myself. Makes no difference to cook a bit more.'

'Maybe I could help, then. Make a salad or something.'

'Sure. But only if you feel up to it.'

If David was making a deliberate attempt to keep the conversation impersonal while they prepared a meal together, Anne had no objection. It was safe territory and as enjoyable as selecting some of the array of fresh vegetables in the crisper bins to slice up for a salad.

'History suggested a straightforward grand mal seizure,' he related during the second case he was telling her about. 'But there was no history of epilepsy and no apparent triggers.'

'On medication?'

'Only some herbal supplements.'

'No recent head injury?'

'Not even an old one. So I'm thinking, poor woman, this could be the first presentation of some nasty brain lesion and I send her off for a CT and request a neurology consult but they're both clear. We're thinking of discharging her but I'm not happy and then she gets up to go to the loo and guess what?'

'Another seizure?'

'Worse.'

Anne forgot about the red onion she'd been slicing finely. Her jaw dropped. 'She arrested?'

'Yep.'

'What happened?'

'We started resus. About to shock her out of her VT when she reverted herself and woke up.' She could hear the smile in David's voice as he slid the steaks into a hot pan.

'And?' Anne raised her voice above the sizzle.

'And we got a cardiology consult. Looks like she had a small MI. Enough to put her electrical circuits inter-mittently out of whack. Could be a congenital conduc-tion abnormality as well. She's been admitted for monitoring and further investigation.'

'So the initial seizure was hypoxic? She'd been non-breathing for long enough?'

'Probably. Maybe the activity of the seizure had been enough to convert the rhythm. Or maybe it was going to happen anyway. She was lucky. Gave my junior staff a good lesson in not taking things entirely at face value, as well. Right. These steaks are done. If you still like yours medium rare, that is?'

Anne nodded. 'They smell fantastic. I think I am hungry after all.'

'Good. Let's eat.'

Conversation ceased after they sat down at the table but it wasn't such an uncomfortable silence this time. Talking about the house and then work had tapped into the kind of communication that had been habitual. A comfort zone. Having a meal together was in that same zone.

Anne was too tired to be really hungry and she'd had enough after only a few mouthfuls. She toyed with her food, thinking about what a different quality her weariness today had compared to last night.

It was only then that it struck her how much her mind had been occupied by things other than her present worries like her body and the babies or even past ones such as David represented. Had she been so appalled at what could be allowed to happen on a remake of this wonderful old house and garden that it had been enough to distract her this much or had her subconscious latched onto it as a means of escape? A chance to rest and heal.

Not that it mattered. The net effect had been a very welcome reprieve. What would happen in a day or two when she returned to her own home? It would be a mess but not one that required imagination to fix. Her brain might be too hormone addled to focus on something academic right now but it needed more activity than simply choosing new carpet or watching tiles being relaid.

And that was when the idea occurred to her.

'I've got a guy who's done a lot of work on my cottage,' she told David. 'Jim. Semi-retired, master builder but he can turn his hand to anything. He'd be perfect for the kind of repairs you need done here, like the windowsills and sticky doors. He could do a bathroom makeover or something, too.'

David was still eating heartily but he paused and swallowed his mouthful. 'Not much point starting if I'm not going to go the whole way.'

'Jim has mates. There's an army of these semi-retired tradesmen out there and I reckon they all drink at the same pub or something. If I give Jim something he can't handle, he can always find someone who can. And they're always good. I had Pete in to do painting and wallpapering a while back and I had no complaints.'

'But I'd still have to make choices about something I'm totally ignorant about. I couldn't pick a colour or a wallpaper pattern to save myself.'

'But I could.'

David's new forkful of food hovered in mid-air. 'Why would you want to?'

'Distraction. My mind is mush. I'd enjoy a project that would keep me busy until I'm well enough to go back to work.'

He was frowning now.

'I'm not suggesting I stay here for weeks, don't worry. I can spend the next day or two thinking and planning and maybe getting fabric and paper samples delivered. It's not that far to my place. I could come over while you're at work and supervise what was being done.'

David was listening now. 'What about the garden?'

'One of my neighbour's sons comes in to do any

heavy stuff I need. He's a student and will be on summer break by now. If he hasn't got a job, I'm sure he'd jump at the opportunity.'

'I wouldn't know where to start in telling him what to do.' David was staring at Anne now. 'Would you?'

'Maybe. I'd like to give it a go.'

'But…why?' There was something dark in his gaze now. Wariness, if not mistrust.

Anne took a deep breath. She needed to choose her words carefully and she wasn't entirely sure what it was she wanted to say exactly. It had something to do with the analogy that she'd picked up on when he'd said he was planning to sell the house. That you had to let things go to move on.

'You want someone to love this house, don't you? To make it a real home again.'

His nod was terse.

'Right now it's not at its best. You might get someone who can't see what it has to offer. Can't see past the…damage, I guess. If you could fix it up and maybe make it even better than it ever was before, you'll find someone who will love it for what it *is*, not what it could be.'

She held her breath. There was no need to hammer the analogy. If there was anything left of that old connection, David would know exactly what she was talking about. What she was offering. A chance at friendship. To repair the damage their relationship might have left them with. Closure perhaps.

Peace.

'Damage does haunt, doesn't it?' he said at last. She

could see the movement in his neck as he swallowed. 'We could give it a try, I guess. See how it goes.'

Anne could only nod. She didn't trust herself to speak for a moment. Even if David was prepared to try repairing something more than what their conversation had ostensibly been about, she couldn't afford that tiny spark of hope reigniting. The one that had flared when he'd said *come home with me*.

'I'll call in the troops,' was all she said finally. 'First thing tomorrow.'

CHAPTER SIX

LEARNING that the removal of damaged floorboards from her cottage had revealed piles in dire need of replacement should have been a cause for dismay.

'I can't move home yet,' she told David. 'Half my floor's been ripped up.'

'Are you in a hurry to get home?'

No. Not if he wanted her to stay...

'Not really. But I didn't intend imposing on you for so long. I could move to a motel or something.'

'You're hardly imposing.' But David shoved his fingers through his hair, unconsciously revealing that the idea of her staying longer might be disturbing. Then he gave her a searching look. Anne said nothing, allowing him time to see whatever it was he was looking for. It only took an instant.

'Seems to me like you've become a project manager in the last few days,' he said. 'For a job I couldn't have tackled to save myself. I should be paying you a lot more than room and board.'

'Don't be daft. I'm having fun.'

Smiling, she waved a hand at the chaos in front of her. The big mahogany table in the dining room was covered with plans for things like an en suite going into the master bedroom and a makeover for the other bathrooms. Sketches of ideas for the garden and paint colour cards were scattered amongst pictures cut from house and garden type magazines. Fabric samples draped the back of chairs and rolls of wallpaper were open and anchored with books on the floor.

This project had become more than fun. At some stage in the last few days Anne had become hooked. She'd never attempted renovation on anything like this scale but then she'd never had the time or the need for distraction. Or an apparently unlimited budget.

Her enthusiasm seemed to be contagious. David returned her smile. 'And I'm enjoying having some company and something happening in the house,' he said. 'It felt like a mausoleum when I first came back. Now it's…'

'A mess?'

'Alive.'

Nothing more had been said about her moving out since then. Day after day went by with the momentum of the renovation project increasing at a pace that mirrored Anne's returning physical well being. She was regaining her emotional strength as well. So much so, that when the prospect of spending a whole day with David when he had his first day off in more than a week was disturbing, Anne decided it was time to stretch her wings.

'I'm going to go and visit Jules and Mac and the babies today,' she informed David when he appeared in the dining room to get an update on progress, a mug of coffee in his hand. 'Daily phone calls don't seem to be enough any more. I'd like to see them all.'

'They live over the back of Governer's Bay, don't they?'

'Yes. Up on the hill with a fabulous view of the harbour.'

'That's quite a drive. You sure you're up to it?'

Anne's nod was confident. 'My car needs a run. The battery's probably getting flat by now.'

'I could drive you over.' Something in his gaze suggested that he hadn't been considering the condition of her vehicle.

'No need,' Anne said hurriedly. Even if he wasn't showing a disconcerting comprehension of how difficult it might be for her to see the babies again, being in car with David would be very different to being in his house like this. Here, there were constant reminders that they weren't alone.

Right now, hammering sounds came from upstairs where Jim and his team were working in the main bathroom. A conversation between a couple of electricians was taking place in the hallway outside what had become Anne's office and through the latticed windows Nick, the university student, gave a wave as he walked past, carrying a serious looking hedge clipper under one arm.

Anne waved back and nodded her approval. The banging overhead got louder.

'It would be a nice drive,' David added. 'I could go for a walk while you were visiting.' He looked up at the ceiling. 'Don't think I'll get much done around here today.'

Anne paused in the sorting of the quotes she'd been reviewing. David might be enjoying how lively the house had become but it had to be unsettling when you couldn't be sure if the water was running or whether a stranger might be in the bathroom you were hoping to use. And maybe it was more to do with him enjoying having company.

Was David lonely?

Like she was a lot of the time when she wasn't at work?

She was going to see her family today. David didn't have any family and he'd always been a bit like her in that his devotion to his career hadn't allowed for the nurturing of close friendships.

When they'd had each other, it hadn't mattered.

'Maybe I'll go and see if I can give that young lad in the garden a hand with something.' David turned to leave and Anne felt the distance stretching between them.

'You're welcome to come with me if you'd like to,' she found herself saying. 'I won't be staying long and I...wouldn't mind a walk somewhere myself.' She rolled her gaze upwards as a particularly loud cracking noise came from directly overhead. 'It is a bit hard to think in here today.'

If Julia and Mac were surprised to see Anne's companion, they hid it well.

'Gidday, mate.' The colloquialism delivered with a strong Scottish accent made them all smile and broke any possibility of ice. 'Come on in.'

Sunshine streamed into the little house on the hill. The living area was taken over by baby gear. Prams and change tables and nappies. A clothes horse was draped with tiny articles drying in the sunshine. The kitchen bench was cluttered with bottles and measuring spoons and tins of formula.

'Good grief!' Anne exclaimed. 'I'd forgotten how completely babies take over your life.'

'We're living and breathing babies,' Julia said happily. 'It's heaven.'

They were so obviously rapt. Anne had given them this gift and she'd never felt so welcome. She hadn't expected that being bathed in this environment would be so over-whelming, however. The whole house actually *smelled* of baby. Of formula and nappies and damp clothes. It took her back. Way, way back to when the centre of her own life had been her small and helpless baby sister. To when there'd been no time for anything for herself but it hadn't occurred to her to feel put upon in any way because that tiny being had been so important. So precious.

She completely understood the intensity of this time in Julia and Mac's life. She didn't expect the conversa-tion to include anything other than the twins and it didn't. They talked of feeding patterns and details of mixing formula and sterilising bottles. Of sleeping— or lack of it on the part of the parents—and of how bathtime got organised each evening. Anne was also quite prepared to admire the infants with the kind of reverence their parents demonstrated.

What was even more unexpected, given the over-whelming environment, was the way she was able to take a step back. The way her body and mind were accepting—possibly with a tinge of relief—that these weren't *her* babies. Her heart was squeezed by the force of love she could feel but her breasts gave no more than a tingle of protest that was easily dismissed, and that heaviness in her belly was gone. So different from how she'd felt in the first days after the birth. That counsellor had been right. It had been hard but it had been the right thing to do to create that initial distance.

The bonding of this new family was so powerful. She wasn't excluded by any means but neither was she in that inner, almost obsessed, circle. She could feel David watching her as she held wee Angus but her smile was genuine.

'He's gorgeous,' she pronounced, handing him back to his dad as he began to grizzle loudly. 'He looks just like you, Mac.'

'He does, doesn't he?' Mac was bursting with pride. 'Chip off the old block.'

'And don't you think Amy looks a bit like me?' Julia asked hopefully. She rocked the baby she was holding as Amy joined her brother in a hungry wail.

'Absolutely.' Anne was still smiling as she noted a hint of a puzzled frown on David's face. He was shifting his gaze from each baby to its parent, clearly making an attempt to find the likeness. Her smile faded as the babies increased the intensity of their demanding cries. She could feel the sound closing in around her. She needed to *do* something. Now.

'There, there, darling,' Julia soothed. 'Lunch is on its way. Mac?'

'Onto it. Come on soldier.' He shifted Angus so that the baby was upright on his shoulder. 'Let's mix that formula.'

'Do…you need a hand?'

'No. We've got this down to a fine art. Unless you want to hang around and help feed them?'

Something like panic edged into the tension. Anne opened her mouth to speak but David answered first.

'I promised Anne lunch somewhere nice. And a walk. If we don't go now we might miss the best of the day weather-wise.'

Julia nodded but her eyes held a question.

Anne hugged her gently, enclosing the baby in the space between them. 'Next time,' she whispered.

'You okay?' The words were almost inaudible.

'I'm good.' Anne tightened the hug a fraction. 'But baby steps, yes?'

She turned to let David know she was ready to leave but he was already heading for the door. Implementing her rescue. Had he been aware that she was reaching her emotional limits? Did he understand, even a little? It was a powerful notion. One that was giving her an ally. A friend. It felt like another bit of tarnish was being polished off the connection between them, making it shine like gold.

The need to escape had been puzzling but real.

Talk about full on!

Still feeling somewhat in shock, David said little as they got back into the car and drove further around the harbour. Some fine tuning of his preconceptions clearly needed to be done.

The experience of the last hour or so wasn't at all what he remembered of encounters with children, which was odd, given that he'd had plenty of contact over the years. Paediatric patients and their siblings, children of colleagues that appeared, albeit briefly, at dinner parties. Had he chosen to only remember some of them in order to fashion his own desires for the future? Or maybe he'd only registered the ones who were old enough to communicate. The ones who had their own personalities. Small people.

Of course, he knew they'd all been newborns at some stage. He'd assumed he had a handle on that as well but given the taste of reality he'd just experienced, his notions were kind of fuzzy around the edges. Had he been spared most of the details by doting parents and nurses who had attended to physical necessities?

'Do all new parents do that?' he asked Anne as they stopped at a corner shop, having decided that the day was nice enough for a picnic.

'What?'

'Talk about what they find in nappies, for instance, as if it was genuinely fascinating?'

'Yeah.' Anne slanted him an amused glance. 'What goes in and comes out of those little creatures is absolutely riveting. So is every twitch and burp and analysis of any differences in the noises they make. It's all part of the bonding process.'

'More like an obsession.' David led the way into the shop. 'I guess it's nature's way of ensuring survival.'

'It's like falling in love,' Anne said quietly, from

behind him. 'When you're the one involved, it's as natural as breathing.'

The bonding theory to ensure survival made sense. But if it was instinctive, why hadn't Anne experienced it after giving birth? Or maybe she had. She'd said as much, hadn't she? He'd been so prepared to slate her for giving those babies away and then turning her back on them and she'd stunned him when she'd said she couldn't go and stay with her sister because she wanted to see the babies *too* much.

And…maybe hope had been born in that instant. Hope that there could be a future for them that gave both of them what they wanted most in life. He wasn't ready to go down that track, however. Not when it might mean setting himself up for the kind of heartbreak he'd spent a year getting over. Not when Anne wasn't herself. They were both vulnerable. Confused. What fate had provided, in their living arrangements, was a kind of breathing space.

Determined to let the topic drop, David parked again at a small bay where a strip of grass led down to a rocky beach. There was a wooden table with built-in benches that was ideal for sitting at to eat the sandwiches and fruit they had purchased. The air smelled of the kelp that was piled up on the rocks below and the sun was warm enough to invite a scramble amongst the rock pools when they had finished eating.

It was Anne who voiced thoughts that were still focused on that visit.

'Poor Mac,' she murmured, watching a family of crabs scuttle into hiding having been disturbed by a shifting rock. 'I don't think he's too keen on having to go back to work next week when his paternity leave runs out.'

David made a sound of agreement but somewhere in the back of his mind another mental rock had been dislodged. Paternity leave? Had it ever occurred to him that he might want to take advantage of such a thing when he had a newborn of his own? Weeks of time away from work? How disruptive would that be? He'd assumed that the mother would be more than willing to make that kind of a sacrifice, though, hadn't he?

Finding a large, smooth, sun-warmed boulder, David sat down to watch Anne crouching to peer into the rock pool.

'He does seem just as enthralled as Julia.'

'He's a natural-born dad.' Picking up a stick of driftwood, Anne poked gently at a sea anemone to watch it flutter shut. 'I know how he feels,' she said a moment later. 'I used to hate having to go to school and leave Jules with the nanny.'

The loose braid of Anne's dark hair lay across her back as she leaned forward, the sun bringing out tiny sparkles of light that made it come alive. Tendrils had come loose and the breeze made them play against her neck and face. David had to fight the urge to reach out and smooth them back. He wanted to see—and touch—the milky smoothness of that skin. It was good to see her relaxing like this, with a childlike fascination for what the rock pool contained.

Such a contrast to the focused energy he'd always associated with her. The sort that was intrinsic to her work and was showing again now in the absorption with the project of restoring his house. The capable, impressive side of Anne Bennett. He'd known her history of raising her sister but had he ever really considered the effect it might have had? Had she really been in the same space that Julia and Mac currently inhabited?

'But you were just a kid,' he said aloud. 'What, six or seven years old?'

'I became a mother.' Anne sat down on the rocks. Her knees were bent and her arms went around them as though she was curling up to comfort herself. And she still stared into the rock pool.

'I was holding her when Mum died,' she said softly. 'Did I ever tell you that?'

'No, I don't think so.'

Anne sighed. 'It was terrifying. But kind of wonderful in a weird way. Taking responsibility for that little baby and looking after her was what got me through the grief. And Dad understood that. He helped but it was always him helping me, not the other way round.'

'And you were still a teenager when you lost your dad, weren't you? That must have been very hard.'

Anne gave a slow nod. 'I was seventeen. Just finishing school and ready to go to uni. Old enough to be able to keep us together without Social Services stepping in and putting Jules in a foster-home, thank goodness.'

The disruption of paternity leave was nothing compared to what Anne had done for her family. It touched him now, as it always had. Maybe it had been her stunning looks and what he'd seen of her skills as a doctor that had attracted him in the first place but knowing her unusual history had certainly contributed to him falling in love with this woman.

She was so capable. So independent. And, at the same time so incredibly giving.

She was still that same person. Even if she couldn't give him what *he* wanted.

Maybe he had been wrong. It was quite possible that he and Anne could be together again. All he had to do was tell her that he'd changed his mind. That being with her was all that mattered. In the wake of that visit to the twins, he could probably sound convincing in admitting he hadn't really thought it through. That maybe he wasn't ready for that kind of disruption to his life. Maybe he would never be ready.

They could both continue their high-powered careers unchecked. They would understand the pressure the other was under and be able to support and nurture success. They would be wealthy enough to have the best of everything. A dream home. Luxurious holidays anywhere they chose. Freedom to choose any hobby they fancied—if they ever found the time.

And perhaps that was the crux. Maybe they wouldn't need or want to find the time for anything as frivolous as a hobby. Life would be two-dimensional. Each other…and work. Quite apart from watching the joy of children growing up, having a family made finding time a priority. It would give life new dimensions. New meaning. Make it bigger, somehow and more worth-while.

Was it being selfish, wanting it all? Everything that life had to offer that was good and meaningful?

He had the possibility of a choice here. To be with the woman he loved or to have the family he dreamed of. He was the one who would have to make the sacrifice, though, and he wasn't ready to do that. Despite this overwhelming awareness of the person he knew Anne to be. She wasn't the only one who'd worked hard to get where she was. Who knew what she wanted the future to hold? Whether or not she would be part of that future, however, she deserved to know how special she was.

'You are amazing, you know,' he said quietly. 'What you've done for Julia has been truly extraordinary.'

'You mean the surrogacy thing?'

'That, too.' He had to touch her. To try and release what was tying him into a knot inside. He held out his hand. 'You had enough fresh air? Don't want you to overdo things.'

Anne took his hand and let him help her to her feet. The rocky surface was uneven, though, and she stumbled. Fell into his arms.

The opportunity was irresistible. David held her and let her get her balance. He waited until she looked up at him, with a mixture of relief and…surprise in her face. Her eyes shone and her lips were parted a little. And her hands were clinging to his shoulders. David didn't wait for common sense to override his response. He bent his head and kissed her.

It was a gentle kiss.

A brief, soft touch of David's lips to her own. Anne didn't have time to close her eyes, even, so she was still looking up at him, stunned, when he pulled back.

For a heartbeat, they simply looked at each other, saying nothing.

Anne could feel her heart hammering but it had nothing to do with the fright of her near fall seconds ago. She could still feel David's hands cradling her back as well, steadying her. And she could feel the strength in the muscles beneath her hands because she was still clutching his upper arms.

She could hear the roll of gentle waves on rocks below and the jagged edge to the breath David was drawing in.

She could smell something more potent than the salt water in the surrounding rock pools or the piles of kelp further away. The same smell she remembered from being carried in David's arms when she'd been barely conscious. The alluring scent of safety.

Her lips were still tingling from that brief touch of his. A sensation that was opening new memories. Awakening desire. She could *taste* it.

Oh…*help*!

She should move, Anne decided in that split second of being aware of little other than what her senses were telling her. She could actually feel the message being sent to her body. An order for action. It complied, sort of. It just seemed to move in the wrong direction.

Closer to David.

An infinitesimal amount, maybe, but it was enough for David to notice. For him to respond by drawing her even closer. Enough to prompt him to bend his head again, and this time it was a real kiss.

His lips moved over hers with the subtle changes of

position and pressure that were a familiar form of communication. It was impossible not to slip straight back into a response that begged for more. For what she knew he was capable of giving her.

Such intense pleasure. Sensations that made her forget she had bones in her body. That made things sparkle and curl deep inside. Tiny lights she hadn't felt for a very long time. A brightness she knew could be turned up until it exploded.

God, she had missed this.

The kiss went on. And on. For too long. For not nearly long enough.

Anne wasn't sure who pulled away first. The one whose common sense had called loudly enough to be heard, perhaps. Those lights began to dim and flicker, leaving her feeling curiously bereft. And shocked at how bright they had been. Was it her own reaction she could see in David's eyes when she met them this time? Or was he feeling the same way?

Who would have thought that the time apart from each other could have magnified physical attraction to that degree? That they were not only still fluent in that very private language but that it seemed to be on an entirely new level.

A dangerous level.

One that made Anne think crazy thoughts.

Like the fact that having those babies for Julia had shown her she was quite capable of being a mother again. That the tape had been peeled away from a maternal switch she had been sure would not be turned on again. That giving birth and nurturing her own child could be fulfilling in a way her career might never be.

That she could have David's baby.

And David.

But part of her mind was fighting back. Pushing opposing thoughts into her head. The kind she had been convinced were the truth when she had given those babies to their real mother. That she had already sacrificed enough. That this was *her* time. The only time she might have in her entire life when she could reach out and achieve her own dreams.

Amazing how fast thoughts could flash. How what was happening in your head could be so at war with what was happening in your heart. And body. No wonder it created a kind of meltdown. A feeling of utter confusion.

Could David see all that happening in the tiny space of time he continued to hold her, with both his hands and his gaze? Was that why she could see what looked like a reflection of her own confusion?

Anne could only be grateful that David took charge of what could have become an awkward moment.

His lips curved in a smile. 'Oops,' he said. 'Where did that come from?'

She could have said something that might have revealed the effect that kiss had had on her. She was tempted to say that she didn't care where it had come from as long as they could find their way back again.

But that would lead to talking about it. She might confess her confusion and even suggest that she'd been wrong about what she wanted in her future.

And what if David didn't want what he had once wanted? He was selling his beloved property. He had a new job lined up to go to very soon. He'd moved on.

This last year hadn't been a picnic for either of them. Was it fair to start something that might simply be a re-run of the past? A relationship that promised everything but disintegrated into the pain of two people pulling in different directions and ripping little pieces off the other as they did so.

Anne couldn't face that. Especially not now when she knew very well that she was more emotionally fragile than she had ever been in her life before. The prospect of adding that kind of pain was terrifying.

So she simply smiled back at David as she began easing herself away from his touch.

'Sea air,' she said lightly. 'It's known for its freshness.'

She took a shaky breath and discovered she could move properly now. She turned to start the short trek back to her car. 'I think you were right,' she added. 'I shouldn't overdo things.'

'Had enough, then?' David's voice was right behind her. His words very quiet.

She chose to ignore the ambiguity in his query.

Or maybe she didn't.

'Yes,' was all she said.

'Fine.'

She couldn't see David's face so she had to guess at what the tone of that word revealed. The best she could come up with was, what…resignation?

'Let's go home,' he added.

No. Not resignation. It was more like relief.

CHAPTER SEVEN

A WEEK went by and some shape began to emerge from the chaos of restoration work on David's house and garden.

Basic repairs had been completed. New plumbing and wiring was in place. Old paintwork was spruced up and faded wallpaper stripped from many rooms. In the garden, new leaves and buds were already appearing to fill in the raw patches where shrubs and roses had been pruned, and the borders had fresh, newly turned soil in places that had only been a tangle of weeds recently.

The weather was glorious and every day Anne could open windows all over the house to let sunshine and fresh air reach every corner and counteract the dust and dirt from the ongoing work. She was making final choices for new wallpaper and curtain fabrics. She had discovered garden centres and filled trolleys with boxes of bedding plants or chosen rose bushes from the glossy pictures on the nursery walls.

The promise of what the finished picture would be like hung in the air, taking shape and urging her to become a little more involved with every passing day. David seemed to be enjoying the process as much as Anne was. He opened accounts at plant nurseries and fabric stores.

'Are you sure you don't want to put a limit on what you're spending?' Anne had to check one day during the following week, having had a wonderful afternoon choosing baby trees.

He shook his head. 'Go for it,' he told her. 'You're doing an amazing job. I think you missed your vocation.'

'I am loving it,' she admitted. 'I never even knew I was interested in this kind of thing.'

'You should be resting, not scraping paint and lugging stuff around. For heaven's sake, Annie, you were holding a *spade* when I got home today and you'd obviously been using it.'

'I needed some exercise. I'm feeling fine. Never better, in fact.' And it was true but her smile had more to do with the way David had said her name than her physical well-being. They were in this project together and it was drawing them a little closer every day. 'You know what they say,' she added.

'What?'

'A change is as good as a holiday.'

'Some holiday.'

'Works for me. This is the longest I've ever had away from work and I'm not remotely bored.'

'Really?' David's glance was curious. 'Aren't you missing work at all?'

'Not yet.' Surprisingly, this was also true. There was

something vaguely disturbing about that but Anne wasn't going to try and analyse what that might be. 'I'm sure I will once this project is finished.'

'Mmm.' David suddenly seemed absorbed in sorting the handful of mail he'd brought inside with him. 'I'm sure you will.'

The moment had been loaded with…something. Again, Anne didn't want to try and figure out what it was because there was something else hanging in the air these days.

That kiss on the beach.

It hadn't been mentioned. It certainly hadn't been repeated but it was there. A different kind of promise, maybe.

But of what?

Anne was trying to ignore it. Trying not to ignite any spark of hope that it was a doorway back to a relationship that might be more than friendship. The kind of spark she'd experienced when David had suggested she come home with him. She wasn't even sure she wanted a repeat of that kiss, despite the messages her body gave her when she lay alone in her bed at night but even if she did, the first move would have to come from David.

He was the one who'd pulled a plug on the relationship in the first place. He hadn't been prepared to compromise on his dreams for his future and he'd made decisive moves to get on with his life. He still was making those moves with his plans to sell his property. If the kiss had changed anything, Anne was sure she would pick up on it and that would be the time to start seriously thinking about where they were headed.

And maybe that was why that particular moment had seemed so loaded. She'd been unable to stop herself looking for clues. David had seemed astonished she wasn't missing work and that she was enjoying the domestic kind of challenge she had taken on with the house and garden. Was he thinking she might be happy to give up work for a longer time and be content to nurture children as well as a garden? Had she been encouraging that line of thought with her accounts of happy visits to see Julia and Mac and the twins over the last couple of weeks? There was no mistaking the way David had lost interest in the conversation when she'd said she would start missing work in due course.

Let it go, she ordered herself. This kind of mental circuit was useless. Damaging. Something had changed for the better in the wake of that kiss because they were more comfortable with each other and Anne was more than happy not to rock the boat. Despite the rapidly increasing level of her physical activity, she *was* still resting emotionally. Content to sidestep both the kind of fierce mental effort her job involved and also the emotional roller-coaster that came with the territory of an intimate relationship.

It was a joy to have a distraction that was both compelling and deeply satisfying. And maybe the promise hanging in the air was the same for both aspects of her life right now—the restoration project and her relationship with David. Basic repairs had been done. The finished picture was unknown but was drawing them both forward because it had to be better than it had been before.

Toward the end of that week, Anne was spending the last of the daylight to empty some of the numerous boxes of plants she had purchased. This was the best time of day for this task. Hot sun would not stress the baby plants. She could give them a good drink and they would have the whole night to settle into their new environment. This was one of the bigger borders, in view of the main living area.

'Part of the vista,' she reminded herself with a giggle.

Her plan had been simple. She wanted to create a colourful mass of blooms. The kind that David's mother had probably taken pride in. After consulting books and experts in the garden centres, she was planting old-fashioned flowers en masse.

Plants like delphiniums and hollyhocks for height at the back, nigella and aquilegia amongst the rose bushes in the middle and a border of gorgeous blue violas along the front.

The house was empty.

So quiet.

Disappointment at not finding Anne in the kitchen where she normally was at this time of day morphed into something even less pleasant as a horrible notion occurred to David.

Maybe she'd packed her bags and gone home. She might have had a phone call today to tell her that the repairs on her cottage were complete and it was ready for habitation again. She might have tried to call him to tell him she was moving home but he'd been so busy he hadn't even glanced at his cellphone for too many hours to count and then the idea of checking for messages had been the last thing on his mind when all he'd wanted had been to get home and unwind after a frantic day.

It had been one major case after another in the emergency department today. A child had been knocked from his bicycle by a careless motorist and the head injury had looked serious enough to have panic-stricken parents and other relatives haunting the department until the little boy had been stabilised and taken to the intensive care unit. A man of only thirty-five had been the victim of a major heart attack and had arrested twice before he could be stabilised enough to be transferred into the care of cardiologists and taken to the catheter laboratory where several stents had been put in to repair blocked arteries.

Another adult had presented with terrifying shortness of breath that turned out to be a pulmonary embolus complicating the recovery from recent surgery. And amidst all the major drama had been the relentless stream of less life-threatening but still serious cases. People who had been in pain and sick and needed medical assistance.

Yes, it had been an exceptionally long day but David had been completely in his element. It might have been stressful and tiring but even in its most chaotic moments he'd been aware of an undercurrent that had added to his job satisfaction. One that he hadn't really been aware of missing for rather a long time.

That undercurrent was the knowledge that at the end of his day he would be going home to someone who would be genuinely interested in hearing all about it.

Funny how that extra dimension could make such a difference. Enough to make it no chore to spend even longer at work. Long enough to make a visit to the intensive care unit and the coronary care unit to follow up on some of those patients so that he could add to their stories when telling them to Anne.

But she wasn't here.

David dropped his briefcase beside the kitchen table, shrugged off his jacket to throw it over the back of a chair and loosened the tie that was starting to feel like a noose around his neck. He wrenched open the door of the fridge and extracted a bottle of icy-cold lager, flipping off the lid and not bothering to pick it up when it skated across the bench to land in the sink.

Moodily, he wandered out of the kitchen. The door to the guest suite was open but he could sense the emptiness beyond. When he'd finished his beer, he'd better unearth his phone and find out where the hell Anne had gone. With a sigh that was more like a low-grade rumble, he skirted the heap of drop sheets and big buckets that were obviously awaiting the return of the decorators in the morning. Their presence prompted him to walk into the main living area in the hope that some visible progress might spark an interest that seemed to have utterly faded since noticing he was alone in the house.

Wallpapering had begun. The huge room looked ghostly in the fading daylight thanks to the pale drop sheets covering all the furniture and the lack of any curtains at the windows. Ghostly and…lonely. He could brighten things up by turning on some lights but why bother? Taking another long swig of his drink, David stepped towards the remaining natural light instead. More out of a sense of duty than interest he looked through the latticed windows to see if he could spot anything new in the garden redevelopment.

And there, right in front of him, he saw Anne crouched on the edge of the biggest border.

Thank God, was his first thought. *She's still here.*

The wash of relief was powerful enough to render him motionless, his drink poised in mid-air. He felt his lips curl into a smile that was entirely unconscious and then both his hand and his eyelids lowered as something much darker than relief took over.

Dismay.

Why did it have to be *this* woman who provoked such overwhelmingly strong feelings in him?

Would he ever be able to get over her?

Did he want to?

Opening his eyes again, David found it was still bright enough outside to make him blink. It would be light for maybe another hour but the sun was low enough to be casting a rosy tinge of sunset on everything, making it look warmer. Softer. Very, very inviting. And Anne was central to that scene.

She was totally intent on her task. She wouldn't have been able to see him standing here, staring at her, anyway, with the sun reflecting off the windows so there was no reason for her to have been distracted. Or for David to move. He could indulge himself for a minute or two and watch her easing tiny plants from a container, cradling each one in her hands before setting it into a hole she had already made in the freshly turned soil. He could see the care she took in positioning them and then pressing earth gently around each new plant.

She'd obviously been out there for some time. The whole border was dotted with small, fragile-looking green clumps. Her arms and face were streaked with dirt and he saw why when she pushed wayward tendrils of hair back from her face before reaching for another plant.

Maybe she was so absorbed with what she was doing that she had simply lost track of the time. She needed to stop. To eat and rest. Unaware of his decisive nod, David headed for the door.

The ache in her back intensified as Anne finally stood up to drop the last, empty punnet into the wheelbarrow. She arched backwards, her hands on her hips to dig her fingers into the spot that hurt, and then she straightened, letting her breath out slowly.

A contented sigh.

She was tired, yes, and her back was a bit sore, but apart from that was feeling great. Fantastic, even. The satisfaction she was getting out of the creative enterprise of the last few weeks was something new and extraordinary. She couldn't wait to show David what she'd accomplished today and share the vision of what it was going to look like in a season or two.

Not that either of them would see the finished picture.

Anne pushed the negative thought aside. How stupid would it be to spoil how good she was feeling right now? Walking towards the nearby tap that had the hose coiled over it was enough to flip the direction of her mood. She dragged in a lungful of the fresh air and noted the spring in her step. She was, possibly, more physically fit than she'd ever been thanks to all the fresh air and exercise in the garden. Hard to believe it was only coming up to a month since she'd given birth to the twins. She'd never expected to recover this quickly, although her back was reminding her that her abdominal muscles still needed a bit more time.

Excess weight was dropping off fast too and that thought made Anne realise how hungry she was. As soon as she'd watered in the new plants she would go inside and start dinner. Having left her watch off, she could only guess at the time but daylight was definitely fading now.

Why wasn't David home yet?

The niggle of concern increased as Anne uncoiled the hose and turned the tap on. It made her turn her head as she pulled the hose towards the garden and it was then she saw him emerge from the house. He had unbuttoned the cuffs of his shirt and was rolling up his sleeves. His tie was gone and the collar was also unbuttoned. His long legs covered the lawn in easy strides and as he got closer Anne could see he was smiling. It was a picture of a man happy to be where he was and doing what he doing.

Something warm curled inside Anne and made her forget any weariness or sore muscles as she smiled back. Had she really thought she was feeling great after that stretch?

She'd been wrong.

This was what feeling great was.

Watching David walk towards her. Feeling like everything was right in the world again. Feeling like she'd arrived home.

Which was stupid. It was David who was arriving home. She didn't really belong here and she wouldn't be here for very much longer. Her smile fading, Anne twisted the nozzle of the hose to send a stronger spray to reach the back of the border.

'Hi,' she called over her shoulder. 'How was work?'

'Flat out.' David stopped beside her and a quick glance showed Anne the glow of sunset on his bare arms as he finished rolling up a sleeve. His hands seemed to glow as well. She'd always loved David's hands. Those long fingers. The mix of strength and cleverness. The ability they had to touch so gently…

She dragged her gaze away. 'Anything interesting?'

'Heaps. I'll tell you all about it over dinner. Speaking of which, have you got any idea of the time?'

'Not really.' Right now, Anne couldn't think of anything other than David's presence beside her. The huge garden around them seemed to have shrunk. Or vanished. It was like a bubble had formed that enclosed herself and this man and there wasn't quite enough air inside it to make breathing easy. Not when that kiss that had been hanging between them had got trapped in the bubble as well. She took a sideways step and pretended to concentrate on where she was directing the water. 'Nick went home a while ago,' she added. 'And he did say something about it being "food o'clock".'

'How long have you been out here?'

'Since lunch.'

'Good grief! You must be exhausted.'

She could feel him looking at her. Taking in her dirty shorts and mud-caked knees. Her hair hadn't seen a brush in way too long either and Anne was suddenly too aware of how scruffy she must look. She didn't *do* scruffy. Never had. It made her feel out of control somehow. Vulnerable.

'We've got heaps done.' She reached for a verbal anchor. Security. 'I got this border sorted and Nick attacked the hedges again. He found a gap that had grown over.' Anne turned sideways, still gripping the hose. 'It leads to a bit that I didn't even know was there. It's round.'

'What is? The gap?'

'No. The bit behind it. It used to be a lawn. Nick cut the grass and got rid of some old compost bins and started on the inside of the hedges and it was then we could see how round it was.'

David had walked around her to the end of the border and then he stopped and stood very still. 'I'd forgotten it was even here.'

'It was overgrown to the point of vanishing. Or was it a secret garden?'

'No...' David seemed lost in thought. 'It was...a pond.'

'Really?' Forgetting about that dangerous bubble, Anne went to stand beside him, the stream of the hose leaving the garden and pointing to the grass beside her feet.

'It got filled in. It was after Dad died and I think

something went wrong with the plumbing and the water drained off and the fish died and Mum didn't have the heart to sort it out. Said she didn't want a pond any more.'

'Oh…' Anne could imagine a water feature tucked away in the quiet, hedge-lined circle. The image was enticing. So enticing she forgot she was even holding the hose until David let out a yelp.

'Oi! My feet don't need watering.'

'Oh, sorry.' Anne tried to turn the hose off but twisted the nozzle in the wrong direction. The jet became a thin line and, to her dismay, it created a hole in the turf, which began to lift. 'Oh, help! I'm ruining the lawn now.'

'Here.' David took the hose from her hands but instead of turning it off he kept it pointing to the same spot. 'Look at that.'

Anne looked. The turf was lifting in a larger piece now.

'It's a paving stone, see?'

'Kind of, I guess.'

David was staring through the gap in the hedge again. He looked back at his feet and then over his shoulder, at the wheelbarrow full of empty plant containers and garden tools.

Moving swiftly, he turned off and abandoned the hose, picking up a spade. With a few decisive sweeps he scraped the turf clear to reveal a large, natural stone paving slab.

'There was a path,' he told Anne, his words tumbling out swiftly. 'And the pond was built of the same kind of stone. There were waterlilies and goldfish and…and it was…just lovely.'

He was looking at her and something in his face made her heart squeeze so hard it was painful. Something poignant. Like loss. She wanted to wrap her arms around him and offer comfort.

Instead, she found herself offering words. 'We could bring it back,' she said softly. 'Make it lovely again.'

There was something else in David's face now. Something that looked like surprise that the possibility might exist. And then hope. And then gratitude for her having thought of it.

It looked a lot like…love.

Maybe it was a trick of the fading light. Anne turned away hurriedly before she could think she saw something that might make her say or do something they might both regret.

David was still staring at her. The tension was unbearable. The bubble was back. So was that kiss. She was getting sucked in. Trapped. If she didn't step out now, she wouldn't be able to.

'I'll…um…get Nick to have a poke around tomorrow, shall I?'

The tension went up a notch but David said nothing. Instead, he seemed to channel the tension into action. He dug his spade into the soil again and Anne heard the clunk of metal striking stone. He walked on a step and repeated the action. Again and again, until the spade made no sound. By now they were well inside the hedge circle and Anne hadn't even noticed she had been following.

'This is it,' David announced. 'The edge of the pond. I'm pretty sure it was lined with stone as well.' He dug out a spadeful of earth and threw it to one side.

'You're not really dressed for digging,' Anne pointed out.

'I don't care. I want to see if I'm right. This is…' David was grinning. Looking so happy Anne had to grin back at him.

'Archeology?' she suggested. She was catching something here. The joy of discovery perhaps. The excitement of finding something that had been lost.

'It's amazing.' David nodded. 'Like I'm unearthing a bit of my childhood I'd completely forgotten.'

'It's going to get dark soon.'

'This won't take long.'

'There's another spade. I'll help.'

'You shouldn't be doing heavy stuff like this.'

'I'm fine, David. Never better.'

'Well…if you're sure. Just for a bit.'

Dusk faded slowly enough for that bit of time to stretch. They worked until it was too dark to really see the stone being uncovered and then carried on, being guided by the sound of their tools scraping the solid stone.

David had rolled his trousers up but his shirt was streaked with mud and his shoes would never be the same.

'Look at you,' Anne said laughingly at last. 'You're absolutely filthy.'

David nodded ruefully. 'And I'm starving.'

'Me too.'

David jammed the spade into the impressive mound of earth they'd created. He looked at the shadowy outline of the old pond they'd revealed. 'Whose silly idea was this?'

'Yours.' Anne was still smiling. 'And it wasn't silly. I love it.' She stepped up from the spot that had had the most earth cleared and David held his hand out to take her spade.

Why didn't she let it go?

If she had, she wouldn't have been pulled so close to this mud-streaked, dishevelled, sweaty, *happy* man. She wouldn't have been inside that bubble again and it wouldn't have had the chance to shrink around them like a skin, moulding them into one entity.

A tangle of limbs and hands and lips. An almost desperate fumbling that only stilled when David's lips found hers and Anne could abandon any rational thought and simply fall into the kiss.

It wasn't enough. Not this time. And they both knew it. When David eased back and took her hand and began to lead her towards the house, Anne was more than willing to follow him.

'We need a shower,' he told her. 'We're very dirty.'

'Mmm.' They both knew they weren't going to be using separate showers. It was just as well Anne was as fit as she was, she decided, otherwise her legs couldn't possibly have kept her upright and walking in step with David. Not when everything inside seemed to be turning into the most delicious liquid imaginable.

This wasn't simply about sex.

As much as David wanted—no, *needed*—to make love to Anne, he knew that physical intimacy was only part of a much bigger picture.

And if he hadn't realised that as he led her into his

house and up the stairs to his newly renovated en suite bathroom, he knew it as soon as he'd finished undressing Anne and taken her into the tiled shower with its multiple jets that surrounded them both.

Rivulets of muddy water trickled away from a body that had changed surprisingly little after the pregnancy. Her breasts were a little larger maybe and her stomach was still soft and generous, but when David soaped his hands and drew her closer to clean off the remaining dirt, her skin still felt like silk. The curves were familiar and delicious. He crouched to rub the engrained mud from her knees, loving the feel of her body beneath his hands but knowing that caring for her like this—making her clean and, later on, feeding her—was just as compelling as any physical fulfillment that could be on the agenda.

Maybe this was a mistake but he was lost in the wonder of being here at all. Being with Anne. Being allowed to care for and touch the woman he loved.

Would always love.

Anne tipped her head back, feeling the warmth of the water on her neck and back and the delicious slide of soapy hands on her skin. It should have been embarrassing having her muddy knees rubbed clean, but David's hands were moving upwards now. Caressing her inner thighs. Slipping behind to cradle her bottom as he stood up and pulled her closer.

His lips felt cool in comparison to the warmth of the shower but they still burned wherever they touched, just like his hands did. On her breasts and neck and mouth. Anne had been trying to return the favour of being washed but the sponge that foamed with shower gel slipped from her hands in the end. She needed everything she had to cling to David and stay upright.

'I want you,' he said simply, his mouth moving against hers.

'I want you, too.'

'It's too soon, isn't it?'

'I don't think so.' She could feel the hardness that was David wanting her, pressing against her. 'No, I'm sure it isn't.' She pressed back, desire so urgent it was unbearable.

David groaned, lifting her. Easing her back so that she was supported against tiles warmed by the rain still falling around and over them.

He was being cautious. Careful. It was Anne's turn to groan then. She wrapped her legs around him and begged for more, hanging on for dear life as her words unleashed the kind of passion she remembered so well. A kind she knew she would never find with anyone else.

It was blinding. A lightning bolt that was over too fast for either of them. So David wrapped them both in fluffy towels and took her to his bed and this time they made love slowly and gently. Retracing maps they both knew but wanted to rediscover in exquisite detail. This time David produced protection, even though Anne was sure she hadn't started ovulating again yet and was at no risk of pregnancy.

'Better safe than sorry,' David murmured.

A tiny comment soon lost in pleasure of each other's bodies but it surfaced again later, as Anne lay in David's arms and let him decide what food he was going to have delivered to the house as soon as possible.

Would she be sorry if she found she was pregnant with David's child?

If only she could answer that question. Because if she could, she wouldn't be feeling so lost right now.

As though she was standing at a crossroads, knowing that the next steps she took would determine the direction she would have to take for the rest of her life. But she was lost and couldn't find anything that resembled a compass.

She wasn't alone.

David was here at the same crossroads. Was history going to repeat itself and have them choose different directions or was it possible that their hands and hearts could stay linked as they moved forward?

Only one thing seemed certain. The time allowed to stay at the crossroads was limited.

And the clock had already been ticking for weeks now.

CHAPTER EIGHT

Choices.

They could be both a blessing and a curse.

'I had no idea goldfish came in so many colours.'

'Neither did I.' David bent down to peer into the tank in front of Anne. There was a huge variety of fish suitable for a garden pond. Big ones, little ones, shiny and speckled. The colours ranged from fluorescent orange and yellow to a deep red. Brown, even.

'How on earth are you going to choose?'

'That's why I dragged you along. Look, even the fins are different shapes. That one's all frilly. Must be a girl fish.'

The pet shop salesgirl, busy with a nearby tank, smiled as she overheard the exchange.

'It's your pond,' Anne told him. 'You get to choose.'

'There wouldn't be a pond if it wasn't for you. *You* choose.'

Anne turned her head, caught by something in David's tone. A note that suggested this was about more than fish. Not that the salesgirl would have picked up on it but, then, she knew nothing of their history.

Or how things had changed in the last couple of weeks since they had begun sharing a bed again. A choice had been made then too but so far neither seemed to be ready to really talk about the implications of what was happening. If they did, more choices would have to be made and there was a very real risk of their rediscovered intimacy vanishing in a puff of smoke that would leave them both burned.

Was that what was underlying David's insistence that she make the choice about the fish? Because the time was coming when she would have to make a rather more personal choice? A choice that was so huge it was terrifying.

To be with David or to be alone.

To be a mother or to continue the career she loved unchecked.

A flash of panic made her break the eye contact with him. Anne stared into the tank again but she wasn't seeing a single fish.

Why was she so afraid? That she would make the wrong choice? Or that she couldn't make it at all? Given how much she knew she loved this man, that choice should have been easy. She loved the way he looked. Her heart skipped a beat every time she saw him when they'd been apart for a while. She loved the sound of his voice. His smile. His dedication to his job and his ability to do it so well. Most of all, she loved the way he cared about *her*. Even now, when she was feeling so fit and well again, he still kept an eye on how much rest she was getting and that she was eating good food. She knew that if she wobbled in any way, he would be ready to scoop her into his arms and make sure she would be all right.

What woman in her right mind would let someone who cared about her like that leave their life? The choice should be a no-brainer. She could choose to be a mother and give David the family he wanted so badly and that would be enough to keep them together, quite probably for ever.

Except it wouldn't be enough, would it?

Why not? Was her career that important to her? And if it was, why had she made life so tough for herself over the last year by having babies for Julia and Mac?

The fish swam happily amongst the oxygen weed and rocks but still Anne couldn't focus.

Love… That was why she'd tipped her life upside down and had those babies. Real, unconditional, forever kind of love. The kind she had for Jules. The kind Julia and Mac had for each other.

Mac had wanted a family. Julia had known she couldn't give it to him and had taken herself away to give him the chance to have that family with someone else. Mac had crossed the world to find her again because being with Jules was more important. It had been his love for her that had been more important than anything else.

Did David feel that way about her? If he did, then anything would be possible. The memory of the way he had carried her in his arms to safety that day by the river was enough to make her believe he might but if he did, why was it *her* that had to make a choice?

She didn't want to. She didn't want to risk losing

what they had. Even if it was only for a few more weeks, she couldn't bring herself to pre-empt whatever was coming.

'I can't choose,' she said aloud, finally. Oh, Lord, was there a note of desperation in her voice? 'It's a big pond. Can't you take some of each colour?'

David gave a huff of laughter. 'That's so like you, Annie. All or nothing.' He turned away from the tank. 'Maybe I'd better get you out of here before you start looking at the kittens.'

'How's the work on the house going, David?'

'Almost done, thank goodness.' In a rare lull in emergency department activity, David had found time to not only eat his lunch but to be enjoying a cup of surprisingly good coffee from the espresso machine in the staff-room.

'Looking good?'

'Amazing. It's exceeded all expectations.' He smiled at the registrar and she smiled back, the eye contact lingering just long enough for David to get the message before she turned to use the coffee machine.

The young doctor was pretty. He knew she was good at her job. He also knew she was doing her emergency department rotation as part of her general practitioner training. She was heading for a career as a family doctor so it could be part time when she might have her own family to factor into her life.

That should have been enough on its own to have made her a blip on David's radar, never mind the fact that she was clever and attractive. He searched hopefully in that instant of eye contact but a heartbeat was as long as it took.

No blip. Not even a glimmer of one. He had absolutely no interest in this woman.

Dammit!

What was it about Anne Bennett that eclipsed other women to such a degree they couldn't even glimmer, let alone shine?

A woman who couldn't even compromise on the colour of fish, let alone juggle the idea of a career *and* a family. So black and white. All or nothing.

It was ridiculous. Couldn't she see that she was shooting herself in the foot as far as a meaningful relationship went? He *loved* her, for God's sake. She was shooting them *both* in the foot. David frowned at his coffee as a disturbing thought occurred to him. Was he guilty of the same sin?

He'd been prepared to walk away from Anne once before because he couldn't have it all. He'd left himself with nothing, hadn't he? Well, he'd still had his career, of course, but had that been enough?

'So…' The registrar sat down at the table opposite David. 'You'll be going on the market soon, then?'

'Sorry?' Good grief, was she asking if he was planning to be available for a new relationship?

She raised her eyebrows. 'The house? With it being finished? Wasn't that the plan?'

'Oh…yes.' It had indeed been the plan.

The house was finished. So was the garden, right down to the pond with its baby waterlilies and a rainbow of fish. Anne's cottage was finished, too. She was going there this afternoon, in fact, to check on the final touches. David had asked her to walk there via the hospital so he could come and see it as well. He was due to finish at 3 p.m. and a leisurely stroll home would be nice.

He wanted to see the cottage. Not to make sure that the workmen had done a good job but because he wanted to see whether he could pick up any vibes that maybe Anne wasn't so excited at the thought of moving back to her own home.

That maybe she would rather stay where she was.

With him.

'I'm not sure,' he said aloud into the silence. 'About selling the house.'

'But aren't you due to leave soon? You've got that flash job in London to go to, haven't you?' The young doctor's eyes were shining. 'I'd *love* to go and work in London. It would *so* exciting.'

'Mmm.' David smiled back in an attempt to catch some of the excitement his junior colleague was emanating.

It should be exciting. All of it. That the house and garden were looking fabulous enough to command a quick, easy sale at a top price. That he had a prestigious position waiting for him in a world-renowned hospital in the one of the most wonderful cities on the globe.

And...he didn't want to go.

He'd been given a choice only that morning. They wanted him to stay on here, in a senior consultancy position. Only a step away from Head of Department and they'd intimated that taking that step would only be a matter of time.

His best intentions—the ones he'd had when he'd come back here—to tie up loose ends and move on with his life had been derailed. He only had himself to blame but there it was. Those intentions hung on one end of a balance and the rekindled romance with Anne hung on the other end.

Where was Anne?

Right in the middle. Depending on which way she moved, the balance would shift and the choice would be easy. Or, if not easy, at least clear.

Maybe he was standing there in the middle as well. Right beside her. He had his own choices that he could make and therefore influence the balance himself. He could decide that being with Anne was more important than having a child.

It *was* more important. There was a principle here that was far bigger than making babies. It was to do with the whole feeling of family. Of loving someone enough for what they wanted or needed to be more important than what you wanted yourself. Was the fact that he and Anne had been pulling in directions different enough to have snapped their relationship once already enough evidence that the kind of love they had wasn't a lasting kind?

He simply didn't know. He desperately wanted to find out and that was what the last weeks with Anne had been about. They were closer than they'd ever been in so many ways but he didn't feel any closer to knowing the answer to what the future held.

Choices still had to be made. And soon.

* * *

Just before 3 p.m. the quiet spell in the emergency department ended dramatically with the arrival of first one and then another ambulance coming from the scene of a multi-vehicle pile-up on the motorway. The trauma bays were already full and every available staff member occupied with the assessment and treatment of the injured people when a third ambulance pulled into the loading bay. Arriving right behind the stretcher that was unloaded from the vehicle was Anne.

'Status 1,' the paramedic confirmed the call that had prompted David and a senior nurse to be waiting out here to meet them. 'Ten-year-old boy who was thrown from a car and then trapped when the vehicle rolled. Chest injuries. Increasing respiratory difficulty. Query pneumothorax.'

'Check Resus 1,' David instructed the nurse. 'Make sure that patient is on the way to CT and the area is clear.'

This little boy was clearly not stable. The tendons on his neck were standing out in his struggle to breathe and the trace on the ECG monitor sitting on the end of the stretcher was showing a sprinkling of abnormal heartbeats.

'Need a hand?'

David was reaching to push the button to open the automatic doors. Thinking ahead to what he would need around him in the next few minutes when they'd transferred this child to the bed in the well-equipped resuscitation area. A chest drain kit, intubation gear, bag mask, X-rays. A central line maybe.

He blinked at Anne as the doors slid open in the wake of her offer to assist.

Was it because she'd been away from work and so engrossed in projects that had nothing to do with medicine that he hadn't made such an instant, obvious connection?

This child was critically ill with major chest trauma.

Dr Anne Bennett was a specialist paediatric cardiothoracic surgeon. The best possible person to take over this case.

'Sure.' This was definitely a no-brainer. This was what Anne did. Who she was. Why did this action of stepping back to let her take over give him the briefest flash of something that felt like…disappointment?

The patient who had been occupying the resus area they were heading for was being wheeled out as they came in but the woman was conscious and cried out as she saw the small figure on the stretcher.

'*Daniel!* Is he…? Will he be…?' Her words became choked by sobs and she covered her face with her hands. 'Oh…*God*…'

David stepped closer to the departing bed. 'We're going to take the best care of him that we can,' he assured the woman, who was presumably Daniel's mother. 'Try not to worry. He's lucky that he's got the best specialist available right here.'

'On the count of three,' Anne was saying, ahead of him now and pulling a paper gown over her clothing as she spoke. 'One…two…three.'

The small body was lifted to the bed and remnants of clothing cut clear. One doctor was in charge of the airway and had an ambu-bag hooked onto the overhead oxygen supply, ready to cover the boy's face and try and squeeze oxygen into his lungs.

'Saturation's right down.' A nurse checked the clips over one of Daniel's fingers. 'Eighty per cent and dropping.'

'Blood pressure's dropping too,' came another voice as new figures appeared on the bank of monitors. 'Systolic down to 93.'

'Run of V tach,' someone else warned as an alarm on the cardiac monitor sounded. 'Okay, back into sinus.'

Anne unhooked her stethoscope from her ears. 'Flail chest,' she reported. 'No breath sounds on the left side. I need a chest drain kit, please.'

The sterile kit was unrolled onto a trolley by the time she had pulled gloves on.

'Check his belly, could you, please, David? And his pelvis. He's losing a lot of blood.'

'I'll get some more fluids up as well and get him cross-matched for some whole blood.'

Anne nodded, now intent on the task of inserting a tube between small ribs to release the air and blood now trapped in the chest cavity and making it impossible for normal breathing. A task made harder by the crush injury that had left so many ribs shattered.

'V tach again,' came the warning as Anne swabbed the boy's chest with disinfectant and was paused with a scalpel in her hand. 'No...V fib... He's arrested.'

'Stand clear.' Anne reached for the life-pack controls. 'Shocking now.'

She watched the screen intently as a normal rhythm emerged from the straight line following the shock. Then she looked up as a newcomer entered a now crowded space. David could sense her relief to see the anaesthetist she probably worked with on a regular basis.

'Good to see you, Bob. This lad needs tubing. I think we're looking at doing a thoracotamy.'

'Tamponade?'

'Looks like it.'

David agreed silently. There was so much bleeding going on in that small chest that it was becoming impossible for the heart to work normally, let alone the lungs. Having checked and found no obvious injuries to the boy's abdomen or pelvis, he was beginning to feel redundant. Daniel's legs and head also seem to have escaped major trauma. It was the chest that had caught the brunt of whatever had trapped this child in the wreckage.

He could—and probably should—go and check the other patients who had come in from this scene but he knew they were well attended by staff who would come and get him if he was needed. And none of them had been anywhere near as critically injured as this young child.

And this was compelling drama. Opening someone's chest in an emergency department was fortunately a rare occurrence. If it had to happen—as was becoming evident it was in this case—because the patient wouldn't survive long enough to get to Theatre without it, then you couldn't hope for anyone better than a surgeon who specialised in doing exactly this kind of procedure.

That so many people were watching and hanging off every movement and word that came from Anne was clearly not fazing her at all.

She had that kind of intense focus that made anything other than the life she was trying to save totally irrelevant. The way she had been that first day David had seen her when he'd come back here. With the backdrop of another case of child chest trauma. Another little life that she'd had the ability to save. Who the hell did he think he was to even consider himself worth compromising such a brilliant career for?

He had the weird feeling that a circle was closing. That something was very close to being complete.

Over.

'Clamp, thanks.' Somehow, amongst the terrible open wound that was this little boy's chest now, Anne had found something that made her tone triumphant. 'Laceration of the left ventricle,' she told her audience. 'I'll put in a temporary suture and we'll get him straight up to Theatre. How's the BP now?'

'Coming up. Systolic 95.'

'Oxygen saturation?'

'Improving. Eight-six per cent and rising.'

'Good.' Anne's hands were making swift, graceful movements, the thread of the suture invisible from where David was standing. She glanced in his direction. 'David, could you alert Theatre that we'll be on the way up in less than five minutes, please?'

'Sure.' Was she intending to go into Theatre with Daniel?

As if reading her thoughts, Anne spoke again. 'Page Jeff, too. If he's not available, I'll scrub. We don't want to lose any time.'

* * *

David had waited for her.

It was nearly 6 p.m. by the time Anne left the paediatric intensive care unit but she found him in his office when she walked past on her way to leave the hospital.

'I thought you might have gone home.'

'I was waiting for you. We had plans, remember?'

He didn't look happy. Why? Because she'd stepped in and taken over a major case in his department?

'Daniel's looking okay,' she told him. 'He'll be on a ventilator for a while but he's oxygenating well and his cardiac function's looking stable. He's got a fighting chance.'

'Lucky for him that you arrived when you did.'

'You could have done it,' Anne said quietly. 'But I'm glad I was there. It was…'

What she'd been missing even though she hadn't realised she was missing it. That adrenaline rush. The amazing zone where you could put every ounce of your skill into making sure no tiny detail got missed. The kind of case that was so unlikely to be successful but when it was…

'It was amazing,' she said aloud. 'Don't you love it when you win against odds like that?'

'Absolutely.' But David's smile looked strained. 'Shall we go? Do you still want to drop in at the cottage?'

Anne was still watching his face. Looking for clues that might explain this odd tension in the room. She had no idea why but she was quite sure that going to the cottage with him would make it worse.

'Not really,' she said cautiously.

'Of course.' David was shutting down his computer.

'You'll want to hang around for a while. In case you're needed for any follow-up on the boy.'

'The boy'? David knew Daniel's name. He was deliberately trying to make this less personal. More professional. To do with the job, not the people involved, as if it was possible to separate them.

The penny dropped and Anne knew what this new tension was all about. No wonder the prospect of going to her old home in David's company had rung alarm bells. That cottage had been the scene of the final unravelling of their relationship. The arguments.

His plans had been unexpectedly disrupted this afternoon and old buttons had been pushed. The ones created by interrupted dates or the inability to leave town for a romantic weekend away. He'd been left by himself. Waiting for her. Anne could almost hear the echo of angry voices in the back of her mind.

'Nothing matters more than your career, Anne. You're selfish.'

'That's the pot calling the kettle black, isn't it? You want me to sacrifice my career to have children. That's worse than selfish. Positively Victorian.'

'If love is involved, it's called compromise, not sacrifice. But you don't know that word, do you? Not the meaning of it, anyway.'

Anne could almost feel the same anger she'd felt then at being accused of being selfish. She'd never been selfish. She'd given up a normal childhood and teenage years to be a mother. She'd given the use of her body to her sister to create a family for her.

Did David still think she was being selfish? Just

because she'd become so involved in this afternoon's case that she'd missed a kind of date with him?

No. Of course he wouldn't be that petty. Maybe the combination of circumstances had given him the kind of flashback she'd just experienced. She was probably looking less than happy herself right at this moment.

'I don't need to stay here,' she said quietly. 'But I have left my mobile number and asked to be called if there are any concerns with Daniel during this post-operative phase.' Her tone rose a little defensively. 'He's become my patient, David. You didn't have to hand him over to me, you know.'

'Oh, but I did.' David was on his feet, coming out from behind his desk. 'A life was at stake, Annie. I would have doing less than my job if I hadn't provided the best care I possibly could.' He put his hands on Anne's shoulders, bent down and kissed her lips gently. 'That was you. The best. I'm not at all convinced that young Daniel would have even made it to Theatre if you hadn't been there. I'm proud of you.'

He sounded sincere. He had used the softened version of her name that only the people closest to her ever used. His kiss had been real. The glow of pleasure lasted until Anne pulled back far enough to meet his gaze but then it spluttered and died. There was something in his eyes that scared her.

Something that reminded her of what she'd seen—or rather, heard—not so long ago. When he'd been talking about the pond. Something beautiful that had been lost. Did he think that he'd lost her? That the pull of her amazing career was something he couldn't—or didn't want—to compete with?

The choice loomed closer. Maybe this was as good a time as any to talk about it. Anne drew in a deep breath and gathered her courage but just as she opened her mouth to speak, the mobile phone in her bag began to trill.

'Daniel?'

'No.' Anne had fished the phone from its pocket and frowned at the screen. 'It's Jules. On her mobile.'

She answered the call but, for several seconds, she could make no sense of what she was hearing. Her sister sounded hysterical. There were babies crying and a loud, mechanical kind of noise. There even seemed to be a siren going nearby.

'Calm down,' she instructed Julia. 'I don't understand. Take a deep breath and start again, hon. Where are you? What's all the noise about?'

She listened carefully. She asked a couple of questions and heard herself automatically saying reassuring things. Then she ended the call and looked at David.

'*What?*' he demanded.

'Oh, my God…' Anne wanted to close her eyes and make this all go away but she couldn't. She clung to David's gaze and tried to get the words from a throat that suddenly felt too tight to breathe, let alone speak.

'What is it?' David said. He was holding her, with both his gaze and his tone. Steadily. 'Tell me.'

Anne swallowed. Hard. She could feel the prickle of tears in her eyes and her voice could only emerge in a whisper.

'Mac's helicopter has crashed.'

CHAPTER NINE

His arms were around her in an instant.

Holding her close.

Giving her that same sense of safety they always did. Advertising David's ability to care for *her*. And, yes, it was other people Anne had to worry about right now. Mac, of course—her dearly beloved brother-in-law. Julia, not only at this point but possibly for the rest of her life, if the worst had happened and she had lost the man she loved so much. And there were two tiny babies, who might have lost their father.

David cared about these people too but his first action was to look after *her*. To be the rock from which she could gather the strength she would need to face this crisis.

How could she ever survive without this in her life?

She couldn't. That was all there was to it but this wasn't the time to be thinking about herself or how she could secure the future she knew she needed. Or imagining how she would feel if her fear had been for David's life and not Mac's. It crept in, though, just for a heartbeat. Long enough for her to know that she loved this man quite probably just as much as Julia loved Mac.

The murmurs of sympathy and encouragement were filtering into the panicked buzzing in Anne's head. Becoming words. Instructions.

'We need to go,' David was saying. 'I'll take you to Jules.'

'No.' Anne shook her head, feeling the solid wall of David's chest against her forehead. Taking in a deep breath that filled her with the warmth and scent of him because she couldn't know how long it might be before she could be this close again. 'She's coming here.'

'What? She's not driving?'

'No.' Anne scrubbed at her face. The tears had gone and she felt calm now. Ready to do whatever needed to be done. 'The news of the crash came through Ambulance Control. Jules has her best friends in the service. They weren't about to let a police officer she'd never met arrive on her doorstep with that news. They dispatched a free ambulance crew.'

'But they're coming here? To Emergency?'

Anne nodded.

David looked pale. 'Why? Is someone hurt? Jules? One of the babies?'

'No.' Anne had to touch him. To find a smile. To offer him just a fraction of what he'd been able to give her. Reassurance. Strength. 'They asked Jules what she needed and she said…' Anne had to take a breath to fight the wobble in her voice. 'She said she needed me.'

'And you said you were here.'

'Yes. We can take her home but maybe this is a better place to be. They haven't found the helicopter yet but when they do… If Mac's injured and not…' Anne had to press her lips together to stop any more words coming out. She had to close her eyes to try not to see the worst.

'If he's injured they might bring him here,' David finished for her. 'Yes. That makes sense. All right, let's go and see if the relatives' room is free. Otherwise we can find another space that will be private.'

He took hold of Anne's hand and led her from the office. Word in the department spread like wildfire and the availability of the relatives' room was guaranteed. When the ambulance pulled into the loading bay a short time later they were both standing there, waiting for the back doors to open.

Julia stumbled out first and almost fell into her sister's arms. It was David who gripped the handles of the two baby car seats and carried the infants inside. Bags that had clearly been hastily stuffed with things the twins might need were carried in by a paramedic who followed the small procession, oblivious to curious stares, as it made its way through the emergency department and into the room set aside for them.

'Thank you so much,' Julia said to the bag carrier. 'I don't know what I would have done if you hadn't been the one to come and tell me.'

'No worries,' the paramedic assured her, giving her a hug. 'Is there anything else I can do?'

Julia shook her head. 'You guys need to get back on the road and I'm okay. I've got Annie now. Just…can you get someone to tell me any news? You might hear something that…that they might wait to tell me.'

The paramedic nodded, his face grim. 'They've sent a search and rescue spotter plane out. If the emergency beacon's working we should hear something soon. One of us will call it through.'

Anne had her arm around her sister again. 'Let me give you my mobile number. And a landline in case we decide to go home.'

It wasn't until she'd recited the numbers and the paramedic was leaving that Anne realised she had automatically given the landline number of David's house as her home.

Because, in the space of the last few weeks, it had become her home, hadn't it?

Where her heart was.

Had David noticed? Turning, Anne saw that he was crouched beside one of the car seats, undoing the safety belt to release one of the crying babies.

Julia had moved to crouch beside the other seat. 'They're hungry,' she was telling David. 'And probably wet.'

'No problem,' David said calmly. 'We'll get them sorted in no time, don't you worry.'

The noise level was escalating. Angus and Amy seemed to think that being taken from the cocoon of their car seats was yet another tribulation. They were both red-faced and howling. Tiny fists punched the air to underline their misery.

This was a nightmare.

Julia needed comfort. Support. A calm environment

would help. What would it be like to be faced with the sense of being unable to cope with the background horror that she might have to parent alone for ever?

Anne started digging in the bags. Looking for nappies and wipes. Formula and bottles and dry clothes.

'Maybe we need some help,' she said. 'I could find a nurse who's not busy, maybe.'

David and Julia both looked at her. Julia looked bemused, as though she didn't quite understand what Anne meant. Weirdly, Anne thought she saw that odd note of sadness in David's expression again.

'We're fine, Annie,' he said gently. 'This is about family. We don't need anyone else.'

He was holding Amy in his arms now. He lifted the baby so that she was pressed against his chest. Close to his heartbeat, as Anne had been herself so recently. The tiny head with its fluffy, dark hair and that endearing bald spot on the back was nestled against David's neck.

Unsurprisingly, the baby's howls started to diminish.

'There you go.' David smiled, turning his head so that his lips brushed Amy's head. 'That's better, isn't it, princess?'

Anne swallowed what felt like a hard lump in her throat. He was right. This was about family. Staying close and looking after each other. Had he seen her offer to find extra help as an admission of failure, perhaps? Did he think that she was trying to avoid dealing with this herself because of some personal issues stemming from the surrogacy? Or, worse, that she was simply being *selfish*?

* * *

'Let me take Angus for you,' she said to Julia.

'Maybe you could make up some formula.' Julia was bouncing Angus gently in her arms. 'Have you found the tin? And the bottles?'

Anne nodded. 'There's a microwave in the staff-room. Or do I need to boil some water? And how many scoops for each bottle?'

'I'd better do it,' Julia decided. 'Here, you take Gus. I know where everything is.'

'I'll come with you.'

'No. They get more upset if they're separated. I'm okay, Annie.' Julia was pale and her eyes huge and dark but her voice was steady. She carefully transferred her noisy bundle into her sister's arms.

'Are you sure?'

Julia smiled. 'I probably know my way around here better than you do. It's part of where I worked, remember? And it's…part of where Mac works. I feel closer to him here and…it'll help if I have something to do.'

Anne was blinking back tears. Good grief, she was supposed to be the strong one. How come she hadn't noticed her baby sister turning into such a strong woman? She felt completely out of her depth here. She should be taking charge and giving Julia strength, not the other way around. This was confusing at some level. Or maybe it was because she was being handed the responsibility of her nephew and she wasn't sure she was ready for this yet.

Ready or not, she had no choice.

* * *

Poor Anne.

She was rocking Angus in her arms, walking round and round the only available space between the couches in this room, looking less and less sure of herself.

'What am I doing wrong?' she asked David.

'Nothing, love. He's sad because he's hungry. And probably because he's got wet pants.'

'Okay. I can deal with that.'

'Sure you can. You're way ahead of me in baby skills.'

Anne knelt on the floor, carefully adjusting her burden so that she could use one hand to sort through one of the bags.

'It's more than a quarter of a century since I changed a nappy,' she said. 'And we used cloth ones, not disposables.' She laid a towel on the floor and put Angus down to unbutton his suit.

'Phew!' She screwed up her nose a moment later. 'Some things don't change. I might need a bathtub here.'

David grinned. 'Wipes should do it. They'll be in that bag there somewhere.'

Anne's face was a picture as she held the baby's feet in the air and started to wipe a small dirty bottom. Her movements were tentative at first and Angus obviously realised that he was in the hands of someone who might not know what they were doing. His shrieks reached an impressive decibel level.

'Want to swap?' he offered.

'No.' Anne sounded as though her teeth were gritted. 'I can do this.'

Of course she could but it was impossible not to

compare this Anne to the woman he'd seen in Resus 1 a few hours ago. That intently focused, brilliant surgeon. She'd been doing what she was meant to be doing then. What she wanted to do. Looking skilled and competent.

Now she was looking lost and miserable. She had to be worried sick about Mac. And Julia. And maybe she hadn't been ready to get this involved with the babies she'd given birth to but wasn't going to parent. And maybe there was another fear that she might not have even acknowledged yet. If the worst had happened and Mac wasn't coming home then she would, by default, become a second parent to her nephew and niece because there was no way she would leave Julia to face the future alone.

Ironic in a way. He'd realised today that he could never ask Anne to compromise her career for the sake of family but fate might be forcing her to do just that.

With children that weren't hers. Or his.

Unconsciously, David tightened his grip on the baby he held. They needed protection, these precious babies. He wouldn't allow himself to think of the worst case scenario.

'You're doing great,' he told Anne, who was reaching for a clean nappy now.

'Which bit goes at the front?'

'I think it's the bit with the sticky tabs. No…maybe it's the other way round.' Good grief, neither of them was exactly qualified to be doing this, were they?

Julia arrived back with two warm bottles of formula as Anne was struggling to keep small, chubby legs still for long enough to stick the nappy in place. She caught David's gaze and her eyebrows rose in a silent query about whether Anne was coping. He smiled.

'Sit down,' he suggested. 'And take Amy. She needs her mum. Give me the other bottle and I'll rescue Annie.'

Anne had picked Angus up. The buttons on his stretch suit were gaping in a peculiar fashion and having a clean bottom hadn't made him any happier. Anne looked over to where Julia was sitting with Amy, who had taken to her bottle, and then she looked at David and he could see despair in her face.

'I'll take him,' he said. 'You need to wash your hands.'

By the time she returned, David was sitting the couch beside Julia and Angus lay in his arms, sucking furiously on his bottle, wide eyes staring up at the unfamiliar man who was feeding him. The only sound in the room was the contented sucking noises the babies were making.

Until Anne's phone rang.

Julia flinched and then froze, watching as Anne took the call.

'They're within range of the beacon,' she relayed moments later.

'Radio contact?' David queried.

Anne shook her head. 'But there's hours of daylight left. They'll find them soon.'

The wait seemed interminable. Having been fed and changed and cuddled, the twins settled to sleep in the cushioned comfort of their car seats, a fuzzy blanket draped over them for warmth. David sat on a couch with a hand on each handle, rocking the seats gently. Anne held Julia in her arms on the other couch. A silent support that spoke of a bond too deep to measure.

And then someone knocked on the door.

'Jules?' It was the same paramedic who had brought her here. 'They've found them.'

David watched the sisters straighten. They both had the same frozen expression on their faces. They were holding each other's hands so tightly it had to hurt.

'They're alive,' the paramedic said. 'Both of them. The radio gear's been knocked out of action but the chopper is pretty well intact and they're both on safe ground. In bush country, so the plane couldn't land.'

'Oh…' For the first time since she'd arrived at the hospital, Julia burst into tears. 'Oh… Thank goodness!'

'They're not hurt?' Anne whispered.

'Not badly, from what could be seen. Mac was lying on the ground but he was waving, apparently. They reckoned he had a big grin on his face.'

Julia hiccupped and smiled. 'That's my Mac.'

'They're sending a chopper. It's about thirty minutes' flight time and I'm on the crew to go. I came to see if you wanted to come with us, Jules.'

'Oh…' Julia sprang to her feet. '*Yes.*'

But then she looked at her babies, asleep in their seats. Her gaze lifted to meet David's and the plea was as eloquent as her turmoil. She didn't want to leave the babies but she had to go to Mac. He was the love of her life and she'd been terrified she might lose him.

And a part of David's heart broke because he knew exactly how she felt. It was the way he would feel about

Anne. They way he would want someone to feel about him. That he was *that* important.

No. Not someone.

Only Anne.

'Go.' David smiled at Julia. 'We'll look after these two, won't we, Annie?'

Anne nodded. She had tears on her cheeks and she got up to give Julia one last, swift hug. 'Go and bring him home,' she said brokenly. 'His family's waiting for him.'

David was so good with the babies.

When Angus woke and grizzled, he soothed him with rocking and soft words. When Amy woke and didn't settle, he picked her up and cuddled her. She fell asleep in his arms and he sat very still on the couch, not wanting to disturb her.

He looked tired. His tie had been abandoned a while ago and his shirtsleeves were rolled up. His hair was tousled and his jaw deeply shadowed. Anne couldn't help remembering the day he'd walked across the lawn towards her, looking a bit like this. The day they'd discovered the lost pond. And each other again.

This situation couldn't be more different. It had nothing to do with sex or even herself and David as a couple. This was a bigger picture. A family picture but, curiously, the bond between them seemed stronger. So powerful it took her breath away and blurred her vision.

Or was that exhaustion kicking in, in the wake of that tense stint in Theatre and then the stress of being so afraid for Mac and his brand-new family? They still didn't know how badly he might be injured. There'd been some delay in getting another chopper off the ground. The rescue team might be lucky to get to the scene before daylight faded completely at this rate.

'We should go home,' David said into the silence of the room. 'That way we could get something to eat and have a rest ourselves. We could be in for a long night.'

'Mmm.' It was a sensible suggestion. They could get back to the hospital quickly enough if they needed to.

But she was reluctant to move. This picture of him sitting there with Amy in his arms was compelling. And confusing. She wanted David to want her as more than a mother for his children but his life wasn't going to be complete without his own family, was it?

He was right. Taking a stand about having children of her own had been selfish. How lucky would that child—or children—be to have a father like him? She already knew how lucky she would be to have him caring for her. Protecting her.

Loving her.

'David?'

He looked up. But his gaze kept travelling when a nurse poked her head through the door. 'Dr Bennett?'

Anne's head turned swiftly. 'Yes?'

'Word is that they're on scene. Mac has a compound fracture of his ankle but is otherwise okay. It'll be an hour or more before they get back and it sounds like he'll be going to Theatre as soon as possible after that.' The nurse hesitated. 'Are you and Dr Earnshaw planning to stay in here?'

'You need the room?'

The nurse bit her lip. 'We've got a man who's terminal. His family's having to take turns to sit with him and they're not getting much privacy in the waiting room.'

'We were thinking of taking the twins home,' David said. 'Maybe you could order a taxi for us?'

David got Amy buckled back into her car seat while Anne packed up all their belongings.

'Are you sure you don't mind?' she asked David. 'You have to walk tomorrow. I could take them back to the cottage.'

'I think they need both of us to get settled at least,' David said. 'Then you'll be able to come back to be with Jules.'

Anne nodded, relieved. She certainly couldn't manage this without David's help. She was zipping up the second bag of baby gear when her mobile phone rang again.

'Maybe it's Jules,' she said hopefully.

It wasn't.

The call was from a registrar in the paediatric intensive care unit. Daniel's blood pressure was dropping. His ECG trace was becoming erratic and his lung function causing concern.

'I'm on my way,' Anne had to say.

And then she looked at where David was standing, holding a car seat in each hand.

'Daniel's in trouble,' she told him. 'I'll have to go and see him. Could we take the twins up to the relatives' room up there?'

'What's going to happen if Daniel needs to go back to Theatre?'

Anne swallowed. Hard. 'I'll have to take him.'

David's face was grim. 'If I'm going to be babysitting for hours by myself, I'd rather be doing it in my own house.'

Anne stared at him. This couldn't be happening. When that nurse had come into this room, she'd been on the point of telling David that she wanted to be with him for ever. That she wanted to have a family with him. But this was exactly what she'd feared all along, wasn't it?

The conflict between her career and family. The last thing in the world she wanted right now was to leave David to look after the babies by himself. Or to be unavailable when Julia had to sit and wait for Mac to come out of Theatre.

The pull of family was overwhelming.

The pull of duty unavoidable. A life was at stake. Someone else's child.

Conflict. Career versus family and child care.

A sound that could almost have been a huff of ironic laughter escaped her lips. She'd been running from making this choice but here it was, right in front of her and, in the end, no matter how agonising it was, she didn't actually have a choice at all.

'I have to go and see Daniel. He's my patient.'

'Of course you do.'

'Will you be all right? With…the babies?'

'Yes.'

'I'm…so sorry, David.'

He grunted an acceptance of her apology but his face was bleak. 'So am I.'

They stared at each other. Echoes of the past whispered around them and stung like an icy breeze.

'It was never going to work, was it?' Anne asked softly.

They both knew what she was talking about.

'No,' David agreed sadly. 'I guess it wasn't.'

CHAPTER TEN

THAT simple exchange had sounded the death knell of their relationship.

It was still ringing in Anne's ears hours later when she accompanied Julia back to David's house to collect the babies.

And her things.

'So…' David was standing in the entrance hall when she came out of the guest suite with her suitcase. 'You're leaving, then.'

It wasn't a question but Anne nodded. 'I need to go home with Jules. She needs me.'

The silence was deafening. What had she hoped she would hear? David saying that *he* needed her, too?

'She tells me Mac's doing well.' His voice was tight.

'We waited until he came round from the anaesthetic. They've done an amazing job of putting his ankle back together but it was touch and go for nerve repair. He may need some more surgery.'

This was easier. A professional kind of conversation.

'He's got external fixation, of course, and they're

worried about infection. He's on a bucket of antibiotics and they think he'll be in hospital for at least a week. Quite possibly longer.'

'He'll be off work for quite a while, I expect.'

'Yes, but once he's home I'm sure they'll be able to cope without me as an extra parent.'

'What about you, Annie?' David's query was soft. 'Will *you* be able to cope with being an extra parent?'

'Yes.' Anne knew she sounded confident. She was. Any grief she might have felt about handing over the babies was well and truly lost in this new pain of losing David.

Again.

Julia came out of the living room, carrying the baby seats.

'Need some help?' David asked.

'I'm good. Thanks so much for everything, David.' Julia looked from him to her sister and a furrow of concern wrinkled her forehead. 'We'll be in the taxi,' she told Anne. 'No rush.'

'You didn't need to get a taxi. I would have taken you all home.'

'I know. But it would have been an hour's drive. It's after midnight and you've got an early start tomorrow. You've helped enough, David.'

His expression was guarded now. 'So it would seem.'

It was Anne's turn to leave but still she stood there, gripping the handle of her suitcase.

This was it. She was walking away from David and it would be for the last time. There would be no going back. The breath she tried to take in got stuck. She swallowed and tried again.

'I don't know what to say,' she whispered.

That she was sorry? That she'd been wrong? Would it help to tell him that Daniel hadn't needed her after all? That it had been bleeding from his spleen that had appeared to be under control but which had started again that had caused his deterioration? Another paediatric team had taken the little boy back to Theatre but by then Julia and Mac had arrived in the emergency department. Anyway, it had been the principle that had done the damage, not this specific incident or case.

'Don't say anything,' David suggested. 'The longer we spin this out, the more painful it's going to be for both of us.'

Anne hated that she was causing him pain. She could see it in his face. In the darkness of his eyes and the lines of strain. By the rigid way he was holding himself so still as he stood there.

'We were chasing the sun, Annie,' he said softly. 'It was inevitable that we would get burnt.'

No way could Anne stem the prickle at the back of her eyes or how tight her throat was now.

'I couldn't have got through the last couple of months if you hadn't been here.'

The tiny tremor of David's lips was the only sign that he was finding this as hard as she was.

'Hey…' His lips firmed and twisted into a rough smile. 'What are friends for?'

The handle of the case slipped from Anne's grasp and she stumbled forward, holding up her arms. David stepped into them and gathered her into the hug she needed so desperately.

But it was different.

She could feel his solidness and the circle his arms made around her. She could hear the thump of his heartbeat but it felt…distant.

Of course it did. He was protecting himself. From *her*.

It gave her a glimpse of this from his point of view. She'd been living a lie ever since he'd come back. He'd seen her pregnant. Giving birth, even. Being content to be away from her job and devoting herself to domestic pursuits like making a home and garden beautiful. She'd reeled him in by allowing their intimacy to rekindle and grow.

And then she'd slapped him in the face when confronted by the choice of being with him and the babies—*family*—or doing her job.

Would he understand if she told him that she hadn't wanted to make the choice she'd been obliged to make? That it had broken her heart? But what difference would it make even if he did understand the cost? The knowledge that there would be lifetime of such conflict was more than enough to show them both that it could never have worked. That it would only have generated heartache and resentment.

That if children were involved, they would suffer too.

If she really loved David, she would let him go. Right now. She would set him free to get on with his life and have a family with someone who would adore him and let nothing get in the way of their time together.

She pulled back from his embrace. Trying to gather her strength so she could give David what he deserved.

'We'll always be friends, won't we?'

He had turned away. He was picking up her case.

Anne couldn't help rushing in to fill this new silence. 'Maybe we could…have dinner or something. Before I go to Sydney. Or you go to London.'

David looked over his shoulder. He cleared his throat. 'We'll be friends, Annie, but I need a bit of space to get my head around things first.'

Of course he did. So did she. Anne followed him outside. This wound was far too raw to think of prodding it yet. It was still bleeding. Badly.

David handed her bag to the taxi driver and bent to smile at Julia who was in the back seat, flanked by her sleeping babies.

'Come and visit us soon,' she told him.

'Maybe.' The word was noncommittal. 'I'm going to be pretty busy. I don't want to let anyone down even if it is the last weeks of my locum. And I've got my work cut out for me if I want to get the house sold before I leave the country.'

And with no more than a nod at Anne, David was gone. As the taxi pulled out of the driveway, she saw the lights of the entranceway cut off as he closed the front door of his home behind him.

For the next ten days Anne's life was taken over by helping to care for the twins and keeping Julia's spirits up. There was the cooking and shopping and housework to take care of and a lot of time was spent travelling to and from hospital visits.

Being this busy was a blessing, however. Anne

didn't have time to agonise over what had happened between herself and David and when she did finally fall into bed at night, she was too exhausted to do anything other than sleep.

Curiously, there was a peacefulness to be found amongst the hectic routine and that was the knowledge that she could help mother these babies and love them but they were not *hers*. She was able to live with them and care for them the same way she'd cared for her baby sister so many years ago. Recognising that, and re-membering the power of the bond her body had shown her after giving birth, she had a glimpse of what it would be like to have her own child. One conceived in love, preferably with the father by her side.

Had she given away the only chance she might have to experience that? Chosen her career instead? It hadn't felt like a conscious choice at the time. She'd been doing her duty. The way she had all her life. Doing the right thing and earning points that would one day allow her to make her own choices.

This was supposed to be her time right now, wasn't it? And here she was doing her duty again and putting her own life on hold. She was living with the babies she'd given birth to. She was in a state of domesticity right up to her eyeballs. Dealing with bottles and nappies and crying babies. She wasn't getting enough sleep and it was just as stressful as she'd known it would be.

And she didn't want to be doing anything else.

How weird was that?

She hadn't seen David. The least she could give him was the space he'd requested. When they took the babies in to visit Mac, they would take the double push-chair with them and Anne would take the twins for a walk to give Julia some time alone with her husband. She would take them out the back of the hospital if the weather was nice and walk near the river. Well away from the emergency department and any chance of running into David.

It was hard enough to know that he came to visit Mac so often and that his news had been passed on until Julia had warned him that he was treading on painful ground. By then she already knew that David was looking forward to heading for London and that the marketing of his house was creating an enormous amount of interest. The agents were confident that the upcoming auction would be a huge success.

Mac did need a second operation on his ankle and by the following week the strain of the frequent visits were starting to show. It was a long drive, with difficult patches over the hills and winding around the bays.

'We've got to shift closer to town,' Julia said on one occasion, as they carried a pair of tired and hungry babies back into the house. 'We've been talking about it off and on since Mac went back to work after his paternity leave.'

'But you love this house. How could you sacrifice a view like this?'

'Family's more important,' Julia said quietly, lifting Angus from his car seat and kissing him. 'We knew Mac was losing family time with all the commuting and that we'd want to be closer to good schools and things when the twins were older. This accident has changed things. We talked about it today. The time we get together is just too precious to waste.'

Anne had picked Amy up. As comfortable with her aunt now as she was with her parents, Amy stopped grizzling and grinned. Anne smiled back, looked up to share the moment with Julia and found that her sister was watching her with an odd expression on her face.

'What?'

'Nothing.'

'Doesn't look like nothing.'

'I was just thinking, that's all. About priorities.'

'You mean do we change wet pants or make some formula first?'

Julia smiled. 'I was looking at a bigger picture. Thinking about how priorities change. That you can think you want something so much nothing else matters but then it changes. It doesn't have to get lost, it just gets…demoted, I guess.'

'You're talking about this house. The views, right? Demotion from an island in the harbour to a park in the city, yes?'

'Yeah…right.' But Julia's tone suggested that Anne was missing the point. That Julia had somehow over-taken her older sister in wisdom.

Maybe she had. Priorities were certainly getting juggled a little for Anne.

The planned month-long visit to the specialist paedi-atric hospital in Sydney was looming closer by the day but the desire to take advantage of the opportunity was fading at an even faster rate.

Finally, Anne sent an email. 'I'm sorry,' she wrote, 'but, due to family circumstances, I'm no longer able to take this time away.'

Julia was shocked. 'But you've been looking forward to this for so long. It was all part of the plan after the babies were born.'

'You said it yourself,' Anne responded quietly. 'Priorities change. You need me right now.'

'Mac's coming home soon. We could cope.'

'I know you could but I *want* to help. This is where I need to be right now. Maybe I need you more than you need me.'

'Oh, hon.' Julia gathered her sister into her arms. 'I'm so sorry things haven't worked out for you and David. I wish there was something I could do.'

'Make me a coffee.' Anne smiled, blinking away tears. 'No…make that tea. I've gone right off coffee for the moment.' She pulled back and then did a double-take at her sister's expression. 'What?'

'That's exactly what you said just before you did your pregnancy test, remember?'

Anne laughed. 'I'm not pregnant again. It's not remotely possible. I'm not even ovulating again yet.'

'How do you know? Some women do it within a couple of weeks of giving birth.'

'I haven't had a period yet, that's how I know.'

Julia was giving her a very strange look. 'Well, you wouldn't, would you? If you were pregnant…'

Anne gave another amused snort. 'I'm not. Two babies is enough in this family. We decided against even the possibility of three way back at the implantation, remember?'

Julia reached for the kettle. 'I'm sure you're right. Just as well, eh? A baby of your own would be the last thing you want right now.'

'Mmm.' But Anne was staring through the window, not seeing the fabulous view of the harbour that Julia was prepared to give up for more important things. She was seeing a very different picture. A much bigger one.

'An iconic house,' the voice announced. 'A piece of our city's heritage that has been meticulously restored to its original glory. A real *family* home.'

From his upstairs bedroom window, David could look down onto the crowded lawn where the auction for this property was taking place on site. There had to be close to two hundred people here, he decided. Prospective buyers and curious onlookers. Agents who were flanking clients or had mobile phones pressed to their ears—in communication with more than one absent bidder who had registered their interest.

Strangers, all of them.

'Imagine entertaining in the glorious drawing room behind me,' the auctioneer continued. 'Looking out on this fabulous vista.'

David snorted, closing his eyes.

Impossible not to think of Anne. The way her eyes had danced with mischief when she'd been telling him the plans those landscape architects had had in mind for his garden.

'*Spheres*,' she'd said, amusement vying with primness.

'*Balls*,' he had countered.

He'd made her laugh and the sound had repaired a thread of connection between them.

The auctioneer had finally finished hyping up the crowd. 'Who wants to start the bidding?' he called.

David crossed the room to sit on the edge of his bed. He took a deep breath in through his nose but that was a mistake. Despite her absence and changing the linen more than once, he was sure he could still catch a hint of Anne's scent here. Not perfume. The scent of Anne. The one he'd filled his senses with that day on the beach when he'd kissed her for the first time in so long. He remembered the feeling of being poised on the edge of a cliff. In danger of falling into a crevasse he'd only just clawed his way clear of. He remembered feeling relieved when Anne had backed away.

Had he really thought he was still in control? That he could save himself from the kind of pain he was feeling now? He should have known he was lost when he'd gone home that day and thought she'd left. The flash of fear should have stopped him in his tracks but, no, he'd hurtled headlong into her arms pretty much, hadn't he?

Well, he had when he'd seen the way she'd looked at him when he'd told her about the pond. The way she had offered to help him retrieve something he'd lost long ago but still cared about.

He would have sworn he'd been able to see love in that look.

The kind of love he'd ached for.

But it had been doomed to failure. He should have known that. He did know it. Even if he gave up the dream of ever having a family, he would have to play second fiddle to Anne's career. There would be time after time when some emergency would take precedence. Like young Daniel that day, who'd fortunately come through the crisis and was apparently happily recuperating in the children's ward now.

He might have thought he was willing to accept whatever crumbs of time were available with the juggling of two high-powered careers but it would be unfair on both of them to try. It was way too obvious where it would lead eventually. There would be resentment and guilt to begin with. And then they would drift apart, intent on their own paths through life. Without a family, the kind of glue that would make compromise a necessity would be missing.

Maybe he could make it work if he wanted it badly enough but Anne would have to want it just as much. Maybe he was just as much of an all-or-nothing personality as she was. But the 'all' he wanted was in his relationship. An equal commitment. To love and be loved in equal measure.

Was it really too much to ask?

Judging by the way Anne seemed to have been avoiding him ever since Mac's accident, apparently so.

The bidding from the crowd outside was heating up. Jumping higher in increments at such a speed David hadn't noticing it passing the reserve he'd set before the auction had commenced.

'Folks…we *are on* the market,' the auctioneer boomed. 'Ladies and gentlemen, who is going to be the lucky family to enjoy this paradise with its country charm in the middle of city convenience? Who will have the pleasure of raising their children here? Or taking their grandchildren for a stroll to feed the fish in that fabulous pond?'

This shouldn't be happening. David shoved his fingers through his hair and then buried his face in his hands with a groan. He was cutting himself off from Anne. From their past. From his own childhood, even. He had no one to blame but himself. He was as selfish as he'd once accused Anne of being. Just as black and white. He'd told her she was incapable of compromise but had he ever actually tried to set a real example?

'*Sold!*' boomed a triumphant sound through the speaker system set up on the lawn. The sound of a gavel hitting the podium punctuated the finale.

Oh…God!

David's head snapped up. What had he done?

What had he been *thinking*?

'*No!*' the word was uttered aloud and it was final. David got to his feet and strode out of the room.

'I'm not going to sell,' David told the startled group of real-estate personnel gathering in his hallway.

'But you already *have*,' the auctioneer insisted. 'It's a legal process, Dr Earnshaw. We have the new owner in the dining room, waiting to sign the contract.'

'I won't sign,' David said stubbornly.

'But why not?' The atmosphere of triumph around him was ebbing. Becoming alarmed. 'The price was more than any of us hoped for.'

'I've changed my mind,' David told him. 'Some things are far more important than money.'

'What kind of things?'

David's head turned at the sound of a feminine voice he knew so well.

'*Annie*...what are you doing here?'

'I came to watch the auction.' She edged through a gap in the group. 'It was a great price. Aren't you happy?'

'No.' David took a step closer to her. 'I'm not selling. This place represents my past. I want it to be part of my future as well.' He turned to glare at the auctioneer. 'You can say all you want about this being such a family home. About swings for children under the elm tree or grandchildren feeding the fish, but you know what?'

'What?' The auctioneer was eyeing him warily.

'It's not the number of people that make a family. It's about what holds them together. It's about *love*.'

'Of course it is.' An agent exchanged a meaningful look with the auctioneer and stepped forward. She had a sheaf of papers in her hand. Probably the sale-and-purchase agreement David was expected to sign. 'The new owners will love this property, I promise you.'

David ignored her. He turned back to Anne.

'I told you we were chasing the sun,' he said. 'And we got burned. I was going about it all wrong. You don't need to chase it. You just need to find a space where you can feel the warmth and see the light. I thought I had to shut myself away to keep safe but who wants to live in the dark?'

'Not me,' Anne said obligingly. The people around them were looking bemused but they shook their heads in agreement as well.

'I love you, Annie,' David said. 'I don't want to live without you. I don't care how big our family is. It's *you* I need.' He held out his hand. 'You're my sun. My warmth. My light.'

'Oh…David…' Anne had tears on her cheeks. 'That's all I ever needed to hear you say. I love you, too.'

'We'll work it out,' David promised, holding her close and kissing her.

'Of course you will,' said the auctioneer with a curiously gruff voice.

'We will,' Anne told him.

'I just need to sort out this mess first,' David groaned.

'What mess?'

'I'll have to find the person who thinks they're buying our home. I need to explain why they can't.'

'You just did.'

David blinked. He frowned at the auctioneer, who'd just spoken, and then looked to Anne's face smiling up at him. He was vaguely aware that everyone around them was also smiling. Grinning, even.

'You?' He blinked again. '*You* bought it?'

Anne nodded.

'Why?'

'It's a family home and…I want a family, David. With you.'

'But…'

'I was wrong. I thought I knew what I wanted but

there I was, finally staring at what I thought was what I wanted, and it didn't look right. It looked empty. Like it was missing something really, really important.'

'Warmth?' David suggested softly. 'Light?'

'Heart,' Anne answered, standing on tiptoe to kiss David again. 'My heart. And you know why it wasn't there?'

'No. Why?'

'Because you have it.'

'And you have mine.' David managed to tear his gaze away from her for long enough to give their audience a firm stare. 'Would you all mind going away?' he asked politely. 'A man could do with a little privacy when he's about to propose.'

Anne watched everybody walking out of the hallway. She saw the auctioneer pull an enormous white handkerchief from his pocket and blow his nose with gusto.

She knew how he felt. Happy endings tended to have the same effect on her.

Except this wasn't an ending.

It was a beginning. For both of them. No, for all of them. Anne caught her breath. Should she tell David now that his dream of a family of his own was much closer than he could imagine?

He was about to propose. Too impatient to wait for everyone to clear the hallway completely, he had taken her hands and pulled her through the nearest doorway, which led into the biggest living area. He was looking down at her with such love in his face that Anne was lost. All she could do was bask in that love and wait for the chance to say 'yes'.

That she would marry him. Live with him and love him for the rest of her life.

There would be plenty of time to share the news of the baby. To make plans that would make it work for them all.

She'd been right after all. This *was* her time. Her chance to do exactly what she wanted most in her life.

'*Yes*,' she whispered.

'Oi!' David's tone was stern. 'I haven't asked yet.'

Anne smiled. 'Are you going to do the down-on-one-knee thing?'

'Good grief! Do you want me to?'

Her smile widened. 'Someone might appreciate it.'

David took his eyes off her for the first time since he'd brought her in here. He turned his head and realised where they were. Right in front of all the windows and French doors that led to the terrace and the lawn beyond. Some of the crowd had gone but there were still a lot of people out there and someone must have told them what was going on because they were all standing there quietly.

Watching. And smiling.

David grinned and went down on one knee. 'I love you, Anne Bennett,' he said. 'Will you marry me? Please?'

'Yes,' Anne said. And then, more loudly, in case her soft response hadn't been heard through the open doors, '*Yes*.'

The auctioneer blew his nose again. And then everyone started clapping.

EPILOGUE

SHE was the happiest woman in the world.

Jean MacCulloch paused for a moment longer in the bathroom, dampening her hand to smooth the grey corrugations of her newly permed hair. Then she pushed her wire-rimmed spectacles more firmly onto the bridge of her nose and went back outside to join her family.

Her family now. All of it.

She stopped on the terrace of this wonderful old house to admire the garden and soak in the party atmosphere. There were balloons everywhere. Rainbows of colour attached to tree branches and joined by twisted streamers. The shiny new red swing and slide set that was Emily Earnshaw's first birthday present was also adorned with decorations. Not that wee Emily was getting a chance to sit in the soft bucket seat of the swing because her cousins were making the most of their ten-month superiority in age.

'Me!' Angus was shouting. 'Me now!'

'No!' It was Amy's new favourite word. She was

gripping the sides of the swing seat, resisting her mother's attempt at prying those little fingers loose. 'No!'

'One more swing,' Julia relented. 'But then it's definitely Angus's turn.'

Emily's parents were smiling at Julia losing the battle temporarily. Anne was busy arranging a party picnic afternoon tea on the child-sized table and chairs that had been set up on the lawn. Pretty cup cakes with pastel icing and marshmallow butterflies on top. Gingerbread people with bright candy-covered chocolate buttons. Platters of fresh fruit pieces and plastic tumblers of juice. There was a cake, too, of course. Pink and white with pretty pink bows and icing flowers and a single candle.

David was holding his tiny daughter who looked every inch the birthday princess in a ruffled pink dress with white socks and sandals and a soft pink headband with a bow to hold back golden curls that were just getting long enough to get in her eyes.

'What do you think, Emily?' he asked, lifting the little girl so that she was in the air looking down at her father. 'Is Amy being a wee bit naughty?'

Emily gurgled with laughter and waved chubby fists.

'Mac!' Julia was trying not to laugh as Amy thwarted new efforts to unclamp her fingers. 'Do something…'

But Mac had spotted his mother and was almost at the terrace steps. 'You all right, Mum?'

'Never better, lad,' Jean assured him. She met him at the bottom of the steps.

'Not too much for you? All these noisy little people?'

Jean smiled. 'It doesn't seem that long ago that you were one of them, Alan MacCulloch. And look at you now.' She had to look a long way up. 'I do wish you'd stop growing.'

Mac laughed and drew her towards the swing. Jean walked slowly. Not because she didn't have more than enough energy but because she wanted to make this moment last a little longer.

'Do you remember when I came to visit with Doreen when you and Julia were first married?'

'Aye. Of course I do.'

'I was so happy for you both but Doreen was trying to spoil it for me. Lording it over me, she was, all the way back to Glasgow, and you know what a long trip *that* is.'

'I certainly do.' Mac was frowning. 'What was Doreen doing to spoil things?'

'Oh, you know, going on and on about how wonderful her Lachlan's family was. Saying that, of course, Julia was a wonderful lassie but wasn't it the greatest shame that you'd never have any bairns? That I'd never be a grandmother?' Doreen clicked her tongue. 'If only I'd known then what Anne had offered as your wedding gift.'

'We didn't tell you because it took us a long time to decide to accept it. It was all too amazing, really.'

'Aye,' Jean said softly. 'So it was. And now I *am* a grandmother. To the bonniest wee bairns in the world.'

'I'll bet that put Doreen's nose out of joint.'

'Aye. And then I told her that I was going to come out here to live.'

'What did she say to that?'

'That I needed my head read. That I was too old to be helping to raise babies and being an adopted grandmother to your wee ones' cousin was just plain daft.'

'You don't mind, though, do you? You're the closest thing to a gran that wee Emily is ever going to have.'

'I'm thrilled, lad. You're all like one family, anyway, what with Julia looking after all the babies on the days that Anne and David are both working.'

'Dadda!' Angus had forgotten he was waiting his turn for the swing. 'Pick me up, Dadda.'

'No,' Amy cried. 'Me!' She gave up the battle to stay in the seat and lifted both arms so that Julia could lift her out. Then she toddled as fast as she could towards Mac, leaving Julia shaking her head.

David had put Emily down. She was standing in front of him and he was holding both her hands. Tentatively, the birthday girl stepped towards her mother who had finished setting out the picnic and was kneeling on the grass, her arms outstretched.

'Look at you.' Anne beamed. '*Clever* girl, Em.'

Mac had a toddler attached to each leg and was moving, with difficulty, towards Anne and the table.

'Food, guys,' he told his children. 'Look…cake!'

Julia caught up with Jean and they both followed, smiling.

David let go of one of Emily's hands when she was close to her mother. Then he let go of the other one. For three whole steps Emily managed to stay upright and then Anne caught her. She cuddled and kissed her daughter but was looking up at her husband to share the joy of the moment.

'Time to light the candle,' David said. 'I reckon we can all make a wish.'

'I don't have anything to wish *for*,' Anne said. I'm the happiest woman on earth.'

Julia was watching Mac as he gave up and sat down on the lawn to let the twins clamber on top of him.

'No,' she said quietly. 'I think I am.'

'Nonsense,' Jean said firmly. '*I* am.' She gazed around at her newly extended family. 'Look at you all.' She beamed. 'And here I am instead of being thousands of miles away. No one could be happier than me.'

But no-one seemed to be listening. Mac had a small child under each arm and he was looking up at Julia, sharing a smile that excluded everyone else.

Anne and David were smiling at each other, too, over the blonde curls of their daughter.

Secret smiles. Full of the kind of love that could make anyone feel like the happiest person in existence.

Jean's nod was satisfied. She was getting to share it all and she knew she was right.

She was definitely the happiest woman in the world.

 MEDICAL™

Single titles coming next month

DATING THE MILLIONAIRE DOCTOR
by Marion Lennox

Vet Tori Nicholls lost everything in a wildfire and doesn't feel she'll ever live again. Until she meets New York doctor Jake Hunter, who's just passing through! But their one night has resulted in pregnancy. Can an Australian country girl renew her life with a Manhattan millionaire…and their baby?

VILLAGE MIDWIFE, BLUSHING BRIDE
by Gill Sanderson

Longing for a new start, midwife Zoe Hilton's plans are thrown into disarray by her new boss, Dr Connor Maitland! Connor is an expert at hiding his emotions, until Zoe quickly breaks down his defences and opens his heart. But he'll need to get down on one knee to make Zoe's dreams come true!

On sale 3rd September 2010
Available at WHSmith, Tesco, ASDA, Eason and all good bookshops.
For full Mills & Boon range including eBooks visit
www.millsandboon.co.uk

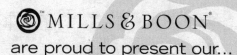

MILLS & BOON®

are proud to present our…

Book of the Month

The Baby Gift
A beautiful linked duet by Alison Roberts from
Mills & Boon® Medical™

WISHING FOR A MIRACLE
Mac MacCulloch and Julia Bennett make the perfect team. But Julia knows she must protect her heart – especially as she can't have children. She's stopped wishing for a miracle, but Mac's wish is standing right in front of him – Julia…and whatever the future may hold.

THE MARRY-ME WISH
Paediatric surgeon Anne Bennett is carrying her sister's twins for her when she bumps into ex-love Dr David Earnshaw! When the babies are born, learning to live without them is harder than Anne ever expected – and she discovers that she needs David more than ever…

Mills & Boon® Medical™
Available 6th August

*Something to say about our
Book of the Month?
Tell us what you think!*
millsandboon.co.uk/community

Secrets. Lies. Time to come clean…

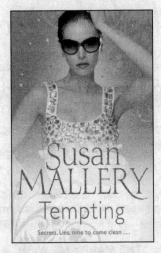

Dani Buchanan is horrified when her father turns out to be a presidential candidate. And then the tabloids find out…

Katherine Canfield is unable to bear children. Dani's a reminder of what Senator Canfield could have had – and Katherine's jealous.

Adopted Canfield son Alex is tempted by Dani. With the scandal of the century brewing, can he pursue a relationship that could tear his family apart?

Available 3rd September 2010

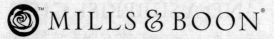

2 FREE BOOKS
AND A SURPRISE GIFT

We would like to take this opportunity to thank you for reading this Mills & Boon® book by offering you the chance to take TWO more specially selected books from the Medical™ series absolutely FREE! We're also making this offer to introduce you to the benefits of the Mills & Boon® Book Club™—

- **FREE home delivery**
- **FREE gifts and competitions**
- **FREE monthly Newsletter**
- **Exclusive Mills & Boon Book Club offers**
- **Books available before they're in the shops**

Accepting these FREE books and gift places you under no obligation to buy, you may cancel at any time, even after receiving your free books. Simply complete your details below and return the entire page to the address below. You don't even need a stamp!

YES Please send me 2 free Medical books and a surprise gift. I understand that unless you hear from me, I will receive 5 superb new stories every month including two 2-in-1 books priced at £4.99 each and a single book priced at £3.19, postage and packing free. I am under no obligation to purchase any books and may cancel my subscription at any time. The free books and gift will be mine to keep in any case.

Ms/Mrs/Miss/Mr _____ Initials _____

Surname _____

Address _____

_____

_____ Postcode _____

E-mail _____

Send this whole page to: Mills & Boon Book Club, Free Book Offer, FREEPOST NAT 10298, Richmond, TW9 1BR